Will Adams worked as a shop salesman and warehouse porter before joining a Washington DC-based firm of business history consultants where he wrote a number of corporate histories and biographies. He would occasionally take time off between projects to travel to remote places in search of exotic settings for his stories. After working in London for a while he resigned and sold his home to give himself a shot at fulfilling his lifelong ambition of becoming a writer.

THE ALEXANDER CIPHER

In 318 BC in the deserts of Libya, Alexander the Great was buried as only a god should be, placed in a Crystal Sarcophagus in a catacomb of chambers, each packed with diamonds, rubies and gold. That's how he should have remained, but time waits for no one . . . It's 2007, and unorthodox archaeologist Daniel Knox is on the trail of Alexander's Gold with Richard Mitchell, ex Australian Special Forces operative turned underwater archaeologist. When a tomb is uncovered on the construction site of a new hotel he believes he has found a clue to what he has been working towards for years. But the discovery has alerted two of the most dangerous men in the world, and Daniel is now a marked man . . .

WILL ADAMS

◆

THE
ALEXANDER
CIPHER

Complete and Unabridged

CHARNWOOD
Leicester

First published in Great Britain in 2007 by
Harper, an imprint of
HarperCollins*Publishers*
London

First Charnwood Edition
published 2008
by arrangement with
HarperCollins*Publishers*
London

British Library CIP Data

Adams, Will
    The Alexander Cipher.—Large print ed.—
    Charnwood library series
    1. Alexander, the Great, *356 – 323* B.C.—Tomb
    —Fiction 2. Treasure troves—Libya—Fiction
    3. Egyptologists—Fiction 4. Suspense fiction
    5. Large type books
    I. Title
    823.9′2 [F]

    ISBN 978–1–84782–266–6

Published by
F. A. Thorpe (Publishing)
Anstey, Leicestershire

Set by Words & Graphics Ltd.
Anstey, Leicestershire
Printed and bound in Great Britain by
T. J. International Ltd., Padstow, Cornwall

This book is printed on acid-free paper

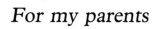

For my parents

Acknowledgements

This book has been over a decade in the contemplation and writing, and during that time I've received help, encouragement and advice from a great many people, too many to acknowledge individually. But I would particularly like to thank my agent Luigi Bonomi and my editor Wayne Brookes, both for seeing something they liked in the original manuscript, and for helping me to make it better. I'd also like to thank Colin Clement for correcting my worst excesses about life and archaeology in Alexandria and Egypt. It goes without saying that where any mistakes remain, they are mine and mine alone.

After his death in Babylon in 323 BC, the body of Alexander the Great was taken in a magnificent procession to Egypt for eventual burial in Alexandria, where it remained on display for some six hundred years.

Alexander's mausoleum was considered a wonder of the world. Roman emperors including Julius Caesar, Augustus and Caracalla paid pilgrimages. Yet after a series of earthquakes, fires and wars, Alexandria fell into decline and the tomb was lost.

Despite numerous excavations, it has never been found.

After his death in Babylon in 323 BC, the body of Alexander the Great was taken in a magnificent procession to Egypt for eventual burial in Alexandria, where it remained on display for some six hundred years.

Alexander's mausoleum was considered a wonder of the world. Roman emperors including Julius Caesar, Augustus and Caracalla paid pilgrimages. Yet after a series of earthquakes, fires and wars, Alexandria fell into decline and the tomb was lost.

Despite numerous excavations, it has never been found.

PROLOGUE

The Libyan Desert, 318 BC

There was a freshwater spring at the lowest point of the cave, like a single black nail at the tip of a twisted, charred and mutilated leg. A thick layer of lichen and other scum clotted its surface, barely disturbed in centuries except to ripple and shiver at the touch of one of the insects that lived upon it, or dimple with bubbles of gas belched from deep beneath the floor of the surrounding desert.

Suddenly the skin burst, and the head and shoulders of a man erupted from the water. His face was turned upwards and instantly he gasped huge heaves of life-giving air through his flared nostrils and gaping mouth, as though he'd stayed underwater beyond the limit of his endurance. His breaths didn't lessen in intensity as the moments passed; rather, they grew ever more desperate, as though his heart was about to burst inside his chest. But at length he reached and passed the worst.

There was no light at all in the cave, not even a phosphorescence of water; and the man's relief at surviving his underwater flight quickly turned to distress that he'd merely exchanged one mode of death for another. He felt around the edge of

3

the pool until he found a low ledge. He heaved himself up, twisted round to sit upon it. Almost as an afterthought, he reached beneath his soaking tunic for his dagger; but in truth, there was little danger of pursuit. He'd had to fight and kick his way through every inch of that watery escape. He'd like to see that fat Libyan who'd aimed to stick him with his sword try to follow; for sure, *he'd* cork in the passage, and it wouldn't spit *him* out till he'd lost some flesh.

Something whirred past his cheek. He cried out in terror and threw up his hands. The echo was curiously slow and deep for what he'd imagined to be a small cave. Something else flapped past him. It sounded like a bird, but no bird could navigate in such darkness. Perhaps a bat. He'd certainly seen colonies of them at dusk, swarming the distant orchards like midges. His hopes rose. If these were those same bats, there had to be a way out of here. He surveyed the rock walls with his hands, then began to climb the gentlest wall. He wasn't an athletic man, and the ascent was night-marish in the dark, though at least the walls were gaunt with holds. When he reached a place from which there was no possible advance, he retreated and found another route. Then another. Hours passed. More hours. He grew hungry and tired. One time he fell crashing to the base, crying out in terror. A broken leg would end him as surely as it would end a mule, but he cracked his head against rock instead, and blackness claimed him.

When he came to, he wasn't sure for a blessed moment where he was, or why. When memory

4

returned, he felt such despair that he considered returning the way he'd come. But he couldn't face that passage again. No. Better to press on. He tried the rock wall once more. And again. And finally, on his next attempt, he reached a precarious ledge high above the cavern floor, barely wide enough for him to kneel. He crawled forwards and upwards, the rock-face to his left, nothing at all to his right, only too aware that a single mistake would plunge him to certain death. The knowledge didn't impede him but rather added sharpness to his concentration.

The ledge closed around him so that it felt as if he was crawling inside the belly of a stone serpent. Soon the darkness wasn't quite so pure as it had been. Then it grew almost light and he emerged shockingly into the setting sun, so dazzling after his long blindness that he had to throw up a forearm to protect his eyes.

The setting sun! A day at least had passed since Ptolemy's ambush. He inched closer to the lip, looked down. Nothing but sheer rocks and certain death. He looked up instead. It was still steep, but it looked manageable. The sun would soon be gone. He began to climb at once, looking neither down nor up, contenting himself with progress rather than haste. Patience served him well. Several times the sandstone crumbled in his hand or beneath his foot. The last glow of daylight faded as he reached an overhanging brow. There was no going back now, so he steeled himself, then committed totally to it, hauling himself up with his fingernails and palms and elbows, scrabbling frantically with his knees and feet, scraping his skin raw on the rough rock, until finally he made it over and he rolled onto his back, staring thankfully up at the night sky.

Kelonymus had never claimed to be brave. He was a man of healing and learning, not war. Yet he still felt the silent reproach of his comrades. 'Together in life; together in death' — that had been their vow. When Ptolemy had finally trapped them, the others had all taken without qualm the distillation of cherry laurel leaves that Kelonymus had concocted for them, lest torture loosen their tongues. Yet he himself had balked. He'd felt a terrible rush of fear at losing all this before his time, this wonderful gift of life, this sight, this smell, this touch, this taste, the glorious ability of thought. Never again to see the high hills of home, the lush banks of its rivers, the forests of pine and silver fir! Never again to listen at the feet of the wise men in the marketplace. Never to have his mother's arms around him, or tease his sister, or play with his two nephews! So he'd only pretended to take his poison. And then, as the others had expired around him, he'd fled into the caves.

The moon lit his descent, showing desert all around, making him realise just how alone he was. His former comrades had been shield-bearers in Alexander's army, dauntless lords of the earth. No place had felt safer than in their company. Without them he felt weak and fragile, adrift in a land of strange gods and incomprehensible tongues. He walked down the slope, faster and faster, the fear of Pan welling in him until he broke into a run and fled headlong before stumbling in a rut and falling hard onto the compact sand.

He had a growing sense of dread as he pushed himself up, though at first he wasn't sure why. But then strange shapes began to form in the darkness. When he realised what they were, he began to wail. He came to the first pair. Bilip, who'd carried him when his strength had failed outside Areg. Iatrocles, who'd told him wondrous tales of distant lands. Cleomenes and Herakles were next. No matter that they'd already been dead, crucifixion was the Macedonian punishment for criminals and traitors, and Ptolemy had wanted it known that was what he considered these men. Yet it wasn't these men who'd betrayed Alexander's dying request about where he was to be buried. It wasn't these men who'd put personal ambition above the wishes of their king. No. These men had only sought to do what Ptolemy himself should have done, building Alexander a tomb in sight of the place of his father.

Something about the symmetry of the crosses caught Kelonymus' eye. They were in pairs. All the way along, they were in pairs. Yet their party had been thirty-four. Himself and thirty-three others. An odd number. How could they all be in pairs? Hope fluttered weakly. Maybe someone else had got away. He began to hurry down the horrific avenue of death. Old friends either side, yes; but not his brother. Twenty-four crosses, and none his brother. Twenty-six. He prayed silently to the gods, his hopes rising all the time. Twenty-eight. Thirty. Thirty-two. And none his brother. And no more crosses. He felt, for a moment, an exquisite euphoria. But it didn't last. Like a knife plunged between his ribs, he realised what Ptolemy had done. He cried out in anguish and rage, and he fell to his knees upon the sand.

When his anger finally cooled, Kelonymus was a different man, a man of fixed and certain purpose. He'd betrayed his oath to these men once already. He wouldn't betray it again. *Together in life; together in death.* Yes. He owed them that much. Whatever it took.

1

I

The Ras Mohammed reefs, Sinai, Egypt

Daniel Knox was dozing happily on the bow when the girl came to stand with deliberate provocation in the way of his afternoon sun. He opened his eyes and looked up a little warily when he saw who it was, because Max had made it clear that she was Hassan al-Assyuti's for the day, and Hassan had a proud and thoroughly warranted reputation for violence, especially against anyone who dared tread on his turf.

'Yes?' he asked.

'So are you really a Bedouin?' she gushed. 'I mean, that guy Max said like you were a Bedouin, but I mean you don't look it. I mean, don't get me wrong, you kind of look it, I mean, your complexion and your hair and eyebrows, but . . . '

It was no surprise she'd caught Hassan's eye, thought Knox, as she rambled on. He was notoriously a sucker for young blondes, and this one had a charming smile and startling turquoise eyes, as well as an attractive complexion, with its smattering of pale freckles and pinkish hints of acne, and a slender figure perfectly showcased by her lime-green and lemon-yellow bikini. 'My father's mother was Bedouin,' he said, to help

9

her out of her labyrinth. 'That's all.'

'Wow! A Bedouin gran!' She took this as an invitation to sit. 'What was *she* like?'

Knox pushed himself up onto an elbow, squinting to keep out the sun. 'She died before I was born.'

'Oh, I'm sorry.' A damp, blonde lock fell onto her cheek. She swept her hair back with both hands, holding it there in a makeshift ponytail, so that her chest jutted out at him. 'Were you brought up here, then? In the desert?'

He looked around. They were on the deck of Max Strati's dive boat, tethered to a fixed mooring way out into the Red Sea. 'Desert?' he asked.

'Tch!' She slapped him playfully on the chest. 'You know what I mean!'

'I'm English,' he said.

'I like your tattoo.' She traced a fingertip over the blue and gold sixteen-pointed star on his right biceps. 'What is it?'

'The Star of Vergina,' answered Knox. 'A symbol of the Argeads.'

'The who?'

'The old royal family of Macedonia.'

'What? You mean like Alexander the Great?'

'Very good.'

She wrinkled her nose. 'You a fan, then? I always heard he was just a drunken brute.'

'Then you heard wrong.'

She smiled, pleased to be put down. 'Go on, then. Tell me.'

Knox frowned. Where did you even start with a man like Alexander? 'He was besieging this

10

town called Multan,' he told her. 'This was towards the end of his campaigns. His men were fed up with fighting. They just wanted to go home. But Alexander wasn't having that. He was first up the battlements. The defenders pushed away all the other assault ladders, so he was stranded up there alone. Any normal man would have leaped for safety, right? You know what Alexander did?'

'What?'

'He jumped down *inside* the walls. All on his own. It was the one sure way to make his men come after him.' And they had too. They'd torn the citadel apart to save him, and they'd only just got to him in time. The wounds he'd taken that day had probably contributed to his eventual death, but they'd added to his legend too. 'He used to boast that he carried scars on every part of his body; except his back.'

She laughed. 'He sounds like a psycho.'

'Different times,' said Knox. 'You know, when he captured the mother of the Persian Emperor, he put her under his personal protection. After he died, she was so upset, she starved herself to death. Not when her own son died, mind. When Alexander died. You don't do that for a psychopath.'

'Huh,' she said. It was clear that she'd had enough talk of Alexander.

She rose to her knees, placed her left palm flat on the deck the far side of Knox, then reached across him for the red and white icebox. She threw off its lid, sampled each of the bottles and cans inside for cool, taking her time, her breasts

11

swinging free within her dangling bikini-top as she did so, making the most of themselves, nipples pink as petals. Knox's mouth felt a little dry suddenly; knowing you were being worked didn't make it ineffective. But it reminded him forcibly of Hassan too, so he scowled and looked away.

She sat back down with a thump, an open bottle in her hand, a mischievous smile on her lips. 'Want some?' she asked.

'No thanks.'

She shrugged, took a swallow. 'So have you known Hassan long?'

'No.'

'But you're a friend of his, right?'

'I'm on the payroll, love. That's all.'

'But he's kosher, right?'

'That's hardly the smartest way to describe a Muslim.'

'You know what I mean.'

Knox shrugged. It was too late for her to be getting cold feet. Hassan had picked her up in a nightclub, not Sunday school. If she didn't fancy him, she should have said no; simple as that. There was naïve and there was stupid. It wasn't as though she didn't know what she was doing with her body.

Max Strati appeared around the line of cabins at that moment. He walked briskly over. 'What happens here, then?' he asked frostily. He'd come to Sharm el-Sheikh on holiday twenty years before, had never gone home. Egypt had been good to him; he wouldn't risk that by pissing off Hassan.

12

'Just talking,' said Knox.

'On your own time, please, not mine,' said Max. 'Mr al-Assyuti wishes his guests to have a final dive.'

Knox pushed himself up. 'I'll get things ready.'

The girl jumped up too, clapped with false enthusiasm. 'Great! I didn't think we'd be going down again.'

'You will not join us, I think, Fiona,' Max told her flatly. 'We have not enough tanks. You will stay here with Mr al-Assyuti.'

'Oh.' She looked scared, suddenly; childlike. She put her hand tentatively on Knox's forearm. He shook her off, walked angrily towards the stern, where the wetsuits, flippers, snorkels and goggles were stored in plastic crates next to the steel rack of air tanks. A swift glance confirmed what Knox already knew; there were plenty of full tanks. He felt stress suddenly in his nape. He could feel Max's eyes burning into his back, so he forced himself not to look round. The girl wasn't his problem. She was old enough to look after herself. He had no connection to her; no obligation. He'd worked his balls off to establish himself in this town; he wasn't going to throw that away just because some bratty teenager had misjudged the price of her lunch. His self-justifications did little good. He felt sick in the pit of his stomach as he squatted down by the crates and started checking equipment.

II

The MAF Nile Delta excavation, Northern Egypt

'Hello!' called out Gaille Bonnard. 'Is there anyone here?'

She waited patiently for an answer, but none came. How odd. Kristos had been clear that Elena wanted help translating an ostracon, but there was no sign of her or her truck; and the magazine, where she normally worked, was closed up. She felt a rare flicker of irritation. She didn't mind making the fifteen-minute walk from the other site; but she did mind having her time wasted. But then she noticed that the hut door was hanging ajar, which it had never been before, not while Gaille had been there at least. She knocked, pulled it open, looked within, allowing in a little sunlight. The interior walls were lined with shelves, stacked with battery lamps, hammers, mattocks, baskets, rope and other archaeological equipment. There was a dark square hole in the floor too, from which protruded the top of a wooden ladder.

She crouched, cupped her hands around her mouth, and called down, but there was no answer. She waited a few seconds, then called down again. When there was still nothing, she stood, put her hands on her hips, and brooded. Elena Koloktronis head of the Macedonian Archaeological excavation was one of those leaders who believed all her team to be incompetent, and who therefore tried to do everything herself. She was constantly running

14

off in the middle of one task to see to another. Maybe that was what had happened here. Or maybe there'd just been a mix-up with the message. The trouble was, it was impossible with Elena to do the right thing. If you went looking for her, you should have stayed where you were. If you stayed, she was furious that you hadn't come looking.

She crouched again, her hams and calves aching from her long day's work, and called down a third time, beginning to feel a little alarmed. What if Elena had fallen? She turned on a battery lamp, but the shaft was deep, and the beam was lost in its darkness. There couldn't be any harm in checking. She had no head for heights, so she took a deep breath as she put her hand on the ladder, reached one foot tentatively onto the top rung, then the other. When she felt secure, she began a cautious descent. The ladder creaked, as did the ropes that bound it to the wall. The shaft was deeper than she'd imagined, perhaps six metres. You couldn't normally go down so far in the Delta without reaching the water table, but the site was on the crown of a hill, safe from the annual inundation of the Nile — one reason it had been occupied in ancient times. She called out again. Still silence, except for her own breathing, magnified by her narrow confines. Displaced earth trickled past. Curiosity began to get the better of apprehension. She'd heard whispers about this place, of course, though none of her colleagues dared speak openly about it.

She reached the bottom at last, her feet

crunching on shards of basalt, granite and quartzite, as though old monuments and statues had been smashed into smithereens and tipped down. A narrow passage led left. She called out again, but more quietly this time, hoping there'd be no answer. Her lamp started flickering and stuttering, then went out altogether. She tapped it against the wall, and it sprang back on like a fist opening. Her feet crackled on the stone chips as she advanced.

There was a painting on the left-hand wall, its colours remarkably bright. It had evidently been cleaned, perhaps even retouched. A profiled humanoid figure dressed as a soldier but with the head and mane of a grey wolf was holding a mace in his left hand, and in his right a military standard, its base planted between his feet, a scarlet flag unfurling beside his right shoulder in front of a turquoise sky.

Ancient Egyptian gods weren't Gaille's speciality, but she knew enough to recognise Wepwawet, a wolf god who'd eventually merged with others into Anubis, the jackal. He'd been seen primarily as an army scout, and had often been depicted on *shed-sheds* — the Egyptian military standard he was holding here. His name had meant 'Opener of the Ways', which was why the miniaturised robot designed to explore the mysterious air shafts of the Great Pyramids had been christened with a version of his name, Upuaut. To the best of Gaille's recollection, he'd gone out of fashion during the Middle Kingdom, around sixteen hundred BC. By rights, therefore, this painting should have been over three and a

16

half thousand years old. Yet the *shedshed* that Wepwawet was holding told a different story. For depicted upon it were the head and shoulders of a handsome young man, a beatific look upon his face, tilted up like some Renaissance Madonna. It was hard to know for sure when you were looking at a portrait of Alexander the Great. His impact on iconography had been so profound that for centuries afterwards people had aspired to look like him. But if this wasn't Alexander himself, it was unquestionably influenced by him, which meant it couldn't possibly date to earlier than 332 BC. And that begged an obvious question: what on earth was he doing on a standard held by Wepwawet, over a millennium after Wepwawet had faded from view?

Gaille set this conundrum to one side and continued on her way, still murmuring Elena's name, though only as an excuse should she encounter anyone. Her battery lamp went out again, plunging the place into complete blackness. She tapped her lamp again, and once more it sprang on. She passed another painting; as far as she could tell, identical to the first, though not yet fully cleaned. The walls began to show signs of charring, as though a great fire had once raged. She glimpsed a flash of white marble ahead, and two stone wolves lying prone yet alert. More wolves. She frowned. When the Macedonians had taken Egypt, they'd given many of the towns Greek names for administrative purposes, often basing them upon local cult-gods. If Wepwawet was the cult-god of this place, then surely this must be —

'Gaille! Gaille!' From far behind her, Elena was shouting. 'Are you down there? Gaille!'

Gaille hurried back along the passage. 'Elena?' she called up. 'Is that you?'

'What the hell do you think you're doing down there?'

'I thought you'd fallen. I thought you might be in trouble.'

'Get out,' ordered Elena furiously. 'Get out now.'

Gaille started to climb. She saved her breath until she reached the top. Then she said hurriedly: 'Kristos told me you wanted to — '

Elena thrust her face in Gaille's. 'How many times have I told you this is a restricted area?' she yelled. 'How many times?'

'I'm sorry, Ms Koloktronis, but — '

'Who the hell do you think you are?' Elena's face was red; tendons stood out on her neck like a straining racehorse. 'How *dare* you go down there? How *dare* you?'

'I thought you'd fallen,' repeated Gaille helplessly. 'I thought you might need help.'

'Don't you dare interrupt me when I'm talking.'

'I wasn't — '

'Don't you dare! Don't you dare!'

Gaille stiffened. For a moment she considered snapping back. It had barely been three weeks ago, after all, that Elena had called her out of the blue and begged her, *begged* her, to take a month out from the Sorbonne's Demotic Dictionary project to fill in for a languages assistant who'd fallen ill. But you knew

18

instinctively in this world how well you matched up against other people, and Gaille didn't stand a chance. The first time Elena had exploded, it had left Gaille shell-shocked. Her new colleagues had shrugged it off, telling her that Elena had been that way ever since her husband had died. She boiled like a young planet with internal rage, erupting unpredictably in gushes of indiscriminate, molten and sometimes spectacular violence. It had become almost routine now, something to be feared and placated, like the wrath of ancient gods. So Gaille stood there and took upon her chin all Elena's scathing and brutal remarks about the poverty of her abilities, her ingratitude, the damage this incident would doubtless do her career when it got out, though she herself would, of course, do her best to protect her.

'I'm sorry, Ms Koloktronis,' Gaille said, when the tirade finally began to slacken. 'Kristos said you wanted to see me.'

'I told him to tell you I was coming over.'

'That's not what he told me. I just wanted to make sure you hadn't fallen.'

'Where did you go?'

'Nowhere. I just checked at the bottom.'

'Very well,' said Elena grudgingly. 'Then we'll say no more about it. But don't mention it to Qasim, or I won't be able to protect you.'

'No, Ms Koloktronis,' said Gaille. Qasim, the on-site representative of the Supreme Council, was every bit as secretive about this place as Elena herself. No doubt it would be embarrassing for Elena to have to admit to him that she'd left the door unlocked and unguarded.

'Come with me,' said Elena, locking the steel door, then leading Gaille across to the magazine. 'There's an ostracon I'd like your opinion on. I'm ninety-nine point nine nine per cent sure of its translation. You can perhaps help me with the other nought point nought one per cent.'

'Yes, Ms Koloktronis,' said Gaille meekly. 'Thank you.'

III

'Are you an idiot?' scowled Max, having followed Knox to the stern of the dive boat. 'Do you have a death wish, or something? Didn't I tell you to leave Hassan's woman alone?'

'She came to talk to me,' answered Knox. 'Did you want me to be rude?'

'You were flirting with her.'

'She was flirting with me.'

'That's even worse. Christ!' He looked around, his face suffused with fear. Working for Hassan could do that to people.

'I'm sorry,' said Knox. 'I'll stay away from her.'

'You'd better. Trust me, you get on Hassan's wrong side, you and your mate Rick can forget about your little project, whatever the fuck it is.'

'Keep your voice down.'

'I'm just warning you.' He wagged a finger, as if he had more to say, but then he turned and walked away.

Knox watched him go. He didn't like Max; Max didn't like him. But they had a valuable relationship. Max ran a dive school, and Knox was a good, reliable dive instructor who knew how to charm tourists into recommending him to others they met on their travels; and he worked for peanuts too. In return, Max let him use his boat and side-scan sonar for what he disparagingly referred to as his 'little project'. Knox smiled wryly. If Max ever found out what he and Rick were after, he wouldn't dismiss it so patronisingly.

Knox had come to Sharm nearly three years before. He'd only been here four weeks when something extraordinary had happened; and it had been prompted by the very same tattoo that had caught Fiona's eye.

While he'd been sitting on the front one evening, enjoying a beer, a powerfully built Australian man had come up to him. 'Mind if I join you?' he'd asked.

'Help yourself.'

'I'm Rick.'

'Daniel. But everyone calls me Knox.'

'Yeah. So I've been told.'

Knox squinted at him. 'You've been asking?'

'They say you're an archaeologist.'

'Used to be.'

'You gave it up to become a dive instructor?' asked Rick sceptically.

'It gave me up,' explained Knox. 'A bust-up with the establishment.'

'Ah.' He leaned forward. 'Interesting tattoo.'

'You think?'

Rick nodded. 'If I show you something, you'll keep it to yourself, right?'

'Sure,' shrugged Knox.

Rick reached into his pocket, pulled out a matchbox. Inside, embedded in cotton wool, was a fat golden teardrop about an inch long with an eyelet at the narrow end for a clasp or a chain. Specks of pink were accreted from where it had been chiselled out of coral. And, on its base, a sixteen-pointed star had been faintly inscribed.

'I found it a couple of years back,' said Rick. 'I thought you might be able to tell me more about it. I mean, it's Alexander's symbol, right?'

'Yes. Where d'you find it?'

'Sure!' snorted Rick, taking it back, replacing it jealously in its makeshift home, then back in his pocket. 'Like I'm going to tell you that. Well? Any idea?'

'It could be anything,' said Knox. 'A tassel for a robe, a drinking cup, something like that. An earring.'

'What?' frowned Rick. 'Alexander wore earrings?'

'The star doesn't mean it belonged to him personally. Just to his household.'

'Oh.' The Australian looked disappointed.

Knox frowned. 'And you found it in these reefs, yes?'

'Yeah. Why?'

'It's odd, that's all. Alexander never came near here. Nor did his men.'

Rick snorted. 'And I thought you said you were an archaeologist! Even I know he came to Egypt. He went to visit that place out in the desert.'

'The Oracle of Ammon in Siwa Oasis. Yes. But

22

he didn't travel via Sharm, believe me. He cut across the north coast of Sinai.'

'Oh. And that was his only visit, was it?'

'Yes, except for . . . ' And Knox's heart suddenly started pounding crazily inside his chest as a wild idea occurred to him. 'Jesus Christ!' he muttered.

'What?' asked Rick excitedly, reading his face.

'No. No. It couldn't be.'

'What? Tell me.'

Knox shook his head decisively. 'No. I'm sure it's nothing.'

'Come on, mate. You've got to tell me now.'

'Only if you tell me where you found it.'

Rick squinted shrewdly at him. 'You reckon there's more? That's what you're thinking, yeah?'

'Not exactly. But it's possible.'

Rick hesitated. 'And you're a diver, yeah?'

'Yes.'

'I could do with a buddy. The place isn't easy on my own. If I tell you, we'll go look together, yeah?'

'Sure.'

'OK. Then spill.'

'Fine. But you've got to remember, this is pure speculation. The chances of this being what I think it is — '

'I get the point. Now spill.'

'Long version or short?'

Rick shrugged. 'I've got nowhere I need to be.'

'I'll have to give you some background first. Alexander came to Egypt only once during his life, like I said, and then for just a few months. Across north Sinai to the Nile Delta, then south

23

to Memphis, the old capital, just south of Cairo, where he was crowned. After that it was north again to found Alexandria, westwards along the coast to Paraetonium, modern Marsa Matruh, then due south through the desert to Siwa. He and his party got lost, apparently. According to one account, they'd have died of thirst except that two talking snakes guided them to the Oasis.'

'Those talking snakes. Always there when you need them.'

'Aristobulus tells a more plausible story, that they followed a pair of crows. Spend any time in the desert, you're pretty much certain to see some brown-necked ravens. They're about the only birds you will see in many places. They often travel in pairs. And they're cheeky buggers too; if they can't find any snakes or locusts to eat, they'll happily scout around your camp site looking for scraps, before heading off back to the nearest oasis. So if you were to follow them . . . '

Rick nodded. 'Like dolphins in the Sea of Sand.'

'If you want to put it that way,' agreed Knox. 'Anyway, they got Alexander to Siwa, where he consulted the oracle, and then it was back into the desert again; but this time he headed east along the caravan trails to Bahariyya Oasis, where there's a famous temple dedicated to him, and then back to Memphis. That was pretty much that. It was off beating up Persians again. But then, after he died, he was brought back to Egypt for burial.'

'Ah! And you think this was from then?'

'I think it's possible. You've got to bear something in mind. This is Alexander the Great we're talking about. He led thirty thousand Macedonians across the Hellespont to avenge Xerxes' invasion of Greece, knowing that he'd face armies ten times larger. He hammered the Persians not once, not twice, but three times, and then he just kept on going. He fought countless battles, and he won them all, making himself the most powerful man the world has ever seen. When his best friend Hephaiston died, he sent him on his way on top of a beautifully carved wooden pyre eighty metres high; like building Sydney Opera House, then putting a match to it, just to enjoy the blaze. So you can imagine, his men would have insisted on something pretty special when Alexander himself died.'

'I get you.'

'A pyre was out of the question. Alexander's body was far too precious to be burned. Apart from anything else, one of the duties of a new Macedonian king was to bury his predecessor. So whoever possessed Alexander's body had a serious claim to kingship, especially as Alexander hadn't left an obvious successor, and everyone was jostling for position.'

Rick nodded at Knox's empty glass. 'You fancy another?'

'Sure. Thanks.'

'Two beers,' shouted Rick at the barman. 'Sorry. You were saying. People jostling for position.'

'Yes. The throne was pretty much open.

25

Alexander had a brother, but he was a half-wit. And his wife, Roxanne, was pregnant, but no one could be sure she'd have a son; and, anyway, Roxanne was a barbarian, and the Macedonians hadn't conquered the known world to be ruled by a half-breed. So there was an assembly of the army in Babylon, and they came to a compromise. The half-wit brother and the unborn child, if he turned out to be a boy, which he did, Alexander the Fourth, would rule together; but the various regions of the empire would be administered for them by a number of satraps all reporting to a triumvirate. You with me?'

'Yes.'

'One of Alexander's generals was a man named Ptolemy. He was the one who made the claim about the talking snakes as it happens. But don't let that fool you. He was a very shrewd, very capable man. He realised that without Alexander to hold it together, the empire was bound to fragment, and he wanted Egypt for himself. It was rich, out of the way, unlikely to get caught up in other people's wars. So he got himself awarded the satrapy, and he bedded himself in, and eventually he became Pharaoh, founding the Ptolemaic dynasty, which ended with Cleopatra. OK?'

Their beers arrived. They clinked them in a toast. 'Go on,' said Rick.

'It wasn't easy for Ptolemy, making himself Pharaoh,' said Knox. 'Egyptians wouldn't recognise just anyone. Legitimacy was very important to them. Alexander was different: a living god of unquestioned royal blood who'd driven out the hated Persians; there was no shame in being ruled by such a man. But Ptolemy was a nobody as far as the Egyptians were concerned. So one of the things he needed was a symbol of kingship.'

'Ah,' said Rick, wiping froth from his upper lip. 'Alexander's body.'

'Ten out of ten,' grinned Knox. 'Ptolemy wanted Alexander's body. But he wasn't the only one. The head of the Macedonian triumvirate was called Perdiccas. He had ambitions of his own. He wanted to bring Alexander's body back to Macedonia for burial alongside his father, Philip, in the royal tombs of Aigai in Northern Greece. But getting him from Babylon to Macedonia wasn't easy. You couldn't just load him on the first boat. He had to travel in a certain style.'

Rick nodded. 'I'm the same way, myself.'

'A historian called Diodorus of Sicily gave a very detailed description of all this. Alexander's body was embalmed and laid in a coffin of beaten gold, covered by expensive, sweet-smelling spices. And a catafalque — that's a funeral carriage to you and me — was commissioned. It was so spectacular, it took over a year to get ready. It was a golden temple on wheels, six metres long, four metres wide. Golden ionic columns twined with acanthus supported a high vaulted roof of gold scales set with jewels. A golden mast rose from the top, flashing like lightning in the sun. At each of its corners, there was a golden statue of Nike, the

27

ancient goddess of victory, holding out a trophy. The gold cornice was embossed with ibex heads from which hung gold rings supporting a bright, multicoloured garland. The spaces between the columns were filled with a golden net, protecting the coffin from the scorching sun and the occasional rain. Its front entrance was guarded by golden lions.'

'That's a whole lot of gold,' said Rick sceptically.

'Alexander was seriously rich,' replied Knox. 'He had over seven thousand *tons* of gold and silver in his Persian treasuries alone. It took twenty thousand mules and five thousand camels just to shift it all around. You know how they used to store it?'

'How?'

'They used to melt it and pour it into jars and then simply smash off the earthenware.'

'Holy shit,' laughed Rick. 'I could do with finding one of those.'

'Exactly. And the generals didn't dare stint on all this. Alexander was a god to the Macedonian troops. Skimping would have been the quickest way to lose their loyalty. Anyway, the funeral carriage was eventually completed. But it was so heavy that the builders had to *invent* shock-absorbing wheels and axles for it, and even then the route had to be specially prepared by a crew of road-builders, and it took sixty-four mules to draw it along.' He paused to take another sip of his beer. 'Sixty-four mules,' he nodded. 'And each of them wore a gilded crown and a gem-encrusted collar. And each of them had a

28

golden bell hanging upon either cheek. And each of these bells would have had inside it a golden pendant tongue just exactly like the one you've got in your matchbox.'

'You're fucking with me,' said Rick, the shock legible on his face.

'And, more to the point,' grinned Knox, 'this entire catafalque, all this gold, simply vanished from history *without a trace.*'

2

I

A hotel construction site, Alexandria

Mohammed el-Dahab kept a framed photograph of his daughter, Layla, on his desk. It had been taken two years ago, just before she'd fallen sick. He'd developed the habit, while he worked, of glancing at it every few moments. Sometimes it gladdened him to see her face. Mostly, as this time, his heart sank. He pinched the bridge of his nose between his thumb and index finger, muttered a short but heartfelt prayer. He prayed for her like this perhaps thirty times each day, as well as during his formal *rek'ahs*. His prayers had done little good so far, but faith was like that. Without testing it was nothing.

There were incongruous noises outside; shouting, jubilant laughing. He glanced irritably through his office window. Work on the building site had come to a halt. His crew were congregating in a corner, Ahmed was dancing like a dervish at a *moulid*. Mohammed hurried out angrily. Allah had cursed him with the laziest crew in all Egypt. Any excuse! He scowled to put himself into the right frame of mind to deliver a proper tongue-lashing, but when he saw what had caused the commotion, he forgot all ideas of that. The mechanical digger had ripped a great

30

gaping hole in the ground, exposing a spiral staircase that wound around a deep, black shaft, still thick with settling dust. It looked yellow, dark, old; old as the city itself.

Mohammed and his men all gazed at each other with the same thought. *Who knows how long this has lain hidden? Who can guess what riches might lie at its base?* Alexandria was not only one of the great cities of antiquity, it boasted a lost treasure of world renown. Was there a man among them who hadn't dreamed of discovering the golden sarcophagus of the city's founder, Iskandar al-Akbar, Alexander the Great himself? Young boys dug holes in public gardens; women confided in their friends the strange echoes they heard when they tapped the walls of their cellars; robbers broke into ancient cisterns and the forbidden cellars of temples and mosques. But if it was anywhere, it was here, right in the heart of the city's ancient Royal Quarter. Mohammed was not given to idle dreams, but gazing down into this deep shaft, his gut clenched tight as a fist.

Could this be his miracle at last?

He beckoned for Fahd's flashlight, lowered his left foot slowly onto the top step. He was a big man, Mohammed, and his heart was in his mouth as he rested his considerable weight upon the rutted stone, but it bore him without protest. He tested more steps, his back turned to the rough limestone of the outer wall. The inner wall that separated the spiral staircase from the great central shaft was built of crumbled bricks; many had fallen away, leaving a black jigsaw.

31

Mohammed tossed a pebble through a gap, waited with held breath until it clattered four heartbeats later at the foot. The spiral closed above him and he saw that the entire staircase was carved from the rock, a sculpture rather than a construction! It gave him confidence. He continued his descent, around and around. The spiral at last straightened out, doubled back through an arched portal into a large, circular room, calf-deep in sand, rock and fallen bricks. At the centre, four sturdy pillars surrounded the open base of the central shaft. The thin, rebounded daylight was thick with chalky motes swirling slow as planets, clotting like salve on his lips, tickling his throat.

It was cool down here, gloriously quiet after the incessant building site din. Including the stair-well from which he'd just emerged, four arched doorways led off this rotunda, one for each point of the compass. Curved benches with oyster-shell hoods were recessed into limestone walls sumptuously carved with prancing gods, hissing medusas, rampant bulls, soaring birds, bursting flowers and drapes of ivy. A dark, downward-sloping corridor showed through the first doorway, humped with rubble and dust. Mohammed swallowed with distaste and premonition as he tore aside its cobweb veil. A low side-passage led off the winding corridor into a large, tall chamber, walls pocked by columns of square-mouthed openings. A catacomb. He went to the left-hand wall, lit up a dusty yellow skull, tipped the dome aside with a finger. A small, blackened coin fell from its jaw. He picked it up,

32

examined it, set it back down. He shone his torch within. At the far end, a high heap of skulls and bones had been pushed back to make room for later occupants. He grimaced at the sight, retreated to the main corridor to continue his survey. He passed four more burial chambers before descending a flight of twelve steps, then another five before he reached the top of another flight of steps and the water table.

He returned to the rotunda. Ahmed, Husni and Fahd had come down too, were now on their hands and knees, scrabbling through the rubble. He was puzzled that they hadn't explored further until he realised it was the only spot with natural light, and he'd taken their one torch.

'What is this place?' asked Ahmed. 'What have I found?'

'A necropolis,' answered Mohammed flatly. 'A city of the dead.'

Obscurely angered by their presence, he walked through a second portal into a large, tall, closed chamber lined with limestone blocks. A banqueting hall, perhaps, where mourners would have come each year to commemorate their loved ones. A short flight of steps led down through the final portal into a small forecourt. Upon a raised step, a pair of tall, blackened, studded metal doors with hexagonal handles were set into a white-marble wall. Mohammed pulled the left-hand door. It opened with a grinding screech. He squeezed through into a broad, high, empty antechamber. Plaster had fallen away in places from the walls to reveal rough limestone beneath. Two lines of Greek characters were carved into the lintel above the arched doorway in the facing wall; they meant nothing to Mohammed. He crossed a high step into a second, main chamber, of similar width and height, but twice as deep. A knee-high plinth stood in its centre, giving the strong impression that something important like a sarcophagus had once lain upon it. If so, it had long since vanished.

A dull bronze button shield was pinned to the wall beside the doorway. Ahmed tried to wrest it free.

'Stop!' cried Mohammed. 'Are you mad? Will you truly risk ten years in Damanhur for an old shield and a handful of broken pots?'

'No one knows of this but us,' retorted Ahmed. 'Who can tell what treasures are here? Enough for us all.'

'This place was looted centuries ago.'

'But not of everything,' pointed out Fahd. 'Tourists will pay mad prices for all kinds of ancient rubbish. My cousin has a stall near al-Gomhurriya. He knows the value of such things. If we bring him down — '

'Listen to me,' said Mohammed. 'All of you listen. You'll take nothing and you'll tell no one.'

'Who gave you the right to make decisions?' demanded Fahd. 'Ahmed found this, not you.'

'But this project is mine, not yours. This site is mine. One word of this gets out, you'll answer to me. Understand?' He faced them down, one by one, until they broke and stalked away. He watched them uneasily. Trusting secrets to such men was like trusting water to a sieve;

34

Alexandria's slums writhed with villains who'd cut twenty throats on the mere rumour of such a prize. But he wasn't going to back down because of that. All his life, Mohammed had striven to be good. Virtue had been a source of great pleasure to him. He'd leave a room after he'd done something particularly generous or judicious, and warmly imagine the admiring words being exchanged about him. Then Layla had fallen ill and he'd realised he didn't give one fig what people thought of him. He cared only for making her better.

The question now was how to turn this find to that end. Looting it was impractical. For all Ahmed's optimism, there wasn't enough to go around; and if he tried to cut out the others, they'd sneak on him to his bosses, maybe even to the police. That would go hard with him. As site manager, he was legally bound to report this find to the Supreme Council for Antiquities. If they learned he'd kept it quiet, he'd lose his job, his licence to operate and almost certainly his liberty too. He couldn't risk that. His salary was pitiful, but it was all that stood between Layla and the abyss.

The solution, when it finally came to him, was so simple that he couldn't believe he hadn't thought of it at once.

II

'Excuse me. You please will help me with this?'

Knox looked up to see Roland Hinz holding

35

up his huge black wetsuit. 'Of course,' he smiled. 'Forgive me. I was miles away.'

He stood behind the big German to make sure he didn't tumble as he tried to pull it on. That wouldn't go down well. Roland was a Stuttgart banker considering investing in Hassan's latest Sinai venture. Today's jag was largely in his honour. He was making the most of it too, giggly with champagne, more than a little coked, getting on everyone's nerves. He shouldn't, in truth, be allowed anywhere near the water, but Hassan paid well to have rules stretched. And not just rules. Getting Roland into his wetsuit was like trying to stuff a duvet into its cover; he kept plopping out in unexpected places. Roland found this intensely funny. He found everything funny. He clearly believed himself the life and soul. He tripped over his own feet and laughed hysterically as he and Knox spilled inelegantly onto the deck, looking around at the other guests as though expecting rapturous applause.

Knox helped him back up with a strained smile, then kneeled down to pull on his booties for him. He had bloated, pinkish-yellow feet with dirt caked between his toes, as though he hadn't washed between them for years. Knox distracted himself by letting his mind drift back to that afternoon when he'd shared his wild ideas about Alexander's catafalque with Rick. The big Australian's initial euphoria hadn't lasted long.

'So this procession came through Sinai, did it?' he'd asked.

'No,' said Knox. 'Not according to any of our sources.'

36

'Oh bollocks, mate,' protested Rick, sitting back in his chair, shaking his head angrily. 'You really had me going.'

'You want me to tell you what we know?'

'Sure,' he said, still annoyed. 'Why not?'

'OK,' said Knox. 'The first thing you need to understand is that our sources are very unreliable. We don't have any eyewitness accounts of Alexander's life or campaigns. Everything we have, we have from later historians citing earlier ones. Second-, third-, even fourth-hand accounts.'

'Chinese whispers,' suggested Rick.

'Exactly. But it's worse even than that. When Alexander's empire split up, each of the various factions wanted to paint themselves in the best light, and all the others in the worst, so there was a lot of propaganda written. Then the Romans came along. The Caesars worshipped Alexander. The Republicans loathed him. Historians were consequently extremely selective in their stories, depending on which camp they belonged to. One way or another, most of what we have is very badly slanted. Working out the truth is a nightmare.'

'Duly noted.'

'But we're pretty sure that the catafalque travelled along the Euphrates from Babylon to Opis, then north-west along the Tigris. A magnificent procession, as you can imagine. People trekked hundreds of miles just to see it. And, sometime in 322 or 321 BC, it reached Syria. After that, it's hard to know. Bear in mind that we're talking about two things here. The first is Alexander's embalmed body, lying in its coffin. The second is the funeral carriage and all the rest of the gold. OK?'

'Yes.'

'Now we know pretty much what happened to Alexander's body and coffin. Ptolemy hijacked it and took it to Memphis, probably with the collaboration of the escort commander. But we don't know what happened to the rest of the catafalque. Diodorus says that Alexander's body was eventually taken to Alexandria in it, but his story is confused, and it seems clear he's actually talking about the coffin, not the catafalque. And the most vivid description comes from a guy called Aelian. He says that Ptolemy was so fearful that Perdiccas would try to seize Alexander back that he dressed a likeness of his body in royal robes and a shroud, then laid it on a carriage of silver, gold and ivory, so that Perdiccas would charge off in pursuit of this decoy while Ptolemy took Alexander's body on into Egypt by another route.'

Rick squinted. 'You mean Ptolemy left the catafalque behind?'

'That's what Aelian suggests,' said Knox. 'You've got to remember, the main prize was Alexander. Ptolemy needed to get him back to Egypt quick, and you couldn't travel quickly with the catafalque. Estimates suggest that it moved a maximum of ten kilometres a day, and that was with a large team of sappers preparing the road. It would have taken months to reach Memphis. And it couldn't exactly have travelled discreetly either. Yet I've never come across any

38

account of it being seen travelling the obvious route south from Syria through Lebanon and Israel to Sinai and the Nile; and surely someone would have seen it.'

'So he left it behind, like I said?'

'Possibly. But the catafalque represented an enormous amount of raw wealth. I mean, put yourself in Ptolemy's shoes. What would you have done?'

Rick considered a few moments. 'I'd have split up,' he said. 'One lot scoots ahead with the body. The other takes a different route with the catafalque.'

Knox grinned. 'That's what I'd have done too. There's no proof, of course. But it makes sense. The next question is how. Syria's on the Mediterranean, so he might have sailed down. But the Med was notoriously infested with pirates, and he'd have needed ships on hand; and if he'd felt it possible, he'd surely have taken Alexander's body that way, and we're pretty certain he didn't.'

'What were his alternatives?'

'Well, assuming that he couldn't move the catafalque as it was, he could have had it chopped up into manageable pieces and taken them south-west along the coast through Israel to Sinai; but that was the route he almost certainly took himself with Alexander's body, and there's not much point splitting up if you're going to go the same way. So there's a third possibility: that he sent it due south to the Gulf of Aqaba, then by boat around the Sinai Peninsula to the Red Sea coast.'

39

'The Sinai Peninsula,' grinned Rick. 'You mean past these reefs here?'

'These very dangerous reefs,' agreed Knox.

Rick laughed and raised his glass in a toast. 'Then let's go find the bugger,' he said.

And that's exactly what they'd been trying to do ever since, though without success. At least, Knox had had a success of sorts. Initially, Rick had only been interested in finding treasure. But the more they'd searched, the more he'd learned, the more he'd caught the archaeological bug. He'd originally been a Clearance Diver in the Australian Navy, the closest they had to Special Forces. Working in Sharm had allowed him to keep diving, but he'd missed that sense of mission. Their quest had restored it to him to such an extent that he'd determined to make a new career in underwater archaeology, studying hard, borrowing Knox's books and other materials, pestering him with questions . . .

Roland's booties were on. Knox stood and helped strap him into his buoyancy control device, then ran through his safety checks. He heard footsteps on the bridge above him and glanced up as Hassan sauntered into view, leaning on the railing and looking down.

'You guys have fun now,' he said.

'Oh, yes,' enthused Roland, giving the thumbs up. 'We have great fun.'

'And don't hurry back now.' He beckoned behind him and Fiona came reluctantly into view. She'd put on long cotton trousers and a thin white T-shirt, as though more modest clothing could somehow protect her, yet still she was shivering. Her moist bikini top had made her T-shirt pearly, and her nipples showed through, pebble-dashed with fear. When Hassan caught Knox staring, he grinned wolfishly and put his arm around her shoulders, almost daring Knox to do something about it.

They said on the streets of Sharm that Hassan had slit the throat of a second cousin for sleeping with a woman he'd put his mark on. They said that he'd beaten an American tourist into a coma for protesting when he'd propositioned his wife.

Knox lowered his eyes and looked around, hoping to share the burden of responsibility. Max and Nessim, Hassan's ex-paratrooper head of security, were checking out each other's dive gear. He'd get no joy there. Ingrid and Birgit, two Scandinavians Max had brought along to keep Roland company, were already suited and waiting by the stern ladder. Knox tried to catch Ingrid's eye, but she knew what he was up to and kept her eyes firmly averted. He glanced back up at the bridge. Hassan was still grinning down at him, aware of exactly what was going through Knox's mind. An alpha male in his prime, savouring the challenge. He ran his hand slowly down Fiona's flank to her backside, cupping and squeezing her buttock. The man had risen from nothing to make himself the most powerful shipping agent on the Suez Canal by the age of thirty. You didn't achieve that by being soft. Now they said he was bored, looking to extend his empire every which way he could, including tourism, buying up

41

waterfront properties in the slump that had followed recent terrorist outrages.

Roland was ready at last. Knox helped him down the ladder into the Red Sea, then kneeled to pass him his fins to pull on in the water. The big German spun backwards like a waterwheel, then splashed to the surface again, guffawing maniacally, slapping the water.

'Hold on,' said Knox tightly. 'I'll be with you in a second.' He kitted himself up, shrugged on and clasped his BCD and tank, goggles loose around his neck, fins in his hand. He started down the ladder and was about to let go when he glanced up at the bridge one final time. Hassan was still staring down at him, shaking his head in mock disappointment. Beside him, Fiona had crossed her arms anxiously over her chest. Her hair was straggled, her shoulders hunched and miserable. She looked her age suddenly, or lack of it; a child who'd met a friendly Egyptian man in a bar and thought she'd worked herself a freebie for the day, confident she could wriggle and flirt her way out of any expectations he might have. Her eyes were wide, lost and frightened, yet somehow still hopeful, as though she believed that everything would work out fine, because basically people were nice.

Just for a moment, Knox imagined it was his sister, Bee, standing there.

He shook his head angrily. The girl was nothing like Bee. She was an adult. She made her own choices. Next time she'd know better. That was all. He glanced over his shoulder to make sure the sea was clear behind him, put his

42

regulator into his mouth, bit down hard and threw himself backwards to explode like fireworks into the womb-warm waters of the Red Sea. He resolutely didn't look back as he led Roland towards the reef, staying a modest four metres deep, in easy reach of the surface should anything go wrong. A masque of tropical fish watched their progress intently but without alarm. Sometimes it was difficult to know which was the show and which the audience. A Napoleon fish, surrounded by a shoal of angels and wrasse, turned regally, effortlessly away. He pointed it out to Roland with exaggerated diving gestures; beginners always enjoyed feeling like initiates.

They reached the coral shelf, a wall of ochre and purple that fell dizzily away into blackness. The waters were still and unclouded; visibility was exceptional. He glanced around unthinkingly, and saw the dark hull of the boat and the menacing blurs of distant big fish in the deeper, cooler waters, and he felt a sharp twinge as he suddenly remembered the worst day of his life, visiting his sister in an intensive care unit in Thessalonike after the car crash. The place had been oppressive with the sounds of life support, the steady wheeze of ventilators, the dull, precarious pulse of monitors, the respectful, funeral-home whispering of staff and visitors. The doctor had tried her best to prepare him, but he'd still been too numb from his trip to the morgue, where he'd just had to identify his parents, and so it had come as a shock to see Bee on the business end of a feeding tube and all the other attachments. He'd felt dislocated, as though he'd been watching a play rather than real events. Her head had been unnaturally swollen, and her skin had been pale and blue. He could remember its waxy pallor still, its uncharacteristic flabbiness. And he'd never before realised how freckled she was around her eyes and in the crook of her elbow. He hadn't known what to do. He'd looked round at her doctor, who'd gestured for him to sit down beside her. He'd felt awkward putting his hand on hers; they'd never been a physically demonstrative family. He'd pressed her cool hand beneath his own, had felt intense and startling anguish, something like parenthood. He'd squeezed her fingers between his own, held them to his lips, and remembered how he'd joked to friends about what a curse it was to have a younger sister to look after.

He didn't any longer.

He tapped Roland on the arm and pointed upwards. They surfaced together. The boat was perhaps sixty metres away. There was no sign of anyone on deck. Knox felt a flutter of nerves in his chest as his heart realised his decision before his head. He spat the regulator from his mouth. 'Stay here,' he warned Roland. Then he set out in strong strokes across the crystal water.

III

Mohammed el-Dahab clasped his case protectively in front of his chest as the woman led him up to the private office of Ibrahim Beyumi, head of the Supreme Council for Antiquities in Alexandria. She knocked once upon his door then pushed it open, beckoned him through. A dapper and rather effeminate-looking man was sitting behind a pine desk. He looked up from his work.

'Yes, Maha?' he asked.

'This is Mohammed el-Dahab, sir. A builder. He says he's found something on his site.'

'What kind of something?'

'Perhaps he should tell you himself,' she suggested.

'Very well,' sighed Ibrahim. He gestured for Mohammed to sit at his corner table. Mohammed looked around, dispiritedly assessing with a builder's eye the bulging wood-panelled walls, the fractured, high ceiling with its missing clumps of plaster, the mildewed drawings of Alexandria's monuments. If this was the office of the top archaeologist in Alexandria, there wasn't as much money in antiquities as he'd hoped.

Ibrahim read his expression. 'I know,' he complained. 'But what can I do? Which is more important, excavation or my comfort?'

Mohammed shrugged as Ibrahim came to sit beside him. He, at least, looked expensive, with his sharp suit and gold watch. He settled his hands primly in his lap, and asked: 'So you've found something, then?'

'Yes.'

'You care to tell me about it?'

Mohammed swallowed. He was a big man, not easily cowed by physical dangers, but educated

45

people intimidated him. There was something kindly about Ibrahim, however. He looked like a man who could be trusted. Mohammed set his case on the table, opened it, withdrew his framed photograph of Layla, laid it facing Ibrahim. Touching and seeing her image restored his courage. 'This is my daughter,' he said. 'Her name is Layla.'

Ibrahim squinted curiously at Mohammed. 'Allah has indeed blessed you.'

'Thank you, yes. Unfortunately Layla is sick.'

'Ah,' said Ibrahim, leaning back. 'I'm sorry to hear that.'

'They call it Burkitt's lymphoma. It appeared in her stomach like a grape and then a mango beneath her skin. Her surgeons removed it. She had chemotherapy. We thought she'd conquered it.'

Ibrahim rubbed his throat. 'Maha said you'd found something — '

'Her doctors are good people,' said Mohammed. 'But they're overworked, under-equipped. They have no money. They wait for — '

'Excuse me, but Maha said you'd found — '

'They wait for her disease to progress so far that there's nothing more they can do.' Mohammed leaned forwards, said softly but fiercely: 'That time is not yet here. My daughter still has one chance.'

Ibrahim hesitated, then asked reluctantly: 'And that is?'

'A bone-marrow transplant.'

A look of polite horror crossed Ibrahim's face. 'But aren't those incredibly expensive?'

46

Mohammed waved that aside. 'Our Medical Research Institute has a programme of publicly funded transplants, but they won't consider a patient unless they've already identified a donor match. But they'll not run tests for a match unless the patient is already in the programme.'

'Surely that makes it impossible — '

'It's their way of choosing without having to choose. But unless I can finance these tests, my daughter will die.'

Ibrahim said weakly: 'You can't expect the SCA to — '

'These tests aren't expensive,' said Mohammed urgently. 'It's just that the chances of a match are low. My wife and I, our closest family, our friends, we've all taken the tests, but without success. I can persuade others, more distant cousins, friends of friends, but only if I organise and pay. I've tried everywhere to borrow money for this, but already this disease has put me so far in debt that . . . ' He felt tears coming; he broke off, bowed his head to prevent Ibrahim seeing.

There was silence for a while. Then Ibrahim murmured: 'Maha said you'd found something on your site.'

'Yes.'

'Am I to understand that you want money for these tests in exchange for telling me about it?'

'Yes.'

'You realise you're legally obliged to inform me anyway.'

'Yes.'

'That you could go to gaol if you don't.'

47

Mohammed lifted his face, met Ibrahim's gaze with perfect calmness. 'Yes.'

Ibrahim nodded, gestured around his shabby offices. 'And you understand I cannot promise anything?'

'Yes.'

'Very well. Why don't you tell me what you've found?'

3

I

Knox reached the dive boat quickly. He took off his flippers, tossed them aboard, climbed up. He could see no sign of Fiona or Hassan. Now that he was here, he wasn't certain what to do. He felt conspicuous and rather foolish. He unbuckled and slipped off his BCD and tank, carried it with him as he walked quietly across the deck to the portside cabins. He tested the doors one by one, looking inside. He finally came to one that was locked. He rattled it. There was a muffled cry inside, then silence.

Some people enjoy and seek out violence. Not Knox. He had a sudden disembodied vision of himself standing there, and it unnerved him badly. He turned and walked away, but then the door opened behind him.

'Yes?' demanded Hassan.

'I'm sorry,' said Knox, without looking around. 'I made a mistake.'

'Come back!' said Hassan, irritably. 'Yes, you. Max's boy. I'm talking to you. Come here now.'

Knox turned reluctantly, walked back towards Hassan, eyes submissively lowered. Hassan didn't even bother to block his view, so that Knox could see Fiona lying on the bed, forearms crossed over her exposed breasts, cotton trousers half pulled down around her clenched and lifted knees. There was a cut above her right eye; her upper lip was bleeding. A torn white T-shirt lay discarded on the floor.

'Well?' demanded Hassan. 'What did you want?'

Knox glanced again at Fiona. She shook her head at him, to say it was all right, she could cope with this, he shouldn't get involved. The small gesture triggered something utterly unexpected in Knox, something like rage. He swung his scuba tank like a wrecking ball into Hassan's solar plexus, doubling him up. Then he clubbed him on the side of his jaw, and sent him reeling backwards. Now that he'd started, he couldn't help himself. He hit Hassan again and again until he collapsed on the ground. It was only when Fiona pulled him away that his mind cleared.

Hassan was unconscious, his face and chest painted with blood. He looked so badly beaten that Knox kneeled and was relieved to find a pulse in his throat.

'Quick,' said Fiona, tugging his hand. 'The others are coming back.'

They ran together out of the cabin. Max and Nessim were swimming towards the boat. They shouted furiously when they saw Knox. He ran to the bridge, ripped wiring from beneath the two-way radio and ignition. All the keys were kept in a plastic tub on the floor. He grabbed the lot. The speedboat was tied by a single rope to their stern. He hurried down the ladder, hauled the speedboat towards them, helped Fiona onto its bow, followed himself, untying the towrope, jumping into the driver's seat, slipping the key into the ignition just as Max and Nessim reached them and started to climb aboard. Knox spun the boat in a tight circle and roared away; the wash of water ripped Max free, but Nessim held on, pulled himself aboard, stood. He was a tough bastard, Nessim, angry as hell, but he was hampered by his wetsuit and his tank. Knox threw the boat into another tight spin and sent him flailing over the side.

Knox straightened out and roared off towards Sharm. He shook his head at himself. *He'd done it now. He'd fucking done it.* He needed to reach his Jeep before Hassan or Nessim could put the word out. If they caught him . . . *Christ!* He felt sick at the prospect of what they'd do. He needed out of Sharm, out of Sinai, out of Egypt altogether. He needed out tonight. He glanced around. Fiona was sitting on the bench seat at the back, head bowed, teeth chattering, a blue towel wrapped tight around her trembling shoulders. For the life of him, he couldn't think how she'd reminded him of Bee. He slammed the heel of his hand against the control panel in anger at himself. If there was one thing he hated, it was memory. You worked your balls off to build a life in a place like this that had no links whatsoever with your past; no friends, no family, nothing to weigh you down. But it wasn't enough. You took your memory with you wherever you went, and it'd fuck you up in a heartbeat.

Ibrahim Beyumi walked Mohammed down to the street to wish him farewell, then thanked him and watched him disappear round the corner. He could have followed him, of course, and found the location of his site that way. But the big man's story had touched him, not least because he'd effectively put his career and freedom in Ibrahim's hands, and Ibrahim always liked to repay such trust. Besides, he'd left a telephone number to call when he had news, so he'd be easy enough to track down, if necessary.

Maha, Ibrahim's assistant, started to rise when he walked over to her desk, but he settled her with a palm, then went to consult the vast street map of Alexandria pinned to the wall behind her. As ever, it filled him with wistful pride, marked as it was with every antiquity in his beloved city, including Pompey's Pillar, Ras el-Tin, the Latin Cemeteries, the Roman theatre, Fort Qait Bey. There were some fine sites among them, and he boosted them vigorously, but he knew in his heart that none of them was in the first rank of Egyptian antiquities. Alexandria boasted no pyramids, no Karnak or Abu Simbel, no Valley of the Kings. And yet, two thousand years ago, its buildings had been something to marvel at. The Pharos lighthouse had been one of the Seven Wonders. The Mouseion had led the world in learning and culture. The Temple of Serapis had awed worshippers with its splendour and the trickery of its flying statues. The Royal Palaces of Cleopatra were imbued with extraordinary romance. And, most of all, it had boasted the mausoleum of the city's patriarch, Alexander the Great himself. If just one of these great marvels had survived, Alexandria would surely now rival Luxor or Giza on the tourist trail. But none had.

'That man,' said Ibrahim.

'Yes?'

'He's found a necropolis.'

Maha looked around. 'Did he say where?'

'In the old Royal Quarter.' Ibrahim traced out the approximate area with his finger, then tapped its heart. Remarkably, it was impossible to be sure even of the broad outlines of the ancient city, let alone streets or buildings. They'd all been victims of Alexandria's particular location. With the Mediterranean to the north, Lake Mariut to the south and west, and the marshy Nile Delta to the east, there'd been no room to expand. When new buildings had been needed, old ones had been torn down to make way for them. Fort Qait Bey was built on the ruined foundations of the Pharos lighthouse. And the limestone blocks of Ptolemaic palaces had been reused for Roman temples, Christian churches and Islamic mosques, mirroring the various ages of the city.

He turned to Maha with a storyteller's smile. 'Did you know that Alexander marked out our city's walls himself?'

'Yes, sir,' she replied dutifully, but without looking up.

'He leaked a trail of flour from a sack, only for birds of all colours and sizes to come feast upon it. Some people might have been put off by such

53

an omen. Not Alexander.'

'No, sir.'

'He knew that it meant our city would provide shelter and sustenance for people from all nations. And he was right. Yes. He was right.'

'Yes, sir.'

'I'm boring you.'

'You said you wanted these letters out today, sir.'

'I do, Maha. Indeed I do.'

Alexander hadn't lived to see his city built. It had been Ptolemy and his progeny who'd benefited, ruling Egypt with gradually diminishing authority until the Romans had taken over, themselves displaced by the Arab conquest of AD 641. The administrative capital had been transferred south, first to Fustat, then to Cairo. Trade with Europe had fallen off; there'd no longer been such need for a Mediterranean port. The Nile Delta had silted up; the freshwater canals had fallen into disuse. Alexandria's decline had continued inexorably after the Turks had taken control, and by the time Napoleon had invaded at the turn of the nineteenth century, barely six thousand people had lived here. But the city had since proved its resilience, and today some four million were packed together into high-density housing that rendered systematic excavation impossible. Archaeologists like Ibrahim, therefore, were at the mercy of developers, still tearing down old buildings to erect new ones in their place. And every time they did so, there was just a glimmer of a chance that they'd uncover something extraordinary.

'He did describe one area in great detail,' he said. 'A forecourt with bronze doors leading to an antechamber and main chamber. What do you make of that?'

'A tomb?' hazarded Maha. 'Ptolemaic?'

Ibrahim nodded. 'Early Ptolemaic. Very early.' He took a deep breath. 'Indeed, it sounded to me like the tomb of a Macedonian king.'

Maha stood and turned, her fingers splayed on her desk. 'You can't mean . . . ' she began. 'But I thought Alexander was buried in a great mausoleum.'

Ibrahim remained silent for several seconds, vicariously enjoying her excitement, wondering whether to deflate her gently now or risk sharing his wilder hopes. He decided to let her down. 'He was, yes. It was called the Sema; the Greek word for 'tomb', you know. Or perhaps Soma, their word for 'body'.'

'Oh,' said Maha. 'So this isn't Alexander, then?'

'No.'

'What is it?'

Ibrahim shrugged. 'We'll need to excavate to find that out.'

'How? I thought we'd spent all our money.'

And that was the nub. Ibrahim's entire budget for the year was already allocated. He'd begged as much from the French and Americans as they could give. It happened like that here, precisely because excavation was such an opportunistic affair. If too many interesting sites were found in the same financial period, he simply couldn't handle them all. It became a matter of triage. At this precise moment, all his field archaeologists were involved directly or indirectly in projects right across the old city. Excavating this new site would demand new money, specialists and crew. And it wasn't as if he could put it on hold until the new financial year. The stairwell was slap in the middle of the hotel's prospective car park; Mohammed could accommodate a couple of weeks of excavation, but any more would ruin his schedule. That was a real concern to Ibrahim. In uncovering ancient Alexandria, he depended almost entirely upon property developers and construction companies to report significant finds. If ever he got a reputation for being difficult to work with, they'd simply stop notifying him, whatever their legal obligations. In many ways, this latest site was a headache he didn't need. But it was also an early Macedonian tomb, quite possibly a very significant find indeed. He couldn't let it slide by. He just couldn't.

There was one possible source of funds, he knew. His mouth felt tacky and dry just thinking of it, not least because it would mean contravening all kinds of SCA protocols. Yet he could see no alternative. He conjured up some saliva to help him speak, forced a smile. 'That Greek businessman who keeps offering to sponsor us,' he said.

Maha raised her eyebrows. 'You can't mean Nicolas Dragoumis?'

'Yes,' he said. 'That's the one.'

'But I thought you said he was . . . ' She caught his eye and trailed off.

'I did,' he acknowledged. 'But do you have a better suggestion?'

'No, sir.'

Ibrahim had been delighted when Nicolas Dragoumis had first contacted him. Sponsors were always welcome. Yet something about his manner had made Ibrahim apprehensive. After putting down the phone, he'd gone directly to the Dragoumis Group's corporate website, with all its links to subsidiaries in shipping, insurance, construction, media, import-export, electronics, aerospace, property, tourism, security and more. He'd found a sponsorship section explaining that the Dragoumis Group only supported projects that helped demonstrate the historical greatness of Macedonia, or which worked to restore the independence of Aegean Macedonia from the rest of Greece. Ibrahim didn't know much about Greek politics, but he knew enough not to want to get involved with Macedonian separatists.

Elsewhere on the site, he'd found a page with a group photograph of the directors. Nicolas Dragoumis was tall, stringy, handsome and well-dressed. But it had been the man standing front centre who'd unnerved Ibrahim. Philip Dragoumis, group founder and chief executive, fearsome-looking, swarthy, lightly bearded, with a large, plum-coloured birthmark above his left cheekbone, and an incredibly potent gaze, even in a photograph. A man to steer clear of. But Ibrahim had no choice. His heart beat a little faster, a little louder, as though he were standing on the very edge of a high cliff.

57

'Good. Then could you find me his telephone number, please?'

III

Knox beached the speedboat near his Jeep and waded ashore. Fiona had pulled herself together, was now insisting on returning to her hotel. From the way she wouldn't meet his gaze, it seemed she'd figured out that Hassan's wrath would be at Knox, not her; and therefore the safest place was anywhere away from him. Not so dumb after all. Knox revved his Jeep furiously. He was glad not to have her to worry about, but it pissed him off anyway. His passport, cash and plastic were in his money-belt. His laptop, clothes, books and all his research were in his hotel room, but he dared not go back for them.

At the main road, he faced his first major decision. North-east to the Israeli border or up the west coast highway towards the main body of Egypt? Israel was safety, but the road was in bad repair, slow and choking with army checkpoints. West, then. He'd arrived here nine years ago on a boat into Port Said. It seemed a fitting way to leave. But Port Said was on the Suez, and the Suez belonged to Hassan. No. He needed out of Sinai altogether. He needed an international airport. Cairo, Alexandria, Luxor.

He jammed his mobile against his ear as he drove, warning Rick and his other friends to watch out for Hassan. Then he turned it off altogether, lest they use the signal to trace him.

He pushed his old Jeep as fast as it would go, engine roaring. Blue oil fires flickered ahead on the Gulf of Suez, like some distant hell. They matched his mood. He'd been driving for less than an hour when he saw an army checkpoint up ahead, a chicane of concrete blocks between two wooden cabins. He choked a sudden urge to swing round and flee. Such checkpoints were routine in Sinai; there was nothing sinister about this. He was waved to the side of the road, felt the bump as he left the road, then cloying soft sand beneath his wheels. An officer swaggered across, a short, broad-shouldered man, with hooded, arrogant eyes; the kind who'd enjoy taunting weaker men until they broke and attacked him, before battering them to pulp and protesting innocently that they had started it. He held out his hand for Knox's passport, took it away with him. There was little traffic; the other soldiers were chatting around a radio, automatic rifles slung nonchalantly over their shoulders. Knox kept his head down. There was always one who wanted to show off his English.

A long green insect was walking slowly along the rim of his lowered window. A caterpillar. No, a centipede. He put his finger in its way. It climbed unhesitatingly upon it, its feet tickling his skin. He brought it up to eye-level to inspect as it continued on its way, unaware of just having been hijacked, the precariousness of its situation. He watched it up and around his wrist with a sense of fellow feeling. Centipedes had had great resonance for the ancient Egyptians. They'd been closely connected with death, but in a welcome

59

way, because they'd fed upon the numerous microscopic insects that themselves feasted upon corpses, and so had been seen as protectors of the human body, guarding against decomposition, and thus an aspect of Osiris himself. He gently tapped his hand against the outside of his Jeep's door until the centipede fell off and tumbled to the ground. Then he leaned out the window and watched it creep away until he lost it in the darkness.

Inside the cabin, the officer was reading details from his passport into the telephone. He replaced the handset, perched on the edge of his desk, waiting to be called back. Minutes passed. Knox looked around. No one else was being kept: cursory inspections and then a wave through. The phone in the cabin finally rang. Knox watched apprehensively as the officer reached out to answer it.

4

A church outside Thessalonike, Northern Greece

'The ram which thou sawest having two horns
are the kings of Media and Persia,' intoned the
old preacher, reading aloud from the open Bible
upon his pulpit. 'And the rough goat is the king
of Grecia: and the great horn that is between his
eyes is the first king.' He paused and looked
around the packed church. 'Every bible scholar
will tell you the same thing,' he said, leaning
forward a little, lowering his voice, confiding to
his audience. 'The ram Daniel speaks of
represents the Persian king Darius. The king of
Grecia represents Alexander the Great. These
verses are talking about Alexander's defeat of the
Persians. And do you know when Daniel wrote
them? Six hundred years before the birth of
Christ, *two hundred and fifty years before
Alexander was even born.* Two hundred and fifty
years! Can you even begin to imagine what will
be happening in the world two hundred and fifty
years from now? But Daniel did it.'

Nicolas Dragoumis nodded as he listened. He
knew the old preacher's text word for word.
He'd written much of it himself, and then they'd
worked together in rehearsals until every word
was perfect. But you could never really tell with

something like this until you took it to the people. This was their first night, and it was going well so far. Atmosphere; that was the key. That was why they'd chosen this old church, though it wasn't an official service. The moon showed through the stained-glass windows. A bird hooted in the rafters. Thick doors excluded the outside world. Incense caught in nostrils, covering the smell of honest sweat. The only lighting came from lines of fat white candles, just bright enough for the congregation to be able to check in their own bibles that these verses were truly from Chapter 8 of the Book of Daniel, as the preacher had assured them, but dark enough to retain a sense of the numinous, the unknown. People knew, in this part of the world, that things were stranger and more complex than modern science tried to paint them. They understood, as Nicolas did, the concept of mysteries.

He looked around the pews. These haggard people. People with compacted lives, old before their time, taking on backbreaking work at fourteen, becoming parents at sixteen, grandparents at thirty-five, few of them making it past fifty; unshaven faces gaunt from stress, sour from disappointment, skin leathery and dark from too much sun, hands callused from their endless struggle against hunger. And angry too, simmering with resentment at their poverty and the punitive taxation they paid on what little they earned. Anger was good. It made them receptive to angry ideas.

The preacher stood up straighter, relaxed his shoulders, continued his reading. 'Now *that being broken, whereas four stood up for it, four kingdoms shall stand up out of the nation, but not in his power.'* He gazed out into his congregation with the slightly manic blue eyes of a madman and a prophet. Nicolas had chosen well. ''Now that being broken',' he repeated. 'That phrase refers to the death of Alexander. 'Four kingdoms shall stand up out of the nation'. And that refers to the break-up of the Macedonian Empire. As you all know, it was broken into four parts by four successors: Ptolemy, Antigonus, Kassandros and Seleucus. And, remember, this was written by Daniel *nearly three hundred years earlier.'*

But unrest and anger weren't enough, reflected Nicolas. Where there was poverty, there was always unrest and anger; but there wasn't always revolution. There'd been unrest and anger in Macedonia for two millennia, as first the Romans, then the Byzantines and Ottomans had oppressed his people. And every time they'd struggled free from one yoke, another had been placed upon them. A hundred years ago, prospects had at last looked bright. The 1903 Ilinden Uprising had been brutally crushed, but then in 1912, 100,000 Macedonians had fought side-by-side with Greeks, Bulgarians and Serbs finally to expel the Turks. It should by rights have been the birth date of an independent Macedonia. But they'd been betrayed. Their former allies had turned upon them, the so-called Great Powers had collaborated in the infamy, and Macedonia had been cut up into three parts under the wretched Treaty of Bucharest. Aegean

63

Macedonia had been awarded to Greece, Serbian Macedonia to Serbia, and Pirin Macedonia to Bulgaria.

'*And out of one of them came forth a little horn, which waxed exceeding great, toward the south, and toward the east, and toward the pleasant land.* The little horn is Demetrios,' asserted the preacher. 'For those of you who may not remember, Demetrios was the son of Antigonus, and he had himself acclaimed king of Macedonia, even though he was not of Alexander's blood.'

The Treaty of Bucharest! Just the name had the power to twist and torture Nicolas' heart. For nearly one hundred years, the borders the Treaty had laid down had remained largely unchanged. And the loathsome Greeks, Serbs and Bulgars had done everything they could to eradicate Macedonian history, language and culture. They'd shut down free speech, imprisoned anyone who showed the slightest defiance. They'd appropriated the land of Macedonian farmers and resettled outsiders on it. They'd razed villages, orchestrated mass murders and rapes, turned Macedonians into slaves whom they'd then worked to death. They'd committed ethnic cleansing on a grand scale, without a peep of protest from the wider world. But it hadn't worked. That was the thing. The spirit of Macedonian nationhood still burned strong. Their language survived, as did their culture and Church, in pockets across this ancient region. They lived on in these simple yet proud people, in the glorious sacrifices they'd already made

64

and would soon be prepared to make once more for the greater good. And then his beloved country would finally be free.

'*And it waxed great, even to the host of heaven; and it cast down some of the host and of the stars to the ground, and stamped upon them. Yea, he magnified himself even to the prince of the host, and by him the daily sacrifice was taken away, and the place of his sanctuary was cast down.* 'And the place of his sanctuary was cast down',' repeated the preacher. 'That's this place. That's Macedonia. The land of your birth. It was Demetrios, you see, who began the chaos that has engulfed Macedonia ever since. Demetrios. In 292 BC. Mark that date. Mark it well: 292 BC.'

In Nicolas' pocket, his mobile began to buzz. Few people had this number, and he'd given his assistant, Katerina, strict instructions not to put any calls through tonight except in an emergency. He stood and walked to the back doors.

'Yes?' he asked.

'Ibrahim Beyumi for you, sir,' said Katerina.

'Ibrahim who?'

'The archaeologist from Alexandria. I wouldn't have bothered you but he says it's urgent. They've found something. They need a decision at once.'

'Very well. Put him through.'

'Yes, sir.'

The line switched. Another voice came on. 'Mr Dragoumis. This is Ibrahim Beyumi here. From the Supreme Council in — '

'I know who you are. What do you want?'

'You've been generous enough to offer

sponsorship in certain — '

'You've found something?'

'A necropolis. A tomb. A Macedonian tomb.' He took a deep breath. 'From the description I was given, it sounds just like the Royal Tombs at Aigai.'

Nicolas clutched his phone tight and turned his back on the church. 'You've found a Macedonian royal tomb?'

'No,' said Ibrahim hurriedly. 'All I have so far is a description from a builder. I won't know what it really is until I've inspected it myself.'

'And when will you do that?'

'First thing tomorrow. Providing I can arrange finance, at least.'

In the background, the preacher was still talking. '*Then I heard one saint speaking,*' he intoned, squeezing every sonorous drop from the biblical prose, '*and another saint said unto that certain saint which spake, How long shall be the vision concerning the daily sacrifice, and the transgression of desolation, to give both the sanctuary and the host to be trodden under foot?* How long shall Macedonia and the Macedonians be trampled underfoot? How long shall we pay the price for Demetrios' sin? Remember, this was written three hundred years before the sin of Demetrios, which took place in 292 BC!'

Nicolas clamped a hand over his ear, the better to concentrate. 'You need finance *before* you inspect?' he asked sardonically.

'We have a peculiar situation,' said Ibrahim. 'The man who reported the find has a very sick daughter. He wants funds before he'll talk.'

66

'Ah.' The inevitable *baksheesh*. 'How much? For everything.'

'In money terms?'

Nicolas clenched his toes in frustration. *These people!* 'Yes,' he said, with exaggerated patience. 'In money terms.'

'That depends on how big the site proves to be, how much time we have, what kind of artefacts — '

'In US dollars. Thousands, tens of thousands, hundreds of thousands?'

'Oh. It typically costs six or seven thousand American dollars a week for an emergency excavation like this.'

'How many weeks?'

'That would depend on — '

'One? Five? Ten?'

'Two. Three if we're lucky.'

'Fine. Do you know Elena Koloktronis?'

'The archaeologist? I've met her once or twice. Why?'

'She's on a dig in the Delta. Katerina will give you her contact number. Invite her tomorrow. If she vouches for this tomb of yours, the Dragoumis Group will give you twenty thousand dollars. I trust that will meet all your excavation costs, plus any more sick children who turn up.'

'Thank you,' said Ibrahim. 'That's most generous.'

'Talk to Katerina. She'll talk you through our terms.'

'Terms?'

'You don't think we'd provide funds on this scale without terms, do you?'

'But — '

'Like I say, talk to Katerina.' And he snapped closed his phone.

'*And he said unto me, Unto two thousand and three hundred days; then shall the sanctuary be cleansed.* Two thousand and three hundred days!' cried the preacher exultantly. 'Two thousand and three hundred days! But that's not the original text. The original text talks about the 'evenings and mornings of sacrifices'. And those sacrifices took place once each year. Two thousand three hundred days therefore doesn't mean two thousand three hundred days at all. No. It means two thousand three hundred *years*. And who can tell me what date is two thousand three hundred years on from the sin of Demetrios? No? Then let me tell you. It is the year of Our Lord 2008. It is now. It is today. Today, our sanctuary is finally to be cleansed. It says so in the Bible, and the Bible never lies. And remember, this was all predicted exactly by Daniel, *six hundred years before the birth of Christ*.' He wagged a finger in both admonition and exhortation. 'It is written, people. It is written. This is our time. This is your time. You are the chosen generation, chosen by God to fulfil His command. Which of you dare refuse His call?'

Nicolas watched with gratification people turning to look at each other, murmuring in astonishment. This was indeed their time, he reflected, and it wasn't a fluke. His father had been working towards it for forty years now, and he for fifteen. They had operatives in every hamlet, town and village. Vast caches of weapons, food and drink were waiting in the mountains. Veterans of the Yugoslavian wars had trained them in ordnance and guerrilla campaigns. They had sleepers in local and national government, spies in the armed services, friends in the international community and among the Macedonian Diaspora.

The propaganda war was in full swing too. The schedules of Dragoumis TV and radio were crammed with programmes designed to stir Macedonian fervour, their newspapers filled with stories of Macedonian heroism and sacrifice, alongside tales of the opulent lifestyles and unthinking cruelty of their Athenian overlords. And it was working. Anger and hatred was building across northern Greece, even among those who had little sympathy with the separatist cause. Civil disturbance, riots, increasing incidents of ethnic assaults. All the telltale trembling of an imminent earthquake. But they weren't there yet. Much as Nicolas craved it, they weren't quite there. A revolution needed people so worked up they *wanted* martyrdom. Break out the guns now, it would look promising for a while, but then everything would fizzle out. The reaction would come. The Greek army would deploy upon the streets, families would be menaced and businesses investigated. There'd be arbitrary arrests, beatings and counterpropaganda. Their cause would be set back years, might even be irreversibly crippled. No. They still needed something more before it could begin. Something very particular. A symbol that the Macedonian people would be prepared to fight to the death for.

And it was just possible that his recent phone call from Egypt might provide it.

II

The Egyptian army officer was still speaking on the phone. He seemed to be talking for a very long time. He came out with a pen and a pad of paper, crouched to jot down the licence plate of Knox's Jeep. Then he went back inside and read it out to whoever was at the other end of the phone.

The Jeep's keys were in the ignition. For a crazy moment, Knox contemplated driving for it. If Hassan caught him, he was finished anyway. But though the Egyptian soldiers looked cheerful and relaxed enough, that would change in a heartbeat if he fled. The threat of suicide bombers was simply too high around here for them to take risks. He'd be shot dead before he made it fifty yards. So he forced himself to relax, to accept that his fate was out of his hands.

The officer replaced the handset carefully, composed himself, walked across. He wasn't swaggering any more. He looked thoughtful, even apprehensive. He gestured to his men. Immediately, they became alert. He stooped a little to talk through the Jeep's open window, tapping the spine of Knox's passport against the knuckles of his left hand as he did so.

70

He said: 'I am hearing whispers of a most remarkable story.'

Knox's stomach squeezed. 'What whispers?'

'Of an incident involving Hassan al-Assyuti and some young foreigner.'

'I know nothing about that,' said Knox.

'I'm glad,' said the officer, squinting down the road to Sharm, as though expecting a vehicle to appear at any moment. 'Because, if the rumours are true, the young foreigner in question has a very bleak future.'

Knox swallowed. 'He was raping a girl,' he blurted out. 'What was I supposed to do?'

'Contact the authorities.'

'We were in the middle of the fucking sea.'

'I'm sure you'll have your chance to tell your side.'

'Bollocks,' said Knox. 'I'll be dead within an hour.'

The officer flushed. 'You should have thought of that before, shouldn't you?'

'I should have covered my arse, you mean? Like you're doing now?'

'This isn't my fight,' scowled the officer.

Knox nodded. 'People in my country, they think that all Egyptian men are cowards and thieves. I tell them they're wrong. I tell them that Egyptian men are honourable and brave. But maybe I've been wrong.'

There was an angry muttering. One of the soldiers reached in the open window. The officer clamped his hand around his wrist. 'No,' he said.

'But he — '

'No.'

The soldier retreated, a little shamefaced, while the officer looked down thoughtfully at Knox, clearly uncertain what to do. A pair of headlights crested a hill behind. 'Please,' begged Knox. 'Just give me a chance.'

The officer had noticed the approaching headlights too. His jaw tightened as he came to his decision. He tossed the passport onto the passenger seat, then signalled his men to stand aside. 'Get out of Egypt,' he advised. 'It's no longer safe for you.'

Knox let out a long breath. 'I'm leaving tonight.'

'Good. Now go before I change my mind.'

Knox put the Jeep into gear, accelerated away. His hands began shaking wildly as his body flooded with the euphoria of escape. He held himself back until he was a distance down the road, then he whooped and punched the air. He'd done a stupid, reckless thing, but it looked as though he'd got away with it.

III

Nessim, Hassan al-Assyuti's head of security, arrived in Knox's Sharm backpacker hotel to find the middle-aged concierge snoring raucously behind his desk. He came awake with a strangled shriek when Nessim slammed down the wooden access hatch.

'Knox,' said Nessim. 'I'm looking for Daniel Knox.'

'He's not here,' said the concierge, breathing heavily.

'I know he's not here,' said Nessim coldly. 'I want to see his room.'

'But it's his room!' protested the concierge. 'I can't just show it to you.'

Nessim reached into his jacket pocket for his wallet, making sure that the concierge caught a glimpse of his shoulder holster while he was at it. He took out fifty Egyptian pounds and set them down on the counter. 'This is me asking nicely,' he said.

The concierge licked his lips. 'Just this once, I suppose.'

Nessim followed the fat man upstairs, still brooding on what had happened on the boat, the humiliation of being bested by some beach-bum foreigner. At first, he'd thought that Knox would be easy to track down, but it wasn't proving that simple. He'd had word back from a contact in the army that Knox had somehow bluffed his way through a checkpoint. When he'd heard about that, he'd felt a spike of intense anger and frustration. How simple it might have been! But he knew better than to make waves. Only a fool took on the army in Egypt; and Nessim wasn't a fool.

The concierge unlocked and opened Knox's door, looking around nervously lest other guests see what was happening. Nessim went inside. He had one night to capture Knox, and he had that only because Hassan was on morphine to manage his pain. When he woke in the morning he'd demand to know what progress had been made.

He'd want Knox.

Nessim fingered the shabby clothes hanging in the wardrobe, checked the side-pockets of the red canvas bag in the bottom, crouched to inspect the books lined up on the floor against the walls. A few comic novels and thrillers, but mostly academic works on Egypt and archaeology. There were CDs, too, some music, others for his laptop. He picked up a cone-bound document. The front page read, in both English and Arabic:

Mallawi Excavation
First Season Notes
Richard Mitchell and Daniel Knox

He flipped through it. Text and photographs of an excavation near an ancient Ptolemaic settlement a few kilometres from Mallawi in Middle Egypt. He put it back thoughtfully. Why would an Egyptologist be working as a dive instructor in Sharm? He checked a few more documents. Maps and photographs of reefs systems, as best as he could make out. He took the canvas bag from the wardrobe and packed all of Knox's documents inside. Then he packed up Knox's laptop too, and his work-related CDs and floppy disks. In the top drawer of Knox's desk, he found photocopies of his passport and driver's licence, presumably in case he lost the originals; and a strip of colour passport-sized photographs, no doubt for the myriad documents foreigners needed to work in Sinai. He scooped these up and tucked them away in his jacket pocket. Then he picked up the canvas bag and laptop to take away with him. The concierge gave a little whimper.

'Yes?' asked Nessim. 'Is something the matter?'

'No,' said the concierge.

'Good. A word of advice. I'd clear the rest of his stuff out, if I were you. I very much doubt your friend will be coming back any time soon.'

'No?'

'No.' Nessim handed the man one of his business cards. 'But call me if he does.'

5

I

The mosquitoes were in a malevolent mood that evening. Gaille had spiked two smouldering green coils onto their tin stands, had buttoned her white chemise tight around her throat and wrists, tucked her long trousers into socks, then sprayed all her remaining exposed skin to a shine with repellent; yet these gossamer fiends still found a way to feed off her, then boast of it afterwards with that infuriating trumpeting of theirs, retreating to the high hotel ceiling well out of range of reprisal even when she stood on a chair. Whatever had happened to the notion of sisterhood? There it was again, that gloating buzz behind her ear. She slapped at her neck but only as a gesture to punish herself for being so easily caught. The damage was done. The side of her right hand began to pulse and redden. Her mouse hand was an easy target as she typed up these damned excavation notes every night. She paused momentarily, glanced at her window. Just one night off wouldn't hurt. A cold beer and a little conversation. But if Elena caught her in the bar —

Her door opened without warning and Elena herself strode in as though she owned the place. She had no regard for anyone else's privacy, but heaven help you if you dared so much as knock upon her door without first giving two weeks' written notice!

'Yes?' asked Gaille.

'I've just had a phone call,' said Elena. She squinted belligerently at Gaille, as though she found herself at a disadvantage and expected Gaille to make the most of it. 'Ibrahim Beyumi. You know him? He's head of the Supreme Council in Alexandria. Apparently he's found a necropolis. He thinks part of it may be Macedonian. He wants me to check it out with him. He also said he was putting together a team for possible excavation, and asked if I could provide specialist support. I had to remind him I had my own excavation to run. Still, I mentioned you were available.'

Gaille frowned. 'He needs support with languages?'

'It's an emergency excavation,' snorted Elena. 'The job is to record, remove, process and store. Translation will come later.'

'Then — '

'He needs a photographer, Gaille.'

'Oh!' Gaille felt bewildered. 'But I'm not a photographer.'

'You've got a camera, haven't you? You've been taking pictures for us, haven't you? Are you telling me they're no good?'

'I only took them because you asked me to — '

'So it's my fault now, is it?'

Gaille asked plaintively: 'What about Maria?'

'And who will *we* be left with? Are you claiming to be as good a photographer as she is?'

'Of course not.' The only reason she'd brought her camera was to photograph badly faded ancient ostraca, so that she could use her laptop's image software to make the writing clearer. 'I just said I'm not a — '

'And Maria doesn't speak Arabic or English,' pointed out Elena. 'She'd be useless to Ibrahim, and all on her own. Is that what you want?'

'No. All I'm saying is — '

'All you're saying is!' mocked Elena spitefully, imitating her voice.

'Is this about what happened earlier?' asked Gaille. 'I told you, I didn't see anything down there.'

Elena shook her head. 'This has nothing to do with that. It's very simple. The head of the Supreme Council in Alexandria has asked for your help. Do you really want me to tell him you refused?'

'No,' replied Gaille miserably. 'Of course not.'

Elena nodded. 'We're doing an initial survey first thing tomorrow morning. Make sure you're packed and ready to leave at seven.' She took a look round Gaille's messy hotel bedroom, shook her head in exaggerated disbelief, then slammed the door behind her as she left.

II

It was a wrench for Knox to abandon his Jeep in long-term parking. It had been his one constant companion since he'd been in Egypt. Eight hundred thousand already on the clock, and more left beneath the bonnet. You grew to love a car when it had done that well for you. He left his keys and the car-park receipt beneath the seat. He'd give one of his Cairo friends a call, see if they wanted it.

The airport was busy. There was so much refurbishment going on, everything was squeezed into half the space. Knox pulled his baseball cap down over his eyes, though it seemed unlikely that Hassan's people would be ahead of him. He had a choice of flights. Many planes arrived in Egypt late at night, turning round to reach their home airports around dawn. He wandered along the bank of check-in desks. London? Screw that. When you'd fucked up your life, the last thing you wanted was to be reminded of it by the success of old friends. Athens was out too. When he'd lost his marbles in the wake of family tragedy, Greece had been put off-limits to him. Stuttgart? Paris? Amsterdam? The thought of such places depressed him horribly.

A dark-haired woman in the queue for Rome caught his eye and smiled coyly. It seemed as good a reason as any. He went to the enquiries counter to see if there were tickets. The man in line ahead of him was moaning about freight surcharges for his computer. Knox tuned out. Go home, that checkpoint officer had urged. But Egypt *was* his home. He'd lived here ten years. He'd grown to love it, for all its heat, discomfort, chaos and clamour. He loved the desert most of all, its searing clean lines, its extraordinary gift of solitude, the kaleidoscopic sunsets and the chill mists in the dune valleys in the moments before

79

dawn. He loved the hard labour of excavation, the thrill of potential discovery, that glorious kick it gave you getting out of bed each morning. Not that he ever got the chance to excavate any more.

The man ahead of him finally paid up. Knox stepped forward, fluttery with nerves. If he was going to have problems, this was where he'd find out. The booking clerk smiled blandly. He asked about seats; she assured him there were plenty. Knox handed across his passport and a credit card. She tapped keys, glanced up. '*Mi Scusi un momento.*' She took his passport and card, vanished through a door at the back of her booth. He leaned forward to see what it said on her screen. He saw nothing to alarm him. He looked around the concourse. Everything appeared normal.

The clerk returned. She wouldn't quite meet his eye. She kept his passport and credit card in her hand, fractionally out of his reach. He glanced around again. Teams of security guards appeared almost simultaneously through doors at either end of the concourse. Knox lunged forward to snatch his passport and card from the startled clerk, then turned, ducked his head, and walked briskly away, his heart pumping wildly. To his left, a security guard yelled. Knox abandoned pretence. He raced for the exit. The doors were automatic, but they slid open so slowly that he had to turn shoulder-first and still crashed into them, forcing his way through, spinning round. A guard on duty outside took his rifle from his shoulder so hastily that he fumbled it clattering to the floor.

Knox fled left, away from the bright lights of the terminal building into the darkness beyond. He vaulted a rail, ran down a steep embankment to a poorly lit airport bus stop, leaped between a group of young travellers sitting on their backpacks, smashed into the wall of an underpass, grazing his palm. Two uniformed janitors sharing a cigarette looked at him in astonishment as he ran between them, the whiff of their black tobacco catching in his throat. He turned left, sprinting hard, ignoring the shouting and the sirens. There were trees to his left; he ducked into their cover, running for another ten minutes until he couldn't manage any more and came to a stop, bent double, his hands on his knees, heaving for air. Car headlights were slowly patrolling the roads, flashlights sweeping through the trees. The sweat on his shirt cooled; he shivered as he caught the scent of himself. This was bad. This was truly fucking awful. If the police got to him, it wouldn't matter if he could prove his case, Hassan would already have him by the balls. He thought through his options. The air and sea ports were clearly on alert. Border crossings would have his photo. You could get any documents in the world forged in Cairo, but Hassan's reach was long. He'd soon know Knox was in Cairo, and he'd put out the word. No. He needed to get away as quick as possible. He could flag down a taxi or a bus, but the drivers would remember him. Trains were often packed with soldiers and police. Better to risk going back for his Jeep.

There was shouting from his left, a single

gunshot. Knox flinched and ducked. It took him a moment to realise they were shooting at shadows. He had his breath back now, and his bearings. He crouched and kept moving until he reached the perimeter wire fence of long-term parking, high but not barbed. He climbed it by a concrete post, dropped down the other side, the joints of his fingers raw from the thin mesh. He ran low between the pools of light and the ranks of parked cars. The place was deserted. Departing passengers were already in the terminal; arrivals had long-since driven off. He drove up to the booth, handed money to a sleepy attendant. The barrier lifted.

Blue police lights flashed away to his left as he pulled out onto the main road. He turned right, instead, heading towards Cairo. The lights shrank and then disappeared from his mirror. Police cars with flashing lights hurtled past on the other side of the highway. He found that he'd stopped breathing, had to make himself start.

Where the fuck was he going to go now? He couldn't stay in Cairo. But he needed to avoid checkpoints too. That cut out Sinai, the Western Desert and the south. Alexandria, then. It was just three hours north, and of all Egypt's cities, Knox liked it most. He had friends there too, so he could avoid hotels. But he was a fugitive; he couldn't inflict himself on just anyone. He needed someone who'd believe in him, someone with strong nerves, who relished a little transgression from time to time, just to keep the blood pumping. Put like that, there was only one contender. Knox felt his spirits lifting for the first time in hours. He stamped down his foot and roared north.

6

I

'*Mais attends!*' yelled Augustin Pascal at whatever bastard was pounding at his door. '*J'arrive! J'arrive!*' He clambered across the naked girl lying with her face down between his pillows. With that long, wavy, tawny hair, it looked like Sophia. He lifted her mane to make sure. *Shit! Shit!* He'd been excited for a week at the prospect of nailing her, and now he'd gone and wasted it while too drunk to remember.

A terrible thing, growing old.

The pounding on the door began again, resonating with the demolition works inside his skull. He checked his alarm clock. Five thirty! Five fucking thirty! But this was unbelievable! '*Mais attends!*' he yelled again.

He kept emergency bottles of water and pure oxygen on his bedside table. He alternated long swallows from the one with deep breaths from the other, until he felt able to stand without keeling over. He wrapped a ragged towel around his waist, lit a cigarette, went to his front door. Knox was standing there.

'The fuck do you want?' demanded Augustin. 'You know what fucking time this is?'

'I'm in trouble,' said Knox simply. 'I need help.'

II

Ibrahim felt in tremendous spirits as he drove through Alexandria. The sun had only just risen, but he'd been too excited to stay in bed. He'd had a dream during the night. No. That wasn't quite right. He'd been lying there half awake, waiting for his alarm to sound, when he'd suddenly been overwhelmed by a sense of exquisite and intense wellbeing. He couldn't shake off the idea that he was on the verge of something momentous.

He pulled up outside Mohammed's address. It was a wretched-looking place, a tall apartment block with pockmarked and discoloured walls, its front doors broken and hanging loose, intestinal wires spilling out of the intercom. Mohammed was already waiting in the lobby. His eyes lit up when he saw Ibrahim's Mercedes and he walked proudly and slowly across, turning around as he did so, like an actor or a sportsman milking their time upon the stage, wanting as many of his friends and neighbours as possible to see him climb in.

'Good morning,' said Ibrahim.

'We travel in style, then,' said Mohammed, pushing back the passenger seat as far as it would go to accommodate his legs, yet still struggling to fit.

'Yes.'

'My wife's very excited,' said the big man. 'She's convinced we have found Alexander.' And he glanced slyly at Ibrahim to gauge his reaction.

'I doubt it, I'm afraid,' said Ibrahim.

'Alexander was buried in a huge mausoleum.'

'And this isn't part of it?'

Ibrahim shrugged. 'It's very unlikely. It wasn't just Alexander, you see. The Ptolemies were buried there too.' He smiled across at Mohammed. 'They wanted Alexander's glory to rub off on them. It didn't work all that well, though. When the Roman Emperor Augustus made his pilgrimage to Alexander's tomb, the priests asked him if he'd like to see the bodies of the Ptolemies too. You know what he replied?'

'What?'

'That he'd come to see a king, not corpses.'

Mohammed laughed loudly. Alexandrians had always enjoyed watching the powerful get taken down a peg or two. Ibrahim was so pleased that he ventured another anecdote. 'You know Pompey's Pillar?'

'Of course. I can see it from my site.'

'Did you know it had nothing to do with Pompey? No. It was erected in honour of the Emperor Diocletian after he led an expeditionary force here to quash an uprising. He was so angry with the Alexandrians that he vowed to revenge himself upon them until his horse was knee-deep in blood. Guess what happened.'

'I can't think.'

'His horse stumbled and grazed its knees, so that they became covered in blood. Diocletian took this as a sign, and spared the city. His officials put up his pillar and statue in remembrance. But do you know what the Alexandrians did?'

'No.'

'They built a statue too. But not to Diocletian. To his horse.'

Mohammed guffawed and slapped his knee. 'To his horse! I like that!'

They were drawing closer to the city centre. 'Which way?' asked Ibrahim.

'Left,' said Mohammed. 'Then left again.' They paused for a tram. 'So where *was* Alexander's tomb?' he asked.

'No one knows for sure. Ancient Alexandria suffered terribly from fires, riots, wars and earthquakes. There was a catastrophic tsunami too. First it sucked away the water from the harbours so that the citizens went out to pick up the fish and valuables just lying there. Then the wave struck. They never stood a chance.'

Mohammed shook his head in wonder. 'I never heard.'

'No. Anyway, the city fell into ruin and all the great sites became lost, even Alexander's mausoleum. And we've never found it since, though we've tried, believe me.' Countless excavators had tried, including Heinrich Schliemann, fresh from his triumphs at Troy and Mycenae. All had come up empty-handed.

'You must have some idea.'

'Our sources agree that it was on the north-east of the ancient crossroads,' said Ibrahim. 'The trouble is, we're not sure where that was. All these new buildings, you see. Two hundred years ago, yes. A thousand years ago, easy. But now . . . '

Mohammed looked slyly at Ibrahim. 'People say Alexander is buried beneath the Mosque of the Prophet Daniel. They say he's in a golden casket.'

'They're wrong, I'm afraid.'

'Then why do they say this?'

Ibrahim was quiet for a moment, collecting his thoughts. 'You know that Alexander appears in the Qu'ran?' he asked. 'Yes, as the Prophet Zulkarnein, the two-horned one. Leo the African, a sixteenth-century Arab writer, talked of pious Muslims making pilgrimages to his tomb, and he said it was near the church of St Mark, like the Mosque of the Prophet Daniel. And Arab legends speak of a Prophet Daniel who conquered all Asia, founded Alexandria, and was buried here in a golden coffin. Who else could that be but Alexander? You can certainly see why people might confuse the mosque with Alexander's tomb. And then a Greek man claimed he'd glimpsed a body wearing a diadem on a throne in the mosque's vaults. It's a very seductive idea. There's only one problem with it.'

'Yes?'

'It's completely wrong.'

Mohammed laughed. 'You're sure?'

'I've searched the vaults myself,' nodded Ibrahim. 'Believe me, they're Roman, not Ptolemaic. Five or six hundred years too late. But the idea has stuck, not least because our best map of ancient Alexandria marks the mausoleum very near the mosque.'

'There you are, then!'

'It was made for Napoleon the Third,' said Ibrahim. 'He needed information on ancient Alexandria for his biography of Julius Caesar, so he asked his friend Khedive Ismail. But there was no reliable map at the time, so Khedive Ismail commissioned a man called Mahmoud el-Falaki to make it.'

'Research is certainly easier if you're an emperor.'

'Quite,' agreed Ibrahim. 'And it's a really fine piece of work. But not perfect, I'm afraid. He fell for the old legends too, because he marked Alexander's tomb near the mosque, and all the modern guide books and histories now reprint it, keeping the myth alive. The poor imam is constantly being pestered by tourists hoping to find Alexander. But they won't find him there, believe me.'

'Where should they be looking?'

'On the north-east side of the old crossroads, like I said. Near the Terra Santa cemetery, probably. A little north-west of the Shallalat Gardens.'

Mohammed was looking downcast. Ibrahim patted his forearm. 'Don't give up hope just yet,' he said. 'There's something I haven't told you.'

'What?'

'I haven't told anyone. I don't want rumours to start, you know. And you mustn't get your hopes up. You really mustn't.'

'Tell me.'

'Alexander didn't have just one tomb in Alexandria. He had two.'

'Two?'

'Yes. The Soma, the great mausoleum I told you about, was built in around 215 BC by Ptolemy Philopater, the fourth of the Ptolemaic kings. But, before that, he had a different tomb, more in the traditional Macedonian style. More, as it were, like the one you and your men found yesterday.'

Mohammed looked wonderingly at him. 'You think this is what we have found?'

'No,' said Ibrahim gently. 'I really don't. This was Alexander, remember. The Ptolemies would surely have built something spectacular for him.' Not that they knew what. They didn't even know when Alexander's body had been brought here from Memphis. The modern consensus was 285 BC, nearly forty years after his death, though no one had satisfactorily explained why the transfer should have taken so long. 'We believe that his body would have been on display, so it's unlikely we'll find it deep underground. Besides, Alexander was worshipped as a god for centuries. The city authorities would never have tolerated even his former tomb being turned into a common necropolis.'

Mohammed looked crestfallen. 'Then why did you say that it might be?'

'Because this is archaeology,' grinned Ibrahim. 'You never know for sure.'

And there was something else too, though nothing he felt like sharing. It was that ever since he'd been a small boy, listening to his father murmur him to sleep with tall stories about the founder of this great city, he'd had a sense of destiny: one day he'd play his part in the rediscovery of the tomb of Alexander. This morning, as he'd lain awake in bed, he'd had a reprise of that feeling, a conviction that the time was upon him. And, for all his intellectual misgivings, he was sure in his heart that it had something to do with the tomb they were on their way to inspect.

III

Nessim had been on the go all night, working furiously to catch Knox before Hassan woke. But he'd failed. He'd received his summons fifteen minutes ago, and now here he was, clenching a fist to steel himself before knocking on his boss's bedroom door at Sharm's medical centre.

Nessim had joined the Egyptian Army at the age of seventeen. He'd become a paratrooper, one of the elite. But a twisted knee had put an end to hopes of active service, so he'd resigned his commission through boredom and had become a mercenary in the endless African wars. A mortar round had landed fizzing in his lap, yet hadn't exploded; instead, it had convinced him that it was time for a change of pace. Back in Egypt, he'd made a name for himself as a bodyguard before being recruited by Hassan as his head of security. If he'd scared easily, Nessim would never have survived such a life. But there was something about Hassan that scared him. Having to report bad news scared him.

'Come in,' muttered Hassan. His voice was softer than usual, and a little wheezy. He'd lost a tooth, and had suffered severe bruising of his ribs too, making breathing painful. 'Well?' he asked.

'Would you please excuse us?' Nessim asked the doctor sitting beside his bed.

'With pleasure,' said the doctor, a shade too emphatically for his own good.

Nessim closed the door behind him. 'We've got the girl,' he told Hassan. 'She was going for a bus.'

'And Knox?'

'We almost had him. At Cairo Airport. He got away.'

'Almost?' said Hassan. 'What good is almost?'

'I'm sorry, sir.'

Hassan closed his eyes. Yelling evidently hurt too much. 'You call yourself my head of security?' he said. 'Look at me! And you let the man who did this wander around Egypt like some kind of *holiday-maker?*'

'You'll have my resignation as soon as — '

'I don't want your resignation,' said Hassan. 'I want Knox. I want him here. Do you understand? I want you to bring him to me. I want to see his face. I want him to know what he's done and what's going to happen to him because of it.'

'Yes, sir.'

'I don't care what it takes. I don't care how much you spend. I don't care what favours you have to call in. Use the army. Use the police. Whatever is necessary. Am I clear?'

'Yes, sir.'

'Well?' asked Hassan. 'Why are you still here?'

'With respect, sir, there are different ways to catch him. One, as you rightly suggest, is by using our contacts in the police and the army.'

Hassan squinted. He was a shrewd man, for all his wrath. 'But?'

'It was easy enough to secure their help last night. We simply told them that Knox had caused a serious incident on a boat but that the details were still unclear. But tomorrow and the day after, if we still want their active help, they'll want evidence of this serious incident.'

Hassan looked at Nessim in disbelief. 'Are you saying what he did to me isn't sufficient evidence?'

'Of course not, sir.'

'Then what *are* you saying?'

'So far, very few people know anything more than rumours. I picked your medical team myself. They know better than to talk. I've had my own people guarding your door. No one has been allowed in without my explicit permission. But if we involve the police, they'll want to investigate for themselves. They'll send officers to interview you and take photographs and talk to the other guests on the boat, including your Stuttgart friend and the girl. And you have to ask yourself if that would be helpful at this particular moment; or indeed whether it would be good for your reputation to have photographs of your injuries reaching the newspapers or the Internet alongside exaggerated reports of how they were incurred, which could easily happen, because we both know you have enemies as well as friends in the police. And you should also ask yourself what it would do for your personal authority if people got to see what a mere dive instructor had done to you, and that he'd managed to escape too,

even if only for a little while.'

Hassan frowned. He knew the value of being feared. 'What's our alternative?'

'We drop the charges. We say it was all a misunderstanding. We get the girl out. You lie low until you've recovered. Meanwhile, we go after Knox ourselves.'

There was a long silence. 'Very well,' said Hassan finally. 'But you're to take personal charge. And I expect results. Understand?'

'Yes, sir. I understand entirely.'

7

I

It was Gaille's first visit to Alexandria. There was congestion along the Corniche. The masts of fishing boats and yachts in the Eastern Harbour jangled like flamenco in a light breeze that brought with it a faint, acidic tang. She rested her head back, shielded her eyes from the early morning sun as it flickered between tall, rectangular, sun-bleached hotels, apartment blocks and offices, pocked with satellite dishes. The place was coming to life like a gigantic yawn. Alexandria had always been the late-riser of Egyptian cities. Shops were raising steel shutters, lowering canopies. Groups of portly men sipped coffees at pastry cafés and watched benignly as ragged boys and girls wended the traffic, selling packs of napkins and cigarettes. The alleys leading away from the front were tight, dark and faintly menacing. A tram already crammed with passengers paused to take on more. A policeman in a dazzling white uniform and flat cap held up his hand to divert them right. An ancient commuter train clanked and rattled with taunting slowness across a junction. Young boys played chase in the open cattle-carts.

Elena glanced pointedly at her watch. 'You're sure this is the right way?'

Gaille shrugged helplessly. Her only map was

a crude photocopy from an outdated backpacker guidebook. Even so, she had a nagging suspicion that she must already have gone badly wrong to have ended up here, though she'd learned enough about her new boss not to admit it. 'I think so,' she equivocated.

Elena sighed loudly. 'At least you could try.'

'I *am* trying.' Gaille couldn't shake off the suspicion that she was being punished for her trespass yesterday, or was at least being opportunistically expelled from the Delta dig because of it.

They were approaching a large junction. Elena looked at her expectantly for directions. 'Turn right,' said Gaille.

'Are you sure?'

'It should be somewhere along here on the left or right.'

'Somewhere along here on the left or right?' snorted Elena. 'That's really helpful.'

Gaille leaned out her window, her brain aching from lack of sleep and coffee. There was a construction site ahead, a huge concrete high-rise with steel bars waggling like spider legs from the top. She said in desperation: 'I think this must be it.'

'You *think* this must be it; or this is *actually* it?'

'I've never been to Alexandria before,' protested Gaille. 'How should I know?'

Elena huffed noisily and shook her head, but she indicated left and swung through double gates, then bumped along a rutted track. Three Egyptian men were conferring animatedly at the far end.

'That's Ibrahim,' muttered Elena, with such obvious chagrin that Gaille had to fight back a smile. *If Elena thought she was gloating . . .*

They parked. Gaille quickly opened her door and jumped down, suffering a momentary, debilitating flutter of shyness. Normally she was confident in professional situations, but she had no faith in her skills as a photographer and consequently felt a fraud. She went around to the back of the flatbed, ostensibly to check her belongings and equipment, but in truth to hide.

Elena yelled out for her. She took a deep breath to compose herself, fixed a smile to her lips, then walked around to meet them. 'Ibrahim,' said Elena, indicating the elegant man in the centre of the group. 'I'd like you to meet Gaille.'

'Our esteemed photographer! We are truly grateful.'

'I'm not really a — '

'Gaille's an excellent photographer,' said Elena, with a sharp glance. 'What's more, she's an ancient languages expert too.'

'Splendid! Splendid!' He gestured to his two companions, who were spreading out a site map on the ground. 'Mansoor and Mohammed,' he said. 'Mansoor is my right hand. He runs all our excavations in Alexandria. I couldn't survive without him. And Mohammed is construction manager for this hotel.'

'Pleased to meet you both,' said Gaille.

They glanced up from their map, nodded politely. Ibrahim smiled distractedly, glanced at his watch. 'Just one more to come. You know Augustin Pascal?'

Elena snorted. 'Only by reputation.'

'Yes,' nodded Ibrahim seriously. 'He's a fine underwater archaeologist.'

'That wasn't what I meant,' said Elena.

'Oh.'

It was a few more minutes before an engine roared at the mouth of the site. 'Ah!' said Ibrahim. 'Here he is.'

A thirty-something man cruised up the approach on a gleaming black and chrome chopper, wending potholes, bare-headed, allowing his long dark hair to flow free. He was wearing mirror shades, two days' worth of stubble, a leather jacket, jeans, calf-high black biker boots. He rode the chopper up onto its stands, stepped off, fetched a cigarette and a brass Zippo from his shirt pocket.

'You're late,' said Ibrahim.

'*Desolé*,' he grunted, shielding the flame. 'Something came up.'

Mansoor asked wryly: 'Sophia, I suppose?'

Augustin grinned wolfishly. 'You know I'd never take advantage of my students like that.'

Elena clucked her tongue and muttered a Greek obscenity beneath her breath. Augustin grinned and turned to her, spreading his hands. 'Yes?' he asked. 'You see something you like, perhaps?'

'How could I?' retorted Elena. 'You're standing in the way.'

Mansoor laughed and slapped Augustin on the shoulder. But Augustin himself looked unruffled.

98

He gazed Elena up and down, then gave her a grin of frank approval, perhaps even of intent, for she was a striking-looking woman, Elena, and anger added a certain something to her colouring. Gaille winced and took half a step back, waiting for the inevitable eruption, but Ibrahim stepped between them just in time.

'Well,' he said, with nervous jauntiness. 'Let's start, shall we?'

The ancient spiral steps looked precarious. Gaille descended warily. But they all reached the bottom without alarm and gathered in the rotunda. The corner of a black and white pebble mosaic showed beneath the rubble. Gaille pointed it out in a murmur to Elena.

'Ptolemaic,' declared Elena loudly, going down on her haunches to brush away the dust. 'Two fifty BC, give or take.'

Augustin pointed to the sculpted walls. 'Those are Roman,' he said.

'Are you suggesting I can't tell a Macedonian mosaic when I see one?'

'I'm suggesting that the carvings are Roman.'

Ibrahim held up his palms. 'How about this?' he suggested. 'It started as a private tomb for some wealthy Macedonian. Then some Romans discovered it three hundred years later and turned it into a necropolis.'

'That would explain the staircase,' admitted Elena grudgingly. 'Macedonians didn't usually build in spirals. Straight lines or squares.'

'And they'd have needed to widen the shaft when they expanded it into a necropolis,' agreed Augustin. 'For light and ventilation, and to lower corpses, and to take out quarried stone. They used to sell it to builders, you know.'

'Yes,' said Elena scathingly. 'I did know, thank you.'

Gaille was barely listening. She was staring dizzily up at the circle of sky high above her head. Christ, but she was out of her depth. An emergency excavation offered no second chances. Within the next two weeks, the mosaic and all these exquisite carvings and everything else in this place would need to be photographed. After that the place would probably be sealed for ever. Artefacts like these deserved a real professional, someone with an eye for the work, experience, sophisticated equipment, lighting. She plucked anxiously at Elena's sleeve, but Elena obviously realised what she wanted to discuss and brushed her off, following Mohammed down the steps into the forecourt of the Macedonian tomb, the dull matt yellow of the limestone shown up by the shining white marble blocks of the façade, and the four engaged marble ionic columns and the marble entablature running across their top. The party paused for a few moments to admire, then pressed on through the half-open bronze door into the tomb's antechamber.

'Look!' said Mansoor, shining his torch at the side walls. They all went closer to inspect them. There was paint on the plaster, though terribly faded. It had been common practice in antiquity for important scenes from the dead person's life to be painted in or around their tombs. 'You can photograph these?' asked Mansoor.

100

'I'm not sure how well they'll come out,' said Gaille wretchedly.

'You must wash them first,' said Augustin. 'Lots and lots of water. The pigment may look dead now. But give them some water and they will spring back to life like beautiful flowers. Trust me.'

'Not *too* much water,' warned Mansoor. 'And don't set up your lights too close. The heat will crack the plaster.'

Gaille looked round desperately at Elena, who was studiously refusing to meet her eye. Instead she shone her torch at the inscription above the portal into the main chamber. ''Akylos of the thirty three,'' said Augustin, translating from the Ancient Greek. The light vanished from the inscription at that moment, as Elena fumbled and dropped her torch, cursing so violently that Gaille glanced at her in surprise.

Ibrahim turned his own torch on the inscription instead, allowing Augustin to start his translation from the beginning. ''Akylos of the thirty three,'' he read out. ''To be the best and to be honoured above the rest.''

'It's Homer,' murmured Gaille. Everyone turned to look at her in surprise. She felt her cheeks burn. 'It's from *The Iliad*,' she said.

'That's right,' nodded Augustin. 'About a man called Glaucus, I believe.'

'Actually, it comes up twice,' said Gaille timidly. 'Once about Glaucus and once about Achilles.'

'Achilles, Akylos,' nodded Ibrahim. 'He evidently thought a great deal of himself.' He was still staring up at the inscription when he followed Mohammed into the main chamber, so that he tripped over the low step and went sprawling onto his hands and knees. Everybody laughed as he picked himself up and brushed himself down with the self-deprecating face of the accident-prone.

Augustin went to the shield pinned to the wall. 'The shield of a hypastist,' he said. 'A shield-bearer,' he explained, when Ibrahim frowned. 'Alexander's special forces. The greatest unit of fighting men in the most successful army in the history of the world. Maybe he wasn't being so boastful after all.'

II

Morning sunlight fell upon Knox's cheek as he lay on Augustin's couch and tried to catch up on sleep. He groaned and showed it his back, but it was no good. The day was already too sticky. He rose reluctantly, took a shower, ransacked Augustin's room for clothes, then ground up some coffee beans for the percolator, and set it brewing. He slathered a croissant with butter and *confiture de framboises*, then wolfed it down as he wandered the flat looking for ways to divert himself. Egyptian TV was gruesome at the best of times, but Augustin's flickering black-and-white portable made it completely unwatchable. And there was nothing to read except tattered newspapers and some comic books. This was not a flat for killing time in. It was a flat for sleeping

102

in, and preferably not alone.

He walked out onto the balcony. Identikit highrises on every side, all in the same disheartened beige, washing hung out to dry on the balconies, ubiquitous grey dishes all bowing to their satellites like the faithful to Mecca. Yet still he felt glad to be here. Few Egyptologists would say it openly, but they looked down their noses at Alexandria. They barely considered the Graeco-Roman era to be Egyptian at all. But Knox didn't think that way. To him, this was Egypt's golden age, Alexandria its golden city. Two thousand years ago, it had been the greatest metropolis on earth, nurturing the finest minds of antiquity. Archimedes had studied here; so had Galen and Origen. The Septuagint had been translated here. Euclid had published his famous works here. Chemistry took its very name from here; *al-Khemia* was the black land of Egypt, and alchemy the Egyptian art. Aristarchus had proposed the heliocentric theory here, well over a millennium before it was rediscovered by Copernicus. Eratostenthes had calculated almost exactly the circumference of the earth by extrapolating from discrepancies in the lengths of shadows cast at the sun's zenith both here and in Aswan, some 850 kilometres to the south, on the summer solstice. What imagination! What intellectual curiosity and endeavour! An unprecedented collision of cultures, an effervescence of thought the equal of Athens, and unmatched again until the Renaissance. It was beyond him how anyone could dismiss such achievements as second best, or think that —

103

His meditations were interrupted suddenly by a noise from inside, as though someone was trying surreptitiously to clear their throat. *Had his sanctuary been discovered already?* He stepped to the edge of the balcony, so that he couldn't be seen through the glass doors, and pressed himself flat against the wall.

III

Ibrahim walked alongside Mohammed as he led this tour of the necropolis. For all that he'd been desperately damping down his hopes before visiting this place, he felt a sense of anticlimax that his hoped-for royal tomb had proved to be the resting place of a common soldier, not a king. But he was a professional, and he concentrated hard, the better to understand what he was dealing with.

The first chamber told him much of what he needed to know. Each wall was cut with columns of *loculi*, like the drawers of a massive morgue; and every one of them was crowded with human remains, half buried in dark sandy dirt, though much more had been scooped out onto the floor, presumably by grave-robbers looking for treasure. Amid the bones and rubble they found a broken faïence figure, some green and blackened coins dating from the first to fourth centuries AD, numerous fragments of terracotta from funerary lamps, jars and statuettes. There were chunks of stone and plaster too. *Loculi* had typically been sealed after burials, but the looters had smashed these seals to get at the contents.

'Will you find mummies, do you think?' asked Mohammed. 'Only I took my daughter to your museum once. She became fascinated by the mummies.'

'It's very unlikely,' answered Ibrahim. 'The climate here isn't kind. And even if they survived the humidity, they'd never have survived the tomb robbers.'

'Robbers stole mummies?' frowned Mohammed. 'Were they valuable?'

Ibrahim nodded vigorously. 'For one thing, people often hid jewellery and other valuables in their body cavities, so the robbers would take them up into the sunlight to tear them apart and search them. But the mummies themselves had real value too. Particularly in Europe.'

'You mean to museums?'

'Not at first, no,' said Ibrahim. 'You see, about six hundred years ago, Europeans came to believe that bitumen was very good for the health. It was the wonder-cure of its time. Every apothecary had to stock it. Demand was so great that supplies ran short. People started looking for new sources. You know how black mummified remains can get; people became convinced they'd been soaked in bitumen. That was where the word 'mummy' came from, you know; *mumia* was Persian for bitumen, and most of the supplies came from Persia.'

Mohammed grimaced. 'People used mummies as medicine?'

'Europeans did, yes,' said Ibrahim, giving the big builder a complicit grin. 'But, anyway,

Alexandria was right at the centre of this trade, which is one reason we've never found even fragments of mummy here, though we know for sure that mummification was practised.'

They moved on to another chamber. Mansoor lit up a plaster seal with his torch. It had faint traces of paint upon it, a seated woman and a standing man clasping right hands. 'A *dexiosis*,' he muttered.

'The wife has died,' explained Ibrahim. 'They're saying goodbye for the last time.'

'Or maybe he's in there with her too,' muttered Mohammed. 'They seem pretty crowded, these tombs.'

'Too many people. Not enough space. That was Alexandria. You know, some estimate that a million people lived here in ancient times. Have you seen Gabbari?'

'No.'

'It's huge. A true city of the dead. And there's Shatby and Sidi Gabr too. But still they weren't enough. Particularly after Christianity became popular.'

Mohammed frowned. 'Why so?'

'Before the Christians, many Alexandrians opted for cremation,' he explained. 'See these niches in the walls? They're designed for urns and caskets. But Christians believed in resurrection, you know. They needed their bodies.'

'This is a Christian necropolis, then?'

'It's an Alexandrian necropolis,' answered Ibrahim. 'You'll find believers in the Egyptian gods, the Greek gods, the Roman gods, Jews, Christians, Buddhists, every religion on earth.'

'And what happens to them now?'

Ibrahim nodded. 'We'll study them. We can learn a great deal about diet, health, mortality rates, ethnic mix, cultural practices. Many other things.'

'You'll treat them with respect?'

'Of course, my friend. Of course.'

They went back out, into another chamber.

'What's this?' asked Augustin, pointing his torch through a hole in the wall to a short flight of steps disappearing down into the dark.

'I don't know,' shrugged Mohammed. 'I didn't see it before.'

Ibrahim had to duck low to get through. Mohammed had to go onto hands and knees. Inside was what appeared to be the tomb of a wealthy family, separated by a line of carved pillars and pilasters into two adjoining spaces. Five stone sarcophagi of different sizes stood against the walls, all decorated with a rich confusion of styles and faiths. A portrait of Dionysus was carved into the limestone above depictions of Apis, Anubis and a solar disc. Stone recesses above each of the sarcophagi held Canopic jars, perhaps still containing their original contents, the stomach, liver, intestines and lungs of the deceased. Other objects glittered on the floor: fragments of funerary lamps and amphorae, scarabs, small items of silver and bronze jewellery studded with dulled stones.

'Marvellous,' murmured Augustin. 'How can the robbers have missed these?'

'Perhaps the door was concealed,' suggested

Ibrahim, kicking at the rubble. 'An earthquake, or just the passage of time.'

'How old?' asked Mohammed.

Ibrahim glanced at Augustin. 'First century AD?' he suggested. 'Maybe second.'

They came at last to the water table. Steps disappeared tantalisingly down into it, hinting at more chambers beneath. The water table had risen and fallen over dramatically over the centuries; if they were lucky, it might have prevented the robbers from looting whatever lay beneath.

Augustin stooped and made ripples with his hand. 'We have budget for a pump?' he asked.

Ibrahim shrugged. Pumping was expensive, noisy, dirty and all too often completely ineffective. It would also mean running a fat pipe along the passage and up the stairwell, which would get in the way of the main excavation. 'If we must.'

'If you want me to explore first, I'll need a buddy. These places are dangerous.'

Ibrahim nodded. 'Whatever you wish. I leave it up to you.'

IV

Nessim's mobile rang as he neared Suez. 'Yes?' he asked.

A man's voice. 'It's me.'

Nessim didn't recognise his caller, but he knew better than to ask. He'd contacted a great many people last night, and few of them were keen on having their connection with Hassan known. Mobile phones were notoriously vulnerable; you had to assume you were being monitored at all times. 'What have you got?'

'Your man has a file.'

Ah! Now he knew. So the Egyptian Security Service had a file on Knox. Intriguing. 'And?'

'Not over the phone.'

'I'm on my way to Cairo now. Same arrangement as last time?'

'Six o'clock,' the man agreed. And the phone went dead.

V

Knox was still standing out on Augustin's balcony, expecting each moment that the glass doors would be pushed open and the intruder would step out. Only now did he realise what a deathtrap this apartment was. The fire escape, lift and main stairs were all outside the front door. Other than that . . . There weren't any other balconies to leap onto, nor any ledge to inch along. He gripped the rail tight, leaned out to look six storeys down to the unyielding concrete of the car park. He could conceivably drop down to the balcony directly beneath his own, but if he mistimed his release . . . his toes went numb just thinking about it.

Inside Augustin's apartment, the coughing was growing worse. A strange intruder to break into an apartment only to stand there hacking away. He risked a quick glance through the glass doors, saw nothing to alarm him. Another cough, then some hissing, and finally he twigged. He went back in, shaking his head at himself, to find Augustin's percolator spluttering out a last few drops of coffee. He poured himself a cup, toasted himself mockingly in the mirror. He wasn't good at this kind of thing, not least because he found confinement hard to bear. Already he could feel a kind of cabin fever building, a slight cramping in his upper arms and the backs of his calves. He longed to take a brisk walk, to burn off some nervous energy, but he dared not go outside. Hassan's men would surely already be showing his photograph at train stations, hotels and taxi companies, scouring car parks for his Jeep. Knox knew he needed to lie low. *But still . . .*

Augustin had rushed off first thing to inspect some newly discovered antiquity. By Christ, he wished he were down there with him.

VI

Ibrahim felt deeply apprehensive as he ascended the spiral stairs back into daylight. He had his report to make to Nicolas Dragoumis, and he was all too aware that more than his excavation funds rested on the outcome; Mohammed's hopes for his poor daughter did too. He squeezed the big man's forearm to reassure him as best he could, then walked a little way off with Elena, Mohammed watching avidly as he dialled the Dragoumis Group switchboard, gave his

110

name and business, was put on hold.

'Well?' demanded Nicolas, picking up.

'It's a fine site,' said Ibrahim. 'There are some wonderful — '

'You promised me a royal Macedonian tomb. Is it a royal Macedonian tomb or not?'

'I promised you something that looked like a royal tomb,' said Ibrahim. 'And it does. Unfortunately, it seems to be the tomb of a shield-bearer, not a king or noble.'

'A shield-bearer?' sneered Nicolas. 'You expect the Dragoumis Group to spend twenty thousand dollars on the tomb of a shield-bearer?'

'The shield-bearers were Alexander's élite,' protested Ibrahim. 'This man Akylos would have been — '

'*What?*' interrupted Nicolas incredulously. 'What did you say his name was?'

'Akylos.'

'Akylos? You're absolutely sure?'

'Yes. Why?'

'Is Elena there?'

'Yes.'

'Put her on. Now! I want to speak to her.'

Ibrahim shrugged and passed her his phone. She walked a little distance away and turned her back so that he couldn't overhear. She spoke for a good minute before returning his phone. 'You have your money,' she said.

'I don't understand,' said Ibrahim. 'What's so special about this man Akylos?'

'I don't know what you mean.'

'Yes, you do.'

111

'Mr Dragoumis wants to be kept fully informed.'

'Of course. I'll call him myself whenever we — '

'Not by you. By me. He asks that I be given unrestricted access.'

'No. I couldn't possibly agree to — '

'Mr Dragoumis insists, I'm afraid.'

'But those weren't our terms.'

'They are now,' shrugged Elena. 'If you want his continued support . . .'

Ibrahim glanced at Mohammed, twisting his hands as he waited. 'Very well,' he sighed. 'I'm sure we can arrange something.' He nodded at Mohammed to let him know he'd got his money. The big man closed his eyes and sagged in relief, then walked unsteadily to his office, no doubt to make phone calls of his own.

Mansoor emerged from the stairwell, walked over to join Ibrahim. 'Well?' he asked. 'Do we go for it?'

'Yes.'

'Destructive or non-destructive?'

Ibrahim nodded thoughtfully. A good question. In a fortnight, if the hotel group got their way, tons of rubble would be bulldozed down the stairwell as a makeshift landfill site, its mouth would be sealed and a car park laid over the top, so that no one could ever get down there again. If that were to happen, then they first needed to remove everything of value, including the wall paintings and sculptures and the mosaic from the rotunda floor. It was perfectly possible, but it took time, expertise and heavy equipment, and

112

they'd need to start planning now. On the other hand, Alexandria was wretchedly short of historic sites, particularly early Ptolemaic ones. If they could negotiate permanent access with the hotel group, this site would make a valuable addition to the city tour; but only if these original features remained in place, and were properly protected during the excavation.

'Non-destructive,' said Ibrahim finally. 'I'll talk to the hotel people. Perhaps they'll realise the value of having an antiquity on their property.'

Mansoor snorted. 'And perhaps they'll give us complementary penthouse suites whenever we ask, out of the kindness of their hearts.'

'Yes. Well. Let me deal with them. But you can handle the excavation, yes?'

'It won't be easy,' said Mansoor. 'I can put Shatby on hold. There's no great urgency with that. We can transfer the crew and the generator and the lighting. But we'll still need more people.'

'Put the word out. You have a budget.'

'Yes, but with a large crew we'll need ventilation; and I don't want people removing artefacts up those steps. That's a recipe for accidents. We'll need to put a lift above the stairwell. And Augustin will want a pump. I know he will. And it's not just what we'll need on site. There are fifteen hundred *loculi* to be emptied, which means six or seven thousand sets of human remains turning up at the Museum or the University over the next fortnight. We'll need to have trained specialists ready to receive them.' He snapped his fingers. 'Our two weeks will be

113

gone like that, you realise.'

Ibrahim smiled. Mansoor always liked to build up a problem in his mind so that his satisfaction at solving it would be all the greater. 'You'd better get started, then,' he advised.

VII

Akylos!

Nicolas could scarcely believe it. Yet, at the same time, he did believe. What was written was written. And the restoration of Macedonian greatness *was* written, and not just in the Book of Daniel.

'What was all that about, then?' shouted Julia Melas over the roar of his Lamborghini Murciélago roadster's engine. She was an aspiring journalist from a Canadian newspaper, interviewing him and his father for a feature on Macedonia. There was a large expatriate community in Canada, a source of both moral and financial support. And she wasn't at all bad to look at, either. Maybe if things panned out well . . .

'We in the Dragoumis Group sponsor historical research all over the world,' he shouted back. 'Truth isn't restricted to one location, you know.' He braked to turn up into the hills, but a white truck appeared around the corner ahead, hurtling downhill faster than its age and size would suggest prudent. Nicolas was in no mood to wait, not with such a pretty girl beside him. He gave the Murciélago a squirt of acceleration

114

and cut in front of it, so that the driver braked and veered and sound his horn impotently. Julia gave a little shriek and glanced admiringly at him. Nicolas laughed exultantly. He felt good. Things were moving at last. Life was like that. Nothing for a year, two years, and then everything all at once.

'You were telling me about Aristander,' she yelled, the wind swirling her skirts up around her thighs, so that she had to press them coyly back down.

Nicolas slowed a little, so that they could talk in more reasonable voices. 'He was Alexander's favourite seer,' he told her. 'After Alexander died, he had a vision that the land in which Alexander was buried would be unconquered through the ages.'

'And?'

'A man called Perdiccas, head of Alexander's successors, wanted to bury Alexander in the Royal Tombs at Aigai, alongside his father, Philip.' They crested a hill, the fertile plains of northern Greece spread out beneath them. He pulled to the side, parked, got out, pointed Aigai out to her. 'The tombs were discovered thirty years ago. They're magnificent. You should go visit.'

'I will,' she nodded. 'But this man Perdiccas: he obviously didn't bring Alexander's body home.'

'No,' acknowledged Nicolas. 'Another Macedonian general, Ptolemy, took it to Egypt instead.' He shook his head regretfully. 'Think of it! But for that, Macedonia would have been unconquered through the ages!'

Julia frowned. 'You can't seriously mean that.'

'Why not?'

'But . . . it's just a prophecy.'

Nicolas shook his head. 'No. It's a historical fact. Consider. Perdiccas was the one man with the authority to hold the empire together. He tried to recover Alexander's body from Ptolemy, but Ptolemy hid behind the Nile, and Perdiccas lost hundreds of men to drowning and the crocodiles trying to cross it. His own officers were so angry that they murdered him in his tent. After that, the empire was doomed. Alexander's legitimate heirs were assassinated. It was every man for himself. But now just imagine if Perdiccas had succeeded.'

'Yes?'

He put his left arm around her shoulder, pulling her to stand beside him, then sweeping his other arm around the magnificent vista, all the way down to the dazzling blue Aegean. 'Look at that,' he said proudly. 'Macedonia. Isn't that a fantastic sight?'

'Yes,' she agreed.

'Perdiccas was an honourable man. He'd have protected Alexander's son from assassination and kept his empire together. And if Alexander the Fourth had been one tenth the man his father had been, Aristander's prophecy would indeed have come true.'

'I thought you said Alexander's body was taken to Egypt,' observed Julia. 'And Egypt hasn't exactly been unconquered through the ages, has it?'

116

Nicolas laughed. He liked a pretty girl with spirit. 'No,' he acknowledged. 'But look at what did happen. The Ptolemies kept the throne for as long as they respected Alexander's remains. But then Ptolemy the Ninth melted down his golden coffin to pay his troops, and that was the end of them. And who took over from the Ptolemies?'

'Who?'

'The Caesars. They revered Alexander, you know. Julius Caesar wept because he fell so far short of Alexander. Augustus, Septimus Severus, Caracalla and Hadrian all made pilgrimages to sacrifice at his mausoleum. He was their hero. But then there were riots, Alexander's tomb was desecrated, and the Romans lost Egypt to the Arabs. The message is clear, isn't it?'

'Is it?' frowned Julia.

'Honour Alexander and prosper. Ignore him and perish. And in Macedonia, of all places on the earth, Alexander would most certainly have been honoured. So it follows that we'd never have been conquered.'

Julia backed away from him, a little disconcerted. She checked her watch and smiled with false brightness. 'Perhaps we should get moving,' she said. 'Your father's expecting me.'

'Of course,' said Nicolas. 'We mustn't keep Father waiting.' He climbed back in his roadster, started her back up, savouring her throaty roar. The way he drove, it was just fifteen more minutes to his father's house.

'Wow!' muttered Julia, as it came into view.

'A re-creation of the royal palace at Aigai,' said Nicolas. 'Only bigger.' His father now rarely left this estate. He'd grown increasingly reclusive with the years, had largely handed over his business empire to professional managers so that he could concentrate on his true ambition.

Costis, his father's head of security, came out to greet them.

'This is Julia,' said Nicolas. 'She's here to interview my father. But I need a few minutes with him first.'

'He's in the vaults,' Costis told him.

Nicolas nodded at Julia. 'Perhaps I can take you back to town later.'

'Thanks,' she said warily. 'But I'm sure I can get a taxi.'

He laughed again, enjoying her discomfort. She'd looked troubled ever since he'd told her about the Aristander prophecy. Westerners today! They took fright at the merest hint of the sacred. It was just as well she hadn't been in church last night, that he hadn't told her about the Book of Daniel. The full prophecy, that was, including the description of the man predicted to bring about Macedonian liberation.

The only way to reach the vaults was via a secure lift. Nicolas stepped into it now. The steel doors closed smoothly. He presented his eyes to the retinal scanner, then it began its slow descent, shuddering a little under its own weight when it came to a halt. An armed guard was standing to attention by the vault inside which his father kept all his greatest treasures. Nicolas punched in his code. The steel door opened. He went through, still thinking about The Book of Daniel, and particularly those verses which twenty-five hundred years before, had promised his people a saviour.

> And in the latter time of their kingdom, when the transgressors are come to the full, a king of fierce countenance, and understanding dark sentences, shall stand up.
> And his power shall be mighty, but not by his own power: and he shall destroy wonderfully, and shall prosper, and practise . . .
> And through his policy also he shall cause craft to prosper in his hand; and he shall magnify himself in his heart, and by peace he shall destroy . . .

His father, as if by some kind of telepathy, was already standing in front of the glass-topped cabinet in which were displayed a few samples of the Mallawi papyri, his hands resting like a priest's upon the walnut frame as he gazed down at the yellowed reeds, the faded black writing. A feeling of intense love, awe and pride burned in Nicolas' chest when he beheld him. *A king of fierce countenance indeed!*

Dragoumis looked up and drilled his son with his emotionless black eyes. 'Yes?' he asked.

'They've found Akylos,' blurted out Nicolas, his excitement almost too much for him. 'It's started.'

8

I

A blue truck cut in front of Elena as she headed back to the Delta, forcing her to slam on her brakes. She blasted her horn until the truck moved back across, then she wound down her window and shook her fist and yelled some choice Arabic phrases at the bewildered driver to let him know what she thought. She was in a troubled mood. It was speaking to Nicolas that had done it. That, and that damned smug Frenchman. Between them, they'd stirred memories of her late husband, Pavlos; and Elena hated that, because each time it happened, she had to suffer once more an echo of her loss.

She'd known of Pavlos long before she'd ever met him; had been infuriated and entertained in equal measure by the tone, anger and wit of his articles ridiculing Macedonian nationalism. She'd been intrigued too by the gossip of besotted women throwing themselves at him. She was a proud and independent woman herself, and, like so many of her kind, she'd yearned to fall helplessly in love. They'd finally met either side of a radio debate in Thessalonike. He'd surprised her from the start. She'd expected someone sharp, assertive, dressy, plausible. Pavlos hadn't been like that at all. Though he wasn't exactly arrogant, she'd never

120

met a man so confident of himself. She'd known from their first handshake that she was in trouble. He had an unsettling way of looking at her, then and later, as though she were completely exposed to him, as though he understood not just everything she said, but all its subtext too. He'd watched her as though she were a movie, and he'd seen her before.

He'd trodden all over her in their debate, defusing her best arguments with humour, hammering relentlessly at her weakest points. Disconcerted, she'd tried to press him back by citing Keramopoullos on the idiosyncratic style of Macedonian ceramics, before remembering that actually Kallipolitis had said this. She'd glanced up fearfully to see him grin. For a terrible moment her scholar's reputation had been at his mercy. That moment — the moment of being at his mercy — had changed her life.

For two days after the debate, Elena had wandered her museum from room to room, never stopping, hugging herself like an addict. Each time she tried to work, a craving like hunger would disturb her within moments. She'd never needed to call men, but she'd called Pavlos. Scared he'd mock her, she'd introduced herself brusquely, remarked that he'd raised interesting points in the debate. He'd thanked her. Then her nerve had failed. She'd held the phone against her cheek, wanting to say something clever or hurtful, but not knowing what. When he'd asked her to have dinner with him, she could have cried.

How had it been? It had been everything. She

remembered little of the detail, as though the intensity of her love had simply been too much for her memory. But she could remember the joy of it. Even now, sometimes, she could experience an exquisite moment of bliss, catching sight of his double on the street, smelling his brand of cigarette in some passer-by's hand, or having some man look at her in the way Pavlos had, like that arrogant Frenchman had, certain he could take her to bed whenever he damned well chose.

Pavlos' death had devastated Elena. Of course it had. She still hadn't recovered from it. How could she? Grief hadn't been as she'd imagined, any more than love had been. She'd imagined grief as a great sea swell that lifted you into wretchedness for a while before setting you back down again much where you'd been before. But it hadn't been like that. Grief had changed the fabric of who she was as completely as blown carbon changes molten pig iron.

Yes, she thought, the metaphor worked: grief had turned her into steel.

II

The woman dropped the manila envelope through the open rear-window of Nessim's Saab as he paused to buy a packet of cigarettes from a vendor. He drove off in a flurry of dust back to his hotel's underground car park, then took it up to his room to read. It was disappointingly thin, as files go, but then he hadn't expected Knox to have a file at all. He flipped through the pages,

122

the print barely legible from being photocopied too often, the photographs almost completely black.

It quickly became clear that the Security Service hadn't really been interested in Knox at all. They'd been interested in another man, a Richard Mitchell, with whom Knox had worked for several years. Mitchell, it seemed, had had a big mouth; he'd accused the extremely well-connected head of the SCA of selling papyri on the black market. A reckless policy that had achieved precisely what one would have expected: his isolation from the Egyptological community and the refusal of any further permissions to excavate.

That at least explained what Knox had been doing in Sharm: killing time until the dust settled, dreaming of treasure on the sea floor. But it wasn't much help when it came to tracking him down. The last sheet in the file, however, was a different matter. It was a list of all Knox's known friends and associates; and it gave their home addresses too.

III

Nur greeted Mohammed at the door. She looked haggard. That meant Layla had had a bad day. 'You look beautiful,' he said, kissing her cheek and handing her a small bouquet of tired blooms.

'How can you afford these?' she protested tearfully.

'They're a gift,' he said gently. 'Sharif wanted you to have them.' He looked past her, down the hallway, to Layla's room. 'Is she awake?'

Nur nodded. 'But tired.'

'I won't be long.' He knocked gently on her door, opened it and walked in. She smiled to see him. He kneeled beside her bed, reached into his pocket, produced a black queen he'd carved and varnished. He liked to whittle. In the rare lulls on site, he'd scour the bins for ends of wood that he could attack with his linoleum knife. It was good therapy. When you could do nothing for your child's health, you could at least do something for her happiness.

Her eyes went wide with wonder and delight. She took the varnished mahogany, licked it with the very tip of her tongue, clutched it tight against her chest, like a doll. For some reason, Layla had turned against dolls since learning of her disease. He couldn't even tempt her with sweets any more. It was as though her life had become too serious for childish distractions.

'You'll read for me tonight?' she asked.

'Of course.'

She snuggled down, seemingly content. They'd called everyone they could think of and begged them to take the tests. That had felt good, as if he was contributing. But now he was dependent on others again. Now he was *waiting*. It was the hardest thing in the world for a parent, waiting.

He felt wretched when he went back out. Nur bit her lip, but she couldn't hold back her tears. She spent her life weeping, drying herself out

124

from the inside. Mohammed took her in his arms, held her tight to comfort her. Sometimes he felt so close to despair, he almost craved for the worst to happen, just so that it would be over. His fine career; his beautiful wife and daughter. Everything that had once seemed so perfect. He murmured tentatively: 'Is she well enough to go out?'

'Out?' There was an edge of hysteria in Nur's tone. 'Where?'

'The site.'

Nur pushed him away. 'Are you crazy?' she cried.

Mohammed embraced her again. 'Listen to me,' he said. 'This archaeologist Ibrahim I told you about, the one with the Mercedes, who is paying for our tests. He has money, he has influence. He moves in a different world from us. Layla needs all the friends she can get in that world.'

'He can help?'

Mohammed hesitated. Nur had a habit of punishing him for promises he made to soothe her through the harder times. 'Who can say?' he murmured. 'But he's a kind man, a gentle man. Once he knows Layla for himself, who can tell what Allah would have him do?'

IV

'Look what I have!' said Augustin cheerfully, hoisting up two plastic bags. 'Falafel baguettes and beer, yes? Just like the old days.'

125

'Great.'

Augustin frowned. 'You don't sound too happy.'

'A little stir-crazy,' admitted Knox.

'One day? You can't even survive one day?'

'It's all these bloody *Tintin* books of yours,' said Knox, helping him unpack. 'Can't you get me something decent to read?'

'Such as?'

'Something archaeological. How about your excavation reports from the harbour? I'd love to know what you've been finding.'

'Sure,' nodded Augustin. 'No problem. I'll bring them back tomorrow night. But if you're suffering . . .'

'Yes?'

'This site I visited today, a necropolis — it goes all the way down to the water table, and then some. But Ibrahim doesn't want to pump. He wants me to explore. I was going to take Sophia, but if you're really going crazy . . .'

A little tremor of fear and anticipation ran through Knox. 'Are you serious?'

'Why not? She's prettier than you, yes, but not so good a diver. You know how dangerous enclosed spaces can be.'

'How would I even get to the site?'

'On the back of my bike,' said Augustin, passing Knox a cold bottle of Stella. 'You can wear my helmet. Someone should. No one will stop us, I promise. The police in the city are a disgrace. Ten years I am here, I am never once stopped. And if we are, *tant pis*! I still have my papers from my last visit to Cyrene. Those

Libyan bastards refused me entry under my real name! Me! Just because of some letter I wrote about that mad fop Gaddafi. I had to go in as Omar Malik, a truck driver from Marsa Matruh, would you believe? If I can pass for a truck driver from Marsa Matruh, so can you.'

Knox shook his head. He couldn't believe he was even considering this. But Augustin had an admirable lack of respect for the ordinary rules of behaviour, and his attitude was infectious. 'And inside the site?'

'No problem. Leave any talking to me. Not that there'll be much. Up top there's a working building site, remember. Down below there are God knows how many chambers, a hundred *loculi* in each, every one stuffed with bones and artefacts, all of which Mansoor wants in the Museum inside two weeks. It's chaos. Excavators from the Museum, from the University, from along the coast. Just one security guard at the mouth of the stairwell, but all you need to get past him is a standard SCA pass, and I can issue you with one of those myself. Some forgettable name. John Smith. Charles Russell. Mark Edwards. Yes! Perfect. Mark Edwards. You look exactly how a Mark Edwards should look.'

Knox shook his head uncertainly. 'You know what Cairo thinks of me. If I'm found out, it could mean trouble for you.'

'Fuck Cairo,' scowled Augustin. 'I still feel sick at what that bastard Yusuf did to you and Richard. Believe me, helping you will be a pleasure. Besides, how will anyone find out? I'm not going to talk. Are you?'

'Someone might recognise me.'

'I don't think so. Ibrahim, maybe, but he's a good man, he wouldn't take it any further. Anyway, he never visits sites any more, he might get his suit dirty. Other than that, no one you know. And they're all friends, except for this gorgeous angry Greek woman called Elena and her — '

'Elena?' Knox put a hand to his brow. 'Elena Koloktronis?'

Augustin pulled a face. 'You know her?'

'No,' snorted Knox. 'Just a lucky guess.'

'How do you know her?'

'You remember what happened to my parents and my sister?'

'Of course. Why? She had something to do with that?'

'It was her husband who was driving.'

'Oh. And he . . . ? He also . . . ?'

'Yes.'

'I'm sorry,' said Augustin. 'I'm sorry both for you and for her. But it's not important. She's not there tomorrow.'

'You're certain?'

'She runs an excavation in the Delta. She only came today to bring in her French photographer girl. Gaille Dumas, something like that.'

'A photographer?' Knox shook his head. 'No.'

'Then we're fine,' said Augustin. He grinned and held out his beer bottle to clink in a toast. 'What could possibly go wrong?'

9

Augustin was right about getting into the site the following morning. It proved a breeze. He was right too about the excitement Knox felt at being part of a proper excavation again. It had been too long. Far too long. Just being on site made him happy. The noise, the smells, the banter. Up top, a generator was roaring away, powering a winch-lift hauling an almost non-stop stream of excavation baskets cut from old truck tyres, filled with rubble to be sifted in sunlight, then sent either to the Museum or to landfill; lamps and ventilator fans were spread throughout the necropolis on miles of white extension leads; and excavators in breathing masks and white gloves were kneeling in the confined tombs, carefully removing artefacts and human remains.

Augustin had brought down all the diving equipment before collecting Knox. They hurried down to the water table, suited up, inspecting each other's gear with great care. People who'd dived as often as they had were sometimes cursory with their safety checks. But in an enclosed labyrinth like this, you couldn't simply dump your weight belt and kick for the surface if things went wrong. There *was* no surface.

Augustin held up a reel of nylon cord, borrowing a trick from Theseus. But there was nothing to anchor it to.

'Stay here,' he said, vanishing briefly, returning with an excavation basket weighted with rubble. He tied the cord to it, gave it a couple of tugs. They hooked themselves together with a lifeline, turned on their dive lamps, then made their way down into the water, Augustin feeding out the cord behind him. Neither man wore fins. They'd weighted themselves to walk. They kicked up more sediment that way, but it made it easier to keep bearings.

Almost at once, they found the entrance to a chamber, most of the *loculi* still sealed. Augustin's torch picked out, on one of them, a haunting portrait of a large-eyed man staring directly back at them. The mouth of the neighbouring *loculi* had rotted away. Their torches glinted on something metallic. Augustin carefully pulled out a funerary lamp, which he tucked into his pouch.

They visited three more chambers. The corridor kept kinking. The cord snagged. Augustin tugged it loose. The water grew murkier and murkier. Sometimes it swirled so badly they could barely see each other. Knox checked his air. A hundred and thirty bar. They'd agreed to dive in thirds; one third out, one third back, one third for safety. He showed Augustin. Augustin pointed back the way they'd come. There was some slack in the cord. He reeled it in. He kept on reeling. Then he turned to Knox, the whites of his eyes bulging with mild alarm inside his mask. Knox frowned and spread his hands. Augustin held up the loose end of the

130

orange cord that should have been tied around the handles of the excavation basket, but which somehow had come free.

II

Children made Ibrahim uncomfortable. An only child himself, he had neither nieces nor nephews, nor any prospects of fatherhood. But Mohammed had bent over backwards to accommodate him and his team on this excavation. Ibrahim could scarcely refuse his daughter a tour, though he thought it crazy to bring a sick child into such a dusty, death-filled place.

One of Mohammed's crew tracked them down in a tomb chamber. 'A call for you,' he grunted. 'Head office.'

Mohammed pulled a face. 'Forgive me,' he told Ibrahim. 'I must deal with this. But I'll be straight back. Could you hold Layla a minute?'

'Of course.' Ibrahim braced himself as Mohammed passed him the bundle of blankets and swaddling, but the poor girl was light as air. He smiled nervously down. She smiled back. She looked terrified of him, painfully aware he must consider her a nuisance.

She asked: 'This man was not Egyptian, then?' Mouth ulcers made her slurp and wince with every word. Ibrahim winced with her.

'That's right,' said Ibrahim. 'He was Greek, from north across the sea. Your father is a very clever man. He knew this man was Greek because he found a coin called an obol in his mouth. The Greeks believed that spirits needed this to pay a ferryman called Charon to row them across the River Styx into the next world.'

'The next world?' asked Layla. Her eyes were large with wonder, as though her skin had been pulled back around them. Ibrahim swallowed, looked away. For a moment, he felt the threat of tears. So young a girl; so harsh a fate.

His arms were beginning to tire when Mohammed finally returned. He beamed at Layla with such affection that Ibrahim felt lost, shamed, as though he had no right to his place in the world, to the air and space he consumed, to his easy life.

He took a pace back into the sanctuary of shadow. 'Those tests we were able to help you with,' he murmured to Mohammed. 'Where might I get one done myself?'

III

Knox and Augustin looked at each other with concern, but they were experienced divers, they didn't panic. They checked their air; they each had twenty minutes, twenty-five if they didn't waste it. Augustin pointed ahead. Knox nodded. They needed to find their way out, or at least a pocket of air where they could wait until the sediment resettled and they could see again.

They reached a dead end. Knox brought his gauge up to his goggles to check air pressure, dropping relentlessly. They kept their hands to the walls to steer through the blinding haze. On night dives in Sharm, his colleagues had talked glibly of zero visibility. With all the muck they'd stirred, this was indescribably worse. Knox could barely see his gauges, even when he held them in front of his mask.

They hit another dead end. Maybe the same one. They could all too easily be going round in circles. Fifteen bar. They began swimming, completely turned around now, their sense of direction gone, the fear building, breathing faster, burning up their precious air, so little of it left, just five bar, deep into the red hazard zone, and then Augustin was seizing his shoulder and thrusting his face into his, tearing out his regulator, pointing desperately at his mouth, Knox passing him his spare, but down to the last few gasps himself and, reaching another fork, Augustin pointing right, Knox sure they'd gone right last time, tugging left, fighting over it, Augustin insisting on going right, Knox deciding to trust him, both men swimming flat out, hitting and kicking each other, scraping rough wall and ceiling, Knox gagging as his tank ran dry, pressure on his lungs, hitting another wall, Augustin wrenching him upwards against steps and then bursting up into open air, spitting out his regulator, breathing in gratefully, the two men lying side by side, chests pumping like frantic bellows.

Augustin laid his head sideways to look at Knox, a glint already in his eye, as though he'd thought of something funny, but couldn't yet get it out. 'There are old divers,' he panted finally.

'There are bold divers.'

Laughter hurt Knox's lungs. 'I reckon you should get a pump, mate.'

'I think you're right,' agreed Augustin. 'And we tell no one about this, OK? Not for a year or two, anyway. I'm supposed to be professional.'

'Mum's the word,' nodded Knox. He pushed himself tiredly up, unbuckled his BCD, dropped it and the empty tank onto the stone floor.

'Look!' said Augustin. 'The basket's disappeared.'

Knox frowned. Augustin was right. In his relief at getting out alive, he'd forgotten what had triggered the trouble in the first place. 'What the hell?' He crouched down where the excavation basket had been. He'd assumed Augustin's knot had just come loose. 'You don't think this was Hassan's doing, do you?'

A rueful expression spread over Augustin's face. 'No,' he said. 'I fear it was simpler than that.'

'What?'

'It was an excavation basket full of rubble,' observed Augustin. 'And what is Mansoor's number-one priority?'

Knox winced and closed his eyes. 'You mean clearing the site of rubble?'

'This is our lucky day, my friend.'

Soft footsteps approached down the corridor. Knox looked up as a slender, dark-haired, attractive young woman appeared out of the shadows, a digital camera on a strap around her neck.

'Your lucky day?' she asked. 'Have you found something?'

Augustin jumped up and walked over, interposing himself between her and Knox. 'Look!' he said, taking out his funerary lamp, waving a hand at the water. 'Chamber after chamber of sealed *loculi*!'

'Fantastic.' She glanced past Augustin at Knox. 'I'm Gaille,' she said.

He had no option but to stand. 'Mark,' he replied.

'Nice to meet you, Mark.'

'Likewise.'

'How's the photography going?' Augustin asked her, touching her shoulder.

'Fine,' said Gaille. 'Mansoor's brought down all his lighting from the Museum so that I can photograph the antechamber, but it gets too hot to keep on long. The plaster, you know. We don't want it cracking.'

'Indeed no.' He put an arm around her shoulder, tried to turn her away from Knox. 'Listen,' he said. 'I understand you're alone in town, yes? Perhaps we could have dinner together? I can show you old Alexandria.'

Her eyes lit up. 'That would be great, yes.' She sounded so enthusiastic, she blushed and felt compelled to explain herself. 'It's just, there's nowhere to eat in my hotel, and they won't let guests take food back to their rooms, and I really hate eating alone in restaurants. I feel so *conspicuous*, you know. As though everyone's watching.'

'And why wouldn't they watch?' asked

135

Augustin gallantly. 'A pretty girl like you. Which hotel are you staying at?'

'The Vicomte.'

'That terrible place! But why?'

She shrugged sheepishly. 'I asked my taxi-driver for somewhere central and cheap.'

'He took you at your word,' laughed Augustin. 'Tonight, then. Eight o'clock, yes? I'll pick you up.'

'Great.' She looked past him to Knox, standing in the shadows. 'You'll come too, yes?' she asked.

He shook his head. 'I don't think I'll be able to make it, I'm afraid.'

'Oh.' She patted her hips and made a shrugging kind of face. 'Well, then,' she nodded, 'until later.' And she retreated up the corridor with a slightly stilted walk, as though she sensed, quite correctly, that she was being watched.

10

I

Back at Augustin's apartment, Knox sat on the couch and tried to kill time. It wasn't easy. *Tintin* was bad enough once. He paced around the sitting room, went out onto the balcony. It seemed forever before the sun set. And still no sign of Augustin. The phone rang at seven thirty. Knox dared not answer, letting the answerphone chug out its message.

'It's me,' shouted Augustin, loud music thumping in the background, along with raucous laughter and the clinking of glasses and bottles. 'Pick up, will you?'

Knox did so. 'Where the hell are you? You said you'd be back hours ago.'

'Listen, my friend,' replied Augustin. 'A difficult situation at work.'

'Work?' asked Knox drily.

'I need you to call that photographer girl for me. Gaille Dumas. The one from the Vicomte. Explain to her that I'm in the middle of a crisis. I'm putting out fires.'

'She's in town all on her own,' protested Knox. 'You can't stand her up.'

'Exactly,' agreed Augustin. 'That's why I need you to do it for me. After all, if she hears this noise, maybe she'll wonder if I'm telling her the complete truth.'

137

'Why don't you ask her to join you?'

'I have plans. You know that Beatrice I mentioned?'

'For Christ's sake! Do your own dirty work.'

'I'm asking as a friend, Daniel. How was it you put it? Yes: I'm in trouble. I need help.'

'OK,' sighed Knox. 'Leave it to me.'

'Thanks.'

'And good luck with your crisis,' said Knox stingingly.

He picked up the phone directory, flipped through it for the Vicomte Hotel. He felt bad for the girl, vicariously guilty. He was puritanical about such things. When you asked a girl out, particularly one who so evidently hankered for company, you showed up. The shadow of a long evening stretched out ahead of him. No one to talk to, nothing to read, nothing to watch on TV. Sod it, he thought. Sod Hassan and his thugs. He went into Augustin's room for a clean shirt and a baseball cap. Then he left a note by the phone, went down to the street, and hailed a cab.

II

Ibrahim couldn't get comfortable at home that evening. His upper arm itched from where the nurse had taken blood for his HLA test. He kept thinking of that poor girl's wide brown eyes. He kept thinking of her predicament, her courage. In the end, he couldn't sit there any more. He went through to his study and plucked a book down from the shelves, one from which his

138

father had read to him as a child. Then he went out to his car.

Mohammed's apartment was on the ninth floor. The lifts were broken. When Ibrahim finally made it, he had to put his hands on his knees a minute, and wheezed for breath. What an effort it must be with an invalid child! It made him think about his own privileged childhood and education, everything made easy by his father's wealth. He heard, inside, the suppressed rancour of a married couple upon whom too much strain has been placed, trying not to let their beloved child overhear. He felt embarrassed, suddenly; an intruder. He was about to walk away again when the door opened unexpectedly and a woman emerged, a scarf over her hair, dressed formally, as if off on a visit. She looked as startled to see him as he to see her.

'Who are you?' she demanded. 'What are you doing here?'

'Excuse me,' he said, flustered. 'I have something for Mohammed.'

'What?'

'Just a book.' He pulled it from the bag. 'For his daughter. Your daughter.'

The woman looked at Ibrahim in bewilderment. 'This is for Layla?'

'Yes.'

'But . . . who are you?'

'My name is Ibrahim.'

'The archaeologist?'

'Yes.'

She bit her lower lip thoughtfully. Then she went back inside her flat. 'Mohammed,' she said.

'Come here. Your archaeologist friend is visiting.'

Mohammed appeared from a side room, ducking his head beneath the low lintel. 'Yes?' he asked anxiously. 'Is there a problem at the site?'

'No,' said Ibrahim, showing a bit more of the book. 'It's just . . . my father used to read to me from this. I thought maybe you and your daughter . . . ' He opened the book, flipped through the pages, showing off the gorgeous illustrations inside, pictures of Alexander from history and myth.

'But it's beautiful,' gaped Mohammed. He glanced at his wife, who hesitated then nodded. 'Layla's been talking about you all evening,' said Mohammed, coming to grasp Ibrahim by the elbow. 'I know it would mean a great deal to her if you gave it to her yourself.'

III

Alexandria was usually one of the most welcoming of Egyptian cities, but the tensions between the West and the Arab world had reached here too, and Knox took a cool nod from a young Egyptian man out with his woman as he paid his taxi-driver on the street outside Gaille's hotel. Normally, he'd have shrugged it off; with Hassan to worry about, it preyed on his mind. All these people. How could he tell which ones were dangerous? The ones who smiled, the ones who scowled?

Gaille's room was on the sixth floor. The old lift rattled and shook as it ascended past floors of

140

gloom and darkness. He pulled back the mesh door and stepped out. The middle-aged, balding concierge was talking with a young bearded man. They both looked at Knox without even trying to hide their disdain.

'Yes?' asked the concierge.

'Gaille Dumas, please,' said Knox.

'The Frenchwoman?'

'Yes.'

'And you are?'

Knox had to think for a moment to remember the name Augustin had given him. 'Mark,' he said. 'Mark Edwards.'

'Sit, please.' The concierge turned back to his friend, picking up their conversation again. Knox sat in a blue armchair, white fluff leaking from the tattered upholstery. A minute went by. Still the concierge made no effort to alert Gaille. A second minute passed. The two men were chatting away, not looking his way, their contempt clear. Knox had no wish to make himself conspicuous, but there came a point when doing nothing was more memorable than doing something, so he stood up, brushed fluff from his trousers, went back over to reception.

'Call her for me,' he said.

'In a minute.'

He put his hand on the counter. 'Call her,' he said. 'Now.'

The concierge scowled but picked up his phone and dialled her extension. A phone tinkled dully down the hall. 'You have a visitor,' he told her. He put the phone back down and resumed his conversation with his friend without a word to Knox.

Another minute passed. A door opened and closed. Footsteps hurried on the hard wooden floorboards. Gaille appeared around a corner, wearing plimsolls, faded jeans and a baggy black sweatshirt. 'Mark,' she frowned, 'what are *you* doing here?'

'Augustin couldn't make it, I'm afraid. Crisis at work. I hope you don't mind a last-minute substitute.'

'Not at all.' She looked down at her dowdy clothes, pulled a face. 'Are we going anywhere smart?' she asked.

'You look fine,' Knox assured her. 'You look gorgeous.'

'Thanks.' She smiled shyly. 'Then shall we just go? I'm starving.'

He ushered her inside the lift. The concierge and his bearded friend glared as he slammed closed the mesh-door a little more vehemently than was necessary. It was dim and tight inside; two people was all it could comfortably take. They stood shoulder-to-shoulder as it clanked slowly down six floors.

'Charming man,' he muttered, once they were out of earshot.

'My guy in Tanta was even worse, would you believe?' said Gaille. 'He gave me those looks, you know, as if he held women to blame for every evil in the history of the world. I felt like asking him, why run a hotel? Why not run a YMCA, or something? Just nice young boys.'

Knox laughed and hauled open the door again

as they reached the ground floor. 'You like seafood?'

'I love seafood.'

'There's this restaurant I used to visit a lot. I haven't been there for a while, but I thought we might give it a try.'

'That sounds great. You know Alexandria well, then?'

'I used to.' Down the building's front steps, he steered Gaille away from the bustling and carnival-like Sharia Nabi Daniel, along a quieter road. With Hassan on his tail, he needed to stay in the shadows. He kept looking around, sensing eyes on him, people frowning, taking a second look. In the darkness behind, a man in pale blue robes was talking quietly but urgently on his mobile, darting glances his way.

'Are you all right?' asked Gaille. 'Is something the matter?'

'No,' Knox said. 'Forgive me. Just a little distracted.'

They came to a fork in the road, a minaret on its corner, giving him the opportunity to cover his jitters with conversation. 'The Attarine Mosque,' he said, pointing it out. 'Did you know that that's where they found the sarcophagus of Alexander the Great?'

'I hadn't even heard they'd found it.'

'Your man Napoleon,' nodded Knox. 'When he had his people plunder Egypt for its treasures.'

'Yes,' smiled Gaille. 'Before you wretched English stole them from him.'

'Saved them for civilisation, you mean.

143

Anyway, they found this huge breccia sarcophagus covered in hieroglyphics, which no one could decipher back then, but the locals swore blind it had been Alexander's. Alexander was Napoleon's hero, so he decided to be buried in it himself and ordered it back to France. But then us Brits diverted it to the British Museum, where it's on show near the Rosetta Stone.'

'I'll look out for it.'

The man was still the same distance behind, talking earnestly on his mobile. Knox felt his anxiety increase. He steered Gaille down a narrow side road to see if that would dislodge him.

'Of course,' he said, 'when hieroglyphics were finally cracked, it turned out that it wasn't Alexander's sarcophagus at all, but Nectanebo the Second's.'

'Ah.'

He glanced around once more, but the road was clear. 'Exactly,' he said, allowing himself to relax a little. 'Sold a pup by the natives. How mortifying! No one even considered that there might be a glimmer of truth to the story. After all, Ptolemy would surely never have put Alexander the Great in the cast-off sarcophagus of some fugitive pharaoh like Nectanebo, would he?'

'It does seem unlikely.'

'Exactly. Do you know much about Nectanebo?'

Gaille shrugged. 'A little.'

'The last native Egyptian pharaoh. He

defeated the Persians in battle and commissioned lots of new buildings, including a temple in Saqqara, city of the dead for Memphis, Egypt's capital at the time.'

'I'm not completely ignorant, you know. I do know Saqqara.'

'He also commissioned this sarcophagus,' grinned Knox, 'though he never got to use it. The Persians came back, and Nectanebo had to flee. So, when Ptolemy took Egypt twenty years later, and needed somewhere to keep Alexander's body while he built him a proper mausoleum in Alexandria, Nectanebo's temple and sarcophagus were both lying empty.'

'You're suggesting he used them as a stopgap?'

The man who'd been following them earlier suddenly appeared ahead of them, still talking quietly but earnestly on his mobile. He glanced their way and immediately dropped his eyes. Knox steered Gaille down a side alley, prompting her to frown at him. He soon regretted his choice. The alley was deserted and dark, and their footsteps rang and echoed on the pavement, emphasising just how alone they were. And when he glanced around, he saw the man entering the alley behind them.

'What is it?' asked Gaille. 'What's wrong?'

'Nothing,' said Knox, taking her arm and hurrying her along. 'I'm just hungry, that's all.'

She frowned, unconvinced, but shrugged and let it go. 'You were telling me about the sarcophagus,' she prompted.

'Yes,' he nodded. He looked around, was relieved to see that they'd put some distance between themselves and their tail. 'Ptolemy certainly needed a stopgap. I mean, it was several decades before he transferred Alexander to Alexandria. And it would explain how the sarcophagus came to be here. I mean, you should see this thing. It's a beast. But perfect for protecting Alexander's body in transit.'

'It makes sense from an Egyptian point of view too,' agreed Gaille. 'You know they believed Alexander to be the son of Nectanebo the Second?'

Knox frowned. 'You don't mean that old *Alexander Romance* story?' The *Alexander Romance* had been a runaway bestseller of ancient times, filled with all kinds of half-truths, exaggerations and lies about Alexander, including a story that Nectanebo II had visited the Macedonian court, where he'd seduced Philip's wife, Olympias, and fathered Alexander.

'It's more than that. When Alexander beat the Persians at Issus, he didn't just make himself *de facto* ruler of Egypt. To Egyptian eyes, it proved he was Nectanebo's legitimate successor. Did you know that one of his Egyptian throne-names was 'he who drives out the foreigners', just like Nectanebo?'

'Hey!' protested Knox. 'I thought you said you didn't know anything about Nectanebo?'

'I said I knew a little,' smiled Gaille. 'In France this counts as a little. Maybe not in England.'

'So you think the *Alexander Romance* story is credible, then?' he asked, steering her to her right, taking another look back as he did so. Their tail was still there; closer, if anything. And then two men appeared around the corner ahead. Knox readied himself to run. But the two men kept on walking, paying no attention to Knox or their tail.

'Well, obviously it's not true,' said Gaille. 'Nectanebo never went anywhere near Greece. But I can certainly believe that such a story gained currency among the Egyptians. Maybe Alexander even encouraged it. He was incredibly skilled at hearts and minds. I've always thought that was one reason he visited Siwa. I mean, everyone assumes that he went because the Oracle of Ammon was so revered by the Greeks. But the Egyptians revered it too, and had done for centuries. Did you know that all the Twenty-Eighth Dynasty pharaohs travelled to Siwa to be acknowledged; and that they were all depicted with ram's horns, just like Alexander?'

They finally emerged onto the Corniche. A breaker crashed against the rocks, spraying spume high over the high wall, leaving the road shining black. Knox glanced round again to see their tail put his phone away in his pocket then look all about, as though he'd arranged a meeting.

'Is that right?' asked Knox.

Gaille nodded vigorously. 'The Egyptians were sticklers for legitimacy in their pharaohs. Alexander succeeded Nectanebo, so in a sense *of course* he was his son. The story about Nectanebo sleeping with his mother was just a convenient way of explaining it.' She smiled apologetically. 'Anyway. Enough shop. Where's this restaurant of yours?'

'Just up here.' He glanced around a final time. Their tail was advancing with a broad smile upon a dark-haired woman and two young children, picking them up, laughing joyfully as he spun them around. Knox breathed more easily. Nothing but paranoia. Then he reminded himself sternly that just because it had proved benign this time, it didn't mean he could afford to relax.

They reached the restaurant, a plush place overlooking the waterfront. Gaille looked at Knox in horror, then down at her shabby clothes. 'But you told me it wasn't smart!' she protested.

'It isn't. And you look beautiful.'

She pursed her lips, as if she knew he was lying, even though he wasn't. She had the kind of looks he'd always found irresistible, shining with gentleness and intelligence. She said: 'I only put on these horrid things because I didn't want to give your friend Augustin any encouragement. If I'd known it'd be you . . . '

A grin spread across Knox's face. 'Are you saying you *do* want to give me encouragement?'

'That's not what I meant at all,' blushed Gaille furiously. 'I only meant that I think I can trust you.'

'Oh,' said Knox gloomily, opening the door for her, ushering her inside. 'Trustworthy. That's almost as bad as being nice.'

'Worse,' smiled Gaille. 'Much worse.'

They climbed a flight of stairs to the dining area.

'Avoid anything freshwater,' he advised, helping her to a seat with a view out over the

Eastern Harbour. 'The lakes around here, it's a miracle anything survives in them. But the seafood will be good.'

'Duly noted.'

He flapped out a napkin as he sat. 'So how's your photography going?'

'Not bad. Better than I expected, if I'm honest.' She leaned forwards over the table, eager to confide. 'I'm not actually a photographer at all, you know.'

'No?'

'I'm a papyrologist, really. The camera just helps me reassemble fragments. You can do amazing things with the software, these days.'

'So how did you get this job, then?'

'My boss volunteered me.'

'Ah. Elena. Very kind of her. So you're working with her in the Delta, yes?'

'Yes.'

'What on?'

'An old settlement,' she said enthusiastically. 'We've found traces of city walls and dwellings and cemeteries. Everything from Old Kingdom up to Early Ptolemaic.'

'Wow. What's the place?'

'Oh.' She looked hesitant suddenly, as though she'd said too much. 'We haven't made a definitive identification yet.'

'You must have some idea.'

'I really can't talk about it,' said Gaille. 'Elena made us all sign agreements.'

'Come on. I won't tell a soul, I swear. And you did just say I was trustworthy.'

'I can't. Honestly.'

149

'Give me a clue, then. Just one clue.'

'Please. I really can't.'

'Of course you can. You want to. You know you do.'

She pulled a face. 'Have you ever heard the expression, putting your head in the wolf's mouth? That's like crossing Elena. You don't do it twice, trust me.'

'Fine,' grumbled Knox. 'So how come you're working for her? I mean, it's a Greek excavation, isn't it? You don't strike me as particularly Greek.'

'Elena's expert fell ill. She needed a replacement. Someone gave her my name. You know what it's like.'

'Yes.'

'She just called up one afternoon. I was really flattered. And I had nothing I couldn't get out of. Besides, it's all very well reading about Egypt in books, but it's not the same, is it?'

'No,' agreed Knox. 'So is this your first excavation?'

She shook her head. 'I hate talking about myself. It's your turn. You're an underwater archaeologist, yes?'

'An archaeologist who knows how to dive.'

'And an intellectual snob too?'

He laughed. 'Raging.'

'Where did you study?'

'Cambridge.'

'Oh!' She pulled a face.

'You don't like Cambridge?' protested Knox. 'How can you not like Cambridge?'

'It's not Cambridge exactly. Just someone who

150

used to study there.'

'An archaeologist?' he grinned. 'Excellent! Who?'

'Oh, I'm sure you won't know him,' she said. 'His name's Daniel Knox.'

11

I

'Marvellous!' laughed Augustin, clapping his hands, when Knox reported back later that evening. 'But that's just marvellous. What did you do?'

'What the fuck could I do?' grumbled Knox. 'I told her I'd never heard of him and changed the subject.'

'And you've no idea why she dislikes you so much? You didn't perhaps fuck her one time, then never call?'

'No.'

'You're sure? That's what it usually is with me.'

Knox scowled. 'Certain.'

'Then what?'

'I don't know,' he shrugged helplessly. 'I can't think. Unless . . . '

'What?'

'Oh, no,' said Knox, his cheeks suddenly ablaze. He put his hand on his forehead. 'Oh, Christ!'

'What?'

'Her name's not Gaille Dumas, you idiot. It's Gaille Bonnard.'

'Dumas, Bonnard, what's the difference? And anyway, who is she, this Gaille Bonnard?'

'She's Richard's daughter,' answered Knox.

'That's who she is.' Then he added bleakly: 'No wonder she hates me.'

II

It was sticky in Gaille's room, even with her balcony doors wide open. That flicker on Mark's face when she'd mentioned Daniel Knox, his hurried change of subject, the way he'd been so ill at ease afterwards. She cursed herself for her big mouth; she'd been having a really good time until then. Of course they'd have known each other. Frankly, it would have been astonishing if two Cambridge-educated archaeologists of similar age hadn't been friends.

Some hatreds are based on principle. Others are personal. Whenever Gaille thought of Knox, though she'd never even met him, she felt a fusion of the two, snakes writhing in her chest. Her mother had been a nightclub singer. She'd had a brief fling with Richard Mitchell, had fallen pregnant, coercing him into a marriage that had never stood a chance, not least because he'd finally realised that he preferred men. Gaille had been just four when her father had given up and fled to Egypt. Her mother, struggling to come to terms with a homosexual husband and a career on the skids, had taken it out on Gaille. She'd also found solace in abusing every substance she could lay her hands on, until, on the eve of her fiftieth birthday, she'd misjudged one of her periodic cries for help and gone all the way.

As a child, Gaille had done what she could to cope with her mother's insecurity, anger and violence, but it had never been enough. She might have gone crazy from the strain of it, except that she'd had a safety valve, a way to relieve the building pressure. It had been the one month every year when she'd joined her father on one of his excavations in North Africa or the Levant, of which she'd loved every second.

Aged seventeen, Gaille had been due to join his second season west of Mallawi in Middle Egypt. For eleven months, she'd been studying Coptic, Hieroglyphics and Hieratic in a desperate effort to prove her value so conclusively that her father would have no choice but to take her on full time. But, just three days before she'd been due to fly out, he'd arrived unexpectedly at their Paris apartment. Maman had thrown one of her tantrums, had refused to let him see Gaille. She'd had to kneel outside the cramped sitting room and listen through its plywood door panels. A nearby television had been loud with sporadic canned laughter, so she'd not heard everything; but enough. He was postponing Mallawi to deal with an urgent personal situation. It wouldn't now take place until after Gaille was back at school.

That season had proved her father's crowning triumph. Just eight weeks later he'd found a Ptolemaic archive so important that Yusuf Abbas, the future Secretary General of the Supreme Council for Antiquities, had taken personal control. Gaille should have been there, but no. A precocious young Cambridge Egyptologist called

Daniel Knox had been recruited in her place. That was her father's urgent personal situation! An itch in his pants. The betrayal had been so hurtful, Gaille had shunned him from that moment on. Though he'd tried to contact her and to apologise, she'd never given him a chance. And though she'd been too committed to Egyptology to see merit in any other way of life, she'd avoided Egypt until he was long dead and Elena's offer had taken her by surprise.

She'd never met Knox; had never wanted to. But he'd written her a letter of condolence, which had included a moving account of her father's last years. He'd claimed that her father had thought and spoken constantly of her, that when he'd fallen to his death rock-climbing in the Western Desert, there'd been nothing anyone could have done to save him, and that his last thoughts had been of her, that his dying request had been of her, asking Knox to contact her himself and tell her so. She'd found this, perversely, both deeply upsetting and immensely consoling.

Then a parcel had arrived from Siwa Oasis, containing all her father's belongings and papers. It had included the police report into the accident and transcripts of statements made by the two guides who'd been on that fateful climb. Both had testified that Knox could have saved her father had he wished, but that he'd stood by and watched instead. They'd both stated too that the fall had been instantly fatal, that his body had already been cold by the time they or Knox or anybody had reached him. That there was no

155

way, therefore, that he could have communicated any last wishes. It had all been a lie.

Before she'd received and read that report, she'd hated Knox only on principle. Since then, it had become personal as well.

III

Nessim had learned as a soldier to be aware of the physiology of fear. Knowing what was happening inside your body was a good way to control it. Your heart beat faster, making your breath hot in your mouth; that metallic tang in the back of your mouth was nothing but your glands flooding your system with adrenalin in preparation for fight or flight; the tingling in your fingers and toes, and the looseness of your bladder and bowels, was blood being reallocated to places that needed it more.

He stood by his hotel window to dial Hassan's number, looking down at the river ten storeys below.

'Have you found him?' asked Hassan, when he was put through.

'Not yet, sir. But we're making progress.'

'Progress?' enquired Hassan acidly. 'Is this the same progress you told me about yesterday?'

'I've put together a strong team, sir.'

'Oh, good. A team.'

'Yes, sir.' It was true too, for all Hassan's scorn. Old comrades, keen for the work, who'd proved themselves both reliable and discreet. He'd given them each Knox's name, his licence

156

plate, copies of his photograph, and the few other details he'd had, then he'd set some to watch the homes of Knox's known associates, others to tour hotels and stations. He'd arranged a trace on Knox's mobile too, so that if he ever turned it on they'd be able to triangulate his position to within a hundred metres. He'd also put a trace on his various bank accounts and credit cards. Anything was possible in Egypt if you had money.

'Listen,' said Hassan. 'I don't want progress. I want Knox.'

'Yes, sir.'

'Call tomorrow. Have good news for me.'

'Yes, sir.' Nessim replaced his handset with a slightly trembling hand and sat down on his hotel bed, shoulders sagging. He wiped his forehead. His wrist came back with the hairs slicked with sweat against his skin. Another of the symptoms. A full house. He contemplated, for a moment, pillaging his bank account and simply vanishing. But Hassan knew too much about him. He knew about his sister. He knew about Fatima and their son. Besides, Nessim's sense of honour balked at running from a professional duty just because he found it difficult or dangerous. So, instead, he got out Knox's Secret Service file and stared at the old, blackened text some more. It hadn't been updated for years. Several of the people on it had changed address, or had left Egypt altogether. Others they couldn't track at all. But it was Nessim's best hope of success, and he prayed that it would come good for him.

157

12

Augustin and Knox headed into the site first thing, eager to get started, hopeful that the pump would have won them enough headroom to explore. They both knew all too well that pumping out an antiquity in Alexandria wasn't easy. The limestone bedrock was extremely porous, holding water like a giant sponge. As soon as they started pumping, therefore, this sponge would start releasing its reservoir, replacing what they were taking out until equilibrium was finally restored. They couldn't hope to beat it, not with the resources they had available. They could only buy a little time.

It was obvious from the moment they arrived on site, however, that something was seriously wrong. The pump engine was wheezing like a chronic smoker chasing after a bus. They hurried down. A seal had evidently failed. Water spilled and sprayed down the camber of the rotunda floor into the Macedonian tomb, where lamps gleamed like pool lights beneath the murky water.

Augustin sprinted back up the stairwell to kill the pump engine. Knox unplugged the power cables, removed his shoes and trousers, collected all the lamps and fans, then coiled them up on the steps, out of the water. The pump stilled; the

158

contents of the pipes gurgled and retreated. Knox waited for silence, then plugged the cables back in, and shed light upon the mess.

Augustin joined him on the top step, shaking his head in dismay. '*Merde!* Mansoor will have my testicles.'

'Can we bring the pump in here?'

'I only arranged for the beast,' grumbled Augustin. 'I don't know how it works.' But a look of inspiration then crossed his face. He vanished and returned with four excavation baskets, tossing two to Knox, then used the others to scoop up water.

'You can't be serious!' protested Knox.

'You have a better idea?' retorted Augustin, already hustling off down the corridor to the water table. Knox did likewise. The heavy baskets strained his shoulder and elbow joints, and left red welts across his fingers. They grinned at each other as they dumped the loads and jogged back up. After a few trips, other excavators began trickling in. They saw what had happened and grabbed baskets for themselves. Soon, a whole crew of them were at it. After a dozen trips, Knox's legs were like rubber. He took a breather in the main chamber, out of the way of the ongoing effort. Despite his initial scepticism, Augustin's idea was working well. The water level had already fallen so far that the high steps between the forecourt and the antechamber, and between the antechamber and the main chamber, were now acting as dam walls, creating three separate reservoirs. Down on his haunches to bathe his throbbing palms and fingers in the cool water, Knox noticed something curious. The water level in the main chamber was lower than in the antechamber, and lower than the step that separated them too.

He frowned, his weariness forgotten, then went out into the forecourt. 'Has anyone got any matches?' he asked.

II

Gaille arrived to find the site in bedlam. She hadn't finished photographing the main chamber yet, so her first reaction was anxiety that she might have missed her chance. She kicked off her shoes, rolled up her trousers and waded in to take a closer look. Her dinner companion from the night before was already in there, throwing broken matchsticks into the corners.

'Skiving, huh?' she asked.

'Look!' he said, pointing at the antechamber. 'See how the water level's higher in there?'

Gaille got the significance at once. 'So where's it draining to?'

'Exactly,' agreed Knox keenly. 'This place is supposed to be quarried out of solid rock.' He threw the last of his matchsticks into the corners, then he and Gaille watched raptly together as they slowly converged.

'I had a really good time last night,' murmured Gaille.

'I did too.'

'Maybe we could do it again some time.'

'I'd like that,' he said. But then he pulled a

face. 'Listen, Gaille, there's something I need to tell you first.'

'It's about Knox, isn't it?' she said. 'He's your friend, isn't he?'

'This really isn't the place to discuss it. Can I come by the Vicomte later?'

She smiled eagerly. 'We'll go out afterwards. My treat this time.'

There was splashing in the antechamber, then Mansoor appeared, bringing Elena with him.

'What's going on?' demanded Mansoor angrily. Gaille turned to her companion, expecting him to explain, but he only ducked his head, grabbed his baskets and fled, leaving Elena and Mansoor staring open-mouthed after him. 'Who the hell was that?' asked Mansoor.

'Augustin's dive buddy,' explained Gaille. 'I think the pump might have been partly his idea.'

'Ah!' said Mansoor. 'I hope he doesn't think I'm angry at him. It's that damned Augustin I want a word with.' He shook his head with a mix of amusement and exasperation. 'What are the matchsticks for?' he asked.

'No one's been emptying from here,' explained Gaille, pointing out the discrepancy in water levels. 'We just wanted to know where it was draining.'

'And?'

'They seem to be converging on the plinth.' They crouched around it, their torches illuminating the dozens of silver trails of air bubbles escaping from beneath. 'Akylos of the thirty-three,' murmured Gaille, struck by a sudden thought. 'To be the best and honoured above the rest.'

'The inscription from above the doorway?' frowned Mansoor. 'What about it?'

'The Greeks loved their puns, you know.'

'Spit it out, girl,' said Elena.

Gaille pulled a face, anxious they might think her crazy. 'It's just, you don't think the inscription could mean that the rest — the other thirty-two, that is — are honoured *below* Akylos.'

Mansoor laughed and squinted oddly at her. 'You're a photographer?'

She blushed, aware of Elena's burning stare. 'Languages, really.'

'I'll get Ibrahim down here,' nodded Mansoor. 'He needs to see this for himself.'

III

Knox found Augustin by the water table, putting on his wetsuit. 'Did Elena recognise you?' he asked Knox.

'I don't think so. Did Mansoor catch you?'

'Not quite.' Augustin flapped his hand as though it had been scalded. 'A close thing, though. *Houf!* I think for sure I am lobster bisque.' He nodded at the water. 'A wise man would stay out of the way for a little while. You want to explore?'

'Let's do it,' agreed Knox.

Despite the pump's failure, it had made good progress during the night, so that the water came

162

up only to their chins. They soon discovered what a maze it was, such an interconnected complex of passages and chambers that they pulled faces of relief at each other, aware of their luck at making it out alive. In one chamber, the far wall had been painted with the outlines of *loculi*, but hadn't been cut. It took Knox a moment to work out why. There was a ragged hole in the ceiling, as though the workmen had accidentally broken through into another space.

'Hey, mate,' he said, shining up his torch. 'Look at this.'

Augustin came to join him. 'What the hell?' he frowned.

'Give us a leg up.'

Augustin made a stirrup of his hands, hoisting Knox up into the new chamber. It was just high enough for him to stand without banging his head. He put his hand on the facing wall, built of limestone blocks, the mortar between them crumbled to dust.

'Help me up, damn you,' said Augustin. 'I want to see for myself.'

Knox reached down for his companion. When they were both up, they set about exploring. A narrow lane led right. There was a narrow gap at its end into a parallel lane flanked by a second block wall, then into a third with an outer wall of solid rock. So: a single chamber, some six metres square and two metres high, divided by internal walls into three lanes connected at one end, forming a capital 'E'. They went together to the end of the central aisle. A flight of five steps led upwards then turned at right angles into a second flight that vanished into the ceiling. Dull thumps sounded from above, shaking dust from the walls.

'Jesus!' muttered Knox. 'What was that?'

Augustin banged his fist against the ceiling. A smile of understanding broke on his face. 'The rotunda,' he said. 'This must be the original staircase. Yes. The Macedonians dug too far; they reached the water table. So? They built these limestone walls for support, they laid a new floor; they covered it with a mosaic. *Parfait!* The builders of the necropolis simply broke in here by accident five centuries later.'

IV

The main chamber had drained completely by the time Ibrahim arrived on site. Bringing heavy lifting equipment down here wasn't easy, so Mansoor had recruited Mohammed instead. The two men worked the tips of crowbars beneath one end of the plinth and levered it up. It made cracking, popping sounds as it gave, protesting after all those centuries of being bonded to the floor. They raised it a few inches, their chests and arms bulging, crowbars arching beneath the strain.

Ibrahim and Elena went down onto their knees to shine their torches beneath. There was a round, black hole in the floor, perhaps a metre in diameter. The plinth was too heavy for even Mohammed and Mansoor to hold long. Mansoor went first, giving a warning cry; then

164

Mohammed too, letting it crash back down, throwing up dust which caught in Ibrahim's nostrils and throat, sending him into a coughing fit.

'Well?' asked Mansoor, flapping his hands.

'There's a shaft,' said Ibrahim.

'You want us to move the plinth?' asked Mohammed.

'Is that possible?'

'I'll need some help and some more equipment, but yes.'

Ibrahim felt all eyes expectantly upon him, but still he hesitated. Nicolas had promised $20,000, but they'd only received half so far, the rest due upon satisfactory completion. Katerina had laid great emphasis on the word 'satisfactory', making it abundantly clear that failure to report a find like this would be considered highly unsatisfactory. And it wasn't as if he could keep it secret, not now that Elena knew. He had a sudden mental image of Mohammed's daughter, her life hanging by a thread.

'Give me a moment,' he said. 'I need to make a call.' He beckoned Elena to follow him up the stairwell, then called the Dragoumis Group, clamping a hand over his ear to shut out the din of the building works. Tinny folk music played as he waited to be connected. He rubbed the bridge of his nose fretfully.

The music stopped abruptly. 'Yes? This is Nicolas.'

'It's Ibrahim. From Alexandria. You said to call if we found anything.'

'And?'

165

'There's something beneath the Macedonian tomb. Perhaps a shaft.'

'A shaft?' Ibrahim could hear the excitement in Nicolas' voice. 'Where does it lead?'

'Almost certainly nowhere. These things rarely do. But we'll need to move the plinth to make sure. It's just, you made it clear that you wanted to be informed at once.'

'Quite right.'

'I'm going to have the plinth moved now. I'll call you back as soon as we — '

'No,' said Nicolas emphatically. 'I need to be there for this.'

'This is an emergency excavation,' protested Ibrahim. 'We don't have time for — '

'Tomorrow afternoon,' insisted Nicolas. 'I'll be with you by one. Do nothing before then. Understand?'

'Yes, but really, it's almost certainly nothing. You'll come all this way and there'll be nothing and — '

'I'm going to be there,' snapped Nicolas. 'That's final. In the meantime, no one goes in there. I want guards. I want a steel gate.'

'Yes, but — '

'Just do it. Send Katerina the bill. And I want to speak to Elena. Is she there?'

'Yes, but — '

'Put her on.'

Ibrahim shrugged helplessly. 'He wants to speak to you.'

She nodded and took his phone and walked off a little distance, making a wall of her back again, so that she couldn't be overheard.

V

Nicolas put down the phone on Elena and sat back in his chair, breathing a little heavily. Well, that *was* a phone call. Daniel Knox in Alexandria! And on his site, too! At this most sensitive of times. He stood and walked to his window, rubbing his lower back hard with his hands, which had suddenly become unaccountably stiff.

His office door opened. Katerina came in with a stack of papers. She smiled when she saw him working his spine.

'What's the matter?' she joked. 'Have you heard from Daniel Knox or something?' He gave her a look that would have peeled onions. 'Oh!' she said, putting the papers down on his desk and quickly withdrawing.

Nicolas sat back down. Few people had ever managed to get under his skin like Knox had. For six weeks, ten years ago, the man had made a series of outrageous slanders against his father and his company, and they'd all stood around and done . . . precisely nothing. His father had granted the man immunity, and his father's word was law, so that had been that; but Nicolas still burned with the humiliation. He rocked forwards and buzzed Katerina.

'I'm sorry, sir,' she blurted out, before he could speak. 'I didn't mean to — '

'Forget about it,' he said curtly. 'I need to be in Alexandria tomorrow afternoon. Is our plane free?'

'I believe so. I'll check.'

'Thank you. And that Egyptian man we bought those papyri through. He arranges other kinds of business too, doesn't he?' He didn't need to spell out for Katerina what kinds of business he was referring to.

'Mr Mounim? Yes.'

'Good. Get me his number, please. I have a job for him.'

13

I

Ibrahim gathered his top team in the rotunda to announce their sponsor's visit. He tried to sound enthusiastic about it. He tried to make out that it had been his idea. He asked people to be available to do show-and-tells, if needed, and promised tea and coffee and cakes, and a buffet lunch afterwards in the Museum, then reminded them all subtly that this man was paying their wages. He suggested they make an event of it. In short, he did everything he could to spin it into a good thing. When he was done, he invited questions. No one said a word. They were archaeologists; they detested sponsors. The meeting broke up and everyone returned to their work.

II

It was late afternoon. Hosni was drowsing in the driver's seat of his battered green Citroën when the black and chrome chopper pulled up outside the apartment block, two men upon it. The driver was in jeans, a white T-shirt and a leather jacket; the pillion passenger in pale cotton trousers, a blue sweatshirt and a red crash helmet that he removed in order to talk to the driver. Hosni grabbed his photograph of Knox, but he couldn't tell for sure at such a distance, not from such a small photograph. The two men shook hands. The passenger went inside, while the driver turned in a tight circle and roared off. Hosni counted storeys. Augustin Pascal lived on the sixth. About twenty seconds later, through his field glasses, he saw the balcony doors open and the pillion passenger step out, stretching his arms wide. Hosni fumbled for his mobile, then speed-dialled Nessim's number.

'Yes?' asked Nessim.

'It's Hosni, boss. I think I've found him.'

Nessim sucked in breath eagerly. 'You're sure?'

'Not one hundred per cent,' said Hosni, who knew Nessim too well to give false hope. 'I've only got this photograph. But, yes, I'm pretty sure.'

'Where are you?'

'Alexandria. Augustin Pascal's place. You know? The marine archaeologist.'

'Good work,' said Nessim. 'Don't lose him. And don't let him know you're on to him. I'll be with you as soon as I can.'

III

Elena had had enough of commuting back and forth between Alexandria and the Delta, so she'd booked herself into the famous Cecil Hotel. It was only ten minutes' walk from Gaille's fleapit, but in every other way it was a different world. She could scarcely waste precious excavation funds pampering a mere languages expert, after all, but for herself it was different. She was here as the senior representative of the Macedonian Archaeological Foundation. She owed it to the dignity of that institution to travel in a certain style.

She spent the early part of the evening catching up on her paperwork. It was extraordinary how bureaucratic running an excavation in Egypt could be. She was beginning to weary of it when she heard a knock upon her door. 'Come in,' she said. It opened and closed behind her. She finished totting up a column of figures, then half turned in her chair to see, with a disturbing little thrill, the Frenchman from the necropolis standing there in his jeans and leather jacket.

'What the hell are you doing here?' she demanded.

Augustin walked to her window as though he owned the place. He pulled back a curtain to gaze out over the harbour. 'Very nice,' he nodded. 'All I have is other people's laundry.'

'I asked you a question.'

He turned his back on the window, leaned against her air conditioner. 'I've been thinking about you,' he said.

'*What?*'

'Yes. Just like you've been thinking about me.'

'I assure you,' she said, 'I haven't given you a moment's thought.'

'Is that right?' he mocked.

'Yes,' said Elena. 'That's right.' But something trembled in her voice, and Augustin's insolent smile grew even broader. Elena scowled. She was attractive, successful and wealthy, well accustomed to being buzzed by womanisers like this. She normally dealt with them without even thinking, by deploying a scornful electric flytrap of a glare that incinerated their interest so efficiently that she didn't even notice any more the sharp spark of death as these little flies tumbled to the floor. But now, when she threw this glare at Augustin, there was no spark and he didn't fall. He simply absorbed it with that offensive smirk of his and carried on staring at her.

'Please leave,' she said. 'I have work.'

But he didn't leave. He just stood there, his back to the window. 'I've booked a table,' he said. 'I wouldn't want to hurry you, but — '

'If you don't leave,' she said coldly, 'I'll call security.'

He nodded. 'You must of course do whatever you think best.'

She felt flutters in her stomach as she pulled the phone towards her. It was one of those old analogues. She dialled the first number, expecting that would be enough for him. But he made no move. He just stood there with that same damned conceited smile on his face. The dial made that low metallic purr as it returned to its starting position. She dialled the second number. The handset felt cool against her cheek. She put her finger in the hole to dial the third number, but then her arm just seemed to die on her, as though all her muscles had atrophied.

He walked across and plucked the handset

from her, rested it back in its cradle. 'You'll want to freshen up,' he said. 'I'll be downstairs.'

IV

'We've found him,' said Nessim.

There was a moment's silence on the other end of the phone. After so many disappointments, Hassan seemed rather thrown. 'Are you sure?'

'Hosni spotted him,' said Nessim. 'He's staying in a friend's apartment. I drove up here as soon as I got the call. He came out fifteen minutes ago, not a care in the world. He must think we've stopped looking. But it's him, all right.'

'Where's he now?'

'In a taxi. Heading towards Ramla.'

'You're following?'

'Of course. You want him picked up?'

That silence again. Then: 'Listen to me. This is what I want.'

V

Knox was surprised and gratified by the warmth with which Gaille greeted him that evening.

'Perfect timing,' she enthused. 'Ibrahim's asked me to do a show-and-tell on the antechamber paintings tomorrow. I need a victim to practise on.' She led him back to her room, defying the toxic glare of her concierge. Her

173

balcony doors were open, a cacophony on the street below, youngsters talking and laughing excitedly in anticipation of their evening, a distant tram clanking on its rails like an overworked kitchen. Her laptop was open on her desk, her screen saver painting weird patterns on the monitor. She nudged her mouse and a colourful wall painting of two men sprang up.

Knox leaned in, frowning. 'What the hell? Is this from the site?'

'The side walls in the antechamber.'

'But . . . they're just plaster. How did you get them to look like this?'

She grinned with pleasure. 'Your friend Augustin. He told me to use water. Lots of water. Not quite as much as you pumped in this morning, maybe, but . . . '

He laughed and softly smacked her shoulder in reproach, triggering an unexpected spark of contact that gave them both a little jolt. 'You've done a great job,' he said, pulling himself together. 'It looks fantastic.'

'Thanks.'

'You know who these guys are?'

'The one on the left is Akylos. The occupant of the tomb.'

Knox frowned. The name Akylos was strangely familiar. But why wouldn't it be? It had been common enough among Greeks. 'And the other?' he asked.

'Apolles or Apelles of Cos.'

'Apelles of Cos?' asked Knox incredulously. 'You don't mean the painter?'

'Is that who he is?'

Knox nodded. 'Alexander the Great's favourite. Wouldn't have his portrait made by any other artist. He often dropped by his studio to bore everyone silly with his views on art, until finally Apelles told him to shut up, as even the boys grinding the colours were making fun of him.'

Gaille laughed. 'That took some courage.'

'Alexander liked people with a bit of brass. Besides, Apelles knew how to flatter as well as mock. He painted Alexander with a bolt of lightning in his hand, just like Zeus. Where is this? Does it say?'

'Ephesus, as far as I can make out, but you can see the lacunae for yourself.'

'It would make sense,' said Knox. 'Alexander went there after his first victory over the Persians.' He reached past her, closed the file, brought up another, soldiers wading through water. 'Perga,' he said. He glanced at her. 'You know about this?'

'No.'

'It's on the Turkish coast, opposite Rhodes. If you want to head south from there, you can hike over the hills, which is hard work, or you can go along the coast. Trouble is, you can only manage this route when a northerly is blowing, because it pushes the sea back far enough for you to get through. There was a southerly when Alexander set out, but you know Alexander, he just kept on going, and the wind switched just in time, lasting just long enough for him and his men to get through. Some people say that it was the seed for the story of Moses parting the Red Sea. Alexander passed through Palestine shortly afterwards, after all, while the Bible was still a work in progress.'

Gaille pulled a face. 'That's a little fanciful, isn't it?'

'You shouldn't underestimate the impact of Greek culture on the Jews,' said Knox. 'They wouldn't have been human if they hadn't been a little dazzled by Alexander.' Many Jews had tried to assimilate, but it hadn't been easy, not least because a centrepiece of Greek social life had been the gymnasium, and *gymnos* was Greek for naked, so everything — by definition — had been on show. The Greeks had prized the foreskin as a fine piece of divine design, and had considered circumcision barbaric. Many Jews had therefore tried to reverse the *mohel's* work by cutting free the skin around the base of their glans or by hanging metal weights from what little they had.

'I don't mean fanciful like that,' said Gaille. 'I'm only saying that bodies of water miraculously drying up to enable the hero to get through aren't exactly unknown in ancient myth. Nor are floods sent to destroy enemies. If I had to put my money anywhere, I'd bet on King Sargon.'

'The Akkadian?'

Gaille nodded. 'A thousand years before Moses, two thousand before Alexander. There's a source describing how the Tigris and the Euphrates dried up for him. And he already has an established point of similarity with Moses.'

Knox frowned. 'How do you mean?'

'His mother put him in a basket of rushes and set him on the river,' said Gaille. 'Just like Moses. He was found by a man called Akki and raised as his son. Mind you, changelings were a common enough motif. It gave the poets a way to show a kind of cosmic justice at work. Take Oedipus. Left out by his father to die from exposure, only to return to kill him.'

Knox nodded. 'It's amazing how the same stories keep cropping up again and again across the entire Eastern Mediterranean.'

'Not that amazing,' replied Gaille. 'It was a massive trading block, after all, and merchants have always loved trading tall tales.'

'And the region was infested by minstrels, of course. And you know what minstrels have always been famous for.'

'Wandering,' grinned Gaille, glancing up and around. Their eyes met and held for a moment, and Knox felt unsettling flutters in his chest. It had been too long since he'd had a woman to share his life and passions with, not just his bed. Far too long. He turned in mild confusion back to the screen. 'So this is a map of Alexander's campaigns?' he asked.

'Not exactly,' said Gaille, a little flustered herself. 'Of Akylos' life. The two just happen to be the same.' Without looking his way, she brought up another picture, a walled city surrounded by water being menaced by an outsize satyr, an anthropomorphic Greek god, part man, part goat. 'This one has me puzzled. I thought it might be Tyre, looking at the walls and water, but — '

177

'It's Tyre, all right,' said Knox.

'How can you be so sure?'

'Tyre was famously impregnable,' he told her. 'Even Alexander had problems with it. One night during his siege he dreamed that a satyr was mocking him. He chased and chased it, but it kept eluding him, until finally he caught it and woke up. His seers interpreted it by pointing out that *satyros* was made up of two words, *sa* and *Tyros*, meaning 'yours' and 'Tyre'. Tyre will be yours. It'll just take time and effort. And so it proved.'

'Unhappily for the inhabitants.'

'He spared everyone who took sanctuary in temples.'

'Yes,' said Gaille tightly. 'Then slaughtered two thousand of them by nailing them to crosses.'

'Maybe.'

'There's no maybe about it. Read your sources.'

'The Macedonians often crucified criminals after they were dead,' replied Knox calmly. 'Like us Brits hanging them on gibbets. To discourage others.'

'Oh,' frowned Gaille. 'But why would Alexander consider the Tyrians criminals? They'd only been defending their homes.'

'Alexander sent in heralds to discuss terms before laying the siege. The Tyrians murdered them and hurled their bodies from the ramparts. That was an absolute no-no back then.' He glanced at Gaille again, puzzled by something. 'This is one hell of a tomb for a shield-bearer, don't you think? I mean, a forecourt, an

178

antechamber and a main chamber. Not to mention Ionic columns, a sculpted façade, bronze doors and all these paintings. It must have cost an incredible amount of money.'

'Alexander paid well.'

'Not that well. Besides, this is how Macedonian kings were buried. It feels, I don't know, *presumptuous*, doesn't it?'

Gaille nodded. 'They're raising the plinth tomorrow afternoon. Maybe that'll give us some answers. You're going to be there, aren't you?'

'I doubt it, I'm afraid.'

'But you must come,' she said earnestly. 'We wouldn't have discovered it without you.'

'Even so.'

'I don't understand,' she complained. 'What's going on?'

There was pain in her eyes, as well as confusion. Knox knew he couldn't prevaricate any longer. He pulled a face to let her know he had a difficult subject to broach, then stood up straight, putting distance between them. 'You know how I said earlier there was something I needed to tell you?'

'It's that damned Knox, isn't it?' scowled Gaille. 'He's your best bloody friend or something.'

'Not exactly.'

'Let's not let him come between us,' she begged. 'I was just shooting my mouth off last night. Honestly. He means nothing to me. I've never even met the man.'

Knox looked steadfastly into her eyes, until realisation began to dawn. Then he nodded. 'Yes, you have,' he told her.

14

It took Gaille a moment to assimilate fully what Knox was saying. Then her expression went cold. 'Get out,' she said.

'Please,' he begged. 'Just let me — '

'Get out. Get out now.'

'Look. I know how you must feel, but — '

She went to her door and threw it open. 'Out!' she said.

'Gaille,' he pleaded. 'Just let me explain.'

'You had your chance. You sent me that letter, remember.'

'It wasn't what you think. Please just let me — '

But the concierge had overheard the commotion. Now he arrived outside Gaille's room, grabbed Knox's arm, dragged him out. 'You leave,' he said. 'I call police.'

Knox tried to shake him off, but he had surprisingly strong fingers, which he dug vengefully into Knox's flesh, giving him no choice but to go with him or start a fight. They reached the lobby. The concierge bundled him into the lift, punched the button for the ground floor, then slammed the mesh door closed.

'No come back,' he warned, wagging his finger.

The lift juddered downwards. Knox was still in

a daze when he stepped out into the ground-floor lobby and down the front steps. The look of anger on Gaille's face had not only shocked him, it had made him realise just how hard he was falling for her. He turned right and right again, heading down the alley at the rear of her hotel, converted, like so many alleys in Alexandria, into an improvised parking lot, so that he had to wend between tightly packed cars.

He remembered, suddenly, the letter he'd sent her, all the deceits he'd filled it with. His face burned hot; he stopped dead in the alley so abruptly that a man walking behind him barged into his back. Knox held up his hand in apology, started to say sorry, but then he caught a whiff of something chemical, and suddenly a damp, burning cloth was clamped over his nose and mouth, and the darkness began closing in. Too late, he realised that he'd allowed himself to stop worrying about Sinai, about Hassan. He tried to fight, to pull away, but the chloroform was already in his system, and he collapsed tamely into the arms of his assailant.

II

It was barely eleven thirty when Augustin brought Elena back to the Cecil Hotel. He'd invited her on to a nightclub; she'd pleaded weight of work. He insisted on escorting her into the lobby all the same.

'There's no need to come up,' she said drily, when they reached the lifts. 'I'm sure I'll be safe from here.'

'I see you to your room,' he announced gallantly. 'I would never forgive myself if anything happened.'

She sighed and shook her head but didn't make a point of it. There was a mirror in the lift. They each checked themselves out in it, and then each other, their eyes meeting in the glass, smiling at their own vanity. She had to admit that they made a striking pair. He walked her right to her door.

'Thank you,' she said, shaking his hand. 'I had fun.'

'I'm glad.'

Elena took her key from her purse. 'I'll see you tomorrow, then.'

'No doubt.' But he made no move to leave.

'You haven't forgotten where the lifts are already?' she asked pointedly.

He smiled wryly. 'I think you're the kind of woman not to be afraid of what she wants. I'm right about this, yes?'

'Yes.'

'Good. Then let me make this clear. If you ask me to leave once more, I truly will leave.'

There was silence for a few moments. Elena nodded thoughtfully to herself as she unlocked her door and went inside. 'Well?' she asked, leaving the door open behind her. 'Are you coming in or not?'

III

Knox slowly returned to consciousness, aware of his lips, nostrils and throat burning, of nausea in his gut. He tried to open his eyes. They were glued shut. He tried to lift a hand to his face, but his wrists were bound behind his back. He tried to cry out but his mouth was taped. When he recalled what had happened, his heart plunged into panicked tachycardia and his body shuddered in a great spasm, arching him off the floor. Something clumped him hard behind the ear and he slumped back into darkness.

He was more circumspect when he came round again. He let his senses gather information. He was lying on his front. Some kind of soft carpet with a lump in the middle that pressed against his ribs. His ankles and wrists were so tightly bound that his fingers and toes tingled. His mouth was coppery and tacky from a cut on the inside of his cheek. The air smelled sickly with cigarette smoke and hair oil. He felt the soft vibration of an expensive engine. A vehicle passed at speed, its sound warped by Doppler. He was on the floor of a car. He was being taken to Hassan. That lurch of panic. Vomit welled in his throat, stopping only at the back of his mouth. He inhaled deeply through his nose until the nausea subsided. He reached for a calm thought. It wasn't necessarily Hassan's men who'd snatched him. Maybe it was freelances after blood money. If he could just get them to talk, he could establish rapport, negotiate, outbid. He tried to sit up, was again clumped

183

brutally on the back of his head.

They swung left, began to jolt over rough terrain. It was all Knox could do to buffer himself. His ribs were banged and bruised. They drove for what seemed an age, then stopped abruptly. Doors opened. Someone grabbed him beneath his arms, hauled him out, dumping him on sandy ground. He was kicked onto his back, fingernails picked at the tape on his cheek. It was ripped from his eyes, taking some lashes with it, leaving his skin tender. Three men stood above him, dressed in black sweaters and balaclavas, turning Knox's guts to water. He tried to tell himself they wouldn't be hiding their faces unless they thought he'd live. It didn't help. One of the men dragged Knox by the legs to a wooden post hammered into the ground. He gathered together several loose strands of barbed wire and wrapped them around Knox's ankles.

Though their car was parked obliquely, Knox could just make out its rear licence. He burned it into his memory. A second man popped its boot, pulled out a coil of rope that he dumped on the sand. He tied a knot in one end, looped it around the tow-bar, tugged it hard to make sure it would hold. He made a hangman's noose in the other end, came over to Knox, slipped it around his neck and tightened it until it bit into the soft skin of his throat.

He'd lost sight of the third man. Now he saw him ten paces away, recording everything on the camera phone. It took Knox a moment to see the significance. He was filming a snuff movie to send to Hassan. That explained the balaclavas too. They didn't want footage of themselves committing murder. It was then that Knox knew he was going to die. He kicked and struggled but he was too tightly bound. The driver revved his engine like a young biker throwing down a challenge. Its back wheels spat sand. Then it began speeding away, rope hissing as it paid out. Knox braced himself; he screamed into his gag. The man with the camera phone moved closer to frame his climactic shot as the rope lifted, shivered and went taut.

15

I

'I trust you have good news for me,' said Hassan.

Nessim, even though talking to a phone, closed his eyes as if in prayer. 'We've had a setback, sir.'

'A setback?'

'Someone else got to him first.'

'Someone *else*?'

'Yes, sir.'

'I don't understand.'

'Nor do we, sir. He went into a hotel. He came out again. He walked around to the back and down an alley. Another man followed him. We thought nothing of it until a black car pulled up and he was bundled into the back.'

'You mean you just let them take him away?'

'We were across the street. There was a tram.'

'A tram?' asked Hassan icily.

'Yes, sir.'

'Where did they go?'

'We don't know, sir. Like I say, there was a tram. We couldn't get past.' The damned thing had just sat there as he'd tooted at it, the fat driver smirking at them, enjoying their frustration.

'Who was it? Who took him?'

'We don't know, sir. We're working on it now. If we're lucky, it's someone who heard what he did to you and thinks they can sell him on to us at a price.'

'And if we're not?'

'According to his file, he has plenty of enemies. Maybe one of them spotted him.'

Silence. One beat. Two beats. Three. 'I want him found,' said Hassan. 'I want him found as a matter of urgency. Do I make myself clear?'

Nessim swallowed. 'Yes, sir. Crystal clear.'

II

Knox felt incomparably older as he trudged north, following tyre tracks in the sand. When the rope had paid out and stretched taut, he'd known he was going to die. It was a qualitatively different thing, knowing you were going to die as opposed to fearing you might die. It did strange things to your heart. It made you think differently about time, and the world, and your place in it.

The rope had been cut clean through, then fixed back together again with duct tape. The tape had ripped free as soon as the rope had gone taut, so that the two sections of rope had pulled apart, and Knox had flopped down on the sand, his bladder venting, his heart bucking like a terrified steer, bewildered by his reprieve. The driver had come around in a great loop over the sand to collect their comrade, who'd been squatting there all the time, filming his reaction, the way he'd pissed himself. They'd all laughed uproariously at that, as though it was the

187

funniest thing they'd ever seen. One of them had thrown an envelope out of the window and then they'd driven off, leaving him tied there to the stake, his trousers soaked, his throat raw with burns from the rope.

It had taken him two hours to free himself from his various bonds. He'd been shivering by then, full body tremors. Desert nights were cold. He'd dried his trousers as best he could by smearing them with handfuls of dusty sand, then gone over to the envelope. Plain white. No writing on it. When he'd opened it, some sand had fallen out. Ballast to stop it blowing away. Apart from that, it had contained only a British Airways compliments slip with four words upon it: 'You have been warned.'

He climbed a small rise. Far ahead, the pinpricks of headlights stretched in both directions on a busy road. He walked with a slow, tired, dispirited pace. It was easy to be bold in the face of notional threats. This was different. And he had others to think of, too, particularly Augustin and Gaille. He couldn't risk putting them in danger.

It was time to get out.

III

Nicolas Dragoumis was an early riser by temperament, but this morning he rose earlier than usual, eager as a child at Christmas. He went straight to his laptop to check his email. There was one from Gabbar Mounim, as promised. He downloaded and decrypted the movie file attachment impatiently while he read the message, nodding approvingly as he did so. His father had always insisted that Knox wasn't to be harmed, and Mounim made it clear that his men hadn't harmed Knox, not in any real sense. A little chloroform, a tap on the skull, a jolt to his system. That couldn't count as harm. On the contrary, it would make him appreciate life all the more.

Nicolas played the movie for the first time. Knox abducted; Knox lying unconscious on the floor of the car; Knox dragged onto the desert sands; the look of terror on his face as the car accelerated away! Nicolas exulted. To think that this wretch had once caused him and his father such grief! And now look at him! Pissing himself like an eight-year-old. He played it again, then a third time, his back soothing with every frame. A good night's work. A very good night's work indeed. Because, unless Nicolas wasn't the judge of character he knew himself to be, that would be the last he ever saw of Knox.

IV

It was growing light when Knox finally reached the coast road, but the traffic was still thin. He ran across, then over a bank of dunes and down the beach to the Mediterranean. He peeled off his trousers and boxer shorts, washing them in the lapping waves, wringing them out as best he could. He draped them over his shoulder and walked along the beach, his feet caking pleasantly with the chill thick sand.

The sun rose orange, laying a fiery comet on the foamy backwash of a wave. He reached a walled compound of holiday homes, a gate swinging on the breeze. It looked deserted. These estates only came alive at weekends and holiday times. Many of the homes had washing lines outside, several draped with swimming costumes, towels and clothes. He went in, wandered amongst them until he spotted an old cream galabiya and headdress, faintly damp, perhaps because of the early hour and the nearness of the Mediterranean. He left his trousers in part exchange, along with as much cash as he could afford. Then he took them and fled before he was spotted.

It was all very well for those men to warn him to get out. But he needed his bank cards, passport and papers, all of which he'd left at Augustin's. Most of all, he needed his Jeep. It took him an hour thumbing for lifts before a three-wheeler stopped. The driver addressed him in gruff Arabic. He replied in kind without even thinking, his mind elsewhere. They talked of football; the man was a passionate Ittihad fan. It was only after Knox had got out that he realised he'd been mistaken for an Egyptian. His Bedouin clothes and genes, no doubt, plus his deep tan and a day's worth of stubble.

He was almost out of money, so he took buses to Augustin's apartment block, walking the last kilometre. He was on alert as he wended his way through the car park or he wouldn't have spotted the two men in the white Freelander, one smoking a roll-up, the other hidden in the shadows. He went closer. Through its rear window, he saw a familiar red overnight bag, a black laptop case and a cardboard box packed with his own belongings from his Sinai hotel room. He spun on his heel and hurried away. He hadn't gone far before he realised that there was no real point in fleeing. If Hassan had wanted him captive or dead, he wouldn't have let him go last night. These men were surely here to make sure he really did leave.

He turned again and walked boldly over to the front steps, his back turned to the Freelander, trusting his Egyptian robes to act like a cloak of invisibility. A janitor was mopping the red terracotta tiles. Knox stepped around the wet patch and risked a glance as he waited for the lift. The men were still sitting in the Freelander. He took the lift up to the seventh floor, walked down a flight, crouching below window level to let himself in. There was no sign of Augustin. He'd evidently been playing away. Knox packed his belongings, then wrote a brief note thanking Augustin for his hospitality, letting him know he'd hit the road, promising to call in due course. He was just finishing up when he heard footsteps outside, then a key scraping in the lock. He watched in frozen horror as the handle turned and the door opened and Nessim came in with a translucent bag of electronic equipment in his left hand.

16

Knox and Nessim stared spellbound at each
other for a moment, each equally startled.
Nessim recovered first, reaching inside his jacket.
The glimpse of his shoulder holster jolted Knox
into action. He charged Nessim, knocking him
over backwards. His gun went skittering away,
tumbling into the stairwell, plummeting six
storeys before crashing at the bottom. Knox
rushed for the stairs. Nessim scrambled to his
feet. They raced down, leaping a flight at a time,
bouncing off the walls as they turned corners,
Nessim barely an outstretched arm behind.
Knox reached the ground-floor lobby, tiles still
slick from their mopping. He slowed just enough
to keep his footing, but Nessim's feet went from
under him and he crashed into the bank of lifts,
turning his ankle, cursing loudly. Knox burst out
of the door and sprinted for his Jeep. He risked a
glance behind. Nessim had emerged too,
hobbling badly. He'd retrieved his gun but was
holding it flat against his side. This place was too
public for such things. He shouted at his
colleague, who started up the Freelander and
drove over to pick him up.

Knox ran to his Jeep, jumped in, turned on the
ignition. The engine caught first time. He was
away at once, up a narrow alley to a main road,

192

which he cut into so sharply that cars behind him had to swerve and brake, getting in each other's way, honking like enraged geese. A glance in his rear view: the Freelander struggling to bull its way through this sudden traffic jam. Knox took advantage, turning left, left again, losing himself in the maze of streets, constantly checking his mirrors, but there was no sign of them. He allowed himself to relax a little. Then he checked once more and there they were. *How the hell had they managed that?* He stamped on the gas, but the Freelander, faster and more manoeuvrable, was catching him inexorably.

Up ahead, at a level crossing, a passenger train crawled into view on his side of the road. Traffic slowed to allow it past. Knox stamped his foot down and swerved into oncoming traffic, tooting furiously to get it to move aside. The train was still coming. There was almost no room, but he kept his foot to the floor and charged across the tracks, the train's engine flicking his rear bumper, nudging him against a wooden gatepost, but then he was through and swerving back into his own lane with nothing but clear road ahead, ignoring the fists being shaken and horns angrily tooted. A glance in his mirror. The train had come to a complete halt across the road. He'd have at least a minute, probably two. He turned a corner, parked.

No way had Nessim picked up his trail just like that. Not in a maze like Alexandria. If Augustin's place had been under surveillance, maybe they'd found his Jeep too. He got down onto hands and knees. The transmitter was taped to his undercarriage. He pulled it free and ran back to the street, flagged down a taxi and paid the driver to deliver it to the Sheraton in Montazah Bay. Then he jogged back to his Jeep and drove off in the opposite direction.

Nessim wasn't a fool. He'd soon realise he'd been tricked. Knox had to make the most of this short window. But Alexandria wasn't like London, with a hundred escape points. His choices were essentially to head south to Cairo, east to Port Said or west to El Alamein. But Nessim would have backup, that was for sure. Hassan didn't operate on the cheap; he'd have those routes watched for an old green Jeep. So maybe he should lie low until they'd dropped their guard. But where? He was toxic; he dared not inflict himself on any more friends. Nessim would certainly check all Alexandria's hotels. And he couldn't stay on the street. Anyone could spot him. He needed to get underground.

The idea, when it came to him, was both so outrageous and so fitting that he gave a snort of laughter and almost drove into the van in front.

II

An unwelcome surprise awaited Nicolas Dragoumis when he and his bodyguard, Bastiaan, drove in from Alexandria Airport to the necropolis site. All he wanted to do was raise the plinth at once and find out what lay beneath, but Ibrahim had evidently decided to make an event of proceedings. Excavators had lined up in a greeting party to shake his hand, and there were tables set up, their white cloths laden with tea and cups and disgusting-looking cream cakes. Clearly he was expected to exchange small talk with these people. It wasn't something he was skilled at, being polite to nonentities. But he was playing for high stakes, so he gritted his teeth, hid his scowl and did his best.

III

Knox stopped at the first cash machine he saw and pillaged it for money. Hassan knew he was in Alexandria anyway; there was no point keeping a low profile. Then he went shopping for supplies: a bulky waterproof bag, food, water, an under-water torch, a battery lamp, spare batteries, books to read. From an automotive store he bought a green tarpaulin. Then he drove off to the forbidding residential district south of the main train station, parked and hid his Jeep beneath the tarpaulin.

He packed all his other supplies into his water-proof bag and strapped it tight around his waist, placing the bulk over his stomach, so that, beneath his robes, he simply looked overweight. Then he hurried to the site, flashing his SCA pass at the security guard on the stairwell, being nodded through without a murmur. Down in the rotunda, two labourers were fixing a steel gate over the entrance to the Macedonian tomb, being supervised by Mansoor, who glanced up as Knox passed.

Mansoor frowned in half-recognition. 'You!' he called out. 'Come here.'

Knox ducked his head and hurried deeper into the necropolis.

'Hey!' cried out Mansoor. 'Stop!'

But Knox kept going, pushing his way past excavators bringing baskets of human remains to the rotunda. Footsteps behind only made him go faster. Several of the chambers had already been completely cleared of artefacts, the lights taken from them and redeployed where they were needed. He'd intended to slip into one and hide in an empty *loculus* until nightfall. Now there was no chance of that.

'Hey!' cried Mansoor behind him. 'Stop that man! I want to talk to him.'

Knox hurried on, down the steps, until he reached the water table and could go no further. Since they'd removed the pump, the level had risen again, so that it is now back as it had started, all the air expelled. He had no time. He walked slowly into the water, so as not to disturb it too much. Bubbles escaped from his robes; the waterproof bag around his waist bellied and tried to float. The search grew closer behind him, checking each of the chambers in turn. He packed his lungs with air, pressed his left hand against the wall, then ducked his head beneath the black water and propelled himself along the corridor, navigating by memory.

His hunger for breath built steadily. He reached the third chamber and swam to its top corner, was relieved to find that his internal compass hadn't let him down. He kicked up out

196

of the water and hauled himself up into the chamber beneath the rotunda, the waterproof bag full of supplies still around his waist. He took off his soaking robes, untied the bag, dried himself, put on trousers and a T-shirt. It wasn't the Ritz, exactly, but it would keep him safe, for a while, at least. A cubic metre of air would last him the best part of an hour, if he didn't exert himself. There were about forty-eight cubic metres in this place, which meant he could stay here tonight and tomorrow. Then he'd head back after the excavators had left, hide overnight in an empty *loculus* before leaving with the others at lunch. As long as no one figured out where he'd vanished to, of course.

He tried to get comfortable, but it wasn't easy. Alone and in the darkness, surrounded by under-water tombs filled with mortal remains, half-expecting someone to pop up at any moment, it wasn't surprising he felt anxious. But as time passed, he felt other emotions too. Envy. Anger. He was the one who'd realised there was something beneath the plinth. Yet here he was, a fugitive, while others got to open it. And he was so close to it! After all, the necropolis came around in a great spiral, so that the Macedonian tomb was just a few metres away from where he was now.

Yes, he frowned. Just a few metres away.

Quarrying stone was brutal work under the best of conditions. It was twice as difficult if your only access was via a narrow shaft. Electricity made it easy to forget how difficult a problem lighting had been for the ancients. Candles and fat-burning lamps had eaten up oxygen, so that rudimentary ventilation systems had been invaluable. Two access points were far better than one, allowing both labourers and air to circulate. And once the quarrying had been completed, and secrecy had become paramount, it would have made sense to seal up for good the larger means of access, maybe by laying stone over it and covering it with a mosaic.

He set down his lamp on the floor, then began a diligent survey of the walls, tapping them with the base of his torch, listening to the echo, hoping to hear a slightly higher pitch that might indicate a cavity behind. He worked from base to apex, then shuffled half a metre to his left, and began again. Nothing. He checked the floors and ceilings, then the staircase. Still nothing. He bit his teeth in frustration. It had made such good sense. Yet it seemed he'd been wrong.

IV

Nicolas had had as much of being polite as he could take. He grabbed Ibrahim by his arm and dragged him to one side. 'Perhaps we could get started,' he said tightly. 'I need to get back to Thessalonike tonight.'

'Of course. Yes. But there's just one more person I'd like you to meet.'

'Who?' sighed Nicolas.

'Mohammed el-Dahab,' said Ibrahim, pointing to a mountain of a man. 'He's site manager for the construction company.'

'And then we can start?'

'Yes.'

'Good.' They walked across. '*Salaam alekum,*' said Nicolas curtly.

'*Wa alekum es salaam,*' replied Mohammed. 'And thank you. Thank you.'

Nicolas frowned. 'What for?'

'The sick girl I told you about,' beamed Ibrahim. 'She's Mohammed's daughter.'

Nicolas looked back and forth in surprise between the two men. 'You mean there really is a sick girl?'

'Of course,' frowned Ibrahim. 'What did you think?'

'Forgive me,' laughed Nicolas. 'I've been dealing too much with your compatriots in Cairo. I assumed *baksheesh.*'

'No,' said Mohammed emphatically. 'This money makes all the difference to us. Your money gives my daughter a chance. We'll hear our results tonight. But whatever the outcome, my family is forever in your debt.'

'It was nothing,' said Nicolas. 'Really.' He turned back to Ibrahim, glanced at his watch. 'Now, really, we must get started,' he said.

V

Knox sat in the darkness with his back against one of the support walls, biting the knuckle of his thumb in frustration. It just made too much sense for this place to be connected to the lower chamber. Yet he'd checked every square inch of

199

the chamber's exterior he could get at, everything except for those areas blocked by the support walls.

He frowned. There had to be at least two feet of limestone above his head, and yet there were support walls. He pushed himself up onto his knees, placed his palms flat against one of them, rested his cheek against it, as though to listen to its secrets. Why on earth would anyone have bothered? This chamber was excavated out of solid rock. The ceiling didn't need props. There were dozens of chambers in this necropolis, and dozens of necropolises in Alexandria. In none of them had Knox ever seen support walls like this. So maybe they weren't support walls at all. Maybe they had another purpose. Maybe they were hiding something.

He walked up and down, inspecting them closely. They were each made up of six columns of six blocks. Each block was perhaps thirty centimetres wide, thirty centimetres high and a metre long, stacked sideways. Each abutted the exterior wall only at one end. If these walls were indeed hiding something, then he'd find it at this junction. The old mortar between the blocks had crumbled away. He pushed hard against the top block. It grated but slowly gave, revealing only solid wall behind. He left it for the time being and went to the second wall. This time, when he pushed back the top block, he revealed a glimpse of space behind. He tried to push both the top two blocks together, but they were too heavy. He rode up the outside wall like a mountain-climber in a rock chimney, then used his feet to push back the blocks as far as he dared, pinned precariously between the remaining blocks beneath and the ceiling above. He dropped down again, went to inspect what he'd revealed. A tight hole into a compact space the size of a broom cupboard, another wall at its far end. He filled his pockets with everything he might need, then squeezed through headfirst, falling hard upon his hands, landing with a grunt.

He turned on his torch, brushed off his palms, went to inspect the far wall. It was built of bricks rather than blocks, small enough for one person to manage with relative ease. Knox felt his breath coming faster as he spread his palm out upon it. Whatever lay on the other side, it had to be connected with the plinth, which Ibrahim was due to raise at any moment. He cupped an ear against it, but could hear nothing. It was crazy even to consider going on. If he were found, he'd be looking at serious gaol-time. But he was so close. Surely one brick couldn't do any harm. Not if he was careful.

He scratched away the dead mortar, then pulled out a single brick and rested it with great gentleness on the floor. He listened intently for half a minute. There was complete silence. He tried to peer through, but the hole was too small for both his eyes and his torch simultaneously. He reached his torch through the gap instead, then squinted as best he could along the line of his arm. But his torch was now pointed in the wrong direction, so he couldn't make out a thing. Trying to twist his hand around, his fingers involuntarily opened a fraction and his torch slipped agonisingly from his grasp. He tried to grab it back but it fell in spirals and landed with a splashy thump in shallow water, its beam making ghostly white ripples on the facing wall.

17

I

Knox had no choice but to retrieve his torch. Ibrahim, Mansoor and others were about to raise the plinth. If they found it, he was certain to be discovered. Besides, he had time. The place was still quiet. He began dismantling the wall brick by brick, placing them precisely on the ground, the old mortar still resting upon them, so that he'd be able to rebuild the wall exactly as he'd found it. When he'd created enough space, he poked his head through, catching a pungent whiff of ammonia. It was a low, arched corridor with a watery floor, like some Victorian sewer. Its walls were even scratched with lines to make it look as though it had been built of bricks rather than excavated, perhaps to disguise the passage he'd just broken through, but possibly because the ancients had simply considered construction more prestigious than excavation.

He stretched down for his torch, but couldn't quite reach it, not without leaning on the wall, which he didn't trust to hold his weight. He removed another two rows of bricks, then straddled what remained. The water felt sharp on his bare foot as he stooped to retrieve his torch. He listened intently. Nothing but silence. He was here now. It would be criminal not to take a quick look.

He splashed along the corridor, brushing aside cobwebs, his imagination sensing eels and night-time creatures around his bare ankles. He came to a compact chamber beneath a chimney shaft, its mouth blocked by some kind of slab. The plinth, no doubt. He went back the other way and came to a marble portal with an Ancient Greek inscription cut into its architrave.

Together in life; together in death. Kelonymus.

Kelonymus. The name was familiar, as Akylos had been. But the memory wouldn't come, and time was short, so he passed beneath it, reaching the foot of a broad flight of stone steps that spread out like a fan as it rose. And at the top . . .

'Jesus Christ!' muttered Knox.

II

'What's going on?' demanded Nicolas, as a large crowd of senior excavators and other guests descended the staircase to the rotunda.

'How do you mean?' frowned Ibrahim.

'All these people?' said Nicolas. 'You can't seriously be inviting them all.'

'Just to watch. From the antechamber. This is a big moment for us.'

'No,' said Nicolas. 'You, me, your archaeologist, Elena. That's all.'

'But I've already — '

'I mean it. If you want the remainder of your

Dragoumis sponsorship money, you'll kick these people out now.'

'It's not that simple,' protested Ibrahim. 'We need Mohammed to lift the plinth. We need the girl to take photographs. Moments like these don't come often, you know.'

'Fine. Those two. No others.'

'But I — '

'No others,' said Nicolas emphatically. 'This isn't a circus. This is supposed to be a serious excavation.'

'Fine,' sighed Ibrahim. And he turned with a sagging heart to disappoint the crowd of excited excavators.

III

Knox's mouth hung open as he played his torch over the chamber like a searchlight over a bombarded city. He struggled to believe his eyes. To his right, a terrace had been hewn in the limestone. Sixteen golden larnaxes or burial caskets stood upon each of two shelves, making thirty-two in all. Glass bowls had toppled and fallen both over the shelves and the floor, scattering their contents of precious and semiprecious stones. Also on the floor, countless precious artefacts: swords and spears and shields and amphorae of silver and clay. White marble had been inlaid into the far wall, a lengthy inscription carved into it, though too distant for him to make out what it said.

But it was the left-hand wall that mesmerised

Knox. It was a huge mosaic, framed at the top by turquoise-painted plaster that represented the sky, and which contoured the main subject matter like a chalk-mark around a corpse. Thirty-three men, clearly soldiers, though not all armed, gathered into two overlapping clusters, one in the foreground, the other further back. They looked remarkably relaxed and cheerful. Some talked among themselves, arms around each other's shoulders. Others wrestled on the sand or played dice. But, kneeling at the centre, was the mosaic's focal point and the group's clear leader: a slight, handsome man with russet hair who looked out of the wall with a purposeful gaze. Both his hands were clasped on the hilt of his sword, plunged deep into the sand. Knox blinked. No one could study Graeco-Roman history without developing a knowledge of mosaic. Yet he'd never seen anything like this.

He had no camera with him, except for the one in his mobile phone. He hadn't even turned it on since Sinai, worried that it would lead Hassan straight to him, but there was no chance of it picking up a signal this deep underground. He tiptoed carefully into the chamber, photo-graphing the mosaic, the burial caskets, the grave goods scattered on the floor, the inscription. He became so completely absorbed in this work that it was only when he heard a grinding, ripping noise from way behind him that he belatedly remembered about the raising of the plinth.

18

Bastiaan and three burly Egyptian security guards kept the disgruntled excavators out of the Macedonian tomb while Mohammed and Mansoor attacked the plinth as they had on the day before, working the tips of their crowbars beneath one end and levering it up. It came more easily this time. They raised it a few inches, just enough for Ibrahim to slide in a hydraulic jack, which they pumped high enough to slide a pallet-trolley beneath. Then they repeated the process at the other end, and simply wheeled the plinth back against the wall.

There was a fat black shaft in the floor, just as Ibrahim had glimpsed. They all gathered around. Mansoor shone down his torch. Light glinted brightly from five metres below.

'Water,' said Mansoor. 'I'll go first.' He turned to Mohammed. 'Tie a noose in a rope. You'll lower me, yes?'

'Yes,' agreed Mohammed.

II

Knox had no time for finesse. He clutched his hand over the bulb of his torch to dim it, yet allow him just enough light to see what he was

207

doing, then he stripped off his T-shirt so that he could erase his footprints in the dust with it as he backed out of the chamber and down the steps. But Mansoor was already being lowered on a rope, flashing his torch all around him and down the passage, so that Knox had to duck back out of sight.

'There's a corridor,' shouted Mansoor, as he splashed into the shallow water and stepped off the stirrup. 'I'll take a look.'

'No!' said Ibrahim. 'Wait.'

'But I'll just — '

'Wait for us.'

The torchlight vanished momentarily. Knox risked another glance, saw the stirrup slithering back up. But then Mansoor flashed his torch again down the corridor, his frustration evident, giving Knox no chance to escape. Someone else was being lowered now, Gaille, twisting this way and that on the rope. Mansoor turned to help her down. It was Knox's only chance. He ran along the corridor to his dismantled wall, trying hard not to make waves.

But Gaille gave a shriek of alarm. 'There's someone there!' she cried.

Knox stepped through the hole in the wall as Mansoor blazed his torch down the corridor. 'There's no one,' he laughed. 'How could there be?'

'I could have sworn,' said Gaille.

'Just your imagination,' said Mansoor. 'Places like this will do that.'

Knox was only half listening, his heart still hammering, frantically rebuilding his wall from within. He couldn't risk his torch, so he had to work by feel and what little light reached him from Mansoor, Gaille and the others as they gathered one by one. But by the time they were all down, his wall was still only three-quarters rebuilt.

'OK,' said Ibrahim. 'Lead on.'

Knox froze. He couldn't do any more now, except press himself back into the shadows and pray. Torchlight flickered and flashed and then grew almost blinding. There was still a great gaping hole in his wall. They had to spot it. But somehow first one then the next walked past with their heads bowed, watching the floor to make certain of their footing. Ibrahim, Mansoor, Elena, Gaille, and then, shockingly, Nicolas Dragoumis. *Nicolas Dragoumis!* Last night's mock execution suddenly had a completely new suspect.

They paused, as he had, to illuminate and read the inscription on the architrave. 'Look!' said Elena excitedly, nudging Nicolas. 'Kelonymus!'

Her tone, and the presence of Nicolas Dragoumis, triggered recognition in Knox, so that he remembered at last why the names Kelonymus and Akylos were so familiar.

III

Ibrahim entered the chamber first. He stood there in silent awe as the others arrived behind him, and took their own places on the bottom step. He gazed almost drunkenly around. It was only when Nicolas made to step up into the chamber that he came back to his senses.

'Stop!' he said. 'No one goes in.'

'But — '

'No one goes in,' he repeated. He felt, suddenly, a surge of authority. He was the senior representative here of the Supreme Council for Antiquities, and this — as no one could for a moment doubt — was a find of historic importance. He beckoned for Mansoor. 'We have to inform Cairo at once,' he said.

'Cairo?' winced Nicolas. 'Is that really necessary? Surely this isn't a matter for — '

'It's a matter for whoever I say it is.'

'But — '

'You're our sponsor and we appreciate your support. This is no longer a matter for you. Is that clear?'

Nicolas had to force his smile. 'Whatever you say.'

'Gaille. You will take photographs, yes?'

'Of course.'

'Mansoor. You stay with her.'

'Yes.'

'I'll instruct Mohammed and the security guards not to let anyone else down. I'll arrange for the necropolis to be cleared. When you're satisfied that Gaille has enough photographs, replace the plinth over the shaft. Then make sure the site is empty and seal off the mouth of the stairwell. I'm sure Mohammed can find a way. Sealed tight, mind. No one is to get in or out. Understood?'

'Yes, sir.'

'I'll have Maha arrange around-the-clock security. You're not to leave until they arrive. Then bring Gaille to my villa. Drive her yourself. And don't let her camera out of your sight.'

'Yes, sir.'

'As for me, I'm going to notify the Supreme Council that we've just discovered the most important antiquity in the modern history of Alexandria.'

IV

Knox quietly finished rebuilding the wall before Ibrahim and the others left. But Gaille and Mansoor remained behind taking photographs, so he didn't dare move, scared the slightest noise would give him away. Cramps built agonisingly in his thighs and calves until Mansoor was finally satisfied, and they left.

There was no time to waste. If he didn't get out quick, he'd be sealed in with all the other corpses. He cleared the area of traces of his presence, then squeezed back into the chamber beneath the rotunda, replacing the blocks as he'd found them. He stripped naked and stuffed everything into his bag, dropped down into the water, breathed deep, then navigated his way back to the steps, pulling the bag behind him. He was lucky. There was no one waiting. In fact, the whole necropolis was eerily dark and silent. He brushed himself dry, pulled on his trousers and T-shirt, filled his pockets with everything of value, then stuffed the rest deep into an empty *loculus.* Then he hurried for the rotunda. Metal screeched and banged as he reached it. He looked up to see daylight already partially eclipsed by the bottom of a blue container, with a second already being positioned next to it to complete the seal. Knox pounded up the steps, his thighs protesting, diving out just as the container was manoeuvred into place. Everyone stared incredulously as he rolled up onto his feet and ran for the gates.

'Stop him!' yelled Mansoor. 'Someone stop him!'

At the site exit, two security guards blocked his way. Knox dropped a shoulder, feinted right, side-stepped left, spinning one of the guards around, bursting out into the street, across traffic, dodging a minibus, putting distance between himself and the chasing pack shouting at people to stop him, yelling into their phones. He cut down an alley towards his Jeep, three men chasing hard. A shopkeeper jumped out to block his path, but he broke through his half-hearted tackle, glanced around to see the three getting closer. And now two soldiers appeared ahead, reaching for their guns. This was turning ugly, fast, but it was too late to stop now. He ducked left, his chest aching, a stitch burning in his side, his legs weighted down with lactic acid. He vaulted a wall, crawled beneath a gate, then ran to the dark alley where he'd left the Jeep, pulling the tarpaulin back just far enough for him to sneak beneath, unlock and open his door, climb inside, sprawling across the front seats, keening for breath while simultaneously struggling for silence, listening to frantic footsteps hurrying up the alley behind him, praying he hadn't been seen.

19

I

Ibrahim greeted Gaille and Mansoor impatiently when finally they arrived at his villa.

'There was a problem at the site,' explained Mansoor. 'An intruder.'

'An intruder?'

'Don't worry. Nowhere near the Macedonian tomb.'

'Did you get him?'

'They're still looking. He won't get far.' He held up his mobile. 'They'll call when they have news.'

'Good. And the site?'

'Sealed. The guards are in place too. It'll be fine for the moment. How about Yusuf?'

'He's in a meeting,' said Ibrahim.

'A meeting?' frowned Mansoor. 'Didn't you have him called out?'

Ibrahim's cheeks flamed. 'You know what he's like. He'll call back soon.' He turned to Gaille. 'May we see your photos?'

'Of course.'

She transferred her pictures to her laptop, opened them one by one. They all gathered around the kitchen table to look. 'Demotic,' muttered Ibrahim gloomily, when she showed him the inscription. 'Why did it have to be Demotic?'

'Gaille knows Demotic,' volunteered Elena. 'She's working on the Sorbonne dictionary project.'

'Excellent,' beamed Ibrahim. 'So you can translate this for us?'

Gaille gave a dry laugh. Demotic was a brute, as Ibrahim had to know full well. Asking her if she could translate this was like asking someone if they spoke English, then jabbering at them in coarse Anglo-Saxon.

Ancient Egypt had had just the one main spoken language, but that language had been written down with a number of different alphabets. The first was Hieroglyphics, the stylised pictograms familiar from temples, tombs and Hollywood movies. These had first appeared around 3100 BC. Pioneering Egyptologists had assumed the language to be pictorial, each symbol representing a single concept. But, after the Rosetta Stone had been found with identical text inscribed in Hieroglyphics, Demotic and Ancient Greek, Thomas Young and then Jean-François Champollion had deduced that these pictograms had had phonetic as well as symbolic value; that they were, in short, letters that could be combined in multiple ways to form words and thus a broad vocabulary; and that this language had its own syntax and grammar too.

Hieroglyphics, while they looked fantastic on the walls of temples and palaces and formal documents, had been far too elaborate to be practical for everyday use. Almost from the start, therefore, a simpler and quicker alphabet had developed alongside. This was known as

Hieratic, and it had become the language of literature, business and administration in Ancient Egypt, which was why it was usually found on cheaper materials like wood, papyrus and ostraka. Then, around 600 BC, a third written language called Demotic had evolved, reducing Hieratic to a series of strokes, dashes and dots, like Egyptian shorthand. To make matters worse, it had neither vowels nor breaks between words, its vocabulary had been large and vernacular, its alphabet had varied significantly from region to region, and it had evolved massively over the centuries, so that it was really a family of related languages, not just one. Mastery took years of dedication and a set of dictionaries the size of a Volkswagen Beetle. Depending how mainstream this inscription was, and what resources would be available to her, decipherment could take hours or days or even weeks. Gaille summed all this up with a wry glance at Ibrahim.

'Yes, I know,' he said, having the grace to blush. 'But still.'

Gaille sighed, though in truth she felt exhilarated by the challenge. It had been too dark in the chamber to make much of the inscription earlier. But her camera had astonishing resolution and her photographs had come out crisply, despite the dust and cobwebs, making the Demotic characters clearly legible. She zoomed out again. Something about the inscription was bothering her, but she couldn't figure out what.

'Well?' asked Ibrahim.

'May I have a minute by myself?'

'Of course.' And he ushered everyone out to give her some peace.

II

Knox lay absolutely still across the Jeep's front seats. The chasing pack had gathered directly outside, and now were discussing plans and catching their breath. Sweat was cooling all over his body, giving him chills despite the warmth of the day. The Jeep lurched as someone sat upon its bonnet. He heard the rasp of a lighter, cigarettes being lit, people gossiping and bantering, chiding each other for being too slow, too old. The Jeep creaked as someone else leaned against it. *Christ!* How long before one of them thought to check beneath the covers? But there was nothing he could do but lie still. Nothing except make plans.

Yet what plans? Hassan, Nessim, the Dragoumises, the police and the army and were all after him, and Christ knew who else. He couldn't risk turning on his mobile phone to review his photographs lest Nessim trace the signal. Besides, he'd barely be able to see anything on his mobile's tiny screen, and anyway, he needed them deleted as soon as possible, because if they were found, they'd prove he'd been inside the lower chamber and earn him ten years in gaol. Ideally, he'd have liked to transfer them to his laptop, but that was in the back of Nessim's Freelander along with the rest of his stuff, and anyway it didn't have a USB port, so his only way of getting the photos to it was by emailing them to his hotmail account, then downloading them. But none of that was going to happen while he was lying in his Jeep with his pursuers on his bonnet.

He turned his thoughts elsewhere: the names Kelonymus and Akylos. When he and Richard had found their Ptolemaic archives in Mallawi, there'd been far too much to translate as they went along. Instead, they'd conserved them, catalogued them and passed them to the SCA for safekeeping and later study. Their preferred method had been to collect all the fragments of a particular papyrus together and photograph them, then assign the fragments and the photograph a single file name, based on where they were found or (if too many had been found in one place) a name of a place or a person from the text. And two names that had cropped up often were Akylos and Kelonymus.

The originals had long ago been taken by Yusuf Abbas of the SCA for 'safekeeping', so God only knew where they were now, but Knox had photographs of them on CDs. Unfortunately, they too were in the boot of Nessim's Freelander, probably under CCTV surveillance in the car park of some top-end Alexandrian hotel; and he wasn't exactly in a position to go hunting hotel to hotel in the hope of a smash and grab. No. He needed another way.

The Jeep lurched as the man got off his bonnet. Footsteps scuffed and faded. Knox waited until there'd been silence for a good couple of minutes, then climbed out and stripped off the tarpaulin. He had no time to waste. He had phone calls to make.

III

Despite staring furiously at the inscription, it still took Gaille several minutes to work out what was bothering her. But finally she got it. The bottom line of text was incomplete, and it was written left to right. Yet Demotic, like Arabic, had been written right to left.

The inscription in the Macedonian tomb had been in Greek. The few words of text in the antechamber paintings had been in Greek. The dedication on the architrave had been in Greek. The shield-bearers had been Greek. The gods they'd invoked had been Greek. This looked like Demotic, but it didn't read that way, not initially at least. And it seemed perverse to switch to Demotic just for the inscription. So maybe it had simply been too sensitive to be written in plain Greek. Maybe the writer had used the Demotic alphabet instead. Codes, after all, hadn't been unknown to the ancients. Alexander himself had used subterfuge to hide sensitive messages. The Admonitions of the Sons of Dawn, one of the Dead Sea Scrolls, had used code for particularly sensitive words. Valerius Probus had written an entire treatise upon substitution ciphers. They'd been simple things, because people had believed them unbreakable. But Gaille didn't.

She copied the inscription out onto a pad,

checking for patterns as she did so. If this was a simple transliteration cipher, and the same word was encrypted more than once, then it would produce identical sequences every time. It wasn't long before she had her first strike, then a second and a third. The third looked particularly helpful: ten characters long, and appearing no fewer than four times. That surely had to be a single word. An important one too. What could it signify? A person's name, perhaps. Mentally, she ran through all the names they'd come across in the upper chamber. Akylos, too short. Likewise Kelonymus and Apelles, Bilip and Timoleum. She had a little surge of excitement when she thought to try Alexander, but that fell short too. Her spirits sank again. She stood up, walked in brisk circuits around the small room, sensing she was missing something, scowling in an almost physical effort to impel her mind to the answer.

When finally it came, her cheeks flushed and she looked around, anxious that her schoolgirl error might have been observed. For Alexander, the name by which the world knew him, was in fact a Latin name. To Greeks, he'd been known as Alexandros. She sat back down and used the letters in Alexandros to begin a transposition alphabet, replacing the Demotic symbols with the matching Greek letters wherever they appeared throughout the text. That gave her enough to guess the word adjacent to the first Alexandros. Macedonia. With half the alphabet now broken, the rest swiftly followed. Ancient Greek was her thing; she made the translation upon her pad, so utterly absorbed in her task that she lost track of time and her surroundings until her name was suddenly called, bringing her back to the real world. She looked up to see Ibrahim, Nicolas, Mansoor and Elena were standing in a semicircle, looking expectantly at her, as though someone had just asked her a question, and they were waiting for her answer.

Ibrahim sighed and said: 'I was explaining to Nicolas how difficult Demotic can be. We want as few people as possible to know about this, so we very much want you to work on it by yourself. How long do you think you'll need? One day? Two? A week?'

It had to be the most gratifying moment of Gaille's professional life. 'Actually,' she said airily, holding up her pad, 'it's already done.'

20

I

Nessim was in his hotel room, discussing plans with Hosni, Ratib and Sami. There was no great zest to their conversation, however. Knox had vanished off the radar, and nothing they'd tried had picked him up again.

It was late afternoon when his phone rang: Badr, Nessim's contact from the phone company, who'd been waiting for Knox to use his mobile. 'He's turned it on,' he said excitedly. 'He's making a call.'

'Who to?'

'No one. At least, he's sending pictures to an email account.'

'Where?'

'Near the railway station.'

'Stay on the line,' said Nessim. 'Tell me if he moves.' Hosni, Ratib and Sami had already risen to their feet. Nessim nodded at them. 'We've got a trace,' he said. 'Let's shift.'

II

'Well?' said Ibrahim excitedly. 'Don't keep us in suspense.'

Gaille nodded. She cleared her throat and began to read out loud.

222

'I, Kelonymus, son of Hermias, brother of Akylos, builder, scribe, architect, sculptor, lover of knowledge, traveller in numerous lands, give homage to you, Great Gods, for allowing me to bring to this place below the earth these thirty-two shield-bearers, heroes of the Great Victor, Alexander of Macedonia, Son of Ammon. I now make good my pledge to bring together in one place the thirty-three who died carrying out the last wish of Alexander, that a tomb be built for him in sight of the place of his father. And to fulfil his wish Akylos and these thirty-two built such a tomb and appointed it with goods fit for the son of Ammon.'

Gaille hadn't properly registered the text until now. She'd been too busy translating it. But, even as she read it out, she realised how explosive it was. She glanced up and saw on everyone's faces the same astonishment she knew must be on her own.

'Go on,' said Elena hungrily.

'And to fulfil his wish they seized his body from the White Wall to take it through the red land of great dryness to the mouth of the place prepared below the earth. And, near that place, Ptolemy, who is styled Saviour, trapped these men so that they took their lives rather than be subjected to his torture. And so Ptolemy crucified them in vengeance and left them crucified for the carrion to feed. Akylos and the thirty-two gave their lives to honour the wishes of Alexander, son of Ammon, in defiance of Ptolemy, son of nothing. I, Kelonymus, man of Macedonia, brother of Akylos, beseech you, Great Gods, to welcome these heroes into your kingdom as you welcomed Alexander.'

She looked up again, to indicate that she had finished. The looks of excitement had given way to a kind of stunned disbelief. No one spoke for a good five seconds.

It was Nicolas who finally broke the silence. 'Does that . . . ' he began hesitantly. 'Does that mean what I think it means?'

'Yes,' nodded Ibrahim. 'I believe it does.'

III

The moment his photographs were sent, Knox deleted the images from his mobile then turned it off altogether and roared away in his Jeep before Nessim had a chance to get to him. Just one more phone call and he'd be in business. He parked near Pompey's Pillar, bought himself a ticket and went inside. The site was a walled enclosure of about a hectare, surrounded by high-density housing. The pillar itself occupied pride of place on the small hillock at its centre, but in fact the whole enclosed area was historic, because it was the one-time site of the famous Temple of Serapis.

Knox had always felt a great fondness for

Serapis, a benign and intelligent deity who'd somehow fused Egyptian, Greek and Asian religious myths into a single theology. According to one thesis, he'd first appeared to Greek consciousness while Alexander had lain dying in Babylon. A delegation of his men went to the Temple of Serapis there to ask whether Alexander should be brought to the temple or left where he was. Serapis had replied that it would be better for him to be left where he was. The delegation had obeyed, and Alexander had died shortly afterwards, that being the better thing. Others, however, asserted that the cult of Serapis had its roots in the Black Sea city of Sinope, while others still claimed that Serapis was Egyptian, because Apis bulls had been sacrificed for centuries and buried in huge vaults known to the Greeks as the Sarapeion, a contraction of 'Osiris-Apis' or 'dead Apis bull'.

Knox glanced around to make sure no one was looking, then hid himself from view behind the base of Pompey's Pillar. He checked his watch, took two deep breaths, turned on his mobile and began to dial.

IV

'What do you mean, you've lost him?' yelled Nessim.

'He's turned off his phone.'

Nessim punched his dashboard so hard, he tore skin from a knuckle. 'What was his last location?'

'As I said, near the railway station.'

'Stay on the line,' ordered Nessim, hurtling through the streets. 'If he makes another call, I want to know at once.' It was five minutes before they reached the station. Nessim drove around for a while, but there was no sign of Knox or his Jeep.

Then Badr spoke again. 'He's turned it back on. He's making another call.'

'Where?'

'South of you,' said Badr. 'He must be right next to Pompey's Pillar.'

Nessim and his men ducked to look out the windows as they drove. Passing a side street, he glimpsed the marble pillar thrusting upwards just a kilometre or so away. 'We're on our way,' he said.

He roared down the road, cut across traffic to Sharia Yousef, then along a wide boulevard, a brownstone wall to his right, Pompey's Pillar on the other side. He pulled a U-turn and swerved up onto the pavement. The four men jumped out and hurried inside to the ticket booth.

'Is this the only entrance?' he asked the woman as he proffered money.

'Yes.'

'Stay here,' he ordered Hosni, as he and the others went into the site. Then he asked Badr on his mobile: 'Is he still on the line?'

'Yes,' confirmed Badr. 'You're right on top of him.'

'Then we've got him,' exulted Nessim.

21

I

Nicolas took Ibrahim to one side. 'Do you have an upstairs bathroom?' he asked, patting his stomach. 'All this excitement seems to have done strange things to my digestion.'

'Of course,' said Ibrahim, pointing him to the stairs. 'First on your left.'

'Thank you.' Nicolas hurried up and locked himself in. Then he took out his mobile to call and brief his father on the blizzard of events, and relay the gist of the inscription.

'What did I tell you?' said Dragoumis.

'You've been right at every step,' acknowledged his son.

'And it was the girl who broke it? Mitchell's daughter?'

'Yes. You were right about her too.'

'I want to meet her.'

'I'll arrange it for once we're done,' said Nicolas.

'No. Now. Tonight.'

'Tonight. You're sure?'

'She worked out there was a lower chamber in the Macedonian tomb,' said Dragoumis. 'She realised the inscription was a cipher, and broke it. She'll be the one to find what we're looking for. I feel it in my heart. She must be on our side when that happens. You understand?'

'Yes, Father. I'll take care of it.' He took further instructions, then finished the call and rang Gabbar Mounim in Cairo.

'My dear Nicolas,' enthused Mounim. 'I trust you were satisfied with — '

'More than satisfied,' said Nicolas. 'Listen. I need something done right now.'

'Of course. Whatever you wish.'

'I believe our friend at the SCA is in a meeting,' said Nicolas. 'When he comes out, he'll have a message on his desk to call Ibrahim Beyumi in Alexandria. Mr Beyumi is going to ask him for an urgent meeting. I want our friend to invite a third party to that meeting, and to look favourably upon what she asks. Her name is Elena Koloktronis.' He spelled it out. 'You may let our friend know that he'll be very generously rewarded, as you will be too. You know I'm a man of my word.'

A chuckle rolled down the phone line. 'I do, indeed. Consider it done.'

'Thank you.' He made several more phone calls, then flushed the toilet, washed his hands and went back downstairs.

'Any better?' asked Ibrahim solicitously, meeting him at the bottom.

Nicolas smiled. 'Much better, thank you.'

'You'll never guess what just happened. Yusuf Abbas called back. He's invited me to Cairo for an immediate meeting.'

'What's surprising about that?' frowned Nicolas. 'Isn't that what you wanted?'

'Yes, but he's invited Elena too. And none of

us can work out how he even knew she was in the country.'

II

Nessim could see no immediate sign of Knox inside the Sarapeion. Little sign of anyone, indeed, except for two Korean tourists taking pictures of each other in front of Pompey's Pillar, and a young family enjoying a modest picnic. He motioned for Ratib and Sami to spread out and comb the site. They went slowly, checking each of the various pits, cisterns and chambers. But they reached the redbrick wall at the far end without a trace of him.

Badr was still on the line. 'Are you quite sure he's here?' Nessim asked icily.

'You must have walked straight past him. I don't understand it.'

Nessim looked over at Ratib and then at Sami. They shrugged and shook their heads. He pointed to the pillar, suggesting they meet at its base. He reached it first. A brown paper bag fluttered in the light breeze. He gave it a wary nudge with his foot, carefully pulled it open. There was a mobile phone inside. He picked it up and turned it around, frowning, wondering what it signified.

There was a tinkle of broken glass the far side of the wall at that moment. It was only when his car alarm began to wail that Nessim realised that was where he'd left his Freelander with all Knox's belongings in the back. An old engine

229

roared and raced away before any of them could react. Nessim closed his eyes and clutched his forehead. He hated Knox. He *hated* him. But he couldn't help but rather admire him too.

III

Nicolas drew Elena to one side to explain how he'd arranged her meeting with Yusuf Abbas, and what she should try to achieve in it. Yusuf was greedy but cautious. If Elena could provide him with an excuse to let her explore Siwa, and thus earn himself his fat commission, then he'd do so. But it would need to look legitimate. A low-level epigraphic survey, say, just her and the girl.

'The girl?' frowned Elena. 'Can we trust her?'

'My father believes so. Well? Can you take care of Yusuf?'

'Leave him to me.'

Nicolas walked over to Gaille who was transferring photographs onto Ibrahim's laptop to show to Yusuf. When she was finished, he asked her for a word, then steered her out into Ibrahim's small garden.

'My father wants to meet you,' he told her.

'Your father?' Gaille looked a little alarmed. 'I don't understand. I don't even know who he is.'

'He's the founder and backer of the Macedonian Archaeological Foundation,' explained Nicolas. 'That makes him your boss. He was also the person who suggested Elena employ you.'

'But . . . why?'

'He knew your father,' said Nicolas. 'He

230

admired him greatly. And he's kept an eye on your career over the years. When Elena needed a replacement, he naturally thought of you.'

'That was . . . very good of him.'

'He's a very good man,' nodded Nicolas seriously. 'And he wants you to have dinner with him this evening.'

Gaille frowned. 'He's in Alexandria?'

'No. Thessalonike.'

'But . . . I don't understand.'

Nicolas smiled. 'Have you ever flown on a private jet before?' he asked.

22

Knox raced through the backstreets of Alexandria, his recaptured belongings piled high on the seat beside him. It had felt good putting one over on Nessim. A man can only run for so long before his pride begins to smart. He drove east towards Abu Qir, putting distance between himself and his pursuers. Then he parked to check what he'd got.

His laptop battery was old and only had an hour's juice. He flicked through his photograph CDs, checking filenames, but he couldn't find a trace of Akylos or Kelonymus. He scowled in frustration. Either Nessim had left them behind or he'd removed them from his car. How unlucky was that? It was a minute or two before another possible explanation occurred to him.

There was a payphone on the corner. He didn't dare telephone Rick directly. Instead, he called a mutual friend who worked at the next-door water sports centre in Sharm, and asked her to fetch him.

Rick came on the line a minute later. 'Hey, mate,' he said. 'You forgotten my number or something?'

'It may be tapped.'

'Ah. Hassan, huh?'

'Yes. Listen. You haven't borrowed some of my

photographic CDs, have you?'

'Christ, mate, I'm sorry. I was just practising my Greek.'

'Not a problem. But I need them. Any way you can get them to me?'

'No sweat. There's nothing happening here. Where do you want to meet?'

'Ras el-Sudr?'

'You mean that dump south of Suez?'

'That's the one,' said Knox. 'There's a hotel there called the Beach Inn. When do you think you can make it?'

'Give me four hours. Maybe five.'

'Perfect. Will you come in your Subaru?'

'Unless there's a reason not to.'

'You might want to check it for tracking devices first. And make sure you're not followed. These guys are serious.'

'So am I, mate,' Rick assured him. 'So am I.'

II

Mohammed and Nur clutched hands as they waited for the phone call to tell them the results of the bone marrow tests. They'd used a private healthcare group with medical centres in Alexandria, Cairo, Assiut and Port Said to make it easier for far-flung friends and family. Especially family. Bone marrow was heritable. The chances of finding a match was significantly higher among kin. They'd tested another sixty-seven people, using up all the funds Ibrahim had made available. Dr Serag-Al-Din had promised to call with the results an hour ago. Waiting for the phone to ring was about the most gruelling experience of Mohammed's life. Nur winced as he squeezed her hand too tightly. He apologised and let go. But she needed the contact as badly as he did, and within moments they found each other's hand again.

Layla was in bed. They'd decided not to inform her of this process until it was done. But she was a sharp child, sensitive to atmosphere. Mohammed suspected she knew all too well what was going on, the sentence of life or death that would shortly be passed on her.

The phone rang. They looked at each other. Nur made a face and started to weep. Mohammed's heart started pattering as he picked up the receiver. 'Yes?' he asked. But it was only Nur's mother, anxious to learn if they'd heard. He bit his lip in frustration and passed her across. Nur got rid of her with promises to call the moment they knew. Mohammed crossed his legs. His bowels felt loose and watery, but he dared not go to the toilet.

The phone rang again. Mohammed breathed deep to pick it up. This time it was Dr Serag-Al-Din. He said: 'Mr el-Dahab. I hope you and your wife are both well.'

'We're fine, thank you. Do you have our results?'

'Of course I have your results,' he said genially. 'Why else do you think I'd call?'

'Well?'

'Bear with me a moment. I seem to have lost my place in your file.'

Mohammed closed his eyes and clenched his fists. *Come on, you son of a dog. Say something. Anything.* 'Please,' he begged.

There was a rustling of paper. Dr Serag-Al-Din cleared his throat. 'Yes,' he said. 'Here we are.'

III

It was dusk when Ibrahim and Elena arrived in Cairo for their meeting with Yusuf Abbas. The great man was waiting for them in an ornate conference room, talking on the phone. He looked up sourly, then waved them vaguely at chairs. Ibrahim set up his laptop while he waited for Yusuf to finish discussing mathematics homework with his son. He found dealing with his boss immensely trying, not least because he was himself a fastidious man, and Yusuf had grown grotesquely fat since he'd orchestrated his palace coup and unseated his energetic, popular and highly respected predecessor. Even watching him wrest himself from his chair was a mesmerising sight, like seeing some ancient ship of war setting sail. He'd prepare for it moments ahead of time, readying his muscles like wind filling the unfurling sails, and the rigging would creak and the anchor would haul and, *yes, yes, yes, movement!* Right now, his forearms rested like giant slugs on the polished walnut table, but every so often he'd lift a finger to his throat, as though his glands were to blame for his obesity, not his incessant consumption of rich foods. And when people addressed him from the side, he'd move his eyes rather than his head to look at them, his pupils sliding to their corners, the very caricature of shadiness.

Finally he ended his call and turned to Ibrahim. 'Such urgency,' he said. 'I trust it has a purpose.'

'Yes,' said Ibrahim. 'It does.' And he turned his laptop to show his boss Gaille's pictures of the lower chamber, while explaining how they'd been found.

Yusuf's eyes lit up when he saw the burial caskets. 'Are those . . . *gold*?' he asked.

'We haven't had time for analysis yet,' said Ibrahim. 'My priority was to seal the site and inform you.'

'Quite right. Quite right. You've done well. Very well.' He licked his lips. 'This is a remarkable discovery. I see I will have to supervise the excavation personally.'

Elena leaned forward. Not much, just enough to catch his eye.

'Yes?' he asked.

'We're both aware of our exceptional good fortune that you could spare time from your other commitments for this meeting, Mr Secretary General, for we know you are a man with extra-ordinary demands upon your time.' Her Arabic was stilted and clumsy, noted Ibrahim, but her posture and use of flattery were impeccable. 'We're glad that you, like us, consider this find to be of historic importance, and are delighted that you'll be involved in its ongoing excavation. However, sharing this

236

exciting news with you wasn't the only reason Mr Beyumi and I were anxious for this meeting. There's something else that needs your wisdom and urgent consideration.'

'Something else?' asked Yusuf.

'The inscription,' said Elena.

'Inscription? What inscription?' He glared at Ibrahim. 'Why haven't you told me about this inscription?'

'I believe I did, Secretary General.'

'Are you contradicting me?'

'Of course not, Secretary General. Forgive me.' He reopened his photograph of the inscription.

'Oh, *this*,' said Yusuf. 'Why didn't you say you were talking about this?'

'Forgive me, Secretary General. The fault is mine. You'll note that the characters are Demotic, but the inscription is actually in Greek.' He nodded at Elena. 'A colleague of Ms Koloktronis' deciphered it. I can explain how it works, if you're interested. Otherwise, here is a copy of the translation.'

Yusuf's mouth worked as he read the text, his eyes going wide as he assimilated the implications. It wasn't surprising, reflected Ibrahim. Memphis had been known to ancient Egyptians as White Wall. The word desert came originally from Desh Ret: the Red Land. Kelonymus referred to Alexander as the 'Son of Ammon', so the place of his father, it followed, was the Oracle of Ammon in Siwa Oasis, where old sources suggested Alexander had asked to be buried. The inscription, therefore, asserted that a group of shield-bearers had stolen Alexander's body from under Ptolemy's nose in Memphis and had taken it across the Western Desert to a tomb they'd prepared within sight of the Oracle of Ammon in Siwa Oasis. Ptolemy, however, had pursued them, and they'd killed themselves rather than fall into his hands. All except Kelonymus, Akylos' brother, who'd avoided capture, and who'd later brought all his comrades' remains back to Alexandria for burial, in fulfilment of his vow.

When Yusuf had finished he blinked twice. 'Is this . . . is this to be believed?' he asked.

'The translation is correct,' answered Ibrahim carefully. 'I've checked it myself. And we believe it to be sincere as well. After all, as you've seen from the photographs of the underground chamber, this man Kelonymus went to extraordinary lengths to honour these men. He wouldn't have done it for a hoax.'

'But it would have been madness,' frowned Yusuf. 'Why would these men throw their lives away on such a venture?'

'Because they believed Alexander's dying wish had been to be buried in Siwa,' answered Elena. 'Ptolemy effectively betrayed that wish when he started to build a tomb in Alexandria. You must remember, Alexander was a god to these people. They'd have risked anything to carry out his orders.'

'You're please not asking me to believe that Alexander is buried in Siwa, Ms Koloktronis,' sighed Yusuf.

Ibrahim knew what was on his boss's mind. In

238

the early 1990s, another Greek archaeologist had announced to the world's media that she'd found the tomb of Alexander in Siwa Oasis. Although her claim had been swiftly and comprehensively rejected. Siwa and Alexander had become something of a joke in the archaeological community.

'No,' acknowledged Elena. 'Alexander's embalmed body was on display in Alexandria centuries after this inscription was made. No one's denying that. However, surely it's possible that they seized his body and set off towards Siwa, where they had a tomb ready and waiting.'

Yusuf sat back in his chair and looked sternly at Elena. 'So,' he remarked, 'the *true* purpose for your presence at this meeting becomes clear. You're not here out of concern for the proper excavation of this Alexandria find. Oh, no. You're here because you believe that somewhere in Siwa there is a tomb appointed with — how does the Alexander Cipher put it again? — yes, with 'goods fit for the Son of Ammon'. And you want my permission to look for them, no doubt.'

'Alexander was the most successful conqueror in history,' said Elena. 'One of Egypt's greatest pharaohs. Imagine what finding his tomb would mean for this country. Imagine what honours would befall the Secretary General whose enlightened leadership made it possible. Your name would rightly be venerated along with the great patriots of this nation.'

'Go on.'

'And you have nothing to lose. I know the chances of finding anything are extremely thin. I know the resources of the Supreme Council are inexcusably tight. But something should be done. Something small. A low-level epigraphic survey of antiquities, say, conducted with the permission of the SCA. Just me and one colleague. Anything more substantial will only provoke rumours. You know what it is with Siwa and rumours.'

Yusuf frowned. 'Every hill in the Oasis has been searched, searched and searched again,' he observed. 'If this tomb does exist, and has lain hidden for twenty-three centuries, do you truly expect to find it in a matter of weeks? Do you know how *wide* the Siwa Depression is?'

'It won't be easy,' admitted Elena. 'But it has to be worth a try. Think of the alternative. When the contents of the Alexander Cipher leak, every treasure hunter in the world will converge on Siwa. If we find the tomb first, we can pre-empt that, or at least announce that there's nothing to it. Either would be preferable to a gold rush.'

'There'll only be a gold rush if word gets out,' pointed out Yusuf.

'But it *will* get out,' insisted Elena. 'We all know it will. That's the nature of these things.'

Yusuf nodded to himself. 'Siwa is the territory of Dr Sayed,' he said sourly, as though he rather resented his colleague. 'And Dr Sayed has his own ways. You'll need his permission too.'

'Of course,' nodded Elena. 'Apart from anything else, I understand he has an outstanding collection of reference materials. Perhaps you might speak to him yourself, ask him to give us access. I know, of course, that it will make no difference whatever to *your* decision, which will be taken solely for the greater benefit of Egypt, but you might perhaps let *him* know that our backers have set aside very significant fees for all our SCA consultants, including yourself, naturally.'

'I cannot agree to an open-ended expedition,' said Yusuf. 'Siwa is small. Whatever your cover story, people will eventually note what you are doing. Your presence will trigger the very result you seek to avoid.'

'Six weeks,' suggested Elena. 'That's all we ask.'

Yusuf rested his hands upon his belly. He liked to have the last word on everything. 'Two weeks,' he declared. 'Two weeks from tomorrow. Then we'll talk again, and I'll decide whether to give you another fortnight or not.'

IV

Nessim paced back and forth in his hotel room, willing his phone to ring, for one of his sentinels to spot Knox before he could go to ground once more. There had to be a good chance. The simple fact that Knox had broken cover to get his belongings back suggested he was after something, that he had a purpose, was prepared to take risks in its pursuit. Yet, for all that, he had no real expectations. There was something about Knox that made Nessim feel fatalistic and inadequate.

He stopped in mid-pace, daunted suddenly by

the prospect of confessing another failure to Hassan. He needed to show he was doing something. He needed to demonstrate that he was *active*. He'd kept the hunt largely in-house up till now. But the time for discretion had passed. He unzipped his money-belt, checked his cash, turned to Hosni, Ratib and Sami.

'Get on your phones,' he told them. 'A thousand dollars to whoever finds Knox's Jeep. Two if he's in it.'

Ratib pulled a face. 'But everyone will know it was us,' he protested. 'When Knox turns up dead, I mean.'

'Do you have a better suggestion?' snapped Nessim. 'Or perhaps you'd like to tell Hassan yourself this time why we haven't found Knox yet?'

Ratib dropped his gaze. 'No.'

Nessim sighed. The stress was getting to him. And Ratib had a point. 'OK,' he said. 'Only people you trust. One in each town. And tell them not to blab, or they'll be answering to Hassan themselves.'

His men nodded and reached for their mobiles.

V

By the time the Dragoumis Group's Lear jet touched down in Thessalonike that night, Gaille had decided that she could get used to travelling like this, despite the twinge of guilt she felt at all these carbon emissions for so whimsical a trip.

White leather seats so comfortable they made her groan with pleasure, a window the size of a widescreen TV, a butler on hand to prepare meals and drinks, the co-pilot coming back to talk her through her preferred arrangements for flying back in the morning. An immigration officer came out to greet her with cloying politeness (any friend of Mr Dragoumis, Ms Bonnard . . .), and a blue, chauffeur-driven Bentley whisked her away up into the hills above Thessalonike, so she could just sit back and admire the night sky.

They reached a walled estate, patrolled by guards. They were waved through, down to a whitewashed palace lit up like *son et lumière*. And then, to cap it all, Dragoumis himself emerged from his front door to meet her, his hands clasped behind his back.

After all she'd imagined of him on her journey, it was a surprise and relief to her to see how short and slight he was. He hadn't shaved; he looked peasant and very Greek. Just for a moment, she thought that she'd be able to handle him easily, that he was nothing to fear. Then she drew closer and realised she'd been wrong.

23

I

Knox cut across country to get to Ras el-Sudr. His route took him through Tanta, the largest town of the Delta. Someone had mentioned it to him recently, but he couldn't think who. It was only when he was out the other side that he remembered Gaille's offhand remark about her Tanta concierge. He pulled to the side to think. He hadn't given much thought to Elena's Delta excavation. Too much else going on. But maybe that had been a mistake. Especially now that Nicolas Dragoumis had appeared on the scene.

It was no secret that Elena's Macedonian Archaeological Foundation was sponsored by the Dragoumis Group. And the Dragoumises had no interest in Egypt, Knox knew, only in Macedonia. If they were financing an excavation in the Delta, therefore, they were after something Macedonian. And just maybe it was connected with what they'd found in Alexandria. It certainly couldn't hurt to find out more.

He headed back into town, found a bar with a phone directory, then rang around all the local hotels asking for Elena. He got a hit on his fifth attempt.

'She not here,' the night clerk told him. 'Alexandria.'

'What about her team?'

'Who you want to speak to?'

Knox ended the call, jotted down the hotel's address, and hurried back to his Jeep.

II

Philip Dragoumis led Gaille through arches and across polished mosaic floors to a drawing room with gorgeous oils and tapestries upon the walls. He made a small, indistinct gesture and Gaille found herself sitting on a yellow upholstered chair without quite being sure why.

'A drink first,' he said. 'Then we eat. Red wine? It's from my estate.'

'Thank you.' She looked around as he opened a bottle and poured two glasses. An oil portrait of a fierce-looking, black-bearded man with a mess of scar tissue around his left eye had pride of place above the huge fireplace. A portrait of Philip II, father of Alexander the Great. Her eyes flickered back and forth between the picture and Dragoumis, and she realised with a slight shock that he was deliberately drawing some kind of parallel between Philip and himself, implying that the birthmark around his own left eye was some kind of stigmata, as though he were Philip reincarnate.

'You don't really believe that?' she blurted out, before she could stop herself.

He laughed loudly and unaffectedly. 'There is a saying: when a wise man does business with the Chinese, he speaks Mandarin.'

'And when he does business with the

245

superstitious . . . ' suggested Gaille.

His smile broadened. He nodded at a second painting, a beautiful young dark woman in ragged peasant clothes. 'My wife,' he said. 'I painted her myself. From memory.'

Gaille smiled uncertainly. 'You've come a long way,' she said.

'I have. My wife hasn't.' He gave a sharp little nod. 'She's buried outside. She loved the view from this hill. We used to walk up here. That is why I bought this land and built my home here.'

'I'm sorry.'

'When I was a young man, I was a troublemaker. I used to go from village to village preaching the Macedonian cause. The Athens secret police wanted to speak with me. You can imagine, it was not a desire I shared. When they couldn't find me, they visited my wife instead. They demanded she tell them where I was. She refused. They poured petrol on her stomach, breasts and arms. She told them nothing. Then they lit it. Still she wouldn't talk. They poured petrol onto our baby son. Finally she talked. My wife was left with terrible burns, yet she could perhaps have survived with proper treatment. But I had no money for such treatment. My wife died because I had chosen to preach rather than to work, Ms Bonnard. The day I buried her was the day I decided to stop playing at politics and become rich.'

'I'm sorry,' said Gaille helplessly.

Dragoumis grunted, as if to acknowledge the inadequacy of words. Then he said: 'I knew your father.'

'So your son told me. But I wasn't that close to him, you know.'

'Yes. I do know. I have always felt badly about that.'

Gaille frowned. 'Why should you feel badly about it?'

Dragoumis sighed. 'You were due to go to Mallawi with him, were you not?'

'Yes.'

'But then he postponed?'

'He had urgent personal business.'

'Yes,' agreed Dragoumis. 'With me.'

'No,' said Gaille. 'With a young man called Daniel Knox.'

Dragoumis made a vague gesture, as if to imply it came to the same thing. 'Do you know much about Knox?' he asked.

'No.'

'His parents were archaeologists themselves. Macedonian specialists. They often visited this part of the world. A charming couple, a delightful daughter. They worked closely with Elena, you know. Ten years ago they visited one of her excavations in the mountains. Elena's husband collected them from the airport. Unfortunately, on the drive up to the site . . . '

Gaille looked at him numbly. 'All of them?' she asked.

Dragoumis nodded. 'All of them.'

'But . . . what's that got to do with my father?'

'It was an accident. A terrible accident. But not everyone believed this.'

'You mean . . . *murder*? I don't understand. Why would anyone want to kill Knox's parents?'

'Not Knox's parents. Elena's husband. Pavlos.'

'But who would want to kill him?'

Dragoumis smiled. 'Me, Ms Bonnard,' he said. 'Me.'

III

Ras el-Sudr was an oil town that had tried to make it as a tourist resort too. Knox loitered near the Beach Inn's car park so that he could make sure Rick hadn't been tailed. When he was satisfied, he went to meet him.

'Good to see you, mate,' grinned Rick.

'You too.'

'Interesting times, eh?' He nodded at a nearby bar. 'You want a drink? You can tell me all.'

'Sure.' They took a table in the shadows, where Knox filled him in on everything that had happened since he'd fled Sharm.

'I don't believe it,' said Rick. 'That bastard Hassan put a noose around your neck? I'll kill him.'

'Actually,' said Knox, 'I don't think it was Hassan. Hassan wouldn't have had the rope cut.'

'Then who?'

'Have I ever told you about what happened in Greece?'

'You mean with your parents? You just told me that there'd been a road accident. You never said there was a story to it.'

'A winding road, an old car, a misty night in the mountains. The kind of tragedy that happens all the time, right? The only trouble was, the

248

driver was a guy called Pavlos. The husband of that woman Elena I was telling you about. A journalist. Very outspoken. A muckraker. He was running a campaign against a very powerful and rich family called the Dragoumises, demanding an enquiry into their businesses, that kind of thing.'

'And you figured he was killed to shut him up?'

'I did at the time,' nodded Knox.

'So what did you do about it?'

IV

Gaille looked at Philip Dragoumis in horror. 'You murdered Pavlos?'

'No,' he assured her. 'I swear to you on my wife's grave that I had nothing to do with his death, or the deaths of Knox's family. All I meant was that certain people believed I had the motive to do it.'

'Why? What motive?'

'You must understand something, Ms Bonnard. I am a Macedonian patriot. This region all used to be Macedonia. Then it was cut up by the Treaty of Bucharest, and handed out to Serbia, Bulgaria and Greece. I have made it my life's work to undo that gross injustice. But others, men like Pavlos, believe this region rightly belongs to Greece. They try to stop me. Pavlos was skilled at insinuation. He wanted an enquiry into my life and businesses not because he thought me corrupt, but because he knew it would leave an indelible smear. When he died, the calls for an enquiry died with him. So you can understand why people believed that I was responsible. But I was not responsible, I assure you. I never even considered Pavlos my enemy, only my opponent, and there is a world of difference between the two. Even if I were a man of violence, which I am not, I would never have sanctioned it against Pavlos. And the truth is, I had no need.' He leaned closer. 'Can I trust you never to tell Elena what I am about to reveal to you?'

'Yes.'

'Good. Then Pavlos had been indiscreet. I had irrefutable evidence of this. The release of this information would have been . . . *problematic* for him. We had spoken together about it. I assure you, he was no longer a threat to me.'

'So you say.'

'Yes. So I say.' There was a trace of impatience in his manner. 'Tell me something, Ms Bonnard. You have been working closely with Elena Koloktronis these past three weeks. Do you really believe that she'd work for me if she thought me guilty of murdering her husband?'

Gaille thought about it for a moment, but there was only one answer. 'No.'

'And you must understand, Ms Bonnard, that Pavlos was everything to Elena. Trust me: if she'd believed me responsible for his death, she'd have made sure the whole world knew about it.'

'She'd have spoken out?'

'Oh, no,' grunted Dragoumis. 'She'd have

killed me.' He smiled at Gaille's startled reaction. 'It's a fact,' he said bluntly. 'It would have been a blood matter. That's still a powerful force in this region. But when you consider how utterly she loved him . . . ' He shook his head. 'I was half fearing she'd do something. So much grief needs vent. But, you see, she knew the truth of it. Her husband was a wild and reckless driver who never serviced his car. No. Elena was broken hearted, but not a problem. It was your father's young friend Knox who was the problem.'

'Knox? In what way?'

'He believed I'd murdered his whole family to silence Pavlos,' said Dragoumis. 'He didn't think I should get away with that. It isn't hard to understand his point of view. So he took up Pavlos' campaign himself. He wrote endlessly to local politicians, newspapers, TV stations. He picketed government buildings and police stations. He spray-painted 'Dragoumis Enquiry' in huge letters outside my head office. He printed it on helium balloons, threw leaflets from tall buildings, draped banners over railings at televised sporting events, rang radio shows and — '

'Knox? Knox did all this?'

'Oh, yes,' nodded Dragoumis. 'It was impressive, especially when you consider that he believed me quite capable of murder. And damaging too. He cut a sympathetic figure, as you can imagine. He set people talking. I asked him to stop. He refused. He was deliberately trying to goad me into doing something rash, as though that would prove his case. I grew worried for him. He was only doing this because he was sick with grief. And there were those, sympathetic with my cause, who wanted to silence him. It reached a point where I couldn't guarantee his safety any more. And if anything happened to him . . . you can imagine. I needed him gone, but he refused to listen to me. So I looked for someone he would listen to.'

'My father,' said Gaille numbly.

'He was a close friend of the Knoxes. And I knew him too. I asked him to come. He was reluctant at first. Mallawi had been about to start, as you know. But I assured him it was a matter of life and death. He flew in. We struck a deal. He'd take Knox away and keep him quiet. I'd put out the word that Knox wasn't to be touched. Your father visited Knox's hotel. Knox apparently gave him a speech about standing up to tyrants. Your father listened politely and slipped knockout drops into his retsina. By the time he woke, they were both captive on a slow boat to Port Said, and your father had time to talk sense into him. And that, Ms Bonnard, is why I feel badly about your falling-out with your father. It would never have happened, you see, had I not asked him to intervene.'

V

In the Rasel-Sudr bar, Rick nodded slowly as he digested Knox's account of his feud with the

Dragoumises, and how he'd come to Egypt with Richard Mitchell.

'And here I was thinking you were just another quiet Brit,' he said. 'Do you have any other international gangsters on your trail, or is that the lot?'

'That's the lot. As far as I know, at least. But guess who I saw this afternoon?'

'This man Dragoumis?'

'His son. Nicolas.'

'And he's as bad?'

'Worse. Much worse. I don't much like the father, but you've got to admire what he's achieved. And he has principles too. When he gives his word, he keeps it. The son's just a wanker with an inheritance, you know?'

'All too well. So you figure this desert lynching was the son getting his own back?'

'Probably.'

'And you're not going to take that lying down, are you?'

'No.'

Rick grinned. 'Cracking. So what's our plan?'

'Our plan?'

'Come on, mate. You're outnumbered. You could use some help. And Sharm's dead, like I say.'

Knox nodded. 'If you're serious, it would be fantastic.'

'Great. Then what's our first move?'

'We head up to Tanta.'

'Tanta?'

'Yes,' said Knox, checking his watch. 'And we're on a bit of a deadline too, so how about I explain when we get there?'

VI

Dragoumis led Gaille through to his dining room. It was a vast space, with a long walnut table running down its middle. Two places had been set at one end, lit by candles. A servant was waiting by a trolley to serve their food, a dark and meaty stew floating with unfamiliar spices.

'Forgive my simple tastes,' said Dragoumis. 'I have never developed a palate. If it's cuisine you enjoy, you must dine with my son.'

'I'm sure it'll be delicious,' said Gaille, prodding at it uncertainly with her fork. 'Excuse me, Mr Dragoumis, but I'm curious. Did you fly me all this way just to talk about my father?'

'No,' said Dragoumis. 'I flew you here to ask for your help.'

'My help?' she frowned. 'With what?'

Dragoumis leaned forward. Candlelight struck his eyes obliquely, making his dark brown irises appear flecked with gold. 'The Alexander Cipher talks of a tomb in Siwa filled with goods fit for the son of Ammon.'

'You know about that?'

'Of course I know,' said Dragoumis impatiently. 'It also says that the shield-bearers killed themselves before Ptolemy had a chance to . . . *learn* from them where this tomb was.'

'Yes.'

'Have you ever heard of such a tomb? A tomb in Siwa filled with goods fit for a man like Alexander.'

'No.'

'Then it remains to be discovered.'

254

'If it ever existed.'

'It existed,' stated Dragoumis. 'It exists. Tell me, Ms Bonnard: would it not be something to discover it? Can you imagine what goods might be considered fit for such a man, the greatest conqueror in history? The weapons he was given from the Trojan wars? His personal copy of Homer, annotated by Aristotle? Be honest: do you not *yearn* to be the one to find it? Fame. Wealth. Admiration. You'd never again need to ask yourself in the dark hours of the morning what your purpose is upon this earth.'

'You misunderstand how these things work,' said Gaille. 'Ibrahim Beyumi is reporting all this to the Secretary General of the SCA. What happens next will be up to them. And it won't include me.'

'Perhaps you have not heard. Elena was at this meeting too.'

'Yes, but — '

'And she has persuaded the Secretary General that she is the best person to lead this search.'

'What? But . . . how?'

'Elena is skilled at negotiation, believe me. However, she is not so skilled at other aspects of archaeology. That is why I asked you here. I want you to go to Siwa with Elena. I want you to find this tomb for me.'

'*Me?*'

'Yes. You have a gift, like your father did.'

'You overestimate my — '

'You discovered the lower chamber, didn't you?'

'Actually that was — '

255

'And you deciphered the inscription.'

'Someone else would have deciphered — '

'Humility does not impress me, Ms Bonnard,' he said. 'Success impresses me. Elena has many virtues, but she lacks imagination, empathy. This is your gift. It is a gift our cause needs.'

'Your cause?'

'You think it old-fashioned to have a cause?'

'I think 'cause' is a politician's word for bloodshed,' said Gaille. 'I don't think archaeology should be about causes. I think it should be about the truth.'

'Very well,' nodded Dragoumis. 'How about this truth? My grandfathers were both born in Greater Macedonia. By the time they were men, one was Serb, the other Greek. To people like you, people without causes, it may seem an excellent thing that families like mine can be cut up and handed out like slaves. But one group of people feels strongly that this is not so good. Can you guess, perhaps, who these people are?'

'I imagine you mean those people who call themselves Macedonian,' answered Gaille weakly.

'I do not seek to change your mind, Ms Bonnard,' said Dragoumis. 'I simply ask you this question: who, in truth, should decide who a person is? They themselves or someone else?' He paused to give her a chance to respond, but she found she had nothing to say. 'I believe that there's a legitimate nation of Greater Macedonia,' he continued. 'I believe that this nation has been illegally divided between Bulgaria,

Serbia and Greece. I believe that the Macedonian people have been unfairly oppressed for centuries, that they've suffered decades of ethnic cleansing, that they are persecuted still because they have no voice, no power. Hundreds of thousands in this region agree with me, as do millions more across the world. They share culture, history, religion and language with each other, not the states to whom they've been allocated. They call themselves Macedonian, whatever world opinion tells them they're called. I believe these people deserve the same rights to liberty, religion, self-determination and justice that you take for granted. These people are my cause. They are why I ask your help.'

He turned his eyes on her. There was something almost triumphal about his gaze, his self-certainty. She tried not to meet his eyes, but she couldn't help herself.

'And you will give it,' he said.

24

I

Knox was keen to stash his Jeep somewhere Nessim wouldn't easily find it. He turned down a narrow country lane just south of Tanta, Rick following in his Subaru. Then they drove in convoy for fifteen minutes or so, until he saw in the moonlight a line of derelict farm buildings in an overgrown field used as a fly-tip. Perfect. He lurched his way down a rutted earth track to a yard of broken concrete. A line of byres stood along the opposite side, open to the elements, their floors muddy, their corners filled with wind-blown litter, their mouths blocked by a line of drinking troughs, partially filled with rainwater. To his left was a low, ugly, concrete-block outbuilding with a wide steel door, which screeched on the concrete when they swung it open on its hinges. It was empty inside, except for the pungent smell of spilled diesel and urine, and white splashes of bat- and bird-shit on the floor. Knox parked inside, took everything he might need to the Subaru, then covered the Jeep with his tarpaulin.

'You ready to explain now?' prompted Rick, as they headed off towards Tanta.

'Sure,' said Knox. 'Did I ever tell you about my Mallawi excavation?'

Rick snorted. 'Did you ever stop?'

'Then you'll remember the basics,' said Knox, opening his laptop and checking the CDs Rick had brought as he talked. 'Richard Mitchell and I found an archive of Ptolemaic papyri. We passed them for safekeeping to Yusuf Abbas, now Secretary General of the SCA. He liked what he saw so much, he took over the whole excavation.'

'And then you spotted some of the papyri on the black market.'

'Exactly. Now, there isn't a wide market for Ptolemaic papyri, even with good provenance. But stolen papyri? I mean, most of the usual buyers are academic institutions. They wouldn't touch anything hot. But Philip Dragoumis is interested in anything Macedonian, particularly if it's got a connection with Alexander.'

'And you think these papyri do?'

'The top tomb in Alexandria was built for a shield-bearer in Alexander's army named Akylos,' said Knox. 'The lower chamber was dedicated by a man named Kelonymus. Both of these names cropped up in the same set of Mallawi papyri. We photographed them and kept them on one of the CDs you borrowed. Look.' He turned the laptop around so that Rick could see the list of file names, dominated by Akylos and Kelonymus. 'And Nicolas and Elena recognised Kelonymus' name yesterday. I'll swear to that.'

'OK. So there's a link between the Mallawi papyri and the Alexandrian tomb. But that doesn't explain what we're doing in Tanta.'

'The Dragoumis Group is funding an excavation near here. They're not people to sponsor digs on the off chance, not in a foreign country. They're looking for something.' They reached the MAF hotel, parked across the street to monitor its front door. 'I think it's all part of whatever brought Nicolas to Alexandria, which means it has to be important. I want to know what it is. But I can't exactly just ring up and ask. All the excavation crew have signed confidentiality agreements, so no one's going to talk, particularly not to me.'

'Ah,' said Rick, nodding at the hotel. 'But they're staying there, are they?'

'Exactly. And, in an hour or so, they'll set off for their day's work. And we're going to follow.'

II

Elena woke early, sunlight streaming in the open window of Augustin's apartment, noises reaching them from below: cars starting, doors slamming, families bickering. She'd had every intention of breaking off with Augustin when she'd returned to Alexandria late last night, before their fling could grow serious. But then he'd appeared at her hotel room to take her out to dinner, and he'd smiled that smile at her, and she'd suffered a moment of exquisite hot cramps, so that she'd known instantly that she'd been fooling herself.

She lay there, staring fondly at him. It was strange — and utterly unfair — how men could look beautiful even when a complete mess. His hair was a medusa, lank snakes all over his face. A thin trail of saliva leaked from the corner of his

260

mouth to darken the pillow. Yet still she desired him. For the first time in a decade, she found herself helpless with lust. And, to think, she and Gaille were off to Siwa later that morning! She needed to make the most of their remaining time together.

She drew back the cotton sheet, the better to look at him. She reached down, began to tickle softly the inside of his thigh from just above his knee all the way up to his scrotum. He swelled, unpeeled, flopped upwards onto his belly. A wicked grin spread across his face, though his eyes were still closed. Not a word was said. She kissed him on his brow, his nose, his cheek, his mouth. His breath tasted sour but not at all unpleasant. Their embraces grew more intimate. They were both too hungry to wait. He turned onto his side, fumbled in his bedside table for a condom that he tore open with his teeth and unrolled adeptly with one hand. He grimaced as he forced himself inside her, resting his weight on both hands, holding himself up high. He half withdrew, jiggled and teased, so that she ached for him and pulled him back in. They found their rhythm. She craned up her neck so that she could look down at the point of junction between them, the long hard black shadow of him drawing out of her, pushing slowly back in. She'd forgotten what a mesmerising sight fucking could be, so ruthlessly animal, so distinct from all the effete ritual of romance that surrounded it. He pushed her back down and they stared hard into each other's eyes until it was too much for her, and she twisted and cried

261

out as she came, and they spilled together onto the floor. They lay there for half a minute or so, wrapped together, grinning, gathering breath.

He jumped up easily to his feet. 'Coffee?' he asked.

'Chocolate.'

He padded naked to his kitchen, discarding his condom into an overflowing bin. A pearly strand yo-yoed from his penis. He wiped it away with kitchen roll, checked his fridge.

'*Merde!*' he scowled. 'No milk.'

'Come back to bed,' she complained. 'I have to go collect Gaille from the airport soon.'

'I need coffee,' he protested. 'I need croissants.' He pulled on yesterday's trousers and shirt. 'One minute only, I promise.'

She watched him out the door. Something like happiness swelled in her chest. All these years of sating her desires with milksops and fops. Christ, but it felt good to have a real man in her life again.

III

It was hard work staying awake. Rick had just bought two cups of sludge coffee for Knox and himself from the first café to lift its shutters when four men and three women in hiking boots, cotton trousers and open-necked shirts came down the hotel steps yawning and carrying rucksacks. A number of Egyptian men who'd been gathering over the last twenty minutes or so went to join them. It was Egyptian law that every

262

dig had to employ local crew. They all climbed aboard two flatbed trucks, squeezing up front or stretching out in the back. One of the men did a quick head count, then they lumbered away along the road towards Zagazig.

Rick gave them twenty seconds, then headed after them. Tailing people was easy in Egypt. There were so few roads, you could afford to hang well back. They turned towards Zifta, turned down a farm track. Rick waited until they were nothing but a cloud of dust, then headed after them. They drove for another two or three kilometres before they saw the one of the trucks parked, and no one in sight.

'Let's get out of here before we're spotted,' suggested Knox.

Rick wheeled around and they headed off. 'Where now?'

'I don't know about you,' yawned Knox. 'But I haven't slept in two days. I vote we find ourselves a hotel.'

IV

The day had passed with wretched slowness for Mohammed el-Dahab, but now it was late afternoon, and time was almost up. He paced back and forth outside the cancer ward of Alexandria's Medical Research Institute. At times he sucked great heaves of air into his lungs; at others his breathing became so short and shallow he thought he'd faint. Waiting for the phone call with the test results had been gruelling enough, but nothing like this. He walked to the window, stared blindly out over the night-time city, the harbour. So many millions of people, none of whom he cared one jot for. Let Allah take them all but leave him Layla.

Dr Serag-Al-Din had given them good news. He'd found an HLA match. Basheer. A third cousin of Nur's mother who'd herself come close to death when her Cairo apartment block had collapsed years ago. Mohammed had thought nothing of it at the time, had been completely indifferent to her life or death. *But if she'd died* . . . He closed his eyes, brought a fist up to his mouth. It didn't bear thinking about.

But the HLA match meant nothing in itself. It mattered only if Professor Rafai now granted Layla a berth for a bone marrow transplant. Mohammed was here to learn of his decision.

'*Insha' Allah, insha' Allah,*' muttered Mohammed again and again. The mantra did him little good. If only Nur was here, someone who understood. But Nur hadn't been able to face it. She was at home nursing Layla, more terrified even than he. '*Insha' Allah,*' he muttered. '*Insha' Allah.*'

The door of the oncology ward swung open. A plump young nurse with huge brown eyes came out. Mohammed tried to read her expression, but it was beyond him.

'Will you come with me, please?' she said.

25

I

Kareem Barak's feet were raw and aching. Too much tramping these wretched roads in tight boots with leaky soles. He cursed himself for having answered Abdullah's summons, and for agreeing his terms. One hundred dollars to whoever found this wretched Jeep! It had seemed too good to be true. But when Abdullah had assigned them districts to search, he'd given him this godforsaken stretch of farmland. How the others had sniggered! As if anyone would park out here! He didn't know why he didn't just give up. But those dollars had him by the throat, not least because for Abdullah to offer a one-hundred-dollar reward, he had to be looking to make five or ten times that for himself, which meant opportunities for a smart young man like himself to exploit. But first he needed some luck.

It was dusk when he saw the farm track and the ramshackle buildings some two hundred metres along it. The way his feet burned, it might as well have been two hundred kilometres. He had a sudden craving for a huge bowl of his aunt's *kushari* with extra fried onions, mopped up with great chunks of *aysh baladi*, then the welcoming embrace of his mattress. No way was the Jeep down there. Enough! He scowled and turned, hobbling painfully back the way he'd come. But he'd barely gone twenty steps when a minibus of schoolgirls rattled past. One of them caught his eye and smiled shyly. She had good skin and huge brown eyes and luscious red lips. Staring after her, he forgot all about *kushari* and bed and aching feet. That was what he truly wanted: a beautiful coy young woman to call his own. And, for all his romantic dreams, he was realist enough to know he'd never have one until he earned some serious money.

He turned, painfully, and trudged up the track to the farm buildings.

II

Mohammed found it difficult even to walk as he followed the nurse. He had to remind himself how it was done, one foot and then the other. She led him to a large office where Professor Rafai was flicking through the dividers of a white filing cabinet. Mohammed had seen him often on his rounds, but had never before been granted a private audience. Mohammed didn't know how to read this. Some men delighted in granting good news; others felt it their duty to break bad.

Rafai turned to Mohammed with a bland, professional smile that gave nothing away. 'Sit, sit,' he said, gesturing to his small round corner table. He pulled out a brown folder, came to join him. 'I hope you've not been waiting long.'

Mohammed swallowed. Did Rafai truly not understand? Yet, suddenly, all Mohammed

266

wanted was to go back outside and wait some more. When hope was all a man had, he fought hard to hold on to it.

Rafai opened the brown folder, peered through his half-moon glasses at a sheet inside. He frowned as though he'd just read something of which he'd previously been unaware. 'You understand what a bone marrow transplant would have involved?' he asked without looking up. 'You understand what you were asking me to put your daughter through?'

It was a numb feeling, catastrophe. Mohammed felt cold and sick, yet at the same time immensely calm. He wondered bleakly how he'd break this to Nur, if Layla would understand what it meant.

Rafai proceeded remorselessly: 'We call this procedure bone marrow transplantation, but that is misleading. In ordinary chemotherapy we target only cancerous fast-dividing cells; but in this procedure we deliberately poison a person's entire system in order to destroy all their fast-dividing cells, cancerous or otherwise. That includes the bone marrow. The transplant is not the treatment. The transplant is necessary because after we annihilate all these fast-dividers, the patient will die without new marrow. It is a traumatic and extremely painful experience, without guarantee of success. Rejections occur despite perfect matches. And even if the new marrow takes, convalescence is extensive. Tests, tests, always tests. This is not the treatment of a few days. Scars stay for life. And then there's infertility, cataract blindness, secondary cancers, complications in the liver, kidneys, lungs, heart — '

Mohammed understood something then. Rafai wasn't here because the task was difficult; he was here because he relished the exercise of power. Mohammed reached forward to push down Rafai's folder.

'Say what you have to say,' he demanded. 'Say it straight. Look me in the eye.'

Rafai sighed. 'You must understand that we cannot give a bone marrow transplant to every patient who needs it. We allocate our resources on the basis of clinical evidence, on who will be most likely to benefit. I am afraid the lymphoma has advanced so far in your daughter — '

'Because you would not do the tests in time!' cried Mohammed. 'Because you would not do the tests!'

'You must understand that everyone here loves your — '

Mohammed rose to his feet. 'When did you decide this? Did you decide before we did the tests? You did, didn't you? Why didn't you tell us? Why did you let us go through that?'

'You're wrong,' said Rafai. 'We didn't make the final — '

'Is there anything I can do?' pleaded Mohammed. 'Anything at all? I beg you. Please. You can't do this.'

'I'm sorry.' Rafai smiled blandly. The interview was over.

Mohammed had never previously understood failed suicides; the ones commonly described as cries for help. But in a moment of insight he realised that some conversations were simply too difficult to broach without some kind of act to demonstrate the overwhelming strength of feeling involved. He couldn't face Nur and Layla with this news. It was beyond him. So he picked Rafai up by the lapels of his jacket instead, and slammed him against his office wall.

<h1 style="text-align:center">III</h1>

The journey to Siwa did little to prepare Gaille for the Oasis itself. It was a seven-hour drive along the flat, scrubby, overbuilt Mediterranean coast, then south through flat and empty desert, nothing to see for mile after mile but the occasional service station or herd of wild camels. But then they topped a rise and the relentless emptiness was suddenly broken by glittering white salt lakes and orchards of silver green. They pulled into Siwa's market square as a muezzin called the faithful to prayer, and the sun vanished behind the dark rose ruins of the old Shali Fortress.

Gaille wound down her window, inhaled deeply. Her spirits lifted. The streets here were wide, spacious and dusty. There were few cars or trucks. People walked, cycled or took donkey carts. After the bustle of Alexandria, it seemed gloriously leisurely and content. Siwa was truly the end of the road. There was nothing beyond it but the great Sea of Sand. The Oasis had no purpose but itself.

They took rooms in a hotel in a date-palm

orchard. Their rooms were newly painted, clean and polished, with sparkling windows and gleaming bathrooms. Gaille took a shower and a change of clothes, and then Elena knocked on her door, and they set off to visit Dr Aly Sayed, Siwa's representative of the Supreme Council for Antiquities.

IV

Knox and Rick ducked down in the front seats of the Subaru as one of the flatbed trucks left for the night, its headlights flickering over the grove of trees where they'd hidden. A good day's sleep had recharged Knox's batteries; and his laptop's too. He reopened it once the flatbed had driven off, resumed his study of the Mallawi papyri.

'I reckon the other one must have already left,' said Rick. 'I mean, they can't excavate in the dark.'

'Let's give it ten minutes. Just to be safe.'

Rick pulled a face, but let it go. 'How you getting on?' he asked.

'Not too bad.' Knox's laptop screen was old and fuzzy. The photographs had been taken for cataloguing purposes, not for decipherment. The lighting was variable, to put it kindly. Most of the papyri were completely unreadable. Yet he could still make out occasional words and even phrases. Often they were vague, almost deliberately so, such as 'and then the thing happened that brought me to Mallawi'. Elsewhere, the author referred again and again to 'the

270

enlightened', 'the truth-bearer', 'the knowledge-able', 'the holder of the secret'. And in other places . . . 'I don't know who wrote this,' Knox told Rick, 'but he wasn't very respectful.'

'How do you mean?'

'The Ptolemaic pharaohs were all called Ptolemy, so they distinguished themselves by their cult-titles. For example, the first Ptolemy was known as Soter, the Greek word for saviour. But here he's referred to as Sotades.'

'Sotades?'

'A scurrilous Alexandrian Greek poet and playwright. Wrote a lot of homoerotic verse, invented the palindrome, then got himself into trouble for mocking Ptolemy Two Philadelphos for marrying his sister. Speaking of which, Philadelphos actually means 'sister-lover', but he's referred to here as 'sin-lover'. Ptolemy Euergetes, 'the benefactor', is 'the malefactor'. Philopator, 'the father-loving', is 'the lie-building'. Epiphanes, 'the manifest god', is 'the manifest fraud'. You get the idea?'

'Not exactly the world's greatest satirist, was he?'

'No. But even *referring* to the Ptolemies like this . . . '

Rick leaned forward in his seat, squinting through his windscreen into the moonlit night, impatient to get moving. 'They must have left by now,' he muttered, turning on his ignition. 'Let's go in.'

'Five more minutes.'

'OK,' grumbled Rick, turning his engine off again. He leaned across to look at the laptop.

'What else are you finding?'

'Lots of place names. Tanis, Buto, Busiris, Mendes. All important Delta towns. But the place that comes up by far the most is Lycopolis.'

'Lycopolis. City of the Wolves, yeah?'

'It was the Greek name for ancient Asyut,' nodded Knox. Asyut was some fifty miles south of Mallawi, where the papyri had been found, so it made a broad kind of sense. But something was knocking at his memory, and it wasn't Asyut.

Another pair of headlights came down the farm track. They both ducked again. 'Looks like you were right,' grinned Rick, his teeth glowing white. The second flatbed came to a complete stop as it reached the road, waiting for a car to pass. They could hear its indicator clicking, and the tired banter of labourers in the back, glad that a long day was over. Then it pulled out onto the Tanta road and was gone.

'Right,' said Rick, turning the ignition on once more. 'Let's do it, yeah?'

'Yes.'

The moon was bright enough for them to drive with only their sidelights on, not wanting to advertise their presence, yet not wanting to look unduly stealthy, either. They reached the line of trees where the flatbed had parked earlier. A stake hammered into the ground declared in Arabic and English that this was a restricted area, reserved by the Supreme Council for Antiquities in partnership with the Macedonian Archaeological Foundation. They retreated a little way, concealed the Subaru in a small copse, then went searching.

Rick had been out shopping while Knox had slept, and now he handed him a torch, though it was still light enough not to need it. A cool breeze rustled and whispered in the branches. A bird hooted. They could see the static umber glow of a distant settlement, and yellow headlights crisscrossing on a road. Their boots clumped with soil as they crossed a field. In its far corner, they found a site in mid-excavation, a honeycomb of roped-off, four-by-four-metre pits divided by baulk walls, then a series of emptied graves, each a metre deep, their contents removed, their bases hidden in shadow from the slanting moonlight, freshly dug earth by their sides. It took them barely fifteen minutes to check it all out.

'Not exactly the Valley of the Kings, is it?' muttered Rick.

'You can't expect them to — '

'Shhhh!' went Rick suddenly, crouching down, a finger to his lips. Knox turned to look at what had caught Rick's eye. Several seconds later, he saw it: a small orange glow between the trees. 'Two people,' whispered Rick. 'Sharing a fag.' He motioned at an empty grave, its foot in darkness. Knox nodded.

They climbed down inside, watching over the rim as two men in dark green uniforms and caps advanced: private security contractors, rather than army or police, but with black holsters on their belts. One of them was holding the leash of a huge German shepherd, growling and baring

273

its fangs as if it had caught a scent, but wasn't yet quite sure of what. His companion was curious enough to turn on his torch, which he flashed around as he and his companion drew closer, discussing some TV movie they'd both watched earlier.

Rick smeared earth on his hands and the back of his neck, gestured for Knox to do likewise, then they lay motionless and face down in the grave as the two guards walked right up to them, the German shepherd getting thoroughly excited, but being hauled back and cursed at. A flare of torchlight bloomed in the bottom of the grave, then was gone. A still-lit cigarette butt landed by Knox's cheek. One of the men, while talking to his companion, unzipped his trousers and took a leak on the earth above, splash-off spattering around them, while his comrade made lewd comments about some actress he fancied. Then the two men turned and trudged away, dragging their agitated dog with them.

Rick was the first to stir. 'Fuck me, that was close,' he muttered.

'We should get out of here,' agreed Knox.

'Bollocks,' said Rick. 'Two men and a German shepherd guarding an empty field? I want to see what they're really protecting.'

'They had guns, mate,' said Knox.

'Exactly,' grinned Rick. 'This is getting interesting.'

'I'm not having you getting hurt,' said Knox. 'Not on my account.'

'Fuck that. I haven't had this much fun in

years.' And he set off before Knox could argue further, keeping low to the ground, using his experience to find the stealthiest path. Knox followed, grateful to have such a friend.

The moon made ghostly shadows through the trees as they mounted a gentle but lengthy rise. Knox glimpsed grey ahead, pointed it out. Rick nodded and motioned for Knox to stay where he was. He vanished for a minute before reappearing out of the shadows.

'Two buildings,' he whispered. 'One large, one small. Made of concrete-block. No windows. Steel doors. Padlocks. But both guards are outside the small one. That's the one we need to get inside.'

'I thought you said it was a concrete-block building with no windows. How the fuck are we going to get inside?'

Rick grinned. 'You'll see.'

V

Dr Aly Sayed lived in an impressive two-storey house at the end of a narrow, tree-lined lane. A dark man with snowy hair, eyebrows and trimmed beard sat outside, a tumbler in one hand, a bulbous fountain pen in the other, his tabletop spread with papers.

'Hola!' he cried cheerfully. 'You must be my secretary general's friends.'

He rested his tumbler on his papers to stop them from being blown away, then bounded across. Siwa had been on the ancient slave route, and he clearly had Negro as well as Arab blood, which he seemed deliberately to emphasise with his open sandals, khaki shorts and short-sleeved gold and scarlet shirt.

'You must be Ms Koloktronis,' he said to Elena, shaking her hand. 'And Gaille Bonnard,' he said, turning to her. 'Yes! Your father's eyes.'

Gaille was shocked. 'I beg your pardon?'

'You are not Richard Mitchell's daughter?'

'Yes, but — '

'Good! When Yusuf tell me to expect Elena Koloktronis and Gaille Bonnard, I think to myself, ah, yes, I recognise this name! When your father dies in his terrible fall, I post to you I think a great package of papers and belongings. You received it, I trust?'

'That was you? Yes. Thank you.'

Aly nodded. 'Your father was my very good friend. He stay with me often. You are welcome for your own sake, of course. But the daughter of such a good man is a thousand times welcome.'

'Thank you.'

'Though I must say I am surprised that Yusuf Abbas commended you so warmly to me.' He raised an eyebrow. 'It couldn't be that he is unaware of who your father is, could it?'

'I don't know,' blushed Gaille.

'Perhaps I should tell him myself next time we speak,' he mused. But then he saw her expression and touched her elbow. 'Of course you know I'm joking. I would never do such a thing. You have my word. Now come inside. You'll honour and adorn my humble home. Inside! Inside!'

276

Gaille and Elena exchanged a glance as they followed. They hadn't expected such exuberant welcome.

He slapped his hand against the rough, yellow exterior wall. 'Kharshif,' he announced. 'Mud and salt. Strong like rock but with one weakness. She turn back into mud again when she rain!' He put his hands on his sides and laughed uproariously. 'Fortunately she not rain like this often in Siwa. Not since 1985! Now Siwa is all one concrete block.' He thumped his chest. 'Me, I like the old ways.'

His front door opened onto a long hallway. Framed photographs jostled for space. More were stacked on the floor. Discoloured patches from previous hangings showed that he often changed them around. He wasn't camera-shy, that was for sure. He appeared in picture after picture: discussing excavation matters on site; out hunting with an army officer, holding up a white gazelle with a gunshot wound in its head; in mountaineering kit halfway up some cliff; sightseeing in Paris, St Louis, Granada, and cities Gaille couldn't place; shaking hands with dignitaries, celebrities and Egypt experts. Not an ego-wall so much as an ego-house.

They reached his kitchen, its broad fireplace open to the night sky. A huge old yellowing refrigerator clicked on and began to rattle loudly as they entered. Aly kicked it and the rattling became more subdued.

'A drink?' he suggested. 'You may not know, Siwa is dry of alcohol. Our young men enjoy too much the labgi, the alcohol we make from dates;

and labgi makes them enjoy too much each other, so — no more alcohol! In this sense, however, my house is the oasis!'

Gaille found his boisterous good humour disconcerting, as though he was laughing up his sleeve at them. He opened the refrigerator door to reveal a jungle of fresh fruit and vegetables inside, stacks of beer and white wine. He wagged a finger at Gaille.

'Your father teach me wicked habits. A terrible thing, the love of alcohol. Each time I run low I must invent SCA business in Cairo. And I hate Cairo. It means I have to pay respects to my secretary general, and — believe me — that is a privilege made all the greater by its rarity.'

He poured them drinks, led them back to the hallway, unlocked a blue door, pushed it open, flipped on a light and stood aside. A wave of delicious cool air wafted out. The room was large and lushly carpeted. A single heavy stand-alone air conditioning machine stood hissing beneath the closed, bolted and shuttered windows. A computer, a flatbed scanner and a colour printer rested upon two archival tables next to three grey steel filing cabinets and white-painted shelving stacked with books above locked, glass-fronted cabinets. Gaille noted the straight lines on the walls. There was no risk of this room, at least, turning back into mud.

'I understand you're here to research our old sites, yes?' Aly waved his hand. 'My collection is at your service. If it is published about Siwa and the Western Desert, it is here. And if not published, either.'

'You're extremely kind,' said Elena.

He waved her thanks away. 'We're all archaeologists here. Why would we keep secrets from one another?'

'Do you have photographs?'

'Of course.' He opened the top drawer of a filing cabinet, withdrew a large map, spread it out. Gridlines ran north to south and east to west, giving each square a unique reference number that corresponded to an indexed folder in the cabinets, containing grainy, black-and-white aerial photographs, as well as occasional colour, ground-level site prints.

While he explained his system to Elena, Gaille wandered along the shelves, fingering sheaves of press-cuttings on the golden mummies of Baharriya, histories of Kharga, Dakhla and Farafra, of the geology of desert. Two entire ranges had been given over to Siwa, the shelves packed so tight that she had to pull hard to pluck out a first-edition copy of Qibell's *A Visit to Siwa*. She turned the crumbling yellow pages with great tenderness. She loved the whimsy of such books, before science had made whimsy unfashionable.

'You know these?' murmured Aly, suddenly at her side.

'Not *all* of them,' she admitted. 'In fact . . . '

He laughed, but there was something gentler, more kindly, more authentic about this laugh. He stooped to unlatch and open a low cabinet. Inside, wire racks bulged with grey and tan folders of loose papers. Notebooks and journals were stacked in separate piles. He found and removed a thick green folder, handed it to her. 'You know the Siwan Manuscript? The history of our Oasis kept by the Mosalims since . . . ' he waved his hand to indicate for ever. 'These notes in red pen are mine. You'll find them valuable, I think.' He set the folder down, returned to his books. 'Ah! Yes! Ahmed Fakhry. A great man. My mentor and my very good friend. You have read his works?'

'Yes.' It was the only research she'd managed so far.

'Excellent. Ah! And this! W. G. Browne's *Travels in Africa, Egypt and Syria From the Year 1792 to 1798.* The first European for centuries to visit Siwa — or to write of it, at least. He thought us nasty, dirty people. We hurled stones at him because he pretended to be a man of faith. How far the world has come! Here's Belzoni, everyone's favourite circus strongman. And Frederick Hornemann. German, of course, but he wrote in English. His journey was sponsored by the London African Society in, let me see, yes, 1798.'

'Is there nothing more up to date?'

'Of course, of course. Many books. Copies of every excavation log. But believe me, when these old people visit, our monuments and tombs were in much better condition. Now many are nothing but dust and sand. 'My name is Ozymandias, king of kings'.' He sighed, shook his head sadly. 'So much lost. You read German, yes?'

'Yes.'

'Good. One never knows these days. Even

reputable universities seem to hand out doctorates to people who can barely speak their own language. Here is J. C. Ewald Falls' *Siwa: Die Oase des Sonnengottes in der Libyschen Wüste*. Cailliaud's *Voyage à Meroe*; you must read that. And that criminal Drovetti! I had to travel to Turin to see the *Canon of Kings*. *Turin*! Worse even than Cairo! They tried to kill me with their trams!'

'When can we start?' asked Elena.

'When you would like?'

'Tonight.'

'Tonight!' laughed Aly. 'Do you never relax?'

'We only have two weeks.'

'Not tonight, I'm afraid,' said Aly. 'I have plans. But I'm an early riser. You're welcome here at any time from seven.'

'Thank you.'

VI

Rick and Knox circled downwind so that the German shepherd wouldn't catch their scent. It was another ninety minutes before the guards set off on their rounds once more. The moment they were gone, Rick hurried into the clearing and over to the smaller building. He examined its two hefty padlocks, produced a hooked length of thick steel wire from his pocket, then proceeded swiftly to unlock them both.

'Where in hell did you learn that?' murmured Knox.

'Australian Special Forces, mate,' grinned

Rick, pocketing the padlocks and ushering him inside. 'They don't teach knitting.' There was a deep hole in the floor, a wooden ladder tied to one wall. 'It's sixteen minutes to the other site,' said Rick. 'I timed it. Sixteen more back makes thirty-two. We need to be out of here in twenty-five tops. OK?'

'We'd better hurry,' agreed Knox, adrenalin pumping as he led the way down. The ladder creaked but held, and he was soon crunching on stone chippings. Rick joined him a moment later. They walked side by side down the narrow corridor, Rick picking out a wall painting with his torch. 'Jesus!' he muttered. 'I thought Wolverine was out of the *Marvel* comics.'

'Not Wolverine,' corrected Knox. 'Wolf god. Wepwawet.'

Rick looked at him strangely. 'What's the matter?' he asked. 'You seen a ghost?'

'Not exactly.'

'Then what? Have you worked out where we are, or something?'

'I think so. Yes.'

'Come on, then, mate. Spill.'

Knox frowned. 'What do you know about the Rosetta Stone?' he asked.

26

'Boss! Boss!'

Nessim glowered at Ratib. Since they'd offered the thousand-dollar reward, their phones had been ringing red hot. Knox's Jeep had been spotted everywhere from Marsa Matruh down to Aswan, as had Knox himself. Nessim was longing for a result, if only so that they call off this damned search and get some peace. But the more time that went by, the lower his hopes fell.

'Yes?' he asked.

'It's Abdullah, boss,' said Ratib. 'You know. From Tanta. Says one of his crew has found the Jeep.'

'Where?'

Ratib shook his head. 'Kid won't say until he's got his money. And he wants more. Kid's demanding a thousand. And now Abdullah is too.'

Nessim scowled. The money itself didn't bother him. It was Hassan's, after all. But being held to ransom did. *Yet if this was for real* . . . He checked his money-belt to see how much he had on him. 'Tell him we want proof,' he said. 'Tell him to send photographs. If it is, they can each have seven fifty.'

Ratib shook his head. 'The kid refuses to go back,' he said. 'Reckons Abdullah will have him

283

followed, and then he won't get anything.'

Nessim barked out a laugh. He'd met Abdullah twice himself, and both times he'd instinctively checked his pockets afterwards to make sure he still had his wallet. 'Ask him to describe exactly what he saw.'

Ratib nodded and complied. 'He says it was covered with a green tarpaulin,' he reported back. 'He says he took a peek inside. He says he saw a box of CDs and books.'

Nessim grabbed the mobile from Ratib. 'What books?' he demanded.

'I don't know,' answered the kid. He sounded terrified, way out of his depth. 'They were in foreigner writing.'

A flashback of Knox's hotel room, the archaeology books he'd taken away. 'Did they have pictures?'

'Yes.'

'What kind?'

'Ruins,' said the kid. 'You know. And those people who dig in the desert.'

Nessim clenched his fist. 'You stay exactly where you are,' he told him. 'We're on our way.'

II

'The Rosetta Stone?' frowned Rick, snapping a couple of shots of the painting with his digital camera, before moving on. 'I know what you'd expect me to know. Why?'

'And that is?'

Rick shrugged. 'It's a large chunk of a

monumental stele. Black basalt, something like that.'

'Quartz-bearing rock,' corrected Knox. 'It should actually be sparkling grey with a pink vein. The black comes from too much wax and London dirt.'

'It's inscribed in three languages,' said Rick. 'Hieroglyphics, Demotic and Greek. And it was found in Rosetta by Napoleon's men. In 1799, wasn't it?'

'Yes.'

They reached a second painting, similar to the first. Rick took two shots, the flash blinding in the darkness. 'They realised it might hold the key to deciphering Hieroglyphics, so they hunted for other fragments. Worth their weight in diamonds, as someone put it.' He squinted at Knox. 'Is that what we're after? The lost pieces of the Rosetta Stone?'

'No.'

'They didn't find anything; but then the stone wasn't from Rosetta originally; it was only transported there as building material.' The walls had turned black with char; great scars scored the baked clay. 'One hell of a fire,' Rick muttered, as he photographed.

'You were telling me about the Rosetta Stone,' said Knox.

'Yes. Copies were made. There was a race to decipher it. Jean-François Champollion made the final breakthrough. He announced his results some time in the eighteen twenties.'

'In 1822.' Friday, September the twenty-seventh, to be exact. Considered by many to be

285

the birth date of modern Egyptology.

Rick shrugged. 'That's pretty much it.'

'Not bad,' said Knox. 'But you know what you haven't mentioned yet?'

'What?'

'The inscription itself. What it says.'

Rick laughed ruefully. 'You're right. How about that?'

'You're not alone. This great monument, this iconic image, and hardly anyone knows what it says.'

'So what does it say?'

Knox flashed his torch ahead. The white marble of a portal glowed pale, and either side lay ghostly wolves. 'It's known as the Memphis Decree,' he said, as they pressed forwards. 'Written to commemorate Ptolemy Five's accession in 196 BC. The Golden Age of the Ptolemies had been well and truly over by then, of course, thanks to Ptolemy Four.'

'The party animal,' nodded Rick, crouching to photograph the wolves.

'Exactly. The Seleukid king Antiochus Three thought he was soft and ripe for plucking. He seized Tyre, Ptolemais and much of the Egyptian fleet.'

'Spare me the detail,' said Rick. 'We're on the clock, remember.'

'OK,' said Knox, as they moved on. 'There was a great battle at Raphia. The Egyptians won. Peace was restored to the land. It should have been good news.'

'But?'

'Taxes were already punitive. Ptolemy had to

286

raise them even higher to finance his war and the victory celebrations. Discord spread. People left their farms. There were massive uprisings across Egypt. Ptolemy was assassinated, and his successor, Ptolemy Five Epiphanes, was only a child. A group of rebels attacked military posts and temples in the Nile Delta. Epiphanes' men went after them. They took refuge in a citadel.'

'That's right,' said Rick, snapping his fingers. 'They thought they'd be safe. They were wrong.'

'They were very wrong,' agreed Knox, as they walked down two steps to a second doorway. 'According to the Rosetta Stone, Epiphanes' men stormed it and put them all to the sword.'

'Charming.'

'You know where it all happened? A place called Lycopolis, in the Busirite nome.'

'The Busirite nome? Wasn't that pretty much where we are now?'

'Exactly,' nodded Knox as they reached the portal. 'Welcome to the citadel of ancient Lycopolis.'

Rick went through first, his torch held out ahead. 'Oh, Jesus!' he muttered, when he saw what was inside. And he turned and looked away, as though about to be sick.

III

'Come,' smiled Aly Sayed. 'This is no evening to waste in a library.'

Gaille and Elena followed him to his outside table. A breeze had turned the evening cool.

Birds chattered distantly. Gaille listened as Elena and Aly chatted amicably, exploring connections, mutual friends, obscure sites they'd both visited.

After a while, he turned to Gaille. 'Your poor father,' he said. 'I think about him often. My esteemed secretary general did not greatly respect him, as you may know. For myself, I work only with people I respect. No man loved this country more.'

'Thank you.'

He smiled and turned back to Elena. 'Now tell me what it is you do in Siwa. Yusuf hinted mysteriously that you'd found something interesting in Alexandria.'

'You could say that.'

'And it has implications for Siwa?'

'Yes.' Elena took a set of Gaille's photographs from her bag. 'Forgive me, but Yusuf insisted I make you promise not to say a word.'

'Of course,' nodded Aly. 'My lips are sealed.'

'Thank you.' She passed them to him, explained how they'd been found, what they meant, then read out a translation of the Alexander Cipher.

'A tomb fit for Alexander,' murmured Aly as he leafed through the pictures. 'And you hope to find it in two weeks?'

'We hope to make progress in two weeks,' said Elena. 'Enough to be granted another two.'

'How?'

'The text gives several clues.' She ticked them off on her fingers. 'It states the tomb was in sight of the Oracle of Ammon; that it was within a hill; that its mouth was beneath the sand; that it was excavated in secret. Tomorrow morning, with your permission, we'll compile a list of all hills in sight of the Oracle. Then we'll visit them.'

He raised his eyebrows. 'Do you know how many sites that will be?'

'We can eliminate a few. This place was built in secret; that cuts out anything near ancient settlements or trading routes. And quarrying is thirsty work. They'd have needed fresh water.'

'This is the oasis of a thousand springs.'

'Yes. But many are salt, and most of the fresh water ones are settled.'

'They could have dug their own well.'

'And we'll search for it,' agreed Elena. 'We've a list of features to look for. For example, as you well know, you can tell quarried rock from the grooves left by the tools. Any significant quantities of such rock will be interesting. Digging in the desert is brutal. The sand's so fine and dry, it runs like liquid. Macedonian soldiers were experienced engineers. Maybe they used a cofferdam. Your aerial photos might help us find its outlines. I'm also having some remote sensing equipment shipped in. A caesium magnetometer; a remote-controlled aircraft for more aerial photographs.'

Aly was still flipping through the photographs. Gaille was watching him idly when his expression froze. He caught himself almost immediately, glanced around with attempted nonchalance, then hurried through the other photographs before passing them back. 'Well,' he said. 'I wish you luck.'

Bright lights flickered between the trunks of

289

date-palms. A canvas-covered truck roared up the drive and stopped in a squeal of brakes. Aly rose to his feet.

'Yusuf suggested you would need guides,' he said. 'I took the liberty of contacting Mustafa and Zayn for you. They are the best in all Siwa. They know everything.'

'Thank you,' said Elena. 'That's most helpful.'

'No trouble. We must work together, must we not?' The truck doors opened, two men jumped down. Aly turned to Gaille and said: 'I thought of them the moment Yusuf told me your name.'

Gaille frowned. 'Why?'

'Because they were the guides with your father on that terrible day, of course.' And, just for a moment, all warmth left his expression. He squinted at her with an almost clinical detachment, curious of her reaction. But then he caught himself and his smile was back and he was the perfect host again, crackling with benevolent energy, making everybody welcome.

IV

Knox shone his torch around to see what had made Rick flinch. There were skeletons lying everywhere on the floor, some of them tiny, many still wearing ragged fragments of clothing, along with jewellery and amulets.

'Oh, man,' grimaced Rick. 'What the hell happened?'

'The siege, remember,' said Knox, more calmly than he felt. 'The men would have fought.

The women, children and elderly would have taken refuge. An underground temple would have seemed perfect. Until they got shut in and someone lit a fire between them and their only escape.'

'Christ! What a way to go.'

Knox nodded, to himself as much as Rick, forcibly reminded of an incident from Alexander the Great's conquests. Samaria had risen in revolt, killing its Macedonian governor. In punishment, Alexander had destroyed the city, executing every rebel he could lay his hands on, then hunting two hundred others to a desert cave. Instead of going in after them, he'd built a fire in the mouth and asphyxiated them all. Their remains had recently been discovered, along with seals and legal documents, considered the oldest cache of Dead Sea Scrolls ever found. Knox had never paid much attention to the incident, an almost inconsequential sidebar of Alexander's campaigns. But suddenly he felt an empathetic sadness for all those people who'd got in the way of Alexander's glory juggernaut.

Rick tapped his arm. 'No time for daydreaming, mate. We're down to ten minutes.'

Knox tore his gaze from the huddled corpses to look around the rest of the space. It was effectively a subterranean Greek temple, Ionic columns embedded in the exterior walls and in front of the pronaos. A wooden walkway had been set up on concrete blocks to enable excavators to move around quickly and without causing damage. Knox went into the pronaos, its walls carved with pastoral scenes, ivy, fruit and animals, then into the naos, dominated by a white marble statue of Alexander on a rearing horse.

'Look!' said Rick, pointing to the far corner. 'Steps.'

They led down into a crypt, a sarcophagus against the far wall, Greek writing upon its side. ''Kelonymus',' read Knox. ''Holder of the secret, founder of the faith.''

'Kelonymus?' frowned Rick. 'That's your friend from the papyri, right?'

'And from Alexandria,' agreed Knox. There were stone vats around the walls, filled with limestone and earthenware ostraca. Knox picked one out, squinted at the faded writing. 'A petition to the gods,' he said.

'So this is a temple? A temple to Kelonymus?'

Knox shook his head. 'To Alexander. It's his cult-statue upstairs. But Kelonymus must have been the founder or chief priest or something.' He crouched down. 'So what have we got?' he asked rhetorically. 'An old man in Mallawi writes about his childhood in Lycopolis. He reveres Alexander, Akylos and Kelonymus. He despises the Ptolemies, dismissing them as liars and frauds. And why were Epiphanes' men so ruthless when they stormed the citadel? Everyone slaughtered or taken for execution.' He glanced at Rick. 'Doesn't that smack of more than an ordinary uprising? I mean, the southern rebels were granted amnesties. So why did these people all have to be killed?'

'They knew something,' suggested Rick. 'They needed to be shut up.'

'The holder of the secret,' nodded Knox. 'Must have been one hell of a secret.'

'Any ideas?'

Knox frowned at the glimmer of a possible answer. 'The Ptolemies were never really taken to Egyptian hearts,' he said. 'They were only tolerated because of their direct succession from Alexander. That's why they tried so hard to associate themselves with him. They spread rumours that Ptolemy One had been Alexander's brother, you know, and built a mausoleum for him and themselves to lie in together. Imagine what would have happened if the legitimacy of that succession came into question.'

'I'll imagine it later, if you don't mind,' said Rick, tapping his watch. 'We need to scoot.'

Knox nodded. They hurried up the steps then back along the walkways and the corridor to the wooden ladder. Rick climbed it first, going for haste rather than quiet, Knox struggling to keep up.

'OK,' murmured Rick, when they'd reached the top. 'Let's do it.' He opened the steel door, ushered Knox out, padlocked it behind them. Away to their left, a flutter of torchlight, the growl of a dog. 'Perfect timing,' grinned Rick.

But then the second guard stepped out from behind a tree directly in front of them, doing up his zip. They all looked at each other in shock.

'Run!' cried Rick. 'Run!'

27

I

Knox and Rick fled headlong into the trees, forearms up to protect their faces from slapping branches.

'Stop!' cried the guard. 'Stop or I shoot.' A shot rang out. 'Stop!' he shouted again.

But they kept going, bulling their way through the woods until they reached a tilled field, then running across it in the approximate direction of the Subaru, their feet plunging deep into the moist soil, their boots growing heavy with accreted mud. Behind them, the German shepherd was barking crazily with excitement. A stitch began in Knox's side. He wasn't as fit as Rick, and began to fall behind. He glanced back. They'd gained good distance on the pursuers, but that damned German shepherd had their scent.

'Keep going,' called out Rick from ahead, sensing that Knox was flagging. 'The Subaru's not far.'

They ran on for another minute before he looked around again. The night had grown overcast, but he could just make out the guards silhouetted upon a low ridge. One of them stopped to aim at Knox, snapping off a couple of rounds that cracked past, making him stumble on the heavy soil, his thighs protesting as he pushed himself back up, finding the running really hard labour now, fighting for every breath, his stitch stabbing brutally in his side, Rick getting further and further ahead of him.

The guards must have realised they wouldn't catch him themselves, so they unleashed the German shepherd instead, then stood and yelled it on. It came bounding over the soft earth, panting as it raced up behind him, gnarling and snapping at his leg. He twisted to kick it away, but tripped and fell, and immediately it sprang on top of him, going straight for his throat, saliva drooling as he desperately held it off, those sharp teeth snapping just an inch from his face. The two guards were closing, wheezing heavily after their long chase. Knox thought he was done for, but then he heard the roar of an engine, and headlights flashed on, and the Subaru raced up beside him. Rick jumped out and charged screaming at the bewildered dog, which leaped off Knox and cowered away for just long enough for both men to scramble back into the car. The dog regained its nerve quickly, however, jumping up at Knox's door, barking furiously. The guards were almost upon them. Rick thrust the Subaru into reverse, stamped his foot down. They accelerated backwards, turning in a crescent out onto the field, then into first and up through the gears. Gunfire cracked. Knox's side window shattered and the windscreen turned opaque. Rick punched out a viewing hole as he raced back to the track, then towards the Tanta road. Knox looked around, but their pursuers were finally lost in the darkness. Private security guards firing off guns would scarcely be keen to contact the authorities, but maybe they had colleagues who'd come out looking for the Subaru.

'We'd better go for the Jeep,' panted Knox.

'You think that's wise? Shouldn't we just lie low for a bit?'

Knox shook his head. 'Kelonymus was constantly referred to as the holder of the secret. I want to know what that secret is. Five will get you fifty that the answer's in that damned inscription from the lower chamber in Alexandria. The one in Demotic.'

'But I thought you didn't know Demotic.'

'I don't,' admitted Knox. 'Which is why we need to go see a friend.'

'Ah! And where's he, then?'

'Ever been to Farafra?'

'Farafra!' protested Rick. 'But that's halfway across Egypt.'

'Then we've no time to lose, have we?'

II

Kareem's eyes bulged when Nessim unzipped his money-belt and drew out a brick of fifty-dollar bills. He'd never seen so much cash. He'd never even imagined it possible. He watched, entranced, as Nessim counted out fifteen notes for Abdullah, then another fifteen that he held tantalisingly out to Kareem.

'Take us to the Jeep,' he said.

Kareem climbed in the back of the Freelander,

296

its rear window smashed and patched with plastic sheeting. It had started raining, making it harder for Kareem to give coherent directions in the unfamiliar landscape. He'd never felt so scared in his life, nor so excited. He was terrified that he'd somehow made a gigantic mistake, or that the Jeep's owner might have returned for it in the past hour. And it wasn't just the reward Kareem stood to lose, he knew. One look was all it took to know that Nessim and his men would want someone to vent their frustrations on.

They reached the track and drove up it to the yard. They parked and trudged through the mud to the outbuilding's steel door, then swung it open on its hinges. For a moment, Kareem saw nothing inside and his heart bolted crazily, but then the Jeep came into view, and he swallowed convulsively with relief.

One of the men lifted up the tarpaulin to check the licence plate. 'It's his, all right,' he announced.

'Good.' Nessim unzipped his belt again, counted out Kareem's cash. 'Now get out of here,' he admonished him. 'And don't come back.'

Kareem nodded vigorously. He clutched the banknotes tight as he splashed off back down the track, the devil on his heels. He glanced around once to see Nessim passing out torches and handguns, then again to see him deploying the Freelander and his men for an ambush. Someone was clearly in mortal danger, but Kareem didn't care. He felt exultant, his life finally about to begin.

III

It had started to rain. Flurries swept through the broken windows and punctured windscreen as Knox and Rick approached Tanta.

'You want to wait it out?' asked Knox.

'Nah,' replied Rick, squinting ahead. 'Shouldn't last long.' He evidently knew his weather, for the squall passed quickly. They turned the heaters on full blast, deliciously warm against their sodden trousers. They cut south of Tanta, turned off the main road.

'Where the hell is this place?' muttered Rick, as they searched for the derelict farm.

'Just ahead,' said Knox, with more confidence than he felt. A young man loomed unexpectedly out the darkness ahead, staring at them with wide mouth and eyes. It was so dark beneath the overcast sky that they drove past the track, had to reverse a little way to turn up it. Rainwater had filled the potholes; they kept lurching violently into them, their suspension creaking, headlights dancing on the trees and byres. Rick hunched forwards over the wheel, peering intently ahead, crawling along.

Knox glanced at his friend. 'What is it, mate?' he asked.

'That kid we passed,' muttered Rick. 'He gave me a bad feeling.'

'Want to turn back?'

He shook his head. 'We won't get ten miles with the windscreen like this; not once we get on the main roads.'

'Take it slow, then.'

'The fuck do you think I'm doing?'

Nerves taut, eyes skinned, they lumbered on down the track to the yard. Rainwater had gathered in shallow puddles on the concrete, their beams reflecting brightly. There was a muddy patch ahead. They both saw the fresh footprints in it together. 'Shit!' swore Rick. He stamped on the accelerator and roared into a violent U-turn, tyres screeching, flinging Knox hard against his door.

Nessim's white Freelander surged out from the trees, headlights springing on full beam, dazzling them both. Rick tried to swerve around it, but he lost traction in the wet and slithered head-on into it instead, bonnets crumpling, glass shattering, airbags deploying, pinning them in their seats. It took Knox a moment to gather himself; a moment he didn't have. His door was hauled open, a cosh crashed into his temple, stunning him. He was hauled out by his collar, dragged roughly along the concrete, too dazed to resist, his ears ringing like a bell tower, until he was inside the outbuilding, and Rick too, the steel door closing like a trap behind them both. Nessim kicked him onto his back, and stood astride him, aiming down at his chest.

'Who's your friend?' he asked, pointing his torch at Rick, groaning and rubbing his forehead, mussing a trickle of blood into his hair. He tried to push himself up onto his knees, but promptly collapsed again, vomiting hard, making the Egyptians laugh.

'Not friend,' mumbled Knox, still hopelessly

disoriented. 'Driver. Knows nothing about this. Let him go.'

'Sure,' snorted Nessim.

'I swear,' said Knox. 'He knows nothing.'

'Then it's his unlucky day, isn't it?'

Knox pushed himself up onto an elbow, his scattered senses beginning to return. 'Good money, is it,' he asked, 'working for al-Assyuti?'

Spots of red flared momentarily on Nessim's cheeks. 'You know nothing about my life,' he said.

'And you know enough about mine to end it, do you?'

'You brought this on yourself,' spat Nessim. 'You must have known what would happen.'

Rick pushed himself up, successfully this time. 'What's going on?' he slurred. 'Who are these people?'

'Don't worry about it,' said Knox.

'They've got guns,' said Rick, sounding fearful and bewildered. 'Why have they got guns?'

Knox frowned at his friend. Somehow his tone didn't ring quite true. Maybe it was simply concussion, but maybe he was trying to lull Nessim and these others into taking him lightly. They'd have no idea of his background, after all. If that was so, then it was down to Knox to buy him some time to go to work. Time and perhaps darkness. The only light in this place was from the various torches, after all, and if he could get them all pointed at him . . .

He glared up at Nessim. 'I overheard you tell that girl in Sharm you used to be a paratrooper,' he said. 'You fucking liar.'

'It wasn't a lie.'

'Paratroops have honour,' sneered Knox. 'Men of honour don't sell themselves to rapists and murderers.'

Nessim slapped Knox hard across the cheek with the barrel of his gun, sending him sprawling. 'Men of honour don't refuse duties just because they dislike them,' he said tightly.

'Honour!' snorted Knox, pushing himself back up onto his knees. 'You don't know what the word means. You're just a whore, selling yourself for — '

Nessim slapped Knox even harder this time, so that he collapsed dazed to the floor, his cheek scraping like stubble on the rough concrete. And it was lying there, in a daze, that he watched Rick blur into action. A single punch sent the first man sprawling. An elbow doubled up the second, Rick wresting his gun from him as he went down, shooting the third through his thigh before turning the gun on Nessim, still standing frozen over Knox.

'Drop it!' yelled Rick. 'Fucking drop it!' Nessim's gun and torch both clattered to the concrete. 'On your knees,' he shouted. 'All of you. On your fucking knees. Now!'

The Egyptians complied, even the wounded man, whimpering piteously with shock, his cream trousers staining red.

'Hands behind your fucking heads!' roared Rick, enraged partly by their treatment of Knox, but more by having been made to fear that he was going to die. The Egyptians must have read their fate in his expression. The colour drained

301

from their faces. Nessim alone showed defiance, bracing himself as Rick aimed down at the bridge of his nose.

Knox remembered the shame on his cheeks earlier, how he'd bridled at the accusation of lacking honour. 'No,' he said, grabbing Rick's arm just before he could pull the trigger. 'We're not like that.'

'You may not fucking be,' retorted Rick, trying to shake him off. 'I am.'

'Please, mate,' said Knox.

'And what the fuck do you suggest we do?' yelled Rick. 'Let them go, they'll come straight after us. This is self-fucking-defence, mate. Nothing more.'

Knox looked again at Nessim. His expression gave nothing away, yet Knox was certain Rick was wrong. Let him go, his personal code wouldn't allow him to come after them. But as for the others . . . He stooped to pick up Nessim's handgun, looked around for inspiration. The outbuilding was small, windowless and built of concrete blocks. Its door was solid steel with strong hinges. He grabbed the tarpaulin from the Jeep, threw it on the floor in front of Nessim, then aimed down at his chest. 'Take off your clothes,' he ordered.

'No,' scowled Nessim.

'Do it,' said Knox. 'If not for yourself, then for your men.'

Nessim's jaw tightened, but he looked around at his men, and seemed to puncture a little. He began reluctantly to unbutton his shirt, motioning his men to do likewise, throwing their discarded clothes into the tarpaulin. When they were down to their underpants, Knox checked to make sure they had nothing concealed, then made a bundle of the tarpaulin and tossed it in the back of the Jeep.

'Can you handle them on your own?' he asked.

Rick snorted. 'Weren't you watching?'

Knox drove the Jeep over to the Subaru and Freelander. The Subaru was dead, but the Freelander came on at the third try, its engine clattering with terminal damage. He wrested it into reverse, bunny-hopped over to the outbuilding. Rick came out backwards, swinging the steel door closed with his foot, allowing Knox to drive tight up alongside it and put on the handbrake. Not perfect, maybe, but it should hold them for a few hours, by which time Knox and Rick would be halfway across Egypt.

They hurried to the Jeep. Rick took the wheel, roaring off unnecessarily fast, as if to burn off his residual anger, not once looking Knox's way. As for Knox, he stared out the windscreen, badly shaken by the revelation that his friend had been prepared to execute those men. The silence grew distinctly uncomfortable, so that Knox began to fear that things between them might never be quite the same.

It was Rick who finally spoke. 'I thought you said those guys were serious,' he muttered.

'What can I tell you, mate?' grinned Knox. 'I thought they were.'

28

Gaille and Elena took Aly at his word, arriving at his house at seven sharp to find him already at work outside, his papers pinned down with a pot of Siwan tea and some cups, as though he'd been expecting them. He greeted them warmly, then showed them into his library and left them to it.

Elena started with the aerial photographs; Gaille with the books. When she pulled down her first volume, it came more easily than the night before, as though the bookshelf was less tightly packed. She looked more closely. Yes. She distinctly remembered a red leather-bound volume that had left stains upon her fingers. She pulled out a modern academic text, checked the bibliography against his shelves. Two standard titles on Siwa were missing. Yet this was supposed to be a definitive collection. Then she remembered that strange look upon his face the night before when he'd been looking through her photographs.

'Elena,' she murmured hesitantly.

Elena looked up crossly. 'Yes?'

'Nothing,' said Gaille. 'Sorry.'

Knowing Elena, she'd go straight out to confront Aly, and bang would go their co-operation. Instead she made a note of the missing titles. She'd call Ibrahim at her first opportunity and ask him to send copies directly to her hotel.

II

Knox was fast asleep in the passenger seat of the Jeep when Rick shook him awake.

'What?' he asked blearily.

'Checkpoint,' muttered Rick.

'Damn it,' said Knox. Checkpoints were so rare in Alexandria and the Delta, he'd stopped worrying about them. But in Middle and Southern Egypt, and in the desert regions, they became commonplace. They drifted to a halt. Two weary-looking soldiers wearing thick uniforms against the morning chill trudged across. One of them rapped the Jeep's window.

'Passports,' he said in English, when Rick lowered it, evidently figuring them both for foreigners. Knox still had Augustin's papers for Omar Malik, but to use them now would only raise suspicions. He fetched out his British passport, handed it across. The soldier yawned as he took it and Rick's to his cabin to check.

The second soldier, meanwhile, remained standing beside the Jeep. He lit himself a cigarette, stamped his feet, then glanced in the rear window. Too late, Knox remembered the tarpaulin bundle containing the clothes and other belongings of Nessim and his men, including their handguns. The soldier opened the back door and leaned

305

inside. 'What's this?' he asked, putting his hand on the bundle.

'Just some clothes,' said Knox, trying his best to sound relaxed.

The soldier pulled back the flaps to rummage inside. He pulled out a jacket, held it up against himself to check his reflection in the glass, before throwing it back and taking a couple of shirts instead, then a pair of trousers, checking through its pockets, pulling out an expensive mobile phone and grinning ingratiatingly at Knox, as if to suggest a gift wouldn't go astray. Knox's mouth was dry. If this prick found any of the guns, they'd have one hell of a lot of explaining to do.

He said: 'Excuse me, but those are our belongings.'

The soldier grunted irritably and threw the trousers and the phone back into the tarpaulin, then slammed the door closed unnecessarily hard. His comrade inside the cabin had finished his call and was coming back out. Knox's heart was banging violently in apprehension, but the soldier handed back the passports without a flicker, waved him and Rick through. They kept the smiles off their faces until they were well away.

'What do you know?' said Rick. 'Maybe Hassan's given up on you.'

'I doubt it, mate,' said Knox. 'I reckon he just doesn't want the authorities knowing he's on the hunt.'

'That's something, at least.'

'Yeah,' agreed Knox. 'It is.' He glanced around

at the bundle in the back. 'But I reckon we should dump this shit before it gets us into grief. What do you say?'

'I reckon you're right,' nodded Rick.

III

Nicolas arrived at Ibrahim's office with delicate business to discuss. His father had charged him with acquiring certain artefacts from the Macedonian tomb for his private collection: at least one golden burial casket, plus a selection of weapons. It was perfectly possible, especially now that Yusuf had taken personal control. It was just a matter of creating convincing replicas and arranging a switch. But Ibrahim was still involved in the excavation, and would need to be dealt with, not least because Yusuf insisted on having a plausible scapegoat in place should their switch be discovered.

'I'm not disturbing you, am I?' he asked.

'Nothing that can't wait,' smiled Ibrahim. 'Just sending some books on Siwa to Gaille. Though I can't believe Dr Sayed doesn't have copies.'

Nicolas settled himself at the corner table. 'I'm sure you must be aware how pleased we are at the Dragoumis Group at the outcome of our partnership,' he began.

'We're pleased too.'

Nicolas nodded and drew a thick envelope from his jacket pocket. 'My family makes it a policy to reward success.' He set the envelope down upon the table midway between them, smiled at Ibrahim to indicate that he should take it.

Ibrahim frowned at the wad of banknotes inside. 'For me?' he asked.

'As a token of our appreciation and gratitude.'

Ibrahim squinted suspiciously. 'And what would you want for this money?'

'Nothing. Just a continuation of our partnership.' Nicolas was, in fact, wearing a miniature camera on his chest, its lens disguised as his second-top button. Everyone in the SCA accepted bribes, but that didn't make it licit. If Ibrahim took this *baksheesh* like a good little boy, the film would be used to coerce him, step by step, until he was completely compromised. If he didn't, Nicolas had many other avenues to explore and exploit.

Ibrahim hesitated, then pushed the envelope back across the table. 'If you wish to contribute further to our partnership,' he said, 'we have a bank account set up for the purpose, as I'm sure you already know.'

Nicolas smiled tightly and took back the money. 'Whatever you think best.'

'Is there anything else? Or may I return to — '

There was noise outside. The door burst open and Mohammed rushed in.

'I'm sorry, sir,' said Maha, gamely hanging on to his arm. 'I couldn't stop him.'

'It's all right, Maha,' said Ibrahim. He frowned at Mohammed. 'What do you mean by this?'

'It's Layla,' said Mohammed, tears streaming down his face. 'They've said no. They've said no. They won't give her treatment.'

'My dear friend,' winced Ibrahim, standing awkwardly. 'I'm so sorry.'

'She doesn't need sympathy. She needs *help*.'

'I'm sorry. I don't see what more I can do.'

'Please. I've asked everyone else. You're her last hope.'

Nicolas stood and backed away. Talk of disease was always uncomfortable to him. The books Ibrahim had collected for Gaille were perched on the corner of his desk. He picked one up, flipped idly through the pages.

'I suppose I can ask around,' Ibrahim was saying. 'But I don't know anyone at the hospital.'

'I beg you. You must do something.'

The book was filled with black-and-white sketches. Nicolas turned to one of a hill, and a lake called Bir al-Hammam. There was something strangely familiar about it. He put the book down and picked up another. It too had a picture of Bir al-Hammam, a photograph this time. He stared at it and stared at it and finally he realised why the images were familiar, and a great orgasmic shudder ran through him.

'Nicolas? Nicolas?' asked Ibrahim anxiously. 'Are you all right?'

Nicolas shook himself back to his senses. Ibrahim was looking strangely at him. He smiled and said: 'Forgive me. Miles away, that's all.' He looked around to see that Mohammed had gone. 'Where's your friend?' he asked.

'He had to leave,' said Ibrahim. 'His wife's in a dreadful state, apparently. I promised to do what I could. But what *can* I do? That poor girl!'

Nicolas frowned thoughtfully. 'If I could help

309

her, you'd be grateful, yes?'

'Of course,' said Ibrahim. 'But I really — '

'Good,' said Nicolas, tucking Gaille's books under his arm. 'Then come with me. Let's see what we can arrange.'

29

I

The Oracle of Ammon proved to be a hump of rock some four kilometres out of Siwa Town. Despite its one-time fame, there was no car park, no concessions stand, no entry charge. When Gaille, Elena and their guides arrived early the next morning, they were alone except for a wizened old man sitting against a wall opposite its base holding out a trembling hand in hope of alms. Gaille reached for her purse.

'You'll only encourage them,' warned Elena. Gaille hesitated, then gave him a banknote anyway. He smiled gratefully.

Two young girls with plaited waist-length black hair came forward offering forearms draped with home-made bracelets. Zayn scowled at them and they ran away giggling.

Gaille had been a little uncertain at first of Mustafa and Zayn. But she quickly warmed to them. Their knowledge of Siwa was impressive. And there was something touching about their friendship: an ancient tradition of homosexual marriage was dying hard in Siwa; local song and poetry still celebrated such relationships. She couldn't help but wonder.

Mustafa was large, with bark-rough skin darkened by sun as much as nature, to judge from the paler bands around his neck and beneath his watch-strap. He was absurdly fit and nimble, despite smoking incessantly. He had a special relationship with his ancient and temperamental truck. No gauges or dials worked any more, and every frill was long gone, from the ball of the gear-stick to the rubber of the pedals and the carpet beneath.

Zayn was a whip of a man, no more than forty, though his hair and beard were streaked with silver. While Mustafa drove, Zayn oiled and polished almost obsessively a thin bladed, ivory-handled knife that he kept folded beneath his robes. Each time he put it away, the slick and spotless blade would scrape against the sheath so that instantly it needed cleaning again, and he'd draw it back out and examine it and mutter Siwan obscenities.

A steep curl of steps led beneath a lintel up into the main body of the Oracle, a skeleton of walls like a wooden ship that had rotted in estuary mud and later dried out. Gaille felt a moment's quiet awe as she stood there. There weren't many places in the world where you could be certain that Alexander himself had once occupied that exact space. This was one of them. The Oracle had been esteemed throughout the Mediterranean during Alexander's time; a rival to Delphi, perhaps even its superior. Legend had it that Heracles had visited, and Alexander had claimed Heracles as his direct ancestor. Perseus was reputed to have made the trek too, and Perseus had been associated with the Persian Empire, which Alexander now claimed for his own. Cimon, an Athenian general, had famously

312

sent a deputation to Siwa to ask whether his siege of Cyprus would succeed. The Oracle had refused to answer, except to say that the person who'd asked the question was already with him. And when his emissaries had returned to the fleet, they'd learned that Cimon had died on that exact day. Pindar had written a hymn of praise to the Oracle; and upon asking it for the greatest luck available to humans, had promptly died. But perhaps the incident that had the greatest impact was the invasion of Egypt by the Persian King Cambyses. He'd sent out three armies: one to Ethiopia, the second to Carthage and the third across the desert to Siwa. This third army had vanished without trace, and the Oracle had gained a certain awed respect as a result.

'Is this where the priests came down?' asked Gaille.

'The chief priest greeted Alexander as o pai dios,' nodded Elena. 'Son of God. Did you know that Plutarch suggested he'd said o pai dion instead? Hah! It would have taken a priest with balls of tungsten to address Alexander as 'my boy'.'

'Unless he was speaking on behalf of Zeus himself.'

'Yes. I suppose.'

'How did the Oracle work?'

'The priests carried the physical manifestation of Zeus-Ammon in a golden boat decorated with precious stones, while young virgins chanted,' said Elena. 'The chief priest read out the questions of supplicants, and Ammon answered them by dancing forwards or backwards.

Unfortunately, Alexander was granted a private audience, so we don't know for sure what he asked or was told.'

'I thought he asked about his father's murderers.'

'That's one tradition,' acknowledged Elena. 'The story goes that he asked whether all his father's murderers had been dealt with, and that the Oracle replied that the question was meaningless, because his father was divine and therefore couldn't be murdered; but all the murderers of Philip the Second had been appropriately dealt with, if that was what was meant. Probably apocryphal, of course. All we know for sure is that Ammon became Alexander's favourite god, that he sent emissaries here when Hephaiston died, and that he asked to be buried here, too.' She picked up a pinch of soil, examined it momentarily, threw it away.

'It must have been a terrible blow to the Oracle's priests,' said Gaille. 'Thinking they were going to get Alexander's body. Then learning it was going to Alexandria.'

Elena nodded. 'Ptolemy soothed their pain. According to Pausanias, he sent them a stele of apology and handsome gifts.'

Gaille climbed as high as she could safely go, then gazed all around. The landscape here wasn't like Europe, where the hills and mountains had been thrust upwards by geological pressure and time. This entire region had once been a sandstone plain high above, but most of it had collapsed. The hills that remained were simply the last men standing. She oriented herself

314

north, Al-Dakrur to her right, the great salt lake and Siwa Town to her left. Ahead, the air was so clear she could see dark ridge lines through her field glasses, many kilometres away. The sand in between was punctured by thrusts of nicotine-brown rock, some no bigger than small cars, others like tower blocks.

'Where will we start?' she wailed.

'All great tasks are just a large number of small tasks,' observed Elena primly. She spread a chart out on flat ground, rested a stone on each corner. Then she set up a tripod, screwed in a camera and telephoto lens, and began a rigorous study, taking a line from the Siwan Hill of the Dead, sweeping her camera to the horizon, then back again, before adjusting it a hair's-breadth to her right. Each time she found a new rock or hill, she photographed it, then invited Mustafa and Zayn to study it through the lens. They squabbled for a while before agreeing a name and marking the chart. Each mark would mean a visit and a survey.

Gaille sat on a hump of rock and stared out over the desert, the breeze buffeting her back, whipping strands of hair forwards into her eyes. And she realised, almost to her surprise, that she was happy.

II

Nicolas asked Ibrahim to drive him to his villa. He needed somewhere private for his base of operations, and his hotel wouldn't do.

'You couldn't excuse me for a few minutes?' he asked, when they arrived. 'I have some . . . *sensitive* phone calls to make.'

'Of course.'

As ever, he rang his father first. He was in a meeting. Nicolas had him called out. 'Well?' asked Dragoumis.

'I've found it.'

'You're sure?'

'I'm sure I've found the place. Whether there's anything inside . . . ' He explained what had happened, how he'd seen the pictures in the books Gaille had asked Ibrahim to send.

'I told you she'd be the one,' said Dragoumis.

'Yes, Father, you did.'

'Well? What's our plan?'

Nicolas told his father how far he'd got. They discussed and refined his ideas, decided on the team, the equipment they'd need, the weapons and logistical supplies. 'I'll take operational charge, of course,' said Nicolas.

'No,' said Dragoumis. 'I will.'

'Are you sure?' asked Nicolas anxiously. 'You know we can't guarantee your safety away from — '

'You think I'd miss this?' asked Dragoumis. 'I've striven my whole life for this.'

'As you wish.'

'And good work, Nicolas. This is well done. This is very well done.'

'Thank you.' Nicolas had to wipe his eyes. It wasn't often that his father congratulated him, but that only made it all the more special when he did. He ended the call and sat there in a glow.

316

Then he shook his head sternly to refocus himself. This was no time to wallow. Nothing had been achieved yet, and it wouldn't be unless he got busy. He rang Gabbar Mounim in Cairo next.

'Yes?' asked Mounim. 'I trust everything is to your satisfaction.'

'As always,' agreed Nicolas. 'But there's something else I'd like you to do for me. Two things actually.'

'A pleasure.'

'Our mutual friend. I'd like him to summon his colleague Dr Aly Sayed of Siwa Oasis to an emergency meeting.' Nicolas couldn't help but suspect that Dr Sayed had deliberately hidden the books from Gaille, suggesting that he must have made the connection too, which meant they needed him out of Siwa while they went to work.

'How much of an emergency, exactly?'

'Tomorrow, if possible.'

Mounim sucked in breath. 'It won't be easy, but I'll see what I can do. And the other?'

'I don't suppose you have influence at Alexandria's Medical Research Institute, do you?'

III

Elena was driving back into town when Nicolas called on her mobile. 'We need to meet,' he said. 'How soon can you get to Alexandria?'

'For crying out loud, Nicolas, I've only just arrived here.'

'This can't wait, Elena. Something's happened. My father wants to discuss it with you.'

'Your father? He's coming to Alexandria?'

'Yes.'

Elena breathed deep. Philip Dragoumis didn't leave Northern Greece on a whim. If he was coming here, it had to mean something truly significant.

'Fine,' she said. 'Where?'

'Ibrahim's villa.'

'When?'

'Tomorrow morning. Nine o'clock.'

'I'll be there.' She snapped closed her phone, already making plans. Leave now, she could be there in time for a night with Augustin.

'I'm needed back in Alexandria,' she told Gaille.

'Alexandria?' frowned Gaille. 'Will you . . . be gone long?'

'How am I supposed to know that?'

'You want me and the guys to start looking?'

Elena frowned. Gaille had a distressing habit of finding things without her help. 'No,' she said. 'Do nothing until I come back.'

'As you wish.'

IV

'You mean to tell me that Knox escaped you again?' asked Hassan incredulously, when Nessim had completed his report.

'He had a friend with him,' said Nessim.

'A friend?'

318

'We'll find them,' said Nessim, striving to sound more bullish than he felt.

His confidence had been utterly shot by what had happened. Having the tables turned so completely would do that to a man, as would a night spent struggling to escape from an outbuilding, or wandering half-naked across farmland with a wounded comrade. But, to Nessim's surprise, the thing that had struck him deepest about the entire fiasco were Knox's words about his lack of honour. Nessim was old enough and wise enough to know that insults didn't hurt unless they rang true, and so now he couldn't stop asking painful questions of himself: *How had it come to this? What was he doing working for a man like Hassan? Was money really that important to him?*

'We'll watch all his friends and associates,' he said. 'We'll put out another reward. It's just a matter of time before we find him again.'

'So you keep telling me,' said Hassan.

'I'm sorry,' said Nessim. 'He's better at this than we imagined possible. But now we know. Now we're prepared. Next time we'll have him.'

'Next time? How can I be sure there'll be a next time?'

'Another week. That's all I ask.'

'Can you give me one good reason why I shouldn't fire you and hire him instead?'

'You'd have to find him first,' muttered Nessim beneath his breath.

'What did you say?'

'Nothing.'

There was a stony silence. Then: 'I think it's

time we discussed this face to face, don't you?'

'Face to face?' asked Nessim bleakly.

'Yes,' said Hassan. 'Face to face.'

V

Mohammed was astonished to see Professor Rafai step out of the taxi and slam its door closed behind him. He'd not expected to see Layla's oncologist again; certainly not on his building site.

'There is somewhere private?' demanded Rafai, trembling with anger.

'Private?'

'To talk.'

Mohammed frowned in bewilderment. 'Now?'

'Of course now! You think I'm here to book an appointment?' Mohammed shrugged, led Rafai to his cabin office. 'I don't know how you do this,' shouted Rafai, as the door closed. He removed his half-moon glasses, jabbed them like a scalpel at Mohammed's face. 'Who do you think you are? I base my decisions on clinical evidence. *Clinical evidence!* You think you can bully me into changing my mind?'

'I'm sorry for my behaviour in your office,' frowned Mohammed, 'but I've already apologised. I was under immense strain. I don't know what else — '

'You think this is about that?' cried Rafai. 'This isn't about that.'

'Then what?'

'Only your daughter!' yelled Rafai. 'Only ever your daughter! You think she's the only one sick. A young boy called Saad Gama waits for bone marrow. A true scholar of Islam. You want to explain to him that we must postpone his treatment because you have more influential friends? You want to tell his parents he must die so that your daughter might live? You think they don't care for him?'

'Professor Rafai, in the name of Allah, what are you talking about?'

'Don't deny it! Don't insult me by denying it! I know you've done this, though how you have the power . . . Well, let me tell you: Saad's blood is on your hands! Your hands, not mine.'

Mohammed went cold. He asked dizzily: 'What are you saying? Are you saying you'll give Layla her transplant?'

Rafai glared furiously. 'I'm saying I won't risk my department over this.'

'But her transplant?' insisted Mohammed. 'Layla will receive her transplant?'

'Tell your friends in Cairo to stay away from me and my staff. If the procedure goes wrong, we'll not be held accountable, you hear? Tell your people that. Tell your people.' He stormed out of the office.

Mohammed's hands were shaking like palsy so that he couldn't even hold his phone steady when he tried to dial Nur.

VI

Nicolas was on the phone with his bodyguard, Bastiaan, when Ibrahim knocked and entered, bringing with him a cup of coffee and a plate of cakes, which he set down on the corner of his desk. Nicolas didn't bother to stop talking, but he slipped into euphemism and turned his back.

'You've arranged for the purchases?'

'Vasileios is flying in with your father. He's been briefed on what we need.'

'And when will you be at the villa?'

'I'm on my way now. Shouldn't be more than fifteen minutes.'

'Good. And make sure — ' Behind him, Ibrahim gave a little gasp. Nicolas turned to see him holding open one of Gaille's books, staring shocked at a picture of Bir al-Hammam. Nicolas closed his eyes in irritation with himself. 'Make it ten minutes,' he told Bastiaan in his coarsest Greek. 'We've got a problem.' He killed the call, plucked the book from Ibrahim's hand. 'There's something I need to tell you,' he said.

'What? But have you seen this picture of — '

'Quickly,' said Nicolas, grabbing Ibrahim's arm and hustling him through to the kitchen.

'What is it?' asked Ibrahim, bemused. 'What's going on?'

Nicolas opened and shut all the drawers until he found what he was looking for. He held it up so that its eight-inch blade glinted.

Ibrahim paled. 'What . . . what are you doing with that?'

Nicolas held the knife out wide in his left hand, so that Ibrahim's eyes followed its glittery menace. Then he punched him with his right, sending him flailing onto his back. He kneeled down and pressed the sharp steel against his throat before he could recover. 'My colleague Bastiaan is on his way,' he said. 'You're going to be nice and quiet until he arrives, aren't you?'

'Yes,' agreed Ibrahim.

VII

Knox had taken over the wheel while Rick caught up on his sleep. It was mid-afternoon when he reached Farafra and nudged Rick awake.

'We're here, mate.'

'Always the way,' grunted Rick irritably. 'Loveliest bloody dream.'

Knox hadn't been to Ishaq's home in several years, but Qasr al-Farafra was small, and it wasn't hard to find. He was looking forward to seeing his old friend. They went back a long way, to their first season at Mallawi. A small and ridiculously intelligent man, Ishaq had spent most of his leisure time in his hammock staring lazily up at the sky. But give him some Demotic to translate, and there was no one better in Egypt.

Unfortunately, when they parked outside his home, everything was shuttered. They banged on his front door, but there was no response. They went a couple of doors down the road to the Information Centre, which doubled as his office, but there was no one there either.

'He must be out on excavation,' said Knox, checking the time. 'He'll be back soon.'

'Let's have a look at these bloody images, then,' muttered Rick.

'I don't have them.'

'You *what?*'

Knox gave him a look. 'You don't really think I'm daft enough to travel halfway across Egypt with enough incriminating evidence on my laptop to get me ten years?'

'So how the hell's your mate going to translate them?'

'It's on the Internet, mate. Ishaq's wired.'

They sat in the shade of a date-palm to wait. Torpor set in. When flies settled upon them, they lacked even the energy to swat them away.

A young boy in robes pushing an old bicycle ten sizes too big approached tentatively. 'You look for Ishaq?' he asked.

'Yes. Why? Do you know where he is?'

'He leave for Cairo. A meeting. A big meeting. All the desert archaeologists are to be there.'

'Did he say when he'd be back?'

'Tomorrow,' shrugged the boy. 'The day after.'

'Bollocks,' muttered Rick. 'What now?'

'I don't know,' said Knox. 'Let me think.'

'I don't believe this Kelonymus bastard. Everything else was in Greek. Why the hell did he have to switch to Demotic for this bloody inscription?'

Knox's jaw dropped; he turned to look at his friend.

'What?' asked Rick. 'What did I say?'

'I think you've only just gone and cracked it,' said Knox.

30

I

Mohammed was still in a daze from his good fortune when his phone rang.

'Yes?' he asked.

'This is Nicolas Dragoumis. You remember, I helped finance the tests for — '

'Of course I remember, Mr Dragoumis. What can I do for you?'

'I believe you should have heard some good news.'

'That was you? You are my friend in Cairo.'

'Yes.'

'Thank you! Thank you! I am in your debt, Mr Dragoumis. I am forever in your debt. I swear, anything you ever want . . . '

'Anything?' asked Nicolas drily. 'Do you really mean that?'

'On my life.'

'I hope it won't come to that,' said Nicolas. 'But tell me: do you have a mechanical digger on your site?'

II

There'd been little for Gaille to do that afternoon. Although they'd recruited Mustafa and Zayn for the next fortnight, she'd given them the day off, then gone to Aly's house, hoping to do some more research, only to find it locked, and a note upon his door saying he'd been summoned to Cairo. She'd gone back to her hotel and lazed away the afternoon in a hammock, before reviving herself beneath a cold shower and hiring a rickety bicycle that she was now pedalling down to a local freshwater spring. Freewheeling one short stretch, she passed a donkey cart carrying three Siwan wives mummified by their dark blue embroidered cotton *tarfottet*. One lifted her cowl and gave Gaille a shy yet radiant smile. She couldn't have been more than fourteen.

Her bicycle tyres were soft. Pedalling was hard work on the road, its surface sticky from the sun. She was relieved when she saw the spring ahead, a small, deep pool bounded by a stone steen, the water clear down to greyish rocks, floating with clumps of lurid green algae. Several *zaggalah* sat around, their work on the date-palms finished for the day, eyeing her with obvious interest. She'd been looking forward to a swim, but she couldn't face their stares, so she went instead into the orchard to share a cup of bitter Siwan tea with the young custodian.

The sun sank behind the great salt lake and the hills beyond, the horizon blazed orange and purple before the colours faded, and another day was gone. She remembered the young Siwan girl on the donkey cart, married at the onset of puberty to spend the rest of her life hidden from the world, her vision reduced to the narrowest of eye-slits, and Gaille had an epiphany; a vivid understanding of the change wrought in herself by the past few weeks. She knew in that moment that she could never again take refuge from life in the physical and intellectual comfort of the Sorbonne, compiling arcane dictionaries of dead languages. Such work was immensely valuable, but it was a step removed from reality; shadows on the wall. She wasn't an academic. She was an archaeologist, her father's daughter.

It was time to make her peace.

III

Rick and Knox found a hotel with a modem jack where they downloaded the photographs of the lower chamber. But decipherment wasn't Knox's strength, and he made little progress. Meanwhile, Rick looked through the other photographs of the lower chamber.

When he came to the mosaic, he frowned and said: 'Haven't we seen this before?'

'How do you mean?'

He fetched out his own digital camera, scrolled through to the painting of Wepwawet holding the banner of Alexander. Knox saw it at once. The skyline in the mosaic and in the painting were identical. In the mosaic, it silhouetted the two groups of soldiers. In the painting, it contoured Wepwawet and his *shedshed*. It was seeing Alexander's face that gave Knox the inspiration he needed to crack the cipher. When he was done, he scrawled out the text, then translated it for Rick.

'A tomb filled with goods fit for Alexander,' murmured Rick. 'Jesus!'

'No wonder the Dragoumises are after it,' nodded Knox. 'And they've got a head start too. We need to shift.'

'Where?'

'The place of Ammon, Alexander's father. Siwa.'

'Siwa!' laughed Rick. 'I might have bloody guessed.' But he was as excited as Knox by the progress they were making.

They consulted a guidebook from the Jeep. Siwa wasn't that far away, not as the crow flew, but it was across unforgiving desert. To reach it by proper roads meant driving all the way up to Alexandria, then along the coast to Marsa Matruh, and south again. Three sides of a square, perhaps 1,400 kilometres in all. Alternatively, they could take the old caravan route. It saved the best part of 1,000 kilometres, but it meant much more hazardous driving.

'What do you reckon?' asked Rick.

'The desert,' said Knox unhesitatingly. 'At least Nessim and his men won't be able to find us.'

Rick grinned. 'I was hoping you'd say that.'

First task was getting permission. There were army posts dotted across the desert with nothing to do but hassle the few hardy tourists who ventured through. Setting off without proper authorisation was asking for grief. But now that Knox's passport had been cleared at the checkpoint, that was only a matter of *baksheesh* and time.

The local army commander begged a couple of hours to arrange the paperwork. Knox and Rick used it to buy supplies: crates of water and baskets of food, an extra spare tyre, cans of oil and petrol. Then they set off, making the most of the cool of the night while it lasted.

IV

Augustin answered his front door with a stained white sheet wrapped like a sarong around his waist. The way his face fell, Elena knew at once. She felt an exquisite calm as she pushed past him into his bedroom. The girl had spiked blonde hair and a brass ring through her lower lip. She had flat breasts with big nipples, and a shaven pubic mound.

'You his wife then?' she asked, reaching down for a soft-pack of Marlboro Lights and a plastic lighter.

Elena turned. Augustin was about to say something when he saw her expression and thought better of it. She hurried down the stairs, walked briskly to her car. She felt no regret at not warning him of her visit. Between ignorance or knowledge, it was knowledge every time. But she grew angrier with every step. At a traffic light, her mobile started to ring. She recognised Augustin's number. She wound down her window and hurled the phone out, watched it spark and skitter on the stone. Traffic was thick. She clenched her steering wheel and yelled, drawing concerned looks from the pavement.

330

She cut up a truck, burned out onto the Cairo road. She had no destination in mind. She wanted only to push the car until it fell apart.

This was not about Augustin. Augustin was nothing, she realised now, merely a screen onto which she'd projected memories of Pavlos. Pavlos was her man, the only man she'd ever truly loved. For ten years, she'd craved to be with him. For ten years, her life had been shit.

An articulated lorry approached fast on the other side of the dual carriageway. Her hands twitched on the steering wheel, she veered towards it. She hit the central reservation, bounced up into the air, had to wrench around her wheel. The lorry driver shook a fist and blared his horn in warning. Not now. Not yet. She'd lost more than a husband when she'd lost Pavlos. She'd lost honour. Dragoumis was flying in. He'd be away from home soil. He'd be vulnerable. They said you could buy anything in the back streets of Cairo. Cairo was just two hours' drive south of here. It was time to put that old maxim to the test.

Elena had a blood debt to settle.

31

I

It had rained during the night. The roads were slick and black. Thin traffic threw up spray that glinted like diamonds in Mohammed's headlights. Before he even reached the outskirts of Alexandria, stress was twisting his spine like a tourniquet. He drove hunched over his steering wheel, consulting his watch and speedometer. He dared not take the flatbed truck and its load over seventy kilometres per hour, yet he dared not be late either. Nicolas had been adamant he reach Siwa by sunset tonight.

It was years since he'd handled a rig this size and weight, but it came back quickly enough, especially once he was out onto the Marsa Matruh highway, where the road became wide, straight and easy. He took Layla's picture from his wallet and laid it on the dash to remind himself why he was doing this. A police car loomed in his wing mirror. It slowed as it came alongside. Mohammed kept his eyes on the road ahead and at last it sped on. His heart settled.

He touched Layla's photo. If all went well, her intense chemotherapy and radiotherapy conditioning treatment would get underway tomorrow. Her condition was so severe, there was no time to waste. Dr Rafai and his medical team would deliberately and systematically fill her system with poisons. In a fortnight or so, if Allah willed it, they'd harvest marrow from Besheer's pelvis, remove fragments of blood and bone, and inject it into Layla. If that worked, Layla would begin months of tests, treatment, rehabilitation. It would be a year at least before they'd know for sure. Until then, he had no choice but to do what Nicolas wanted; because Nicolas had made it quite clear to him that what had been given could just as easily be taken away.

Mohammed had had a mechanical digger on site. It had been finding the heavy-duty flatbed transporter truck that had proved difficult. All his usual suppliers had been out, but he'd kept on the phone, calling friends and friends of friends until finally he'd found one. Then it had been a matter of filling in paperwork, collecting it and bringing it to his site, loading and securing the mechanical digger all by himself, because Nicolas had been adamant that he let no one else know what he was up to.

And all the while Mohammed had brooded on why Nicolas would want such equipment in Siwa. None of the answers made him feel any better. The rising sun threw his own shadow far ahead of him upon the black highway. Mohammed drove into it like a dreadful premonition.

II

Knox stared through the Jeep's windscreen at the sands stretching out before him. The desert was at its most beautiful in the early morning and the late afternoon, when the angle of the sun created chiaroscuro shadows in the golden dunes, and the heat was less intense. But during the rump of the day, when the sun was up, it turned the landscape monochrome and flat, except for those areas covered by a layer of salt crystals from some long vanished sea, where it was so dazzling he had to squint to protect his eyes.

The track he was driving had been used since ancient times, an old caravan trail from the Nile to Siwa. The bones of camels lay either side; empty petrol cans, burst tyres, discarded water bottles. Perhaps they'd been here a week; perhaps decades. The Western Desert didn't recycle like other places. It froze like a time capsule. His lips were cracking badly with dehydration; his tongue kept gluing to the roof of his mouth. He took another swig from the water bottle he kept clamped between his legs, swilled it around before swallowing. Within seconds, however, his mouth was as dry as before. He glanced over his shoulder to reassure himself they had sufficient supplies.

On one of his trips with Richard, retracing the tracks of the Zerzura Club explorers who'd mapped the Western Desert and the Gilf Kabir, Knox had encountered the remains of a man in Bedouin dress sitting by the ashes of a fire in a dune valley, who'd seemingly died abruptly of a heart attack; and his hobbled camel nearby, which had perished with him, unable to move.

'What's that?' frowned Rick, pointing ahead.

The Jeep's windscreen had smeared so badly that Knox had to lean his head out the window to see it clearly. There was a low darkness on the horizon, like rain, except that there were no clouds in the sky, and rain was the least of your worries out here in the Western Desert.

'Trouble,' muttered Knox.

III

Elena was in a fiery mood when she reached Ibrahim's villa fresh from her trip to Cairo.

'You're late,' said Nicolas angrily, leading her into the kitchen, where Philip Dragoumis was at the table discussing plans with Costis, his longtime head of security, and several of his team, battle-hardened veterans of the various Balkan conflicts. 'I told you to be here at nine.'

Just the sight of Dragoumis made Elena's bag weigh heavier on her shoulder. But this wasn't the moment.

'I had something to do,' she said. 'What's the rush, anyway?'

'We need to be in Siwa by nightfall.'

'Siwa!' she protested. 'You made me drive all the way up here just to drive straight back down again.'

'It's for your own good,' said Nicolas, nodding at the security monitor. 'You've been recorded arriving. Tomorrow evening you'll be recorded leaving. And Ibrahim will swear you've stayed here all the time in between.'

'Then how — '

'There's a back gate,' said Nicolas. 'We've rigged the camera on it to show nothing.' He glanced at his watch. 'But we need to get moving. Can I have your mobile, please?'

'Why?'

'Because if you use your mobile while we're travelling, you can be traced,' he said with exaggerated patience. 'There's not much point in having an alibi if you're going to blow it with a phone call.'

'Then how will we communicate?'

'We have mobiles in the cars,' said Nicolas. 'Now please just give it to me.'

'I don't have it,' admitted Elena, a little sheepishly. 'I threw it away.'

He frowned. 'You threw it away? Why?'

'Does it matter? Now what's this about? It had better be good.'

'I think you'll find it good,' growled Dragoumis. She frowned at him. He beckoned for her to join him at the table. He opened the two books on Siwa for her to see, and laid them alongside a photograph of the mosaic.

'Christ!' murmured Elena.

'Yes. We've found it at last. Now all we have to do is bring it home.'

She looked at him in horror. For all that she sympathised wholeheartedly with the Macedonian cause, she was an archaeologist too. Sites and artefacts were sacred to her. 'Bring it home?'

'Of course. What else do you think we've been working for?'

'But . . . this is crazy. You'll never get away with it.'

'Why not?'

'For one thing, it may not be there.'

'If it isn't, it isn't,' shrugged Dragoumis. 'But it is. I know it in here.'

'But an excavation like this can take months. Years.'

'We have one night,' grinned Nicolas. 'Tonight. A mechanical digger will meet us there. Eneas and Vasilieos are bringing other equipment and a container lorry. One of our ships is headed to Alexandria. It'll be docked by morning, in plenty of time to load whatever we find. Believe me, our captains are skilled at playing the three-card trick with sealed containers. Within days, it will be back in Thessalonike, and then we can announce.'

'Announce? You can't! Everyone will know we stole it.'

'So? They won't able to prove it. Especially once you claim that the MAF made this discovery in the mountains of Macedonia. As a respected archaeologist, people will accept your word.'

'I don't believe this!' protested Elena. 'I'll be an international joke.'

'I don't see why,' said Nicolas. 'If it's possible Alexander had a tomb prepared for him in Siwa, why not in Macedonia?'

'We have an explanation for Siwa. The Alexander Cipher.'

'Yes,' said Dragoumis. 'And what does it say, exactly? That the shield-bearers prepared a tomb for Alexander in the place of his father; and that they crossed the desert to take him there. That applies to Siwa, certainly. Ammon was Alexander's divine father and Siwa lay across the Western Desert. But it applies to Macedonia too. Philip was Alexander's mortal father. And the shield-bearers would have had to cross the Sinai Desert to reach it.'

Elena's mouth fell open. She couldn't refute the logic, yet still she felt appalled. 'But people would know,' she said weakly.

'We certainly hope so,' grinned Nicolas.

'How do you mean?'

'What do you imagine the reaction will be when Athens tries to wrest it off us, as international pressure will force them to do. Can you imagine the outcry? Macedonia will never stand for it.'

'There'll be war,' said Elena numbly.

'Yes,' agreed Nicolas.

Elena turned to Dragoumis. 'I thought you were a man of peace,' she said.

'And so I am,' he agreed. 'But every nation has the right to defend itself. And we are no different.'

IV

The place where Gaille's father had fallen to his death was at the eastern edge of the Siwa Depression, some three hours' drive from Siwa

Town. They took the Bahariyya track for the best part of a hundred kilometres, then turned north. It was a beautiful, if slightly eerie, setting. High cliffs jutted from the great Sea of Sand. There was no greenery out here. A white snake slithered away from them down a steep dune. Apart from that, Gaille saw no life at all, not even a bird.

It was a five-minute scramble from where they parked to the foot of a high, sheer cliff. A cairn of stones marked the exact spot. His full name, Richard Josiah Mitchell, had been scratched crudely into the top one. He'd always hated being called Josiah. His closest friends — knowing this — had teased him mercilessly with it. She picked it up, asked her guides if either of them were responsible. They shook their heads, suggested it must have been Knox. She set it back as she'd found it, uncertain what to think.

As she stood there, Mustafa explained how they and Knox had hurried down here to find her father already cold, his blood everywhere; how they'd offered to help Knox take his body back to the truck; how he'd snarled at them.

She looked around at where they'd parked. 'You mean *that* truck?' she asked.

'Yes.'

She felt a little weak. 'My father's body was in your truck?'

Mustafa looked a little sheepish. He told her how much he and Zayn had respected her father, what a tragedy it had been, how unnecessary. Gaille stared upwards while he talked. The rockface rose sheer and high above them. It

339

made her toes tingle. She felt light-headed, a little nauseous. She'd never been good with heights. She took a step back, stumbled, might have fallen had Zayn not grabbed her by the arm, restored her to balance.

Her sense of vertigo stayed with her as she and Mustafa climbed the rock-face. Zayn elected to stay behind with the truck, in case of robbers. Gaille had snorted softly when she'd heard that. Robbers! There was no one for fifty miles. But she couldn't blame him. The growing heat and the gradient made the climb far more difficult than she'd anticipated. There was no path, just a series of steep shelves of rock, too sandy to provide secure footing. Mustafa led the way, dancing up in his ragged flip-flops, careless of his thick white robes and heavy pack, five times bulkier than her own. Each time he'd got far enough ahead, he'd squat like a frog on an outcrop to smoke one of his foul cigarettes and watch amiably as she laboured to catch up. She grew increasingly indignant. Didn't he know that men his age shouldn't be able to ingest tar so relentlessly and still be fit? Didn't he realise he should be a physical wreck? She scowled up at him. He waved cheerily back. Her feet ached despite her leather boots; her calves and thighs were trembling with exertion, her mouth tacky with thirst.

She reached him at last, slumped down, fetched out her water bottle, swilled and swallowed a mouthful, asked plaintively: 'Are we nearly there yet?'

'Ten minute.'

She squinted suspiciously at him. He'd said that every time.

V

The sandstorm hit relatively lightly at first. Rick sat back in his seat with a relieved smile. 'This isn't so bad,' he said.

'If it doesn't get any worse.'

It was still light enough outside that Knox could see the track, despite the sand being blasted against his door and window. Sandstorms tended to fall into two broad categories. One was effectively a dust storm, hundreds of feet high, that blocked out the sun and was disorienting without being particularly brutal. The other — like this one — was a true sandstorm, a fierce wind picking up grains of sand from the dunes and firing them like shotgun pellets.

It wasn't long before Rick was regretting his complacency, the wind buffeting them so hard, they were creaking back and forth on their suspension, the bodywork and windows being assailed by a non-stop barrage, loud and frantic, that seemed certain to break through the fragile old glass. Visibility deteriorated so badly that Knox could barely see the track any more. He kept on skewing into soft sand that cloyed beneath their wheels, or over stray sharp rocks that threatened their tyres, so that he had to go down into first gear and slow almost to a crawl.

'Shouldn't we stop?' asked Rick.

Knox shook his head. Stop for even a minute, the wind would blow away the sand beneath their tyres, making them sink into the created pits, until they were stuck. Then it would pile up a drift against their side until they were completely buried and their doors pinned, effectively dependent on being rescued. And there wasn't much chance of that out here.

The winds grew indescribably fierce. They were rocking precariously back and forth. Their left-hand wheels dropped suddenly just as a gust blew viciously hard, so that for a moment it felt as if they were about to be blown onto their side.

'Christ!' muttered Rick, clutching his door handle, as they slammed back down onto four wheels. 'Have you been through one like this before?'

'Once,' said Knox.

'How long did it last?'

'Seven days.'

'You're fucking with me.'

Knox allowed himself a small smile. It wasn't often he'd seen Rick rattled. 'You're right,' he admitted. 'It was more like seven and a half.'

VI

A waft of tobacco smoke tickled Gaille's throat and made her cough. Mustafa held up a hand in apology, then screwed the butt into the dust with his flip-flop. Gaille dribbled water onto her palm, ran it over her brow, rose reluctantly to her feet.

'How much further?' she asked.

342

Mustafa nodded keenly. 'Ten minute,' he said.

She bit her teeth together. Damned if she'd give him the satisfaction of begging for more recovery time. She followed him wearily up a gully in the hillside. After a little while, it suddenly sheared away, so that she could see for tens of kilometres over the golden desert. It looked endless.

'You see,' said Mustafa with an impresario's whirl of the hand. 'Ten minute.'

By God, they were high up. Gaille inched closer to the edge. It fell away beneath her direct to the rocks below, fawn cliffs riven by black shadows. A ledge ran above the precipice before reaching again the safe embrace of a gully. But it was ridiculously narrow, more stepping stones than path.

'You crossed that?' she asked.

Mustafa shrugged. He kicked off his flip-flops, walked quickly across, left hand against the cliff wall, soles of his feet moulding themselves to the meagre holds. He dislodged a small stone. She put a hand against the cliff wall and leaned out to watch it fall. It hit a knob of rock and bounced away from the cliff. Still it fell. And still. She could barely see the cairn on the rocks far below.

Mustafa reached the far side. 'See,' he grinned. 'Is nothing.'

She shook her head. There was no way she could do it. Her balance was poor; her ankles tired. It would be difficult enough at ground level. But up here . . .

Mustafa shrugged, came back across. Chills

cramped Gaille's toes just watching him. He placed his hand on her back to give her courage. She reached her left foot tentatively onto the first small outcrop, brought her right foot to join it. She looked for an age at the place where she had to set her foot next. She made that step jerkily, and then another. The world warped and grew indistinct around her. It sheared away from her at the same time as it rushed up at her face. She wanted to go back but she couldn't move. She closed her eyes, pressed her back against the cliff wall, stretched out her arms for balance. Her fingers and toes felt bloodless and weak; her knees threatened to buckle. It was then that she understood at last what had happened to her father, and Knox's part in it. Tears sprang from her eyes as she realised how wrong she'd been about him, about everything.

'I can't do this,' she said. 'I can't — '

Mustafa grabbed her hand, pulled her to safety. 'You see,' he grinned. 'That was all Knox must do.'

She shook her head at him, collapsed dry-heaving into a bowl of rocks from which she couldn't possibly fall. She turned onto her back, covering her eyes with her hand, while wiping away the tickle of tears from her cheeks. Her father's life insurance policy had included a handsome bonus for accidental death, enough for Gaille to buy herself an apartment. *An apartment!* She felt wretched. She struggled to her feet and, with weak, rubbery legs, followed Mustafa on the long, silent walk down.

32

I

Knox and Rick drove through the sandstorm for what seemed like hour after hour. The whine and screech and roar got to them both, furious harpies clawing at the Jeep's metalwork, trying to get at them. The engine was increasingly strained too, unsettling glugs and belches coming from the radiator. But finally the storm began to abate; and then, in what seemed little more than a moment, the wind died away altogether and they were through, nothing but open desert around them.

They'd driven off the track some time before, and there was no sign of it either, or any landmarks to give them guidance. They had neither GPS nor a decent map against which to plot it.

'You know where we are?' asked Rick.

'No.'

'Then what the fuck do we do now?'

'Don't worry,' said Knox. He climbed up onto the Jeep's bonnet, scoured the horizon through field glasses. People thought of the desert as a single flat landscape, bereft of personality and recognisable features. But it wasn't like that at all, not once you'd been out here a few times. Every region had its own personality and look. Some parts were like those American salt flats where land-speed records were set. Others were like raging high seas frozen into dunes; and though the sands shifted, the underlying shapes themselves were immortal and unchanging. And there were numerous cliffs and ridges too, many of which Knox had climbed.

The air was still hazy, but away to the north, he spotted a familiar escarpment. Half an hour's drive, and they'd be back in business.

'We should eat,' he told Rick. 'Give the engine a rest.'

They sat in the shade of the Jeep and washed cold rice and vegetables down with water, the engine creaking and groaning as it cooled. When they were done, they topped up the radiator and set off again, reaching the track where Knox had known they would, then drove on through the seemingly endless desert. Yet it wasn't endless. In fact, it was only a little after dusk that they reached a sealed track, and then progress was swift. Within another hour they pulled into Siwa's main square.

'I could kill a cold drink,' muttered Rick.

'Not if I see it first,' answered Knox.

II

Mohammed refuelled fifty kilometres north of Siwa, then drove for half an hour with his mobile on the seat next to him, waiting for it to pick up a signal. When finally it did, he pulled off the road to call Nur. It did him good just to hear her voice. His premonitions of his own doom had been growing stronger with every passing minute. But then Nur mentioned Layla's name and Mohammed blurted out suddenly how much he loved them both, that if something went wrong and she shouldn't see him again —

'Don't talk like that!' The distress in Nur's voice shocked him.

He breathed in to calm himself, assured her that he was fine, he'd see her tomorrow evening. He rang off, switched off his mobile before she could call back, checked his watch. He'd made excellent time. He jumped down, walked back along the side of the road, crouched. He scooped up a handful of sand, let it trickle away, watched the peaks that remained upon his fingers, the valleys between them. The sand was so hot from a day of baking sun that it left his skin reddened. He scooped up another handful, as though he believed that by punishing himself now, he could avoid more grievous punishment later.

A Bedouin in a dusty white truck honked his horn and leaned out of his window to ask cheerfully if he needed help. Mohammed thanked him but waved him on. He was so tired, time seemed to move at half its usual speed. The sun lowered to the horizon and finally set. It grew dark quickly. He kept glancing up and along the road to the coast. It was so straight and flat, it would have made a Roman weep for joy.

When he saw the two 4×4s and a container lorry approaching, he stood, brushed sand from his trousers, climbed back into his cab. The vehicles slowed as they drew alongside. An interior light came on in the leading 4×4.

Nicolas leaned out of its window and motioned for Mohammed to fall in behind. He gave him the thumbs up, pulled out. He followed the convoy a few more kilometres along the road to Siwa, then across the sands and deep into the desert.

III

Gaille was out walking when she saw Knox and another man glugging bottles of ice-cold water under the awning of a cafè. She hesitated, then walked over. He looked up, startled to see her.

'Gaille,' he said awkwardly.

'Daniel,' she nodded.

'This is Rick,' said Knox, nodding at his companion.

'Nice to meet you.'

'Likewise.'

She turned back to Knox. 'Can we talk? In private?'

'Sure.' He gestured at the road. 'Want to take a walk?' When she nodded, he turned to Rick. 'You don't mind, do you, mate?'

'Take your time. I'll get something to eat.'

Knox and Gaille walked off side by side. 'Well?' he asked.

'I went out there today.'

'Out where?'

'To where my father died. Mustafa and Zayn took me.'

'Ah.'

She turned to face him. 'I want to know what

happened, Daniel. I want the truth.'

'I'm sure they told you the truth.'

'I'm sure they told me what they saw,' replied Gaille, walking on again. 'But that's not quite the same, is it?'

He gave her a sideways glance. 'What's that supposed to mean?'

'You stuck with my father when no one else did. You wouldn't have done that unless you'd cared about him. So why did you let him fall?'

'I didn't.'

'Yes, you did. And you must have had a reason. And I think I know what it was. He was already dying, wasn't he?'

'I don't know what you're talking about.'

'What was it? Aids?'

'It was an accident.' said Knox.

She shook her head. 'Mustafa and Zayn told me you snarled at them when they offered to help you with his body. All that blood. That's why I'm thinking Aids.'

'It was an accident.'

'And then of course you had him cremated so quickly.'

'I told you, it was an accident.'

'You'd have to say that, wouldn't you, or you'd be complicit in insurance fraud.' Knox opened his mouth to speak, but nothing came out. In the darkness of the back street, it was tough to read his expression. But she persevered anyway. 'He made you promise to write to me, didn't he? To tell me he'd been thinking of me? Please. I just need to know.'

Knox was silent for a while. 'Yes.'

She nodded several times. Although she'd known it in her heart, it still took some effort to assimilate. 'Tell me,' she said. 'Tell me everything.'

'It wasn't just Aids,' sighed Knox. 'His whole body was in meltdown. He had cancer. His organs were failing. It was just a matter of time. Time and pain. He was never the kind of man to eke things out in hospital, or be a burden. You should know that. He wanted to go on his own terms, in a place he loved. And he wanted to do something for you, to make up for being a bad father.'

'A bad father?' asked Gaille bleakly. 'Is that what he said?'

'Yes.'

'And you just let him . . . go ahead with it?'

'He didn't give me a choice. At least, my choice was to be there or not to be there. He was my friend. I chose to be there.' Then he added mulishly: 'I'm sorry if you think that was wrong.'

'I don't,' she said. 'I just wish I could have been there too.'

'You had your chance.'

'Yes,' she agreed. 'You don't need to tell me I've behaved badly. I know that. And I'm sorry.'

They'd looped around in a circuit. Rick saw them and waved. They went to join him.

'Cracking chicken and chips,' he said. 'So you're this famous Gaille, then?'

'Gaille, yes,' she acknowledged. 'I don't know about famous.'

'You are to me. Your man Knox here talks about you non-stop.'

'Shut it, Rick,' said Knox.

Rick laughed. 'So how you getting on with your search?'

'What search?'

'Come on, love. Goods fit for the Son of Ammon.'

She looked back and forth between them. 'How do you guys know about that?'

Knox shrugged and smiled. 'You're not the only one who's been behaving badly.'

'How do you mean?'

'Remember when you got lowered beneath the plinth?' He pulled a face and mimicked her voice outrageously: 'There's someone there!'

Her eyes went wide. 'That was you!' she laughed. 'Daniel, that's *awful*!'

'I know,' he grinned. 'So have you had any luck?'

'I can't talk about it. I gave my word.'

'Who to?' scoffed Knox. 'Elena? Nicolas Dragoumis?'

'No. Yusuf Abbas.'

Knox laughed out loud. 'That crook? The man's corrupt, Gaille.'

'He's the head of the SCA.'

'He destroyed your father.'

'I don't know,' sighed Gaille, putting her hands on her head. 'I don't know who to trust any more.'

'You can trust me,' said Knox. 'Your father did. Or if you want to talk to someone in authority, try Dr Sayed. You can trust him with your life.'

'Are you sure?'

'How do you mean?'

She hesitated, then said. 'He saw something in my photographs of the lower chamber. I'll swear he did. And then some books went missing from his shelves.'

Knox frowned. 'And you think he took them to stop you making some kind of connection?'

'Maybe.'

'Believe me, Gaille, if that's the case, it wouldn't have been to stop you. It would have been to stop Yusuf. Let's go see him.'

She shook her head. 'He's not here. He's been called to Cairo. And his house is locked.'

'Then it's just as well we've got Rick,' grinned Knox. 'He's got a talent we can use.'

33

Ibrahim's nerve, never particularly strong, had completely failed him since Nicolas had pressed that sharp blade against his throat. Courage was easier in daydreams. He'd let himself be bullied into calling in sick, then writing out and signing multiple authorisations on SCA paper for an excavation in the Western Desert, even though the Western Desert was completely outside his jurisdiction. Since then, he'd been forced to stay by his phone in case Nicolas was challenged and he was called to verify his signature.

He hadn't been left alone. Manolis and Sofronio, Nicolas' pilot and co-pilot, were with him. They'd locked all the exterior doors and windows, pocketed the keys and confiscated his mobile. Now they followed him everywhere, to his bedroom, even to the bathroom. And Sofronio spoke enough Arabic to listen in on his conversations whenever the telephone rang, his finger poised to disconnect should Ibrahim try anything.

Nicolas and his men were clearly intent on looting a priceless historical treasure from Siwa. Ibrahim had dedicated his life to Egypt's heritage, yet now he was helping these gangsters pillage it. He turned abruptly and walked towards his office. Manolis followed.

'I only fetch my work,' Ibrahim sighed. Manolis came with him all the same. Ibrahim pulled some papers from his top drawer, glanced at the lock as he left. The key was on the inside, as he'd thought. He walked back out with Manolis, then tutted at himself. 'My pen,' he said.

Manolis waited while Ibrahim returned to his office, picked up a bulbous red fountain pen from his desk, held it up for Manolis to see. His heart began pounding unhealthily fast and his mouth went dry. His sedentary life had rendered him hopelessly unfit. He put his hand on his office door, told himself that this was the moment. His mind urged his hand to slam the door and twist the key, buy himself some time, allow him to redeem himself . . . but his hand didn't obey. He lost his nerve and walked on out. His heart-rate slowed. The adrenalin ebbed. He felt an urgent need to urinate. He bowed his head in shame at the truth of himself. A coward, a failure, a nothing. A man's life was the gift of Allah: what a waste he'd made of his.

II

Bir al-Hammam. Twin peaks connected by a low rock ridge. Steep slopes of sand that fell away like a pyramid on every side. A freshwater lake at its southern foot, bounded by reeds and vegetation. The gibbous moon shimmered off waters rippled by the skipping of insects and the fish that hunted them. Fruit bats shrieked as they left their caves in the worn limestone to gorge themselves on the nearby orchards.

Nicolas arranged his vehicles in a semicircle around the base of the hill in order to conceal their activity. Not that anyone was likely to be passing. They were ten kilometres north of Siwa, after all, and three from the nearest road or settlement. He supervised the unloading of equipment, distributing shovels, picks, torches and weapons. He ordered Leonidas to take one of the AK47s and climb onto the container, the better to keep lookout.

Moonlight gave Mohammed enough light to work by. He munched great scoops out of the desert with his mechanical digger and dumped them behind him, his vehicle gradually tipping forwards so that he had to reverse out and then dig himself an approach trench. The hill was an iceberg, most of its mass hidden beneath the sand. After three hours, his entire digger had been swallowed by the pit he'd created. But still he found nothing.

Nicolas and his men had watched eagerly at first, but their interest ebbed as the hours passed without success. Every so often Nicolas asked Mohammed to pause, then went to inspect the newly uncovered rock. Mohammed looked around during these intervals. The dunes were so cold and white, you'd think them snowdrifts. Leonidas came down from sentry duty on the top of the container, moaning about how bitter it was. No one went up to replace him. The men hunched their shoulders and cupped cigarettes.

Mohammed filled another scoop, dumped it

behind him. The sand cascaded hard down the slopes; it sounded like rain. His mind fizzed and blurred with tiredness. He was by now so deep in his own pit that he couldn't help but imagine that he was digging his way down to hell. Nicolas held up a hand to ask him to idle his engine once more, then went forward with his father to inspect the sandstone. He shook his head in frustration and kicked the rock angrily. Mohammed tried not to show gladness. His best hope was to obey orders and find nothing. Nicolas trudged out of the pit, came over to him. Mohammed lowered his window.

'Enough,' said Nicolas. 'There's nothing. We must leave.'

Mohammed nodded at the vast trench he'd created. 'Do we fill it in?'

Nicolas shook his head. 'The first wind will take care of it for us.'

'As you wish.' Mohammed looked over his shoulder to back out of the trench. He was so tired, he forgot to change gear and jumped forwards instead, clattering the rock of the hill with his scoop. A sheet of solidified sand cracked and fell away. He shook his head in annoyance as he changed gear and reversed away.

There was a shout of excitement, then a chorus. The Greeks all clustered round the rock, shining torches. Mohammed stood up in his cab. He could just make out a smooth piece of pink marble the size of an outspread hand. His heart sank. Whatever it was these men were looking for, he'd just found it for them.

III

It was dark and quiet at Aly's house. The windows were shuttered and the front door locked. Rick produced his steel wire, and soon they were inside.

'I don't like this,' said Gaille nervously.

'Trust me. Aly's a friend. He'll understand. Let's just find these books.'

It was Rick who did so, beneath Aly's mattress. There were five volumes, all told. They took one each, flipped through the pages. Gaille spotted the line drawing of Bir al-Hammam.

'Look!' she said, setting it on the bed. 'The silhouette of the hills. It's the same as the mosaic.'

'And the Wepwawet painting,' said Knox.

Gaille stared at him in surprise. 'You've been there too?'

'We've been everywhere, sweetheart,' grinned Rick.

'The holder of the secret,' muttered Knox. 'So now we know what it was: the location of the tomb the shield-bearers built for Alexander, with all the grave goods still inside.'

'The *exact* location,' added Rick, pointing out the two outcrops of rock that mapped exactly onto Akylos' splayed knees and Wepwawet's outspread feet, and between which both sword and standard were planted.

Gaille sucked in breath anxiously. Knox squinted at her. 'What?' he asked.

'It's just, I asked Ibrahim to send me copies of

these books. And then Elena was summoned to Alexandria. And Aly to Cairo. You don't think someone's . . . *trying* something, do you?'

'I don't know,' said Knox grimly. 'But I think we should make sure.'

34

I

It was the small hours, so Knox took it easy on his Jeep until they were out of town, then he opened her up over the rutted desert track, the old suspension groaning and squeaking as they bounced and jarred. Icy air blew through the cracks in the doors and the empty ventilator slots. Rick was in the back, leaning forward between the front seats, while Gaille clamped her hands beneath her armpits.

'We must be mad!' she shivered. 'Why don't we come back in the morning?'

'We can't risk it.'

'Risk what?' she grumbled. 'Even if people know about the tomb, they can't exactly just loot it.'

'Trust me: the Dragoumises will do exactly that, if the prize is big enough.'

'But is it big enough? I mean, they're certain to be found out. Would they really risk international condemnation and life in prison just for some goods fit for Alexander?'

'Maybe that's not what they're after. Maybe there's more.'

'Like what?' asked Rick.

'There's only one thing they'd risk everything for.'

'Come on, mate. Spill.'

'Dragoumis wants an independent Macedonia. That's only going to happen through an all-out war. He knows that. But nations don't go to war for nothing. They need a cause. Something greater than themselves that they can all believe in. The Jews followed the Ark of the Covenant into battle. Christians followed the True Cross. If you were Macedonian, what would you follow?'

'The body of Alexander,' said Gaille numbly.

'The immortal, invincible lord of the world,' agreed Knox.

'But that's not possible,' protested Rick. 'Alexander was on display in Alexandria hundreds of years after the shield-bearers all died.'

'Was he?'

'Of course,' said Gaille. 'Julius Caesar visited him. Octavian. Caracalla.'

Knox waved impatiently. 'Thanks for the history lesson, guys,' he said, 'but think about it from a different perspective for a moment. Imagine you're Ptolemy, just settling in to Egypt. News comes that these bastard shield-bearers have made off with Alexander's body. You *need* that body. It's the only thing that gives your reign legitimacy. You set off after them. But by the time you catch them, there's no sign of Alexander, and the shieldbearers have all killed themselves. What the hell do you do now?'

'A double?' frowned Rick. 'You're suggesting he used a double?'

'It has to be possible, doesn't it? I mean, Ptolemy had already used a decoy once to send

360

Perdiccas off in the wrong direction. Surely the idea would at least have *occurred* to him.'

'But Alexander had the most famous face in antiquity,' protested Gaille. 'Ptolemy couldn't just embalm a substitute and hope no one noticed.'

'Why not? There was no TV, remember. No photography. There was memory and there was art, all of it idealised. Listen, Ptolemy kept Alexander in Memphis for thirty or forty years before he moved him to Alex. That's baffled archaeologists for decades. Do you really believe it took that long to build an appropriate tomb? Or that Ptolemy held the transfer back deliberately so he'd have a grand state event for his son's succession? Bollocks. Maybe *this* is why. Maybe Ptolemy couldn't risk bringing the body to a Greek city because it wasn't Alexander at all, and he had to wait until everyone who'd known Alexander well was either dead or too gaga to remember what he looked like.'

'You're dreaming.'

'Am I? You showed me the painting yourself.'

'What painting?'

'In the antechamber of the Macedonian tomb, of Akylos with Apelles of Cos. Tell me this: why would Alexander's personal portrait painter waste time on a humble shield-bearer? Could it be because Akylos was sitting in as Alexander's model? I mean, we never found his body in Alexandria, did we? And you saw the mosaic. Akylos was short and slight with reddish hair. Now describe Alexander.'

'No,' said Gaille weakly. 'It can't be.' But chills ran through her.

Knox read it on her face. 'What?' he asked. 'Tell me.'

'It's just,' she said, 'it always seemed odd that Kelonymus buried the shield-bearers in the Royal Quarter. I mean, that was the absolute heart of Ptolemy's power. Taking them there would have been suicidal.'

'Unless?'

'Kelonymus wrote in the Alexander Cipher that he'd pledged to reunite the thirty-three in death as in life. If you're right, I mean if it really was Akylos buried as Alexander in Alexandria, then the necropolis would have been as close as Kelonymus could possibly have got the other shield-bearers to him. This was his effort to reunite them.'

Knox stamped his foot to the floor. They roared across the sand.

II

Elena watched raptly as Mohammed cleared the marble slab of sand and set the teeth of his scoop between the top of the marble and the limestone lintel, then toppled it forwards. She flinched as it fell, professionally appalled by such cavalier vandalism, but the sand was soft and it didn't shatter. She was still as determined as ever on her vendetta; but she also had to see what lay inside. In every way possible, this was the climax of her career.

They each took torches, shining them down into the black mouth. A flight of a steps almost entirely submerged beneath a slant of sand led down to a rough-hewn corridor just tall and wide enough for two men to stand shoulder to shoulder. Elena followed Nicolas and Philip Dragoumis fifty paces into the hill before the corridor opened out into a cavernous chamber. But, as they shone their torches eagerly around, they soon realised it was empty, except of dust and detritus: a broken drinking vessel; an earthenware amphora; the hilt of a dagger; the bones and feathers of a bird, presumably trapped here centuries before. Only the walls repaid in any way the efforts they'd made to find this place, the raw sandstone handsomely sculpted like the stations of the cross, scenes from Alexander's life in deep relief, furnished with real artefacts.

In the first, to their left, Alexander was a gurgling infant in his cot, strangling snakes like Hercules — and evidently there'd once been real snakes there, though time had disintegrated them, leaving only wafer-thin translucent skins in his clenched paws. In the second, he was leading his famed horse Bucephalus away from his own shadow, the better to tame him. The third showed him with other young men around the feet of an elderly man, perhaps Aristotle himself, reading from what would once have been a parchment scroll, but which had long since crumbled into fragments that lay at his feet. The fourth showed Alexander on horseback exhorting his men to battle. The fifth had him plunging

363

a wooden-shafted javelin through the chest of a Persian soldier armed with a bronze axe. Then came the celebrated Gordian knot. Legend had promised sovereignty over all Asia to the person who could untie it, even though untying it was impossible; a conundrum that Alexander had resolved with his customary directness by cutting straight through the rope, represented here by a carved trunk of wood, one end looped around the metal yoke of a chariot, the other anchored inside a slot in the rock wall. The next scene showed him consulting the Oracle of Ammon itself, the chief priest assuring him of his divinity. And so it went on, his victories, setbacks and his deathbed, all beautifully recorded. The final scene showed his spirit ascending a mountain to join the other gods, being welcomed as an equal.

Their flashlights played amongst these mesmerising sculptures, creating shadows that stretched and danced and ducked and darted with life after twenty-three hundred years of utter stillness. No one dared speak. For though this was a remarkable find, it wasn't what they'd come for, it wasn't what they needed. Either the shield-bearers had never made it this far with Alexander's body, or someone had been here before them.

'I don't believe this,' muttered Nicolas, balling his fist. 'I don't fucking believe this. All our work! All our work!' He gave an inarticulate cry of frustration and kicked the rock wall.

Elena ignored his tantrum and crouched down instead by the foothills of the mountain up which Alexander's spirit was ascending. 'There's an inscription,' she told Dragoumis.

'What does it say?'

She wiped away the dust, held her torch at an angle to accentuate the shadows and make it easier to see. ''Go up into the secret skies, Alexander,'' she translated out loud, ''while your people here mourn.''

'There's another one there,' said Costis, pointing his torch at the base of the relief of the infant Alexander strangling the snakes.

Dragoumis translated this one himself. ''You do not know your strength, Alexander. You do not know what or who you are.'' He glanced doubtfully at Elena. 'Does it mean anything to you?'

'It's from *The Iliad*, isn't it?'

Dragoumis nodded. 'They both are. But what are they for?'

Elena went down on her haunches by a third scene, a depiction of fierce fighting. ''Shield clashed against shield, and spear with spear. The clamour was mighty as the earth turned red with blood.''

Dragoumis was by the Gordian knot, he and Costis working their torches in tandem, the better to see. ''Whichever man undoes the knot that fixes this yoke will find himself the Lord of all Asia.''

''Talk not of running, nor of fear,'' said Elena, ''for I know of neither.''

They went on around the walls, deciphering the inscriptions. When they were done, Elena looked at Dragoumis. 'What do you think?'

'I think we need more — '

A heavy thump from outside reverberated up the passage at that moment. The floor shook; dust shivered from the walls. Nicolas looked around, then closed his eyes in anger as he realised what it was.

'Mohammed,' he muttered.

III

Opportunity had taken Mohammed by surprise. The Greeks — every last one of them — had gone inside the hill. Curiosity had got the better of them. He'd waited a minute or two, half expecting one or other of them to realise their mistake and come back out. When they didn't, his courage began to mount. If he could block them in, he could go into Siwa and bring back the police. They'd all go to gaol for years, unable to affect Layla or exact revenge.

His first idea was to ram the mouth of the passage with one of the vehicles, but they were all the wrong shape. He decided instead to reseal the passage with the marble slab, then swamp it beneath sand. He slid the teeth of his hydraulic scoop beneath it and tried to lift it. But it was so heavy, his back wheels left the ground, his hydraulic mechanism screeched and stalled, the slab slipped sideways and clapped loudly on the sand. He cursed himself. They were bound to have heard that. Shouts of alarm came from within. It was too late to back down now. He reversed a little way, then accelerated forwards, using momentum to pick up the marble slab. A

366

Greek arrived at the mouth just as it tipped back neatly into its slot. Mohammed felt exultant as he scooped more and more sand upon it. The pink marble quickly disappeared, imprisoning them all inside. He was unable to believe how simple it had been. Nur was right; she always said that if you faced your demons you could conquer any —

A muffled burst of gunfire. A second burst. Mohammed watched numbly as a cone was sucked out of the sand in front of him, as it widened and deepened. A small black hole appeared. A man clambered through. Mohammed swung his scoop at him, but he ducked it easily, then simply aimed his AK47 at Mohammed's face. Mohammed took his hands off the controls, raised them numbly. A second man crawled out, a third. He thought of Layla, what would happen to her now, and felt despair. More Greeks scrambled out, like so many rats. Costis opened his cab door, switched off his ignition, took away the keys.

Nicolas appeared, brushing down his sleeves and trousers. He said: 'If any of my people knew how to work this machine you would be dead now. Do you understand?'

'Yes.'

'You have a daughter,' he said. 'Her life depends upon our goodwill. Do you understand?'

'Yes.'

'You will co-operate?'

'Yes.'

He nodded at Costis, who'd returned with a

367

pair of handcuffs. He closed one cuff around the steering wheel, the other around Mohammed's left wrist, allowing him enough movement to work his controls, but not enough to escape. He added the key to a keyring chain on his belt. Then he frowned and looked over his shoulder out over the dunes.

It was a moment before Mohammed heard what had distracted him: the faint growl of an engine coming from Siwa. Costis glanced at Nicolas, who held up his hand for silence. The noise died away momentarily, then returned even louder. Nicolas grimaced with foreboding. It was the early hours of the morning. No one should be out driving in the desert, not unless they had a very specific purpose.

'You want us to check it out?' asked Costis.

'Yes,' said Nicolas.

Costis signalled to Leonidas, Bastiaan, Vasilieos and Dimitris to go with him. They grabbed weapons and sprinted for their 4×4s.

35

There were old ruts and tyre tracks in the sand.
Knox used them like a water-skier uses wake,
jolting all three of them so that they bounced in
their seats. It was a point of pride for Gaille that
she wouldn't remark upon it, even though the
passenger-side seat belt had broken years ago
and Knox had to fling out his arm every so often
to hold her in her seat. The Jeep's antique
suspension squeaked, squealed and banged.
Knox downshifted, turned and roared up a
dune, straining his old engine the last few yards.
As they crossed the crest, she could see the
now-familiar silhouette of Bir al-Hammam
ahead. Then they were on the down slope, taking
it at such an oblique angle that their two
right-side wheels left the ground for a moment,
hanging in space. Knox pinned Gaille in her seat
until they bounced back onto four wheels. She
threw him a grin. But then he glanced in his rear
view and frowned in obvious concern. She
turned to see a 4×4 coming up fast behind them,
its headlights off, evidently not wanting to give
itself away.

'What the hell?' muttered Rick.

'It's those bloody Greeks,' said Knox. He
raced down a dune, gaining speed to climb its far
bank. They flew over the top, bounded down the

other side, roaring away along the compact valley sand.

'There's a second one,' said Rick, as another 4×4 appeared over the dune to their left, plunging down the bank, forcing Knox into an evasive skid, their wheels throwing up sprays of sand that brought them almost to a stop. He shifted up through the gears, turning back the way he'd come, but the Jeep was no match for the 4×4s. They gained inexorably, pulling up alongside on either flank, motioning for him to stop. Knox spun hard and cut left, forcing the driver to slam on his brakes, making the sands turn red for a moment, the vehicle's back end quivering. He roared up another dune, but the gradient was steep and the sand soft, and their balding tyres lost traction and began to churn.

Knox stopped fighting, let gravity roll them back down, then swung the Jeep around. A 4×4 nosed into their right-hand side so that both their wheels left the sand. It nudged them again, harder this time, tipping them up onto their side, ploughing a short furrow in the sand before crashing onto their roof. Gaille shrieked and threw up her hands to protect her head as Knox tried to hold her in her seat, but momentum was too much for him and she smacked the windscreen hard.

They came to a stop. Gaille felt dizzy and sick. The passenger door opened. A man stood above her aiming an AK47 at her face. She looked numbly up at him. He motioned for her to get out. She tried to obey, but her limbs wouldn't function. He grabbed her by a hank of hair and hauled her viciously out, ignoring her cries of pain. Knox crawled out after her, bracing himself to spring at the man, but another of the Greeks was waiting in ambush and he clubbed Knox on the back of the head with the butt of his gun, so that he collapsed face-first on the sand.

Rick came out next, hands over his head, looking cowed. But it was only an act. His first punch knocked the first Greek clean onto his backside. Rick wrenched his AK47 from him, twisted it around at the second man, his finger already pulling the trigger. But he didn't quite make it. A yellow burst of flame spat from the second man's muzzle, the percussive noise of automatic gunfire, and Rick's chest exploded red, and he was thrown backwards onto the sand, the AK47 falling from his grasp.

'Rick!' cried Knox, crawling over to his friend. 'Oh Christ! Rick!'

'Jesus, mate,' slurred Rick, trying to raise his head. 'What the fuck . . . ?'

'Don't talk,' pleaded Knox. 'Just hold on.'

But it was already too late, his wounds far too severe. The tension went from his neck and his head slumped lifelessly.

Knox turned round, hatred in his heart, purpose in his eye. But the Greek gunman was watching him with perfect self-assurance. He spat negligently onto the sand, as if to indicate that was all Rick's death meant to him, then pointed his weapon at Knox's chest.

'Hands behind your head,' he said. 'Or it's the same for you and the girl.'

Knox glared at him, but there was nothing he

could do. He made a silent vow that he wouldn't leave Rick unavenged; then he clasped his hands behind his head, while another of the Greeks bound him hand and foot.

II

Ibrahim couldn't sleep. He'd lain awake brooding for hours. Every time he'd managed to soothe himself to relative peace, he'd suffered another spasm of shame. He'd dedicated his whole life to the study of ancient Egypt. To be complicit in the rape of a tomb — and such a tomb! — would blacken the Beyumi name for ever. He couldn't allow this further stain upon his honour. He couldn't. Yet each time he sat up resolved to do something, his nerve wilted. He wasn't that kind of man. He was no kind of man at all. And what could he achieve anyway? They'd removed his mobile, his bedside phone, his modem jack. They'd locked his doors and windows, taken the keys. He rose once more, went to his bedroom door, stood there with his hand upon the handle. He returned for his dressing gown. He took three deep breaths for courage, opened his door.

Manolis was asleep on a mattress in the corridor outside. Ibrahim stood still, waited for his heart to calm. He reached his left leg over Manolis. A floorboard creaked beneath the carpet. Ibrahim froze.

Manolis' eyes opened. Ibrahim could see the luminous white rings of his corneas. 'What are

372

you doing?' he grunted.

'My stomach,' said Ibrahim. 'I need tablets.'

'Wait. I come with you.'

'It's OK. I — '

'I come with you.'

III

The two 4×4s pulled up in front of Nicolas with a screech of brakes and a squirt of sand. Bastiaan threw open the back door of the first and hauled two figures out onto the sand. The first was some lifeless stranger wrapped in a rug, his chest shot to pieces, a mess of blood and pulp. Then the girl, Gaille, dizzy and pale, her wrists and ankles tied with rope. She looked around, evidently terrified, and her eyes locked on someone standing behind him.

'Elena!' she cried plaintively. 'How *could* you?'

'Because she's a patriot,' retorted Nicolas coldly, when Elena didn't speak.

Costis was hauling another man from the back of the second 4×4. He glared up from the sand. *Knox!* Nicolas felt a little nauseous suddenly, as though he'd eaten something that disagreed with him. There was something about the man that made him feel just that little bit helpless.

Knox's gaze slid past Nicolas to where his father was standing. 'So!' he said contemptuously. 'A common tomb robber.'

'Scarcely a *common* tomb robber,' replied Dragoumis, unruffled, 'as I suspect you know full well.'

'Have you found him, then?' asked Knox, despite himself.

'Not yet,' admitted Dragoumis.

'Not yet?' frowned Nicolas. 'What do you mean, not yet? There's nothing there.'

Dragoumis looked sourly at his son. 'Have you learned nothing about this man Kelonymus?' he asked impatiently. 'Do you really believe he's the kind to surrender his greatest secret to the first breach?' He pointed at Gaille, then said to his men, 'She understands his mind better than anyone. Bring her inside.'

'Don't do it, Gaille,' said Knox tersely. 'Don't give them anything.'

Dragoumis turned to him. 'You know I am a man of my word. So let me make you an offer. If you two help me find what we're looking for, I vow I'll let you both go free.'

'Sure!' scoffed Knox. 'After everything we've seen!'

'Believe me, Daniel, if we find what we're looking for, the more you two talk, the better it will be for us.'

'And if we refuse?'

Dragoumis gave a small, sorrowful shrug. 'Do you really want to put that to the test?'

Nicolas kept his eyes on Knox as he debated his response. It was clear that he was still burning with rage for what they'd just done to his friend, was only waiting for an opportunity to gain revenge. He turned to warn his father, but his father silenced him with an acerbic look, as though he was already five steps ahead. He shrugged and turned back to Knox. The man

374

was still struggling with himself, with his conscience; but then he glanced at Gaille, her face ashen with fear and streaked by tears, silently pleading with him to do nothing rash, and he blinked and sighed and put his hatred back in its box for the moment.

'OK,' he said. 'We'll do what we can.'

'Good,' nodded Dragoumis. He turned to Costis. 'Untie their ankles. But not their wrists. And keep a close eye on this one,' he added, gesturing at Knox. 'He's more dangerous than he looks.'

Costis nodded. 'I know,' he said.

IV

Ibrahim and Manolis walked downstairs together. The carpet was lush, but the soles of Ibrahim's feet felt icy. He glanced down, almost expecting them to be glowing blue-white, like diamonds. Sofronio was snoring on the couch. When Manolis turned on the lights, he sat up, disoriented with sleep, then cursed Manolis in Greek and covered an expansive yawn.

Ibrahim made a show of looking through his kitchen cabinets, slamming drawers, muttering. He heard the two Greeks conferring. Their Greek was so guttural, he couldn't understand a word, but the way they looked suspiciously at him . . .

'They're not here,' he said brightly. 'They must be in my desk.' He walked briskly towards his office. Sofronio and Manolis were still muttering. It was now or never. Ibrahim leaned his weight forward and broke into a run.

V

'Move, damn you,' said Costis, jabbing Knox in the base of his spine with the muzzle of his AK47.

Knox glowered over his shoulder. 'You're going to pay for what you did to Rick,' he promised.

But Costis only snorted and jabbed him harder. And, truly, Knox was in no position to make threats. Walking along this dark passage into the belly of the hill, the flicker and glare of torchlight all around, having to duck every so often to avoid scraping his scalp on the low ceiling, he felt sure that it wasn't just Alexander's tomb he was walking into, but his own, and Gaille's too, unless he could somehow turn this situation round.

The passage opened out abruptly. Evidently the Greeks had been here before, for they expressed no surprise at the marvellous sculptures around the walls. But to Knox they were so remarkable that for a moment he almost forgot about his predicament. His wrists were still bound, but his hands were in front of him. He took a torch from one of the Greeks, then went over to a sculpture of Alexander leading a charge. Gaille came with him, and then Elena and Dragoumis too, creating the surreal impression of four academics at a conference discussing some obscure artefact.

Gaille stooped to translate the inscription. ''Then Pallas Minerva gave him courage that he might outdo all others. Fire blazed like the summer sun from his shield and helmet.'' She turned to Elena. 'Is that what you made of it?' she asked.

'Pretty much,' agreed Elena. Then she added, a touch uncertainly: 'It's from *The Iliad,* isn't it?'

'Yes,' agreed Gaille. 'Adapted a little, but yes.'

Elena nodded more confidently. 'He certainly likes his Homer,' she said. 'All of the inscriptions are from *The Iliad.*'

'Not all,' corrected Dragoumis. He nodded at the far wall. 'The Gordian knot wasn't in *The Iliad.*'

'No,' agreed Knox. He walked over to it, stooped to read the inscription. ''Whichever man undoes the knot on this yoke will find himself the Lord of all Asia.'' He snorted and glanced around at Dragoumis. 'You gave us your word, yes?' he asked.

'Yes,' said Dragoumis.

'Good,' said Knox. He walked over to the tableau of Alexander spearing the Persian and grabbed the bronze axe in both hands. It was cool to the touch, and surprisingly heavy.

'Stop him!' cried Nicolas.

'Be quiet,' said Dragoumis irritably.

Knox took the axe to the Gordian knot, bringing the blade down hard, slicing splinters out of the wood. He struck again, and then a third time, the blows sending shivers up his fingers and palms. But the dull blade still did its work, for the old wood shattered and tore apart. One end lay still; the other slithered like a fugitive snake into the rock wall, attached to some kind of weight. There was a low scratching sound, then silence. They waited expectantly, but seconds ticked by and nothing more happened.

'Is that it?' sneered Nicolas. 'I hope you don't think that — '

And then it started, a low rumbling in the rock above their heads, growing louder and louder, shaking dust from the ceiling, making tiny vibrations in the floor. Everyone looked up, and then apprehensively at each other, wondering what it was. The noise stopped. There was silence again. Everyone shrugged and began to relax and —

The wall to Knox's right suddenly exploded, shards of stone flying everywhere. He had virtually no time to react. He dropped the axe and threw himself to the ground, taking Gaille down with him, hugging her face against his chest as fragments of rock thudded and crashed into his legs and back, glancing off his scalp, leaving him with the sharp pulse of drawn blood.

It was over almost before they'd realised it was happening at all. The shrapnel settled, the thunderous noise died, leaving their ears ringing. People began muttering and coughing and choking with the dust and powdered sandstone, gingerly checking themselves for injuries. One of the Greeks was cursing, but not too seriously, as though he'd sprained a wrist or turned an ankle. Other than that, and a few cuts and bruises, it

378

seemed they'd been lucky. It took Knox a moment to realise what an opportunity this was for him and Gaille to make a break for it. But when he glanced around, the first thing he saw was Costis grinning knowingly at him, and pointing his gun.

Knox picked himself up, helped Gaille up too. Someone retrieved a torch and shone it at where the wall had been, a great, gaping hole now torn in its heart. There was blackness beyond, indicative of an even greater space, and the glint of metallic objects on the floor. They edged closer, treading tentatively on pulverised sandstone littered with fragments of a tougher stone like marble that crackled beneath their feet.

Knox looked up at the circular shaft that rose almost vertically above him into the hill before vanishing into darkness. Cutting the Gordian knot must have triggered a rock-fall. But then he was through to the other side, and other matters took his attention. The hewn passage zigzagged left and right, shielding it from the blast of the falling rock. Then it began to funnel open. Niches were cut in the walls, and in them life-sized painted alabaster statues of nymphs and satyrs, a rearing horse, Dionysus on a couch, his head thrown back, drinking from a goblet, surrounded by tendrils of ivy and fat bunches of purple grapes. They passed other objects too. Attic vases of brown, red and black painted with scenes from Alexander's life, too crude to be the work of Kelonymus, perhaps the personal tributes of the shield-bearers themselves. A wooden model of a chariot. Some crude pottery figurines. A silver wine jug and matching drinking vessels. A bronze cauldron. A golden bowl containing fists of uncut precious and semiprecious stones: ruby, turquoise, lapis lazuli, amethyst, diamond, sapphire. A golden cup inscribed with a sixteen-pointed star, and next to it a golden handbell that reminded Knox poignantly of Rick. And then, set in the right-hand wall, a painting of Alexander in his chariot carrying a golden sceptre, just like the frieze described by Diodorus Siculus as part of the funeral catafalque, enabling Knox to answer at last the question of how Kelonymus and the shield-bearers had financed all their endeavours. They'd had the catafalque. Perhaps these shield-bearers had been the very unit Ptolemy had tasked with bringing it back to Egypt, only for them to change their plans once they realised he'd betrayed Alexander's last wish.

Costis nudged Knox in the back again. They moved on. Now they reached and passed what could only be described as an ancient library: scrolls bound with ivory holders, and stacked in *loculi* cut in the sandstone walls, and books in open silver and golden caskets, handwriting still faintly visible on the yellow parchment and papyrus, as well as drawings of herbs, flowers and animals.

'My God!' muttered Gaille, looking at Knox with wild eyes, all too aware of the intrinsic and historic value of this find.

The passage opened up again. They came into a great domed chamber, twice the size of the previous one, its floor glittering like shattered quartz with metallic artefacts, its walls and ceiling decorated with gold leaf, so that their torches reflected dazzlingly from all sides. And there were grave goods here too, set on twelve altars — rings and necklaces and amphorae and coins and caskets. Weapons too: a shield, a sword, a helmet, a breastplate, a crested helmet. And, in the centre of the chamber, at the heart of all the altars, at the focal point of their torches, there was a high pyramid, rising in steps on every side to a peak upon which rested a magnificent golden anthropoid coffin.

No one could be in any doubt now about what it was they'd found.

36

Ibrahim slammed closed his office door and turned the key in the lock just as Sofronio charged it with his shoulder. Ibrahim jumped back and cried out as the panels bulged and the frame shivered. But the door held. Sofronio charged again. Still it held. Ibrahim gained in confidence. He strode to his desk, picked up his phone, dialled 122. It rang twice before it was answered. He gave his name and address, began to explain his situation when the line suddenly went dead. His eyes tracked the white wire to the point where it pierced the wall out into the main body of the house. He stared at it numbly. A different kind of pounding started upon the door, sharp and loud; a boot, not a shoulder; two men taking it in turns. The frame by the jamb at last began to give.

Ibrahim dropped the telephone handset, backed away, watching sickly as the wood began to splinter. There was nowhere to hide. The door into the main room was the only way out, except for the windows, but they were locked and Manolis had the keys. A paperknife and a paperweight lay on his desk. The knife was sharp and steely but he knew in his heart he lacked the nerve to wield it in anger. He hurled the paperweight through the window instead, then jumped up onto his desk. The doorframe finally gave way, the jamb a streak of yellow beneath its coat of gloss. The two men charged in. Ibrahim dived for the open heart of the shattered window, but Sofronio grabbed his ankle, stopping him dead, so that he plunged down onto a long, jagged shard. It was a strangely dull sensation, more blow than cut. All strength ebbed from his limbs. He was dragged back into the room, his chin thumping onto his desk and carpet. He felt his stomach wall flap open as he was turned onto his back, saw with a certain perverse pride the deep shock on Manolis' face as he pressed his hands either side of Ibrahim's belly in a futile effort to stem the evisceration. Sofronio simply closed his eyes.

Ibrahim lay there as the two men discussed what to do. Manolis tipped books from the shelves while Sofronio left the room and returned with a large, translucent bottle of white spirits, which he splashed over the papers, carpet and wooden desk. He stooped to set fire to it with his plastic yellow lighter, then both men hurried away.

A teaching of the Prophet came irreverently to Ibrahim's mind, that a Muslim should keep inviolate his blood, property and honour. He almost managed an abstract chuckle at this, to have lost all three in such spectacular fashion. His fingers and toes began to tingle like a good tonic water. He'd long been queasily fascinated by the mechanics of death — whether oblivion would follow instantly from his heart stopping or whether his mind would fade out like an antique wireless. Fire filled the room with choking thunderclouds. His eyes burned. He heard sirens, a screech and clash of metal, gunshots, and then men in masks and uniforms rushing in, kneeling beside him. But too late; far too late. To his surprise, he felt a mild but growing euphoria. He'd brought indelible dishonour on his name, his family and his city; but at least people would say that he'd given everything he could to put it right.

II

In the chamber within the hill, Knox, Gaille and all the Greeks climbed the pyramid together to the summit. There was a moment's awed silence as they stood around the coffin, raised to waist level upon a white marble plinth, its lid lushly carved with scenes of hunting and war. With the side of his hand, Knox brushed away the skin of sand and dust that had settled over the millennia. You could tell gold from bronze because bronze tarnished over the centuries. This was gold.

Dragoumis rested his palms upon it, like a high priest. 'Open it,' he ordered.

The lid was so heavy, it took all of them heaving together to raise it and shift it sideways, then lay it on the floor beside the coffin. They all stared down hungrily inside, pressing and craning past each other, the better to see. A man's body lay snugly within, deep in dust and the traces of petals and spices, a giant ruby diadem around his brow, his arms folded across his chest, a sword on one side, a golden sceptre on the other. He'd evidently once been covered in gold leaf, but it had peeled away in places, exposing blackened, parchment skin and limbs shrunken down to the bones beneath. Black and gold, like so many of the world's most dangerous creatures.

In the dappled, moving light, Knox looked for the signature scars on the body. Yes. Even after all these centuries, it was possible to discern faint traces of the throat slash of Cyropolis, the shoulder puncture of a Gaza catapult, the nipple piercing of a Multan arrow and the gashed thigh of Issus. His skin prickled. He felt weak. There could be no question.

'It's him,' he murmured. 'It's Alexander.'

Dragoumis' eyes were wet when he looked around. 'Then it's time to bring him home,' he said.

III

It was easy enough taking the coffin lid out to the container lorry. That was just a function of exertion and time. The coffin itself, however, was another matter altogether. It was far too heavy for them to lift, so they slung ropes around it to lower it carefully down the pyramid, using sand as a lubricant on the steps and the passage floor, dragging it behind them, all pulling together, even Knox and Gaille, yet still only making a foot or so with every heave. But they brought it finally to the passage mouth, already turned into a ramp-by the sand Mohammed and dumped. They tied a thick rope to the towbar of a 4×4 and tried to drive it out, but its wheels spun uselessly. They brought in the second 4×4, and all heaved together, and managed to haul it to the lorry.

Getting it up into the container was even more problematic. Mohammed tried to lift it with the hydraulic arm of his digger, but only tipped forwards.

In the end it was Dragoumis who suggested the solution. Mohammed dug a trench in the sand in front of the coffin. The lorry reversed into it, so that the mouth of the container was below the coffin. Then they plugged the intervening gap with sand and dragged the coffin down and in until it was over the front axle, as stable as they could make it.

Nicolas wiped his brow, well pleased, then looked over to his father for approval. But his father only gestured towards the east, where the sun was already beginning to rise on the horizon. Nicolas nodded. Perhaps one day they might come back for all the other treasures inside the hill. For the moment, they had what they needed, and it wouldn't pay to be greedy.

IV

No one noticed when Elena slipped away from the container and walked across to the 4×4s to collect her bag. She'd bought her gun last night by the simple expedient of flagging down the first taxi she'd seen in Cairo and thrusting cash at its driver until he'd realised she was serious and had begun a relay of telephone calls. Two hours later, a dealer had shown her his collection. She'd known the one she wanted before he'd even picked it up. It was black and chunky and just looking at it gave her confidence. When she'd pointed it out to him, he'd nodded keenly. A shrewd choice, he'd enthused. The Walther P99. A semiautomatic with two magazines. He'd begun to explain how it was put together. She'd told him not to bother. Instead, he'd taken her out into the alleys of the City of the Dead and shown her how the safety catch worked. She'd pumped four bullets into a wall. It had given her a warm glow in her belly. It gave her the same warm glow now as she took the gun in her hand.

Three lives to take. Then her blood debt would finally be settled.

She turned around. Mohammed was reburying the mouth of the tomb beneath sand. Knox and Gaille were being herded by Nicolas, Leonidas and Bastiaan to the 4×4s. The other Greeks were sitting on the back of the container, smoking well-earned cigarettes. Costis and Dragoumis were standing together, watching benignly. Costis had an AK47 slung over his shoulder, but he looked relaxed, not expecting trouble. Elena couldn't have asked for a better opportunity. She walked towards them, the Walther hidden behind her back. The men turned when they saw her coming. Dragoumis frowned, as though puzzled by her expression.

'Yes?' he asked.

She took Costis first, pulling the trigger even as she was raising the gun. The round punctured his ribcage. The recoil kicked up her hand so that the second round tore through his upper chest beneath his throat, flinging him onto his back. Her sense of time and space distended. To her left, men yelled in panic and scrambled for their weapons. She paid them no heed. She felt strangely invulnerable, protected by destiny. Costis was making strange, high keening sounds. He raised his head to look down at his punctured front, then tried to hold his hands over himself. She stepped astride him, aimed at his nose and fired once more. The bullet tore through the ridge above his eye. His head slumped lifelessly to the sand.

She turned to Dragoumis. His face was white. He seemed frozen. She walked up to him and pressed the muzzle against his heart.

'Tell your men to be still,' she said. Dragoumis said nothing. She raised and pressed her gun against the forehead. When she saw him tremble, she felt a great gladness inside. Then she realised he wasn't trembling with fear, but with anger.

'I didn't kill Pavlos,' he said flatly.

'Yes, you did.'

He shook his head. 'You have my word: that crash was an accident.'

'It was no accident,' she assured him. 'Believe me. I know everything. I know you hired a whore to seduce Pavlos. I know you had them filmed together, that you showed him the footage. I

388

know you threatened to send me a copy unless he stopped calling for an enquiry.'

'Then you know, also, that I had no need to kill him.'

Elena could feel tears prickling on her cheeks. 'Did you really believe you could control Pavlos? Not a chance. Not you. Not me. Not anyone. He came to me. He confessed everything. That's how I know you were responsible.'

A muscle flickered on Dragoumis' temple. 'I give you my word,' he said. 'I swear on Macedonia. On the body of Alexander. On the death of my wife. I never ordered for Pavlos to be killed.'

'No,' said Elena. 'But *I* did. I had him killed because of your fucking film.'

She smiled as Dragoumis assimilated this, worked out the import, looked at her for the first time in the certain knowledge of his own death; and seeing that, savouring it, she shot him once through his forehead, scattering bits of his brain and bone like seed corn over the sands. Then, thinking of Pavlos, longing for him, she stuffed the hot muzzle against the roof of her mouth, closed her eyes, uttered his name, and pulled the trigger one final time.

37

I

Nicolas Dragoumis flinched and closed his eyes a millisecond before Elena killed his father and then herself. When he opened them again, his father was lying on his side, one arm splayed out, the other tucked awkwardly beneath him, legs folded like two parts of a swastika. Nicolas found himself staring and staring, unable to take in what he saw. It was impossible that such a man could be so quickly and comprehensively extinguished. He stepped unsteadily across Elena's prostrate corpse to stand beside him, waiting for him to move, to rise, to brush himself down, give orders.

He jumped as someone touched his elbow. He turned to see Leonidas talking to him. He could see his lips move but could make no sense of his words. He looked down again. Slowly, his brain began to recover. All men died; but their missions lived on. His father's mission lived on. It was up to him to complete it. The thought strengthened Nicolas. He looked around again. The sun had already cleared the horizon. The mouth of the tomb had already vanished beneath sand. His men were gazing expectantly at him.

'Dig a pit,' he said. 'We bury Costis and Elena

390

here.' The calmness and authority of his voice surprised him. But then, why should it? His father had been Philip the Second reincarnate, the father of Alexander the Great. And what did that make him? Yes. *What did that make him?*

'And your father?' frowned Leonidas.

'You think I'd leave him here?' snapped Nicolas. 'We bring him with us. He is to be buried with full honour.'

'What about those two?' asked Leonidas, nodding at Gaille and Knox, being herded by Bastiaan into the back of one of the 4×4s.

Nicolas felt a resurgence of his anger, and an opportunity to vent it. His jaw tightened. He stooped to pick the Walther from Elena's loose grip. He checked the magazine. Five gone. Four left. He walked over to the 4×4.

'Get Knox out,' he ordered.

Bastiaan dragged Knox out by the arm, throwing him on the sand. Nicolas aimed down at his chest. The girl cried out, pleading for mercy. Bastiaan punched her on her temple, so that she fell sprawling unconscious across the rear seats.

Nicolas stared down at Knox. 'No one can say we didn't give you fair warning,' he said.

'Your father gave us his word he'd let us go if we helped you find Alexander.'

'My father is dead,' said Nicolas.

'Yes, but he — '

He got no further, however, Bastiaan slamming the butt of his gun into the back of his skull, so that he collapsed face down upon the sand.

'Thank you,' said Nicolas. He smiled as he aimed at the back of Knox's head and tightened his finger on the trigger.

II

Mohammed rubbed his left wrist where the hard steel handcuff chafed. He didn't recognise the man Nicolas was about to shoot, but he recognised Gaille, who'd always been nice to him during the necropolis excavation, enquiring after Layla and wishing them all well; and he recognised murder too, and that he was colluding in it.

He'd thought Layla's life worth any price. Now he realised he'd been wrong.

The cuff was too tight to slip his hand free. And though he was a strong man, he wasn't strong enough to rip the steering wheel from its mount. But the handcuff key was on a chain on Costis' belt. That, at least, gave him a fighting chance. He started up the digger, thrust it into gear, accelerated forwards.

The suddenness of his charge caught the Greeks by surprise. Nicolas turned and fired twice, but Mohammed used the scoop as a shield and the bullets pinged and whined away, and then he was upon Nicolas, so that he had to dive aside, rolling over and over. Bullets sprayed; Mohammed ducked as he worked his controls to scoop Costis up from the sand. Then he turned down the slope, using gravity and the gradient to help him speed away, glancing over his shoulder to see the Greeks streaming down after him on foot and in the 4×4s. The digger bucked and jolted. Costis danced in the scoop but didn't fall.

Mohammed reached flatter terrain and dumped Costis to the sand, then pulled up alongside him, placing the bulk of the digger between himself and the Greeks. He threw open the cab door and stretched down. He couldn't quite reach Costis. He twisted the steering wheel as far as it would go, tried again. Still no good, only able to brush him with his fingertips, however hard he strained. The Greeks were yelling as they hurtled down towards him, loosing off wild shots, roaring their vehicles. He hooked his right boot beneath Costis' head, lifted him high enough to snatch a hank of his hair. He grabbed his chin, collar, finally his belt, the chain, the keyring. Four keys. Two bore BMW insignia. The others were small, unmarked.

He had to lift Costis bodily from the sand to get the first key up to the cuff. No good. He was trying the second when something exploded behind his ear and his world went black.

III

Nicolas felt demons screaming in his chest, but he managed somehow to keep them penned inside.

'New plan,' he said tightly, as he arrived to find Mohammed unconscious, blood leaking from a cut in his scalp. 'Put the bodies in the flatbed. Dump it and the digger in the lake.'

Vasilieos pulled up in the second 4×4. He nodded at his back seat. 'And the girl?'

Nicolas peered in. Gaille was sprawled unconscious across the back seats. It made him realise suddenly that he'd forgotten about Knox in the chaos, and he suffered a sudden lurch of premonition. He looked around. All his men were down here with him, every last one of them. Without Costis or his father to lead them, they'd degenerated into an undisciplined rabble.

'Where's Knox?' he demanded, even though in his heart he already knew the answer. 'Who the fuck was looking after Knox?'

No one spoke. Their eyes wouldn't meet his when he glared their way. He clenched his fists as he gazed up to where Knox had been. There was not a sign of him, except — at least — for the ropes with which he'd been bound, lying discarded on the sand. He closed his eyes for a moment to let the swell of fury pass. Sometimes it almost seemed as though God wasn't on their side.

He jumped in the 4×4 with Vasilieos and Bastiaan, drove back up. The place was a mess of footprints, impossible to track. Knox could have vanished anywhere. He could have hidden himself beneath sand, climbed the hill, be on the other side of it by now. The sun was getting higher all the time. Daylight wasn't safe. You could see for ever in the desert on a clear day. Their vehicles would stand out like beacons. The tourists and the bird-watchers would already be leaving their hotels. Reveille would have sounded in the army barracks. They had to leave now.

Nicolas half pulled Gaille out of the back seat, pressed the muzzle of the Walther against her temple. 'Hear this,' he shouted. 'The girl dies if you give us trouble. You hear? Any trouble at all, your old friend's daughter dies.'

His voice echoed off the hill, then faded to silence.

38

Knox watched from his ledge as Nicolas and several of his men drove off north in the container lorry and one of the 4×4s, leaving others behind to load Rick, Elena and Costis into the flatbed, which they then drove out into the lake. It ploughed up a great white wash as it floated, before tipping onto its side, belching out air and then sinking. Knox felt sickened watching the body of his old friend Rick consigned so unceremoniously to the deep; and guilty too, because Rick had only come here to help him. But this wasn't the time for regret or mourning or vengeance. Those would come later. Right now he had work to do.

The Greek driver swam in a leisurely breaststroke back to the bank. He shook himself down, walked over to the mechanical digger, started it up and repeated the trick. The driver hauled himself out the window as the cab vanished beneath the surface. He was halfway back to the bank when the lake erupted behind him and the big Egyptian spluttered up, coughing and choking. His revival lasted only a few moments until the digger dragged him back down beneath the surface, still handcuffed to the wheel. One of the Greeks cracked a joke. They all laughed as they climbed into the second 4×4

396

and set off after their comrades.

Knox waited until they were out of view, then scrambled down the cliff face and bounded down the sand dunes to the lake, stripping as he went.

II

Choking had shocked Mohammed back to consciousness but, it seemed, only so that he could experience terror. The digger pulled him remorselessly down. He managed a last despairing breath before it tugged him beneath the murky water. His engine stalled. The door was hanging open, the whole vehicle tilting at a precarious angle as though it might tip over on the soft lake bed. He pulled himself inside. A little air had been trapped against the cab's curved roof. He breathed in, felt for and switched on the roof-light. It cast rings of reflected yellow light upon the disturbed water, revealing how small his supply was. He ducked back down, strained to pull his hand free of its cuff, but his thumb prevented him. He tried to wrench the wheel from its mount. Useless. The exertion was only burning through his meagre supply of oxygen. The key was in the ignition. He turned it but the engine didn't respond. He went up for another breath. The digger lurched and tilted further. Precious bubbles streamed away. He remembered reading about some mountaineer who'd sawed off his arm with a penknife to free himself from a rock-fall. Yes. He could do this for Layla. He took a breath, ducked down, fumbled the floor for shards shattered by gunfire, but found only pebbles of safety glass. He went back up.

A flurry of water, a tug on his sleeve. He almost died of fright when a man's head bobbed up beside him. The man Nicolas had wanted to kill.

'Where's the key?' he asked curtly.

'The dead Greek,' gasped Mohammed. 'On his belt.'

The man nodded, ducked and vanished.

There was so little air, it was already beginning to go bad. He pressed his cheek against the exposed metal roof and tried to keep calm. An eternity seemed to pass. The air grew fetid. His mind fuzzed. A headache pounded between his eyes. He prayed for Layla, that somehow she would get through this, that her life would be good once this dreadful disease was behind her. What could stop her then? All fathers were proud of their daughters, but which of them had such cause?

The cab lurched again. A small shriek escaped him as more air bubbled away. That was the trouble with hope; it came at the cost of intense fear. He had to pull his cuffed wrist almost taut to reach the remaining air. It was rank, it was poisoning him, he had to breathe harder and faster to harvest any oxygen from it at all. The cab lurched and tipped remorselessly sideways. His last supply of air bubbled away. He clamped his mouth with his hand as long as he could, but then he couldn't fight his lungs' need any more, he had to open it. Water flooded in. He choked once, but then sucked in again, and the liquid poured down his throat. A swirl of random yet comforting colours, patterns, sensations, aromas; bathed in the warm love of Nur and Layla; and then a burst of bright white light.

III

Nicolas called Ibrahim's villa as he led his small convoy north on the Marsa Matruh road. There was no reply. He called Manolis on his mobile, and then Sofronio. Neither of them answered. Something was wrong. Anxiety gnawed at his stomach. He glanced at Vasileios.

'What is it?' asked Vasileios.

'I don't know.'

He looked around at the container lorry immediately behind. Burdened by its precious cargo, it struggled to reach and maintain 70 k.p.h. At such a rate, it would take them at least ten hours to reach Alexandria. Ten hours. Christ! Who knew what might happen in that time, especially with Knox on the loose? And he'd thought everything would go so smoothly! He picked up his mobile, intending to try Ibrahim and the guys again, only to see his signal fading and dying altogether. If their journey down was any way to judge, it wouldn't pick up again until they neared Marsa Matruh and the coast.

There was nothing for it but to press on.

IV

Streams of released air and lake-bed gasses simmered the surface of the lake. Slicks of oil and algae and detritus made overlapping circles. Knox swam from one to the other, kicking down. The flatbed truck had made it further into the lake than the digger. The water, usually so clear, was badly muddied. Knox had to work by feel. His lungs were about done when he touched something metallic. He surfaced for more air then dived once more, pulled himself through an open window into the flatbed's cab. He searched with his hands.

The first corpse he found was Rick. That sickness in his gut again. He squashed it down.

The second body had long hair. A woman. Elena. He pushed her aside and grabbed hold of a foot instead, followed it up a trouser leg to a belt. He fumbled along it, found a key chain. He unbuckled the belt, slipped off the key chain.

Clutching it tight, he pulled himself out of the cab, kicked for the surface, heaving in breath, then swam back until he judged himself to be above the digger. He packed his lungs with air and kicked down. His eyes were raw and burning. The excavator had tipped onto its side. He pulled himself in the broken window. All the air had escaped. Mohammed was slumped and lifeless. In his haste, Knox dropped the keys. By the time he found them and picked them up again, the pressure was building relentlessly in his own lungs, his brain screeching for air. He took Mohammed's wrist. The first key didn't fit.

The second neither. In panic, disbelief, he tried the keys again. Still nothing. He wanted to scream. He needed air. The other cuff was locked around the steering wheel. He tried the first key on that, then the second. This time it went in. He turned it, the cuff released, he grabbed the big man's collar, dragged him to the window, out and up to the surface, then swimming with one arm to the shallows, hauling Mohammed behind him with the other, pulling him up onto the bank.

He put one hand on his chest, his other on his throat. The big man's heart had stopped. Of course it had fucking stopped. He'd been breathing nothing but water for the last three minutes. Knox thought back to the drowning and near-drowning course he'd attended as a diving instructor. When water enters the airways, people automatically experience larygnospasm; which was to say that their throats constricted to divert the inhaled water to their stomachs. But after cardiac arrest, the airways often relaxed again, allowing water belatedly to enter the lungs. Kurt, a beanpole Austrian with a beard down to his nipples, had taught no-drainage cardiopulmonary resuscitation straight from the book; but in an acerbic aside had remarked that if *his* life depended upon it, he'd want the Heimlich first, whatever the current thinking was, because if your airways were blocked, that was your brain fucked anyway. Knox stretched both arms around the big man's waist, made a fist of his right hand, pressed his thumb below the ribcage, squeezed his abdomen with a sharp upward thrust. Frothy dark water pulsed like blood from his mouth and nose. He pumped until nothing more came out, then tilted back his head to open his airway, pinched his nose, ventilated him twice. He checked for a pulse, found nothing. He kept pumping and ventilating, pumping and ventilating, until the big man suddenly convulsed, choked, gasped, expelled a dribble more water from his throat and mouth, began again to breathe. Knox slumped onto the muddy sand beside him, naked and drained and trembling.

Then he remembered with weary horror that Nicolas had Gaille. *Let her be alive. Please God, let her be alive.*

He pushed himself to his feet, gathered his clothes. His legs were weak and rubbery. Even so, he forced himself to run across the dunes to see if he could salvage his Jeep.

39

I

Nicolas leaned out his window to direct the container lorry to pull to the side of the road. He needed to refuel and make phone calls, but he couldn't exactly pull into a service station with Gaille lying across his back seats. His men opened up the back doors of the container. The sun was still low enough that it hadn't heated up inside yet.

They waited until the road was clear in both directions, then dragged Gaille inside, gagged her and tied her to the steel handrail at the cab end. Then he ordered Eneas to stay inside with her to make sure she didn't try anything.

Back in the 4×4, they raced on ahead. The road was straight and true and untroubled by uniforms. Vasileios turned on the radio and searched for music. Nicolas turned it off again. They finally reached a service station, a couple of trucks parked outside, on their way to or from Siwa. Vasileios refuelled while Nicolas made calls. There was still no answer from Ibrahim, Sofronio or Manolis. What the hell was going on?

He called his office in Thessalonike and ordered Katerina to look into it. But his apprehension was growing worse all the time as he climbed back into the 4×4.

403

II

Knox's Jeep was still lying at an angle on its roof a third of the way up a dune. He pushed and pushed, achieving a little back-and-forth resonance, but he couldn't quite take it to its tipping point. He dug sand from beneath the roof with his bare hands to increase the angle of tilt, then tried again. With a great crash, it fell onto its side and then almost onto its wheels, teetering there for a moment before threatening to fall back. Knox hurled himself against it, his feet slipping and slithering on the soft sand, but he refused to give way, and finally he won and it clattered upright, throwing up clouds of sand and dust.

The key was still in the ignition. He turned it with trepidation, but it caught first time. Tears of gratitude moistened his eyes. What a beautiful, wonderful fucking car. He raced back to the lake. Mohammed was breathing shallowly but regularly, though he hadn't regained consciousness. Even with Gaille to worry about, Knox couldn't just leave him. The man weighed a ton. It was all Knox could do to heave him into the back. Then he set off back to Siwa and its General Hospital, devising plans as he went.

III

It was late morning when Nicolas drew close enough to the coast to pick up a signal on his mobile. He called Ibrahim's home number at once, then Manolis and Sofronio. Still nothing.

He called Thessalonike, but now Katerina wasn't answering either. Fear was a pool of acid in his gut. Manolis and Sofronio were his pilot and co-pilot — without them, they'd be stuck in this shit-hole of a country. Alexandria was still six hours away, but he had to know what was going on so that he could make contingency plans. He called the other 4×4 on their mobile. Bastiaan answered. He ordered them to drive on ahead and investigate.

IV

Knox pulled up outside Siwa General Hospital, tooting his horn frantically. A nurse came out, shielding his eyes from the morning sun. Knox flung open the rear door, showed him Mohammed, a handcuff still locked around his wrist.

'What happened?' asked the nurse, moving already into diagnosis.

'His heart stopped,' replied Knox. 'He almost drowned.'

The nurse ran back inside, reappearing a few moments later with a doctor and a trolley. 'The police will want to talk to you,' said the doctor.

'Of course.'

They loaded Mohammed gently, wheeled him inside.

'Come with us,' said the doctor. 'You'd better wait inside.'

'In a moment,' said Knox. 'I need something from my Jeep.' He went back out. Police be fucked. It wasn't just Nicolas' warning about

405

what he'd do if he encountered trouble. It was that the Egyptians were notoriously trigger-happy in hostage situations and no way was he about to entrust Gaille to their care. Anywhere else in the world, he wouldn't have had a hope of catching Nicolas after the head start he had. But this wasn't anywhere else. This was Siwa, and Siwa was unique. There was no way the container lorry could cross the desert. That meant it only had one possible route out. North to the coast, then east to Alexandria. Once in Alexandria, all Egypt would open up, but that was still many hours away.

He put his hand on the dashboard. 'Just one more journey,' he pleaded. 'Just one more.' Then he roared away.

V

Nicolas' mobile rang when he was passing by El Alamein. 'Yes?'

'Bastiaan here. We're at the villa.'

'And?'

'It's burned out. No sign of the guys. But there are uniforms everywhere. Fire. Police. Medical.'

Nicolas fell silent as he realised the extent of this disaster. The alibis that had been meant to protect them were now going to hang them. They'd all been filmed entering the villa on the security cameras. And even if the fire had by some miracle destroyed the tape, the rental cars outside would still lead the police inexorably to the airport, to their immigration details, to their

406

plane. Going for it now would be like salmon leaping for the net. He ordered Bastiaan to head back and meet them outside Alexandria. Then he called Katerina in Thessalonike again. She answered this time, but he'd barely said a word when she cut in and told him primly she wasn't at liberty to discuss company policy on that matter, but she could get someone to —

'There are people with you?'

'Yes.'

'Police?'

'Yes.'

'They're listening in?'

'No.'

'Recording calls?'

'Not yet.'

'You can get somewhere and call back?'

'Not immediately, sir.'

'As soon as you can.'

Nicolas chewed knuckles while he waited. It was twenty minutes before she rang back.

'I'm sorry, sir,' she said breathlessly. 'There are police everywhere. They have warrants. Apparently the Egyptians asked them to — '

'You've heard from Manolis and Sofronio?'

'Not directly, sir. But I overheard a policeman. I think there's been a fight with the Egyptian police. I think Manolis is hurt. He had to go to hospital. Sir, they're saying he killed a man. What's going on? They're accusing us all of terrible things. Everything's going crazy. People are terrified. They're searching our files. They're freezing our accounts. I heard two of them talking about ordering our ships back to port.'

'They can't do that,' protested Nicolas. 'Put Mando onto it.'

'I already have. He says it's going to take him a couple of days to — '

'I don't have two days,' yelled Nicolas. 'Sort it out now.'

'Yes, sir.'

'And call me. Call me the moment you learn anything.'

'Yes, sir.'

'And I need Gabbar Mounim's phone number again. Quick as you can.'

'Yes, sir.'

VI

The dread was building in Knox. He'd been pounding his poor Jeep for seven hours and still he hadn't caught up with the lorry, and Alexandria was now only thirty kilometres ahead. Was it possible he'd miscalculated? Was it possible Nicolas had got here already, or found another route out? A plane from Marsa Matruh? Across the border into Libya? No. Both of those would be madness, let alone impossible to organise on such short notice. This *had* to be their route. He just had to keep on going.

Five kilometres shy of the first main road junction, he glimpsed a container lorry ahead. He sped up. Yes. And one of the 4×4s in front of it. He took his foot off the gas at once, dropped back to a discreet distance, and followed.

40

The moment Bastiaan and his crew returned from their Alexandria sortie, Nicolas ordered everyone off the road. They took a sandy track to the edge of a lake, mist rising from its water, shabby fishermen poling their weather-beaten punts along narrow channels between reed-covered islets. He'd intended to explain the situation to them all, canvass their ideas, discuss plans, but nerves were so strained by fear as they realised the extent of their predicament that they quickly began shouting, jostling, blaming each other. It was just as well that Katerina called at that moment, giving everyone a chance to calm down.

She had Gabbar Mounim's number for Nicolas. He called it at once. A woman answered. He asked for Mounim, gave his own name. Without even checking, she told him politely that Mr Mounim couldn't come to the phone right now. He asked her more forcefully. She repeated her message. He screamed at her. She repeated it once more, completely unperturbed. Nicolas breathed deep, asked as politely as he could when Mr Mounim might be able to call him back. Mr Mounim was very busy all this week, apparently. Perhaps next week or the week after.

Nicolas killed the call, fearful suddenly they might run a trace. News of leprosy travelled so fast in his world, it defied Einstein. He slammed the heel of his hand against the side of the container. It rang dully. Their plane was tainted, their ship. Their names, descriptions, passport numbers and licence plates would already be spreading like disease along the wires. He closed his eyes. Dismay curdled to anger.

Knox. It could only be Knox. Knox had blabbed.

He went to the rear of the container. He'd made the penalty of interference clear. It wasn't his fault now. If you wanted people to take you seriously in this world, you had to be prepared to execute your threats. The container's door was open. It was still hot and stifling inside. The girl was lying gagged on the floor, her wrists bound around the interior handrail, her lips dry and chapped. Nicolas untied her and dragged her by her ankle to the mouth of the container. She struggled limply, weak with dehydration. He dumped her onto the sandy earth. Surplus baggage. Dangerous baggage. Baggage with a mouth.

He'd left the Walther in the 4×4. He held out his hand to Leonidas. 'The AK, please.'

Leonidas blinked. 'She's just a girl.'

'Are you stupid?' shouted Nicolas. 'She's seen everything. You want to spend your life in a Gippo fucking gaol?'

The girl spat out her gag so that it hung like a noose around her neck. 'Please,' she sobbed. 'Please.' Her face was ugly with tears and mucus.

Nicolas couldn't bear to look at her. 'Don't kill me,' she wailed, shuffling towards him on her knees. 'Oh God, I won't talk. I swear. Don't kill me. Please don't kill me. I don't want to die. I don't want to die.'

'Your father rejected violence,' said Leonidas. 'Your father — '

'My father is dead,' snapped Nicolas, his hand trembling. Weaken now, he'd be a joke. 'Give me your fucking gun.' He snatched it from Leonidas' grip. Leonidas looked nauseated, turned his back. It was just as well to know who had the stomach for the hard tasks.

The girl was still mewling, clawing at his trousers. He clubbed her with the butt, took a step back, raised it to his shoulder. He'd never killed anyone before. He'd given orders, sure. And they'd brought a few corpses from the morgues up into the mountains for training purposes. Puncturing human flesh helped harden you, even if it was lifeless. He'd come almost to enjoy the sensation of plunging a bayonet into a stomach. You had to attack it with commitment, or the blade would push back rather than penetrate the skin. But this was different. He'd thought it would feel clean and sharp and fine to kill. In truth it felt squalid and deformed.

She was kneeling, hugging and kissing his feet. It was better when he couldn't see her face. He filled his sights with the dark hair on the top of her skull. Her face bobbed up again. Again he balked. Shooting her through her eyes or forehead made him feel distinctly uncomfortable. Why couldn't she just keep her face down? Didn't she have any consideration? He menaced her again with the gun. She fell onto her back, wailing. Her face was grey and harrowed with terror. He gestured for her to roll onto her front. She wouldn't. She lay there, mewling perversely, as though she knew the turmoil she was putting him through. He gritted his teeth. This was the price of leadership. This was the price of Macedonian liberation. He steeled himself by imagining all the accolades and glory that would be his due. Then he pressed the butt into his shoulder and filled his sights with her face once more.

II

Knox had followed the convoy off the road at a safe distance, concealing his Jeep behind a rocky bank, then watching the Greeks argue and panic. Though he was too far to hear their exact words, it was clear from their confrontation that their plans had gone seriously awry and they were scared.

Nicolas vanished purposefully into the container. A minute later, he dragged Gaille out, then demanded an AK47 from one of his men. Knox watched sickly, but there was nothing he could do. He had no mobile to summon the police or army. And he was unarmed and alone. Trying to save her now would be nothing but suicide. His only sane option was to go fetch help. He'd done his best, after all. It was someone else's turn. No one would blame him.

He crouched over to his Jeep, started her up, the highway traffic close enough to muffle the sound. Then he just sat there a moment, because he knew in his heart that going for help was condemning Gaille to death. And he couldn't accept that. He just couldn't. It wasn't simply the debt he owed her father, though that was part of it. It was Gaille herself. It was the way he'd come to feel about her.

His skin prickled with fear as he realised what he was going to do. Don't be an arse, he told himself. It did no good. He took a deep breath and closed his eyes, almost in prayer. Then he stamped his foot to the floor, like some old knight spurring on his faithful steed, and charged.

III

An engine roared behind Nicolas. He whirled around to see an old Jeep hurtling directly at him. *Knox!* He was standing there in numb disbelief when Leonidas snatched back his AK47 and sprayed a burst at the Jeep's bonnet. The hood sprang up; the engine spouted geysers of steam and licked with flames. He could hear Knox revving futilely, but the Jeep rolled slowly to a stop in front of them. The hood clanged back down. Knox opened the door and fled, but a round hit him in the leg, and he cried out with pain and fell headlong, and a moment later he had Bastiaan and Eneas upon him.

Nicolas wrested back the gun from Leonidas. Killing the girl was one thing. Killing Knox another. He walked over, lifted the gun to his shoulder, aimed down.

'Wait!' cried Knox desperately, turning onto his back, holding up his arms as if that could protect him. 'Listen! I can get you out. I can get you out of Egypt.'

'Of course you can,' mocked Nicolas, his finger on the trigger. 'You can sprout wings and fly us, no doubt.'

But Leonidas pushed down the muzzle of Nicolas' gun. 'How?' he asked.

'I'll ask the questions,' snapped Nicolas. He turned back to Knox, raised his gun once more. He felt ridiculous suddenly. 'How?' he asked.

'I know people,' said Knox.

'Oh, you *know* people?' sneered Nicolas. 'We all know people.'

'I know Hassan al-Assyuti,' said Knox.

Nicolas frowned. 'The shipping agent?'

'I saved his life,' nodded Knox. 'A diving accident. I gave him mouth-to-mouth. He said if I ever needed a favour — '

Nicolas squinted at him. 'You're lying.'

'Take me to see him. He's in Suez. Ask him yourself. He'll tell you.'

'*Take* you to see him?' snorted Nicolas. 'He's your best fucking friend and you don't even know his phone number?'

'I've never had to call in the favour before.'

Nicolas hesitated. Knox was up to something. He was sure of it. But if there was any truth whatever to his claim ... He opened up his mobile again, called Katerina, asked her to find a number for al-Assyuti. He walked in circles as he waited for her to call back, stamping his feet. When finally she did, he dialled it himself. He didn't trust Knox one bit. He asked for Hassan al-Assyuti, was put on hold. He kept his eyes on Knox all the time, waiting for him to blink, back down, admit this was bullshit. A woman picked up and tried to fob him off with a practised spiel about Hassan being in a meeting and could she please take a message, which she would make sure he received at the very first —

'I need to speak to him now,' said Nicolas. 'Tell him it's Daniel Knox.'

'Daniel Knox?' She was clearly taken aback. 'Oh. Yes. Right. I ... I'll put you straight through.'

Nicolas couldn't hide his astonishment. He held the phone in such a way that Knox could talk, but so that he could listen in as well. Hassan came on.

'Knox?' he demanded. 'Is that really you?'

'That's right,' said Knox quickly. 'Listen, I want to come see you.'

There was a pause. Then Hassan asked incredulously: 'You want to come to see me?'

'That's right. I need something shipped out of Egypt. If I come to see you, will you take care of it for me?'

There was silence. 'You'll come yourself? In person?'

'If you agree to help me get this shipment out.'

'What kind of shipment? Where headed?'

'I'll tell you when I see you.'

'Very well. Can you get to Suez?'

'Sure. Give me six hours.'

'Six hours then. At my container terminal.' He snapped off directions that Nicolas jotted down. The line went dead. Nicolas closed his phone.

'Well?' asked Leonidas.

'He agreed to help,' admitted Nicolas reluctantly. Something stank, though he wasn't quite sure what. But it was a lifeline, and he had no option but to grab it. 'You'll stay in the container until Suez,' he told Knox. 'One sound and you're dead. Understand?'

'Yes.'

'Get us out of Egypt and you and the girl can go. You have my word.' He smiled as he spoke, and looked directly into Knox's eyes. He couldn't afford him realising there was no way on earth he'd allow two witnesses to all this mayhem simply to walk away.

41

I

Knox and Gaille were gagged and tied to the handrail at the cab-end of the container. One of the Greeks, a burly man they called Eneas, was handed a flashlight and ordered to watch over them. Knox's thigh throbbed with his gunshot wound; but from the quick examination he'd been allowed, it looked worse than it felt, ploughing a deep furrow along his skin, but missing muscle and bone.

The container was stiflingly hot once the rear doors were closed, and stuffy too, particularly when Eneas lit himself a cigarette. After he'd stubbed it out, he drank great gulps from a water bottle, then splashed it profligately over his hair and forehead. Just the sound of it was torment. Knox closed his eyes and dreamed of waterfalls and crushed ice.

The coffin and lid were so heavy that the container lorry's brakes shrieked when they slowed to refuel. Eneas stood above Knox, menacing him with the butt of his AK47 until they rumbled off again, so that he rocked back ever so slightly on his heels. Gears crunched and the engine whined as they struggled to pick up speed. Just as well Egypt was so flat.

Gaille began sobbing behind her gag. She'd had two or three such bouts already, interspersed with long periods of calm. Terror was too intense to sustain. Knox too had had two periods of icy shudders when his shirt saturated with sweat, exacerbating his dehydration. In between, however, his mind felt clear as he sought a way to get himself and Gaille out of their dire predicament. But nothing came to him.

He stopped trying to force it. Experience had taught him that answers often came when he allowed himself to think of something else. Their guard lit another cigarette, the flame of his lighter glowing red-gold off Alexander's coffin. Knox found himself staring at it. What an end for such a man, a pawn in the never-ending game of politics and personal advancement. But there was a certain appropriateness too. Alexander's life itself had ended in anticlimax in Babylon, triggered perhaps by the horrors of the Gedrosian Desert, into which he'd led 40,000 men, and out of which he'd brought just 15,000. There'd been death in the air. An elderly Indian philosopher called Calanus had joined Alexander on his campaigns, but he'd fallen sick. Unwilling to rot away, he'd burned himself alive instead, assuring Alexander they'd meet again soon. In a drinking contest to celebrate his life, forty-one Macedonians had died, including the winner. Then Alexander's closest friend Hephaiston had died too, the greatest blow of all. And then there'd been Alexander's visit to the tomb of Cyrus the Great at Pasargadae. Cyrus had been the greatest conqueror and emperor before Alexander, a semi-divine figure worshipped throughout Persia. Yet Alexander discovered his bones lying scattered on the floor by bandits who'd tried unsuccessfully to steal his golden sarcophagus. The inscription on Cyrus' tomb had read: 'O man, whoever you are and from wherever you may come — for I know that you will come — I am Cyrus who won the Persians their Empire. Therefore do not begrudge me this little earth which covers my body.' But his plea had gone unheard.

They said that when Alexander was lying on his deathbed in Babylon, aware his end was upon him, he'd tried to drag his failing body down to the river that ran by the palace, so that he'd be swept away by the waters, that the world might believe him taken up to his rightful place among the gods. But perhaps he'd also sought to deny his successors the chance to treat his mortal remains with the disrespect they'd shown Cyrus. So maybe that was the fate Alexander had wanted for his body. Not Siwa, nor Alexandria, nor Macedonia, but the oblivion of water.

The oblivion of water. *Yes.* And, finally, the germ of an idea came to Knox.

It seemed forever before the lorry next stopped. The back of the container shrieked as it was opened. Knox leaned his head back against the steel wall. Fear tickled his chest like the beads of a rosary. Stars lay low on the horizon. The day was gone. Perhaps his last.

Nicolas climbed up inside. One side of his hair was spiky, as though he'd napped against the window. He pointed the Walther at Knox. 'We're in Suez,' he said, as Eneas untied Knox's bonds and pulled out his gag. Knox clenched and unclenched his hands to get the circulation back. He stood gingerly and rubbed his thigh.

Nicolas gestured Knox to go to the mouth of the container. Knox ignored him. He picked up Eneas' water bottle. There were still a few mouthfuls left. He removed Gaille's gag, held the bottle to her lips, tipped it up for her until it was empty. Then he kissed her on her crown.

'I'll do my best,' he promised her.

'I know you will.'

'Move,' said Nicolas, jabbing him with the Walther's muzzle.

Knox hobbled to the end, making more of his injury than it really warranted, hoping to convince Nicolas he was badly hurt. He helped himself gingerly down onto tarmac, giving a little cry of pain as he landed, then hopping a couple of times on his good leg. They were in the corner of a huge, empty car park. It stank of stale fumes and scorched rubber. Arabic music drifted from a distant petrol station. Over a wall of trees, the sky glowed orange.

'This is how it's going to work,' said Nicolas. 'You and Leonidas will go to see al-Assyuti. You'll negotiate our safe passage back to Greece. When Leonidas is satisfied, he'll call me and — '

'Fuck that,' said Knox. 'I do nothing until Gaille is safe.'

Nicolas gave a tight smile. 'When Leonidas is satisfied, he'll call me, and both you and the girl can go free.'

'Forget it. Let Gaille go now and I'll do my best for you. You have my word.'

Nicolas sighed. 'The girl's our leverage. You

can't expect us to release her.'

'And Hassan's my leverage,' replied Knox. 'I'm not going to deal with him for you until the girl's safe.'

A siren wailed out on the main road. Flashing blue and red lights. They all turned as casually as they could, competing to show the least alarm. It was only an ambulance. They waited until it was out of sight.

'We keep the girl,' said Nicolas. 'That's not up for discussion.'

Knox shrugged. 'Then how about this,' he suggested. 'I go see Hassan, like you want. And I take your man with me. But Gaille comes too.'

Nicolas snorted. 'What kind of fool do you take me for?'

'You want to get out of Egypt, don't you? All I want is this over and done with. We'll all go in together, if you don't trust me.'

'Sure!' mocked Nicolas. 'Straight into your trap.'

'What trap? How on earth could I have arranged a trap? Besides, you're going to have to trust yourself to al-Assyuti at some point.'

Nicolas glared at him for a few moments, trying to read what he was up to. But then he shook his head and beckoned for Leonidas and Bastiaan to come with him. The three of them walked off a few paces, conferring urgently but quietly. When they were done, Nicolas came back.

'We'll all go in together,' he said, as though it had been his idea. 'But the girl will stay in the container with Eneas.' He held up his mobile.

'Try anything — if I even *sniff* a trap — it'll be the end of her. Understand?'

Knox looked into his eyes. The devil and the deep blue sea, rocks and hard places, Scylla and Charybdis. Hurling nitro at glycerine in hopes of crawling out of the resulting crater wasn't much of a strategy, but he had no alternative.

'Yes,' he said.

Nicolas gestured at a 4×4. 'Good. Then come with me.'

'If Gaille's in the lorry, I'm in the lorry.'

'Very well,' scowled Nicolas. 'We'll ride up front with Bastiaan.'

II

Oncoming headlights spiked into Knox's eyes as he sat between the two Greeks in the container lorry's high cab. Adrenalin added lustre to the ink-blue night sky, and his mind felt almost unnaturally sharp. Bastiaan drove anxiously, grinding the gears, muttering and cursing, perhaps uncomfortable with such a heavy load, or perhaps with the situation he found himself in. Nicolas kept the muzzle of his Walther pressed unnecessarily hard into Knox's ribs, while giving Bastiaan directions at the same time.

They turned off the main road into an industrial estate of low warehousing and cracked concrete. There was no other traffic. All the offices were closed. Every twenty metres or so, streetlights made yellow pools in the sea of black.

A line of tall cranes marked the waterfront. A series of 'PRIVATE: KEEP OUT' signs bearing the logo of al-Assyuti Trading ran along a high chain-link fence.

Bastiaan checked his wing mirrors and slowed as they neared the entrance. The brakes began to sing. He released them to hush them. When he turned to make the approach, their front wheels bumped pavement. They pulled up at a wooden barrier. Bastiaan lowered his window to attract the attention of the elderly security guard playing checkers against himself in a glass-walled booth, watched by a Doberman on a leash. He sighed, hobbled across, squinted up at Bastiaan and asked in Arabic what he wanted. Bastiaan shrugged and looked at Knox and Nicolas for assistance.

'I'm Daniel Knox,' said Knox. 'Mr al-Assyuti is expecting me.'

'All of you?' asked the man.

'Yes.'

A ship's horn sounded distantly. The guard shrugged and shook his head, then returned to his booth, made a call. With the window open, cool night air flooded in, bringing the smell of diesel, salt and rotting fish. A security camera whirred and focused. The barrier lifted. Bastiaan drove on through, struggling to pick up speed. The office buildings were at the far end of the terminal. There were stacks of coloured containers everywhere, like a gigantic set of child's building blocks. There was no one in sight, no navvies, no fork-lift truck drivers, no truckers, no crane operators. Emptiness and silence. The

4×4s fanned out like wing men either side of the lorry. A huge ship lumbered along the canal. The lights of its bridge and deck doubled in the water, and Knox had a disembodied yet overpowering sensation that the past decade of his life was now reaching its climax. The deaths of his parents and of his sister, his conflict with the Dragoumises, his years with Richard, the quest for Alexander. And Gaille too. Gaille most of all.

As if reading his mind, Nicolas punched a number into his mobile. A moment later, Knox heard it ringing in the container behind. When Eneas answered, Nicolas held it up for Knox to see.

'I'll do it,' he warned. 'I'll have her killed if you try anything. I swear I will.'

Something about his choice of words made Knox frown. A memory of Elena came unexpectedly to his mind, of her standing before Dragoumis in the moment before she shot him, and the words she'd used to explain herself.

'Elena didn't *kill* Pavlos,' he muttered. 'She *had* him killed. That's what she told your father.'

Nicolas scowled. 'So?'

'Elena was an archaeologist, not a Mafia wife. How would she have someone killed?'

'How the fuck should I know?' But there was an edge of anxiety in Nicolas' voice.

'How long has Costis worked for you?' demanded Knox, certain he was on to something.

'Shut up!'

'I bet he was working for you back then,

424

wasn't he? Did Elena know him?'

'Where do you get this bullshit?' protested Nicolas shrilly.

'Elena went to Costis,' asserted Knox. 'She hired him to kill Pavlos.'

'Stop this!'

'And that's why Elena shot him. Not because he was standing next to your father, but because he was the one who actually arranged the crash.'

'I said stop it!'

'And Costis was on your payroll.'

'I'm telling you: this is your last warning.'

'He'd never have accepted a job like that without clearing it with you first.'

Nicolas smacked Knox's temple with the barrel of the Walther. 'I warned you,' he yelled.

'Did you know my family would be in that car?' demanded Knox.

'For fuck's sake! Shut up, will you!'

'Did you know my sister would be in it?'

'Just fucking shut up!'

'She was sixteen years old,' said Knox. 'She was sixteen fucking years old.'

'This is war!' shrieked Nicolas. 'Don't you understand? War! Sacrifices have to be made.'

There was a moment of shocked silence, as though neither man could quite believe the confession. Nicolas pointed the Walther at Knox's brow, his hand trembling with shame and fear, his finger on the trigger, ready to murder him merely to avoid his reproach. But then the lorry's brakes began to sing as Bastiaan pulled up outside the office building, and a man pushed through the darkened double doors ahead,

425

letting them swing closed behind him.

'Who's that?' muttered Nicolas. 'Is that Hassan?'

Knox shook his head. 'Nessim.'

'Nessim?'

'Hassan's head of security.'

'Security?' Nicolas' voice went flat, deadened by presentiment.

Nessim waited until all the vehicles had come to a halt. Then he gave a signal and all around them, on the roofs of containers, men armed with automatic weapons stood up, aiming down, poised to fire. Sash windows were raised in all the offices, and more gun-barrels slithered out.

'You're completely surrounded,' shouted Nessim, hands cupped around his mouth. 'Turn off your engines. Put away your weapons. Place your hands on your heads. Open your doors slowly. Then come out one by one. No one needs to die.'

Nicolas glared at Knox with utter loathing. He raised his mobile. 'It's a trap,' he snarled. 'Kill the — '

Knox smashed the mobile from Nicolas' hand before he could finish his command, but Nicolas still had the Walther, and he turned it on Knox as he pulled the trigger. Knox flung back his head so that the bullet only scorched his cheek before shattering the driver's side window. It was like a starter's pistol, setting everyone off. Bursts of gunfire flashed orange from the 4×4 to their left. Nessim flung himself down. A countering firestorm erupted from on top of the containers and the office windows, turning the 4×4 instantly into a sieve, bullets clanging and whistling and shrieking through the metal and off the asphalt. Knox grabbed Nicolas' wrist and twisted it until he dropped the Walther, while Bastiaan crunched the lorry into reverse, gunning the engine in a desperate effort to pick up speed. There was yelling all around, cries of pain, people running, constant gunfire, but somehow the lorry remained unscathed. The second 4×4 turned in a circle, automatic weapons blazing from its window. The firestorm turned its wrath upon it, glass and metal puncturing and shattering. A back door opened, a man jumped out. He ran five paces, firing blindly behind him, before being cut down, crashing to the ground.

The lorry was finally picking up some pace. Nicolas and Knox fought for the Walther as it slid around the floor beneath the cab's seats. A single bullet put a cobweb in the windscreen. Bastiaan grunted and was thrown back, a small hole in the front of his forehead. Then he slumped forwards, revealing the great red crater in the back. They began at once to lose speed. Nicolas seized the Walther and turned it on Knox. Knox butted him on the bridge of his nose, then grabbed his wrist and slammed it repeatedly against the dashboard until he dropped it. He pushed Bastiaan aside, reached his foot across to stamp on the gas. They accelerated once more. He wrenched the steering wheel round, reversing them towards the canal. Nicolas picked up the Walther again and turned it on him just as their rear wheels dropped off the jetty's edge and their undercarriage scraped and screeched on the canal wall. The weight of gold in the container used the jetty's edge as a fulcrum to hurl the cab into the air. Nicolas shrieked as they were flung upright, then plunged down into the water. The lorry shuddered as it hit, then again as gravity threw Alexander's golden coffin and lid like twin battering rams into the rear doors, tearing them off their hinges, then spilling out into the canal, plunging down through the water.

The lorry bobbed twice, then flopped onto its belly. Without the golden coffin weighing it down, there was enough trapped air to keep it afloat. Nicolas tried to wrest open the passenger door to get out, but the weight of water wouldn't allow it. He wound down the window instead, letting the canal gush in, frothing silver. He tried to climb out but Knox grabbed his ankle and wound the window back up, pinning his waist. The cab tipped onto its side, trapping Nicolas underwater. He kicked and kicked in an effort to break free, but Knox reminded himself of his sister, of his parents, of Rick, and hardened his heart. It seemed an age before Nicolas finally went still. Knox climbed out the other window, keeping the container between himself and the gunmen now lining the jetty. His eyes were soon on fire from the polluted water so that he had to feel his way around. But when he opened them in a blurry squint, he was sure for a moment that he could see the twin eye sockets of a skull staring back at him before it fell on its side, releasing bubbles like a dying breath, and swirling away down into the deeps.

He shook his head to clear it. Let the dead bury the dead. He had Gaille to save. The container's rear doors had been ripped off. He pulled himself inside. It was already two-thirds underwater, and filling fast. Everything had tipped out during the plunge, everything but Gaille, saved by her rope cuffs around the handrail, as he'd prayed she would be. But the water was already up to her throat, so that she had her head tilted back, straining upwards for air.

Knox ducked underwater to find and then untie her bonds, but the wet knots had pulled tight, and the water level was rising all the time, over her chin now, her mouth, her nostrils. He kept on at the rope until he felt at last a little give in it, enough to work in a nail and then a fingertip, and suddenly the knots were loose and Gaille slipped her wrists free, and she and Knox turned and swam for the mouth of the container, emerging from it together, gasping for breath, turning around to watch the container vanish underwater with a final belch of released air.

A line of men stood along the waterfront, rifles raised and aimed. Nessim, standing out front, pointed them to a flight of steps that led up out of the water. The fight that had kept Knox going finally deserted him. He knew it was all up for himself. All he could hope for now was to give Gaille a chance. He swam tiredly across, helped her out by her elbow. She took his hand. He tried to pull free, to put distance between them, but she realised what he was up to and refused to

429

let go. They climbed the steps silently together, still holding hands, giving each other courage.

'Follow me,' ordered Nessim.

Knox's leg had started bleeding again. It pulsed with pain so that he couldn't help but limp. Hassan's men were pulling bodies out of the 4×4s. A rear door fell open and Vasilieos' head flopped out, his AK47 rattling onto the concourse. Weapons immediately were turned towards the noise, safety catches released. Then they realised there was no danger, and someone cracked a joke and everybody laughed, relief from the nervous tension of combat.

Knox's sodden clothes grew increasingly chill. He put his arm around Gaille, squeezed her shoulder, kissed her temple. She smiled bravely at him. The polluted water burned tears from his eyes that ran freely down his cheeks. He wiped them away. He kept thinking about the moment Nicolas had shuddered and died, the door between life and death that they were now standing at themselves. Despite his fear, he had no urge to run. It was out of his hands; the jury had retired. Nessim showed them into a drab office with a huge stuffed fish in a glass case and tattered charts of freshwater and marine species on the wall. He left for a moment, returned with two dirty hand towels, tossed them one each. They wiped dry their faces, their arms. Knox sat down and clamped his towel over his leg. 'What happens now?' he asked.

'We wait,' said Nessim.

'For what?'

'Mr al-Assyuti was in Sharm when you called.

He'll be here any minute.'

'This has nothing to do with the girl,' said Knox. 'Let her go.'

'We wait for Mr al-Assyuti,' said Nessim.

'Please,' begged Knox. 'I let you and your men go in Tanta. You owe me. Let her go.'

But Nessim only shook his head. Knox closed his eyes, weary, frightened and dismayed. It galled him that al-Assyuti of all men would be the one to benefit. He'd have no trouble dredging the sarcophagus and lid from the mud and murk of the canal bed, and once he did, he'd prise out the gemstones and melt down the gold, destroying forever one of the great finds of modern archaeology. And who could say that he wouldn't get his hands on the rest of the Siwa treasure too; he or Yusuf Abbas or the two of them together? The thought of such corrupt men turning so glorious a find to their own benefit made him feel physically ill.

His whole life, Knox had searched for such objects, not for their intrinsic value, but for the knowledge they brought with them; yet first by cutting the Gordian knot, then by reversing the container lorry into the canal, he'd wilfully played his own part, just to give himself and Gaille a chance of life, where there'd seemed no chance at all. And it hadn't even worked. Then he looked sideways at her sitting beside him and he felt a certain peace; because he knew absolutely that if he had to do it all again, even knowing what he knew now, he wouldn't hesitate. He took her hand again, interlaced fingers, gave her a little squeeze of reassurance.

She smiled and reciprocated, caressing his skin with her thumb.

Fifteen minutes passed; headlights sprang through the window. Knox's heart accelerated. He glanced again at Gaille, who was looking as frightened as he felt. Footsteps grew loud. Nessim opened the door and Hassan al-Assyuti walked through, hands clasped behind his back. He looked bigger than Knox remembered. His eye and jaw were both puffy, and he grimaced as he moved, as though still feeling the beating he'd taken.

'Let the girl go,' said Knox at once. 'She knows nothing about this.'

Hassan smiled wolfishly, showing a flash of gold where previously there'd only been white. 'You're a hard man to find, Mr Knox. My men have been scouring all Egypt.'

'We had a deal,' said Knox. 'I said I'd come to see you. You said you'd get a shipment out for me. I'm here. She's the shipment. Keep your word. Get her out.'

'You don't think you've breached the terms of that particular contract? You don't think three vehicles filled with armed and hostile men allows me to — '

'Please,' said Knox. 'I'm begging you. Do what you want with me, but let the girl go.'

'What? So she can walk straight out of here and sell her story to the press?'

'She won't do that. Tell him, Gaille. Give him your word.'

'Fuck him,' said Gaille, through chattering teeth. 'I'm staying with you.'

Hassan barked out a laugh, amusement and admiration mixed. 'You prefer looks to intelligence in your women, I see.'

'You won't get away with this.'

'Get away with what?' shrugged Hassan. 'All I've done so far is rescue you from a situation of extreme jeopardy. You should be thanking me. As for what I'm going to do next . . . '

'Yes?' asked Knox.

'You humiliated me in Sharm, Mr Knox,' said Hassan, tendons tautening in his neck. 'People have been *laughing* at me. At me, Mr Knox. At *me*. I'm sure you appreciate that I can't allow such things to go . . . *unremedied*.' He came a step closer, leaned down so that the tip of his nose was almost touching Knox's, his breath sour in Knox's nostrils. 'It's a simple matter of respect.'

'Respect!' snorted Knox. 'You were raping a girl.'

Hassan's eyes narrowed. He stood up once more, his fists clenched. Knox braced himself for a punch, but Hassan restrained himself, even managed a taut smile. 'I'd almost given up hope of finding you,' he said. 'But then, this afternoon, you called out of the blue. I thought it was a joke at first. I thought you were *taunting* me. You had to be aware, after all, of what I'd do to you. But then an extraordinary news story began to break. A man recovering in Siwa Hospital began babbling about discovering the tomb of Alexander the Great and golden coffins and a conspiracy of Greeks and how a young man called Knox had come to his rescue. And

433

suddenly your telephone call began to make some sense. What else could your shipment be but these renegade Greeks, this plundered treasure?'

'How happy you must have been,' said Knox bitterly. 'Having me deliver it straight to your door! Don't you have enough gold?'

'A man can never have enough gold, Mr Knox,' retorted Hassan. 'And yet you're right, in a way. Money has never been a problem for me. There are other things, however, that I've found more difficult to acquire. Do you see where I'm going, Mr Knox?'

'My guess would be to prison for life.'

Hassan laughed. 'You couldn't be more wrong. This isn't some crude heist. This is an official operation. Semi-official, at least. Those men out there are paratroops, Egypt's finest, old comrades of Nessim's. After all, you don't really imagine I have thirty armed marksmen to call upon at such short notice, do you? And why do you think your convoy wasn't challenged on your approach to Suez? And why do you think no one shot at your container, except when your driver tried to get away?'

'I don't understand,' protested Gaille. 'What's he talking about?'

'I'm talking about a way for you two to walk out of here alive,' he told her. 'I'm talking about a way for everybody to win.'

'Go on,' said Knox.

'The ambitions of youth aren't the same as the ambitions of maturity, Mr Knox. You've probably realised that for yourself. When I was a young man, I craved only money, because money is like air — if you don't have it, nothing else matters. But once you have it . . . ' he made a dismissive gesture.

'So what *do* you want?'

'Legitimacy. Respectability. A place in the hearts of my people. An opportunity to serve.'

'An opportunity to serve!' snorted Knox. 'I don't believe this! You're going into *politics?*'

Hassan allowed himself a smile. 'Our nation is led by an ageing generation,' he said. 'A generation out of touch with its people. Egypt is crying out for new leadership, for people with fresh ideas and energy, for people who understand the new ways. I intend to be one of those people. Yet politics in Egypt is not an easy world to penetrate, particularly for a man with my . . . background. Egypt is riddled with nepotism, as you know. Too many sons are already waiting in line. And I'm sure you realise that patience isn't my strongest point.'

'So that's it,' muttered Knox. 'You're going to make yourself the hero of the hour. The saviour of Egypt's heritage.'

'And you're going to help me, Mr Knox,' nodded Hassan. 'You're going to tell the world that the reason you contacted me earlier today was because when you realised that these great Egyptian treasures were in danger, you knew I was the person to go to, because I always put my country and my people ahead of anything else; and you've been proved right by events, because I've done exactly that.'

435

'And if I don't?'

Hassan reached out to stroke Gaille's cheek. 'It's already a blood-bath outside, Mr Knox. Do you really believe that two more corpses would make any difference?'

'You're bluffing.'

'Is that a challenge, Mr Knox?'

Knox stared at him, trying to read behind his eyes. But the man was made of stone; he gave nothing away. He glanced instead at Gaille, bracing herself for the worst, yet prepared to suffer it on his account; and he knew then that he had no choice. 'Fine,' he said. 'You have a deal.'

'Good,' said Hassan. He nodded at Nessim, still standing stolidly by the door. 'You have my head of security to thank, you know. This was his idea. I was *angry* with you, Mr Knox. You have no idea how angry. After your call came, I wanted you shot. But Nessim persuaded me this was the wiser course.' He leaned in close once more, as if to confide a secret. 'I'm a bad enemy to make, Mr Knox. You'd do well to remember that.'

'I will,' Knox assured him. 'Believe me.'

Hassan looked back at him, amused by his defiance, and the two men locked gazes for long enough for both to realise that it wasn't over between them just yet, that unfinished business remained. But it could wait. It would wait. They each had too much to lose.

Knox stood, helped Gaille to her feet, put his arm around her. They walked together to the door, held open for them by Nessim. Knox nodded fractionally at him as they passed, and Nessim nodded back, an acknowledgement of debts settled, perhaps even of mutual respect. But then he and Gaille passed through the door and into a whole new life.

EPILOGUE

So this is what fame feels like, thought Knox, roasting beneath the arc lights as he gazed out over the bank of microphones to the squatted rows of photographers and the TV crews and the press journalists perching forwards on their chairs, taking notes with one hand while straining to be noticed with their other, eager to pose their questions, if only to show their bosses they were doing their jobs, because they must have realised by now that they wouldn't get any answers worth a damn.

'I'm sorry,' declared Yusuf Abbas for the umpteenth time. 'It's far too early to know exactly what we've found. Archaeology doesn't work that way. We need time to secure and examine the sites. We need time to retrieve and study what we find. In a year or two, perhaps, we'll know a little more. Now. Just three more questions, I think. Who wants to — '

'Daniel!' shouted out a young red-headed woman. 'Daniel! Over here!' Knox turned towards her, was momentarily dazzled by the flash of a camera. 'How can you be sure it was Alexander?' she yelled.

'Is it true there's more gold?' called out a Japanese journalist.

'Gaille! Gaille!' cried a grey-headed man. 'Did you think you were going to die?'

'Please,' begged Yusuf, holding up both hands,

438

loving every moment. 'One at a time.'

Knox scratched his cheek, itching with tiredness and accumulated stubble. How bizarre this all was. To think that, at that very moment, people around the world would be watching him on TV. A few would almost certainly be old acquaintances. They'd squint at the screen in disbelief, or maybe mutter an obscenity beneath their breath, or hoot with laughter and pick up their phone to alert mutual friends. *Have you seen the TV? Remember that guy Knox! I swear to God, it's him!*

He glanced across at Gaille. She smiled and raised an eyebrow back at him, as though she understood exactly what was going through his mind. The past twenty-four hours had been bewildering. Their police debriefing in Suez had initially been conducted in a jubilant, self-congratulatory mood. Jokes cracked, hands shaken, he and Gaille treated as heroes. Mohammed's story seemed to have captured the popular imagination. And to make things even sweeter, they'd watched Yusuf Abbas on live TV struggling haplessly to explain his relationship with the Dragoumises, and why he'd given the MAF permission to excavate in the Delta and conduct a survey in Siwa, and why Elena Koloktronis had visited him in Cairo.

But then, suddenly, the tone had changed. A new investigator called Umar had arrived at the police station. His first act had been to have Knox and Gaille locked up in separate cells. Then he'd proceeded to interrogate them unrelentingly. He'd had scimitar sideburns and sharp eyes, and he'd seemed absurdly suspicious of everything Knox had told him. He'd tried to trick him into contradicting himself, and to twist his words against him. He'd showed no interest at all in Nicolas Dragoumis and his men, as though robbery and multiple murder were unimportant to him. He'd focused instead on Knox's own movements, pressing him particularly on the SCA sites in Alexandria and the Delta, trying to force him to admit that he'd broken into them.

'I don't know what you're talking about,' Knox had insisted. 'I know nothing about those sites.'

'Really?' Umar had said, frowning theatrically. 'Then perhaps you can explain how photographs of them were found on a laptop and a digital camera in your Jeep.' Knox's heart had plummeted. He'd forgotten completely about those. To clam up now, or ask for a lawyer, would be tantamount to admitting he had something to hide. To lie to a man like this would be madness; but so would be coming clean. And he'd had Rick's reputation to worry about too. No way could he allow his friend's good name to be tarnished as a tomb robber, not after the sacrifice he'd made. Umar had smiled with infuriating smugness. 'I'm waiting,' he'd said.

'I've done nothing wrong,' Knox had protested.

'That may be your opinion. In my country, we consider breaking into historic sites a very serious crime. Especially for a man already known to have sold antiquities on the black market.'

'That's bullshit!' Knox had protested furiously. 'You know that's bullshit.'

'Explain the photographs, Mr Knox.'

Knox had scowled and sat back in his chair, arms folded across his chest. 'What photographs?'

Umar had snorted. 'Do you know the penalties for antiquities theft? Even for *attempted* theft, you could serve ten years.'

'This is ridiculous. I've just helped save a great treasure for Egypt.'

'Nevertheless,' said Umar, 'a wise man would be aware of the seriousness of his position. Are you a wise man, Mr Knox?'

Knox had narrowed his eyes, sensing subtext in Umar's words. 'What do you mean?'

'I mean that there is *one* explanation for your presence in these sites that I would gladly accept.'

'And that is?'

'That you were there with the authority of the SCA. Specifically, with the knowledge and blessing of the secretary general, Yusuf Abbas.'

Knox had closed his eyes as finally he'd caught on. 'So that's it,' he'd laughed. 'I say I was working undercover for Yusuf, and suddenly he wasn't best friends with the Dragoumises any more. He was *investigating* them. Tell me: what do you get out of it?'

'I've no idea what you're talking about,' Umar had replied primly. 'But perhaps we should go through your statement one more time. The

441

media are clamouring for the full story, as I'm sure you appreciate. Only this time, why don't you start by describing the phone call you made to Yusuf Abbas to alert him to your suspicions about the Dragoumises, and the authority he granted you to act covertly on his behalf?'

'Or?'

'Or everyone loses. Yusuf. You. The girl.'

Knox had felt sick. 'The girl?'

'Egypt needs someone to punish, Mr Knox, and the Greeks are all dead. But your friend Gaille was working for them. She was flown to Thessalonike on a private jet just days ago to meet Philip Dragoumis. She was with Elena Koloktronis in Siwa. Trust me, I can make her look guilty as the devil with far less material than this. Such a sweet young thing too! Can you imagine what even a month in an Egyptian prison would do to her?'

'I don't believe this.'

Umar had leaned forwards. 'And think of this too. If you agree, you'll be a hero. I've been authorised to tell you that the SCA will welcome you back into the fold with open arms, and look favourably upon any future excavation applications you might choose to make.'

For a moment, Knox had felt the urge to hurl the offer back in Umar's face. Five years before, younger and more headstrong, he would have done so. But the wilderness was a good teacher. 'If I agree,' he'd said, 'it'll be on one condition.'

'And that is?'

'A new SCA award. The Richard Mitchell Award, presented annually to a promising young

442

archaeologist by the secretary general himself. The first to go posthumously to Rick.'

Umar had allowed himself a small smile. 'You will excuse me one minute?'

Knox had stretched out his leg as he'd waited for Umar to return, the bullet wound feeling pleasantly tight and sore. Nothing but flesh, he'd been assured. In a week, it would be only a scar and a memory.

Umar had come back in. 'Not the Richard Mitchell Award,' he'd said. 'Just the Mitchell Award. A recognition of the contribution the whole family have made. My contact assures me any more would be impossible. I believe him.'

Knox had nodded. Frankly, he'd been surprised Yusuf had buckled even that far. It was effectively an acknowledgement that Richard had been innocent; and if he were innocent, then who but Yusuf could be guilty? He had to be really feeling the heat. For a moment, for precisely that reason, Knox had considered rejecting the deal. But it hadn't been just his own skin at stake.

'Fine,' he'd said. 'But you'll need the girl's agreement too.'

'I already have it,' Umar had told him, patting his pocket. 'It seems she didn't want you in gaol any more than you wanted her.'

'May I see her?'

'Not yet. Once we've rewritten your statement, we'll hold a press conference. You, the girl and Yusuf will tell the world how you worked together with Hassan to foil those dastardly

Greeks. After that, you and she can do as you please.'

'Once we're irretrievably compromised, you mean.'

Umar had only smiled.

And so here they all were, Yusuf Abbas wrapping up the press conference, thanking the journalists for coming, insisting they contact him directly with any further questions, not Knox or Gaille. Then he rested his palms flat on the table, clenched his jaw, braced his hams, and launched himself up out of his chair onto his feet, before beaming around the room as if expecting applause. When it didn't come, he beckoned Gaille and Knox to stand beside him for a few final group photographs, an arm around each of their shoulders as though they were the best and oldest of friends. The cameras clicked their fill. Arc lights started going out. Journalists called friends and offices on their mobiles as they filed out in a muted hubbub. The world's attention moved on, leaving Knox feeling oddly deflated. He'd never sought the spotlight, yet there was something undeniably intoxicating about it.

Yusuf kept his arms around their shoulders as he steered them through the rear doors of the conference hall, enquiring solicitously about their plans. The moment the doors shut behind them, however, he scowled and stepped back and shook his hands with distaste, as though he suspected Knox and Gaille of carrying diseases.

'Don't even think about talking to the press without my permission,' he warned them.

'We gave our word.'

444

Yusuf nodded sourly, as though he knew how much the word of such people was worth. Then he turned his back emphatically on them and lumbered away.

Knox gave a little shudder as he turned to Gaille. 'Want to get out of here? I arranged for a taxi.'

'Then what are we waiting for?'

They made their way along a maze of corridors.

'I can't believe Yusuf's going to get away with it,' muttered Knox.

'We had no choice,' Gaille reassured him. 'There's no evidence against him. There is against us. And it's not our fault Egypt appointed him secretary general.'

'Your father would never have agreed.'

'Yes, he would. He made a deal with Dragoumis, didn't he?' She smiled and took his arm. 'Anyway, it's done now. Please let's talk about something else.'

'Such as?'

'Such as what are you going to do now?'

He thought bleakly of Rick. 'I've a funeral to attend.'

'Oh, Christ. Of course.' She bowed her head a moment, then asked: 'And afterwards?'

'I haven't thought about it,' shrugged Knox, though this was a lie. The prospect of excavating again had been in his nostrils ever since Umar had made his offer. 'And you?'

'I'm off to Paris, first flight I can get.'

'Oh.' He stopped dead. 'Really?'

'I've decided to leave the Sorbonne,' she said.

445

'I owe it to them to tell them in person, don't you think? They've been very good to me.'

Knox couldn't prevent a smile from spreading across his face. 'And then?'

'I'm planning to come back here. Find myself some excavating work. Learn the ropes, you know. I understand that Augustin is always looking for new assistants. Maybe I could — '

'Augustin!' protested Knox, appalled. 'That old goat! You can't be serious!'

'I thought he was your friend.'

'He *is* my friend. That's precisely why I don't want you working for him.'

'I need a job,' insisted Gaille. 'Do you have a better suggestion?'

They reached the back doors, pushed through them and down the steps to the waiting taxi. Knox opened the back door for Gaille, climbed in alongside her, giving directions to the driver. He wound down his window as they pulled away, allowing in the scents of Egypt, the spices, the fumes and the sweat. This was more like it. Away from the politics, the ambition, the bargaining, the corruption, the deceit. In pursuit of the raw truth once more.

He turned to Gaille. 'I'll be needing a partner myself, as soon as all this has blown over,' he told her.

'Really?'

'Yes. Someone who'll work for a pittance, just for the love of it. Someone with the right skills to complement my own. A languages expert, ideally. Preferably one who can take a half-decent photograph too. Two employees for the price of one, you know. I'm cheap like that.'

Gaille laughed, her eyes sparkling. 'And may I ask what the two of you will be going in search of?'

He grinned at her. 'Don't you mean, what will the two of us be going in search of?'

'Yes,' she said happily. 'That's exactly what I mean.'

We do hope that you have enjoyed reading
this large print book.

Did you know that all of our titles
are available for purchase?

We publish a wide range of high quality
large print books including:
Romances, Mysteries, Classics
General Fiction
Non Fiction and Westerns

Special interest titles available in
large print are:
The Little Oxford Dictionary
Music Book
Song Book
Hymn Book
Service Book

Also available from us courtesy of Oxford
University Press:
Young Readers' Dictionary
(large print edition)
Young Readers' Thesaurus
(large print edition)

For further information or a free
brochure, please contact us at:
Ulverscroft Large Print Books Ltd.,
The Green, Bradgate Road, Anstey,
Leicester, LE7 7FU, England.
Tel: (00 44) 0116 236 4325
Fax: (00 44) 0116 234 0205

Other titles published by
The House of Ulverscroft:

CORSAIR

Tim Severin

1677. Snatched from an Irish village by Barbary corsairs, seventeen-year-old Hector Lynch is sold at auction in Algiers. He is befriended by fellow captive Dan, a Miskito Indian from the Caribbean. The two friends escape the horrors of the slave barracks, and serve aboard a Turkish ship, which is sunk at sea. By a savage twist of fortune they are condemned to further slavery — when they are chained to the oar bench of a French galley with vagabonds and convicts for company. Hector is driven by the need to find out what happened to his sister, Elizabeth, who was also kidnapped by the corsairs. He learns the chilling truth when he and his colourful band of brothers are shipwrecked off the coast of Morocco.

THE SLEEPING DOLL

Jeffery Deaver

Daniel Pell is a contemporary Charles Manson. Obsessed with controlling people, he had formed a quasi cult with a group of women in central California. Eight years ago, he slaughtered a family, though the three women in his own 'Family' were absolved of any part in the deaths. Now, Pell has escaped and Kathryn Dance, interrogator and kinesic analyst, must work with her team to find him. She brings together the three women, now leading normal lives, to help her find out what Pell is up to. Dance must also find the 'Sleeping Doll', the one surviving daughter of the original murder eight years ago. Meanwhile, Pell, with a young woman he has manipulated to help him, tries to fulfil his mission . . .

THE FACE OF DEATH

Cody Mcfadyen

The girl is sixteen, at the scene of a grisly triple homicide, and has a gun to her head. She claims 'The Stranger' killed her adoptive family, that he's been following her all her life, killing everyone she ever loved, and that no-one believes her. And no-one has. Until now . . . Special Agent Smoky Barrett is head of the violent crimes unit in Los Angeles, the part of the FBI reserved for tracking down the worst of the worst. In the wake of her own personal tragedy, she's finally spinning the fragile threads of a new life. But when The Stranger finally does show his face, if she's not ready to confront her worst fear, Smoky won't have time to do anything but die . . .

THE WALKING DEAD

Gerald Seymour

A young man begins a journey from Saudi Arabia, believing it will end with his death in England. If his mission succeeds, he will go to his god a martyr — and many innocents will die with him. For David Banks, an armed protection officer, charged with neutralizing the threat to London's safety, his role is no longer clear-cut: one man's terrorist is another man's freedom fighter: dangerous distinctions to a police officer with his finger on the trigger. Soon the two men's paths will cross. Before then, their commitment will be shaken by the journeys that take them there. The suicide bomber and the policeman will have cause to question the roads they've chosen. Win or lose, neither will be the same again . . .